ON DEADLY GROUNDS

BY KAYE D. SCHMITZ

ON DEADLY GROUNDS BY KAYE D. SCHMITZ
Lamplighter Mystery and Suspense is an imprint of LPCBooks
a division of Iron Stream Media
100 Missionary Ridge, Birmingham, AL 35242

ISBN: 978-1-64526-261-9
Copyright © 2020 by Kaye D. Schmitz
Cover design by Elaina Lee
Interior design by Karthick Srinivasan

Available in print from your local bookstore, online, or from the publisher at:
ShopLPC.com

For more information on this book and the author, visit:
kayedschmitzauthor.com

Brought to you by the creative team at Lighthouse Publishing of the
Carolinas (LPCBooks.com):
Ramona Richards, Shonda Savage, Darla Crass, Sally Shupe

Library of Congress Cataloging-in-Publication Data
Schmitz, Kaye D.
On Deadly Grounds / Kaye D. Schmitz 1st ed.

Printed in the United States of America

PRAISE FOR *ON DEADLY GROUNDS*

A tale of family intrigue and grand misfortune—a historical escapade, packed with menace and peril—one you're going to enjoy.

~ **Steve Berry,**
#1 Bestselling Author of *The Warsaw Protocol*
The Malta Exchange

Kaye Schmitz's *On Deadly Grounds* is an intriguing mystery that will keep you turning the pages until 'The End!'

~ **Patricia Bradley**
Award-winning author of *The Logan Point Series*
Memphis Cold Case Series

Kaye Schmitz' suspense novel, *On Deadly Grounds*, hits all the right notes: an old Southern mansion guarding generations of secrets; several mysterious deaths, a small boy suddenly mute, a hidden key and a race against time, and a young woman, haunted by violence and loss, finding her way. But at its' heart, this is a story of family and courage, of moving on – and coming home.

~ **Helaine Mario author of Maggie O'Shea mysteries**
The Lost Concerto
Dark Rhapsody

What a great read! The action and intrigue kept me moving forward . . . I wanted to solve the mystery with Mattie. The ending was fascinating and clarified the role of all the characters. The attention to details is impeccable. I really enjoyed this novel and hope there is a sequel coming soon. GREAT JOB!!!

~ **Larry McDorman**, Florida reader

Kaye Schmitz has created engaging characters and a compelling story of mystery and intrigue. Don't start this book if you haven't finished your chores...you won't want to put it down! A truly great read.

~ **Kelly B. St. Clair, Esq.**, Virginia reader

I just LOVED this story, so rich in details, and a masterfully woven plot. I enjoyed every page of it. The historical connection to Russia and the oil scandal added much to the extra flavor, I loved it!

~ **Candi Lennox**, Florida reader

I loved reading this book. It is a fantastic read, full of excitement and equally full of deep family connections. The love that is shared among the three generations of Maguires is something that I, coming from a huge Arkansas family, can certainly relate to.

~ **Glenda Blake**, Georgia reader

Mattie Maguire is my new favorite book character! She had me hooked from chapter one. Emotion, suspense, fear, and finally justice.....everything I enjoy in a great book!

~ **Lorna Jones**, Florida reader

From the very first chapter, Kaye Schmitz sparks our curiosity about the Sinclair Mansion history filled with love, tragedy, murder and intrigue right up to the surprise ending.

~ **Cheryl Dangelo**, Florida reader

What an intriguing mystery! I love stories that draw me in and make me feel and see everything as the characters do. Having been to Asheville, this took me right back to the beauty and history of that area. I also enjoyed the twists and turns of the characters up through the very end!

~ **Ellen Reese**, Florida reader

Loved *On Deadly Grounds*! The fast paced story-line offered several surprises along the way that kept me on my toes. The author did a great job of weaving the past with the present to help put together the pieces of this murder mystery. She paints the setting so clearly, that this fictional place now exists in my head, as if it were a real place. I would now like to read this book again, knowing the ending, so that I can look for all of the clues that I missed along the way. Delightful book! I couldn't put it down!

~ **Keri Orndorff**, Florida reader

The story telling in this novel is so captivating and immersive in its description of another era that readers feel naturally like they are there, rather than just being told they are there. While the story has murder, mystery, and intrigue, I find the small details and minor characters just as satisfying as the larger concepts. I struggled to put the book down and wanted to read it all in one sitting so I could have resolution about the characters I came to care so much about.

~ **Stephani Dykes**, Kansas reader

Written with clarity and precision, ON DEADLY GROUNDS proves to be an intriguing thriller full of twists and turns at every corner. While writing of the present and the past, the author creates a complete history of the Sinclair family from North Carolina, and their Estate, Clairmont Place. ON DEADLY GROUNDS has bad things happen to good people, and author Kaye Schmitz doesn't shy away from strikingly vivid and detailed descriptions. A bona fide page-turner.

~ **Ron Dykes**, Florida reader

I just finished reading *On Deadly Grounds* by author Kaye D Schmitz. The journey this book took one on kept us guessing and second guessing "who done it." The twists and turns made for an interesting read and the research for this book became apparent from the beginning. I hope all will enjoy trying to be an armchair sleuth and solve the mystery.

~ **Susan Byrd**, Maryland reader

Wow! I forgot just how much I enjoy reading until I could not put this book down. The vivid descriptions took me back to western North Carolina - my home for almost 27 years.

~ **Genie McBride**, Florida reader

On Deadly Grounds is an entertaining mystery with many twists and turns. The vivid descriptions of the characters and the multiple settings make the book very relate-able to the reader. The action and intrigue will keep the reader engaged to the very end.

~ **Georgiann Ellis**, Florida reader

A fast reading romp through mystery land that I couldn't put down. I could easily visualize the places and characters. This is a winner.

~ **Judee Brooks**, Georgia reader

The book caught my interest from the first paragraph - a murder, tragedies over several decades, and a hidden treasure in a magnificent mansion. How can you not want to find out the mysteries held in the pages that follow?

~ **Judy Thomas**, Florida reader

It's a rare novel that weaves such wonderful characters and descriptive storytelling with edge-of-your-seat suspense. Kaye has done just that in "On Deadly Grounds." I couldn't turn the pages fast enough to see what would happen next. And just when I thought I had it figured out and loose ends were wrapping up—she reveals a few more surprises. A fantastic read!

~ **Kristin Balcita**, Florida reader

To
My darling husband, Michael,
With whom I have been joined at the hip
Through every step of this path.
May we travel many more of these roads together.

ACKNOWLEDGMENTS

Writing this book was actually more fun than writing my first book. Maybe because I had one published and out there, but also, I think, because I had gotten such good feedback and my readers seemed to want more.

So, regardless of the fact that an author is responsible for writing every word of a manuscript, help, support, and inspiration come from many different places. I want to begin by thanking two people I consulted for technical guidance—my niece, Kelly St. Clair, an attorney who helped me with legal language, and my neighbor, Ovie Belt, a former fire chief, who taught me how and why different things might burn. While the final story doesn't contain a lot of the language we discussed, the help those two gave me still sent me along the right path.

One of my favorite parts of writing this book was working with the core members of my "Street Team." So a huge thank you to Sue Foster, Kathy Granieri, and Lorna Jones. They made the journey through the story with me many times and their feedback and wisdom helped shape its believability. Not only are they lovely ladies and a hoot to work with, but before I released the manuscript to them the first time, we all signed contracts with each other. Their part was a promise to tell me the truth about what they read and what needed improvement, and my part was a promise to them that I wouldn't take it personally—or be offended—when they did. We have a great time getting together to make the story better.

I also want to thank The Seymour Literary Agency and my agent, Julie Gwinn, as well as my general editor at Lighthouse Publishing of the Carolinas, Sally Shupe. Sally had a heck of a time trying to wean me away from "head hopping" when I used more than one point of view in the same chapter. And I will be eternally grateful to my managing editor, Darla Crass, at Lighthouse's Lamplighter Mysteries and Suspense Imprint. Darla guided me through crafting a stronger story and even offered storyline ideas from time to time. Her knowledge of her craft was evident from the first time we talked, so it was easy for me to trust her judgment. Throughout the process, I always appreciated her tenacity and encouragement.

As always, my darling husband, Michael, receives my loudest thanks. He read countless versions and kept me on track about what makes the story compelling and satisfying to readers. I will never forget the day when he was going through the last few chapters and made a beeline for my office door. "What have you done?" he wailed. "I loved this character, but you made me hate him! You have to change it." So I did. He's my best barometer of what will work and what won't, and I will never release a story to the world that doesn't contain his stamp of approval. To this day, he is my best reader and my most trusted sounding board. If I get stuck, he is magical about listening and is always spot on with his ideas. He has been and still is my most ardent fan, my loudest cheerleader, and always, my best friend. Thank you, my darling Mikey … for my life.

CHAPTER ONE

2017

Sinclair Station, North Carolina

Murder or not, Mattie Maguire decided, the Clairmont Place mansion exuded an aura of grandeur. Oh sure, it had witnessed its share of tragedies during the past several decades, but the mansion's magnificence, coupled with the beauty of the fall morning, diminished those memories to wispy mists and banished them to the Sinclair family cemetery where they belonged.

She pointed herself toward the event tent, erected the previous day on the grounds outside the mansion, and stumbled on a loose stone in the path. For the second time in an hour, she paused to re-tie her trusty old tennis shoes.

"It's Miss Matilda, is it not?"

The voice startled her. She thought she was alone.

She pushed her bangs out of her eyes and rose from the cobblestone path beside the hundred-year-old mansion. A friendly face accompanied the voice and she returned his smile with one of her own.

"Mattie, please," she said. "Mattie Maguire. No one's called me Matilda since the president of Wake Forest handed me my diploma ... and that was more than ten years ago."

He stood only three or four inches taller than her five feet seven ... and with heels, she figured she'd look him straight in the eyes.

She brushed her hand on the back of her jeans and held it out, assuming he would shake it. But instead he left it hanging in mid-air and bent from the waist in a very courtly bow.

Old school, she mused, hiding her smile. *Definitely old school.*

But that fit. Everything about him shouted old school. He wore his thick hair, more silver than brown, slicked straight back from his strong

1

forehead and his dark eyes crinkled and then widened to match his smile. His age, she figured, ranged somewhere between her father's mid-sixties and her grandfather's mid-eighties.

"How can I help you, Mr. ..." Mattie asked.

"Bill," he answered. "William, actually. William Carson. But please, call me Bill."

"Oh! Bill! You're the one Gramps told me about for the new position. What are they calling it—Archival and Records Officer?" She grabbed his hand and shook it anyway. "Boy, am I glad to meet you."

"Yes," Bill answered. "That's the one. I start tomorrow."

"I am so glad the Clairmont Place Management Board finally took action and created that position," she said. "My poor gramps has done a great job of keeping things under control, but he's in his eighties now. I understand you'll also be monitoring any necessary internal maintenance, too, right?"

"Yes. But what I'm most looking forward to is going through all of those documents."

"I have loved that, too," Mattie said, "ever since the board granted me permission to work inside the mansion. Did they tell you this property has been selected as the site of the next International G7 Summit when it cycles back to the States?"

"Yes," he said. "Congratulations."

"Thanks. It was quite an ordeal to make that happen."

Mattie spent months in committee meetings and then weeks on proposals to the Summit Final Selection Committee. The level of detail the committee sought struck her as incredible. And somewhat ridiculous.

At least, that's what she thought until one of her meetings covered the history of the Summits—and the security surrounding them. With leaders from the seven member countries that represented the most advanced economies in the world and the highest percentage of global wealth together in one place, security was always a primary concern. But it took precedence over everything else after Russia was ousted from the G8 Summit Group in 2014.

The Russians, she'd been told, remained ticked off about being kicked out of the group. So a large bank of proposal questions focused on handling Russian infiltrators.

As if I would even recognize a Russian infiltrator, for goodness' sake.

Knowing that she had no expertise in that area, she worked with Sinclair Station's newly elected sheriff, Bryan Bennett, and security organizations from around the area to complete that section.

"There's still a ton of stuff to do," she added. "But the board also agreed to let me submit a restoration grant to the State Historic Office. Did they tell you that part?"

At his nod, she continued. "I'm hopeful we'll get some funding to help fix the house up prior to the summit since it's been closed for so long. And to add Clairmont Place to the National Register of Historic Places."

She pushed her bangs out of her eyes again. "But you're right about the documents," she added, "all those valuable pieces of history just lying around." She shook her head. "They should have been archived to a vault years ago. I'd love to help you with that."

"I would welcome it. And I can help you with your restoration grant submission. If you're interested, that is. I recently retired from the State Historic Office and still have lots of friends there."

"If I'm interested? Are you kidding? That would be outstanding," Mattie said.

"Everybody at the office loves this old place, Miss Matilda, just like they love Biltmore. And your reputation is very well known and respected, too, so you shouldn't have any trouble getting the grant approved. Especially since your family has worked with the Sinclair family for the past eighty years. That's correct, isn't it?"

"Eighty years," she breathed in a half whisper. "I forget it's been that long. But yes," she said, "four generations of Maguires have worked for the Sinclairs. Originally at the first Mr. Sinclair's textile mill, then as groundskeepers here on this property. My grandfather, Michael—whom you met—took over the groundskeeping when his father, Melvin, retired. And now my dad—I assume you've met him, too—is president of the Sinclair Bank & Trust."

She checked her watch. "I'm really pressed for time right this minute, Bill. I'm setting up for tomorrow night's Halloween Gala, our primary fundraiser for the Visitors and Conventions Bureau. But maybe I could meet you at the mansion's East Portico entrance in the morning. I've already assembled a small stack of documents that I used for the summit application, and I'd love it if you could tell me what we'll need for the restoration grant. Will that work?"

"Perfectly," he said.

"I have to tell you," Mattie added, "I am totally stoked to get the house opened up again. It's been a fantasy of mine for years."

She left Bill standing there, but her mind continued to dwell on the fact that the mansion had been closed to the public for more than sixty-five years, since shortly after the murder of Henry Sinclair, son of the city's founder.

His story was so sad.

Henry Sinclair married again after his first wife died, but was killed less than two years later. Murdered. Shot while he slept. By his secretary, of all people. With the second Mrs. Sinclair standing beside him, trying to wrestle the gun from his hand and terrified she would be next.

But the secretary turned the gun on himself instead.

Mattie shivered involuntarily. Except for the killer killing himself, the story was far too close to her own.

She shook off the thought.

With her husband gone, the house must have held nothing but sadness for her. Probably why she closed it and moved the rest of the family to Greece. Thank goodness she leased the grounds to the city.

But access to the inside of the house had been denied to everyone except Mattie's grandfather, who monitored interior maintenance, and more recently to her while she worked on the G7 Summit application. The Clairmont Place Management Board and her boss at the North Carolina Visitors and Conventions Bureau were thrilled when the town of Sinclair Station won the venue bid. And as event director for the Bureau, she would be front and center in ensuring that everything ran smoothly.

Mattie continued along her path toward the event tent and flipped through pages on her clipboard. She made a note to check on the permission document sent to Greece for Mrs. Sinclair's signature. On the summit application, the Selection Committee accepted her father's signature, as president of Sinclair Bank & Trust and chair of the property's management board. But they still required Mrs. Sinclair's signature at some point. It wouldn't look good for her father if they didn't get it soon, since he had assured Senator Bradley there wouldn't be a problem. And the senator had assured the president.

She forced her focus back to her remaining tasks before the next evening's Halloween Gala. She skirted the gardens, exploding with fall blooms, and her heart swelled as she drank in the beauty surrounding her. The mansion itself was beyond beautiful from an architectural standpoint. *And why not?* It was designed by the same man who created Biltmore, a mere twenty-two miles to the west.

But the Sinclair murder, committed all those years earlier, continued to pop up in people's minds before anything else at the mention of Clairmont Place. It proved to be a great catalyst for filling chairs at the Halloween Gala on the property.

She passed the koi pond and turned quickly as movement to her left caught her eye. A black blur disappeared behind one of the beech trees that lined the drive. She stood perfectly still. But nothing else moved. Regardless, her arms tingled with gooseflesh as she bent to tie her shoe again, lowering her head and scanning the area.

She hated the cloud of fear that accompanied so many of her waking hours, but her near brush with death before returning to her hometown six years earlier had resulted in a persistent skittish state.

She stepped into the huge tent just as two men in black uniforms entered from the back. The words "Ellison Electrical," embroidered on their shirts, became visible as she neared them.

Oh ... it must have been these guys I saw earlier.

But her gooseflesh remained.

"You know where the cables are supposed to go?" she asked them. "I hope these won't be in your way," she added, pointing to the tall heaters that lined the temporary structure as insurance against a chillier than normal evening.

"No, ma'am," the taller one said. "We can work around them. The lighting company will deliver the chandeliers tomorrow. Then we'll be back to install them."

She inspected several other items and signed the electrician's work order. Then she left the tent area and surveyed the grounds to make certain they were ready for guests, smiling as she passed the house.

Regardless of its splendor, she had always thought Clairmont Place looked more like a family home than its larger counterpart, Biltmore. In her mind, there should have been children running around, playing games and skinning their knees.

But that never happened. No child had lived there past the age of ten.

Then the beautiful house was closed.

5

For almost seventy years, Clairmont Place's lovely rooms collected dust rather than memories.

What a colossal waste.

She needed to get back to her office, so she took the shortcut to the parking lot—a dense canopy of locust trees that shaded the cobblestone path beside the hundred-year-old mansion. Daylight dimmed in the shelter of the thick foliage and she hurried through the shadows. But her shoelace, untied again, tripped her up and she threw out her arms to keep from falling.

Her fingers brushed against something unfamiliar in the semi-darkness … something that didn't feel like leaves … and her heartbeat spiked to high alert. She wanted to scream … started to scream. But before the sound could leave her throat, pain slammed into the back of her head and shot through her skull.

The semi-darkness faded to total black.

She didn't know how long she lay in the arbor path, but finally opened her eyes and sat up gingerly. She felt a small bump on the back of her head and looked up to find out what she had hit. The low light revealed nothing out of the ordinary, so she tried to stand. But when her right foot didn't cooperate, she saw her shoelace snagged on one of the locust roots.

Oh … that's why I fell. Wonder what I fell against that bumped my head? Who knows.

She freed her foot, tested each leg and shook her arms to find everything working properly. So she continued along the path until she reached daylight at the other end of the canopy, and then emerged close to the parking lot.

She rubbed her head again as she got in her car, a sheepish expression on her face for her clumsiness.

The light-haired man stayed hidden among the thick branches that formed the canopy and kept watch on the woman to make certain she was okay.

He hadn't intended to hurt her. He simply needed to make certain she didn't see him.

His code name was "The Operative"—TheO for short—and he'd

prepared for the upcoming events scheduled to take place on the property his whole life.

He couldn't let his cover be blown now. He had to be more careful. Discovery at this point would ruin everything.

It was too soon.

CHAPTER TWO

As a child, Mattie had spent a great deal of time at the caretaker's residence where her grandparents lived on the grounds of Clairmont place. Ironically called The Cottage, it was a spacious and lovely four bedroom, four-bath home. But it didn't compare to the magnificence of the mansion itself, and her fantasy of living in the house was legendary in her family.

The best she'd been able to do until the summit application, however, was to spend time outside the house—on the grounds. So she held as many Bureau events there as possible. Of course, daily trips inside to work on the summit proposal fueled her passion for it to fever pitch.

Mattie was thrilled that Bill Carson had offered to put in a good word with the State Historic Office on the restoration grant. With his experience and contacts, the grant was almost certain to be funded, and the mansion could be restored to its former glory. Or close, anyway.

Mattie had breakfast with her grandparents at The Cottage the morning after she met Bill, but she purposely didn't mention her clumsiness in the arbor the previous afternoon. She was still embarrassed.

"I think he'll be really good, Gramps," she said. "The fact that he loves the house as much as we—well, I—do, tells me he'll fit right in."

"Did he tell you why he loves the house so much?"

"No, why?"

"His mother was Rachel Carson. Cook Carson for the Sinclair family before they moved and closed the house."

"Oh. I had no idea. Did he and his mother actually live there?"

"Mm-hmm. They had a little apartment behind the kitchen. I think he was around eight when the house was closed up."

"I'm meeting him there this morning to help him get started. And then it's back to final preparation for the gala. Your guys will have the grounds finished in time?"

"Mattie Mat," he said, "have I ever let you down?"

Mattie smiled and blew him a kiss, then shrugged into her jacket and walked toward the mansion where she unlocked the door to the East Portico. Bill met her outside.

"Good morning," she said. "I had planned to take you on the 'grand tour,' but Gramps told me you used to live here, so you're probably already familiar with the interior."

"Not at all, unfortunately," he said. "My mother was the cook and I was only eight when the family stopped returning from Greece and closed the house for good. Children of the hired help weren't allowed on the floors occupied by the Sinclair family. So, no, I really haven't seen much of it."

"You're in for a treat, then," she told him.

When Mattie first received permission to enter the mansion, her grandfather had acted as her tour-guide.

"I'll show you the house the same way Gramps showed me. But you should probably know that I have always had a little-girl desire to actually live here. In fact, when Gramps brought me here last year, I had trouble believing I actually walked on the floors of the house I had loved all my life."

They entered the East Portico and a long hallway rolled out before them. They walked past a laundry room, a butler's pantry and a number of other rooms currently used as storage. Every inch of space was cluttered, and many items lay virtually invisible under draped sheeting. But everything, covered or not, wore a thick layer of dust.

"The rooms on this floor won't be used during the summit, so they won't be updated until after the rooms on the upper floors. Same with the level below this one," she added. "I won't take you downstairs today, but you should see it when you can. I've only been down there once, but there's a complete Roman spa with a small indoor pool—empty, of course, and a wine cellar—also empty. Down that hallway"—she pointed to the right—"is a card room and a billiard room."

They turned left and reached a large, open space with flagstone flooring and stairs that climbed the walls on both sides.

9

"What was this used for?" he asked.

"Gramps explained it as a sort of receiving room," she answered, "primarily for staff, chauffeurs, grooms, the women who attended to the grand ladies who came to visit. But he also said it was seldom used by the time the house was closed. Here we are," she added, turning toward the closest set of stairs.

They ascended the first part of the stairs then crossed a landing, still adorned with patterned carpets that released a plume of dust with each footfall, and climbed the second level of steps. Few windows broke the stone surface of the walls, so the stairs rested in shadow. When they reached the top step, blinding sunlight filled their faces.

They stepped into the huge entrance hall that rose two stories above them.

"Just look at that," Mattie said. "Isn't it beautiful?"

Bill followed her gaze. High up and in the middle of the foyer hung a huge crystal chandelier, centered in the middle of a curved marble staircase with wrought-iron decorative balusters under a teak banister.

"It is, indeed." He walked toward the stairs. "I actually have seen this part of the house," he added. "My mother brought me here on the day we moved out. I totally understand your love for this place, Miss Matilda."

"On my twelfth birthday," she said, "Gramps snuck me in here. That was more than twenty years ago, but I remember being blown away even then. I felt like a princess in an enchanted castle." She put her hand on the newel post. "I pestered my poor Gramps to let me slide down this banister." She turned toward Bill. "It's still on my bucket list. Someday I'm going to."

Bill threw his head back and laughed.

"Come on," Mattie said to him. "I'll take you to Henry Sinclair's office. It's a good place to work."

Bill followed her around the stairs to the left and down a hallway wider than the one they had entered on the floor below. Mattie paused at one of the doors that opened into a large, ornate room, the back wall of which consisted entirely of floor-to-ceiling windows that curved outward in a semi-circle.

"I thought this room would be great for the main meeting room of the summit." Each window, flanked by Corinthian columns crowned with gold leaf trim, sported dozens of small panes that showcased the manicured lawn ablaze with fall flowers—the handiwork of her grandfather's ground crew.

On their way down the hall, they passed several other large rooms, including a library with more books than the public one that served their small town.

She opened two tall narrow doors to her left and swung them into the room. "Henry Sinclair's office," she said. "The first time I came in here, the dust was so thick, the furniture appeared almost white rather than the rich mahogany and cherry hues you see now. I've tried to keep it somewhat cleaned up since then."

A massive desk occupied one side and a fireplace commanded the entire wall across from it. A large portrait, featuring a red-haired woman holding the reins of a horse, hung above it.

"Oh," Bill said, looking at the portrait. "That must be Miss Lily and Prince. That's exactly how my mother described them."

As always happened when she was in Henry's office, Mattie studied the portrait. It had always bothered her that a picture of Henry's first wife still hung in his office well after he had a second wife. It seemed insensitive.

She wanted to believe Henry Sinclair had been a good guy, but she couldn't help wondering if that lack of sensitivity could have contributed to his secretary being upset enough about something to shoot him.

Maybe, she thought as she picked up a document from his desk and put it down again, the answer is here. Among the family history. Just waiting to be found.

CHAPTER THREE

1944

Henry Sinclair focused on the portrait across from him, centered over the massive fireplace that dominated the room. A beautiful red-haired woman smiled down from the picture and held the reins of her chestnut horse, a profusion of flowers in colors of the rainbow blooming behind her. Sunlight from Henry's window reflected from her hair and radiated bronze highlights to every corner of the room.

His heart filled with love at the memory of her reaction when he had presented the portrait to her the previous year on her twenty-fifth birthday. "Oh, Henry," she said, tears spilling down her face. "You've captured one of my happiest memories—my wonderful Prince and my favorite flower gardens. The only things missing from making this a perfect representation of my life are you and Jeffrey."

The most gentle soul he'd ever met, his darling Lily spread sunshine and happiness to everyone at Clairmont Place. To the whole town of Sinclair Station, actually.

Lily's laughter reached him through his open window and Henry went to take a look. Dressed in her emerald-green riding habit, Lily stood with two young boys; Michael Maguire, the twelve-year-old son of Henry's head agronomist, and their own six-year-old son Jeffrey.

"Cook Carson has lunch ready for you—both of you," Lily said to the boys. "I'll see you when I return from my ride." She mounted Prince and turned the big stallion toward her favorite forest trail.

"Mikey, look at this," Jeffrey said. The older boy joined him at the base of a large wisteria bush, its purple blooms hanging heavy to the ground.

"It's a robin's nest," Michael said. "We should put it back. But we need to be really careful or the mother bird won't take care of her babies."

Henry watched as Jeffrey held the branches aside and Michael slid the nest back into place, careful not to touch the baby birds.

"We did it, Mikey," Jeffrey said when they finished. "I'm going to wait at the stables for Mommy to come back so I can tell her about it. I can go with you, Mikey, right? To put the hay out for the horses? And be there when she comes back?"

"Sure," Michael said. "Right after lunch."

Henry smiled and returned to his desk.

He had no idea that in less than two hours, his world would be devastated.

After their lunch, the boys left the kitchen with chocolate-chip cookies, still warm from the oven. Chocolate coated Jeffrey's fingers and outlined his mouth.

"Ready?" Michael said.

"Yeah," Jeffrey answered. He wiped his hands on his shirt and skipped behind Michael on their way to the stables. An only child, Michael loved it that Jeffrey wanted to hang out with him, and he poked out his chest as he led them down the path.

Michael's duties on Clairmont Place included putting out hay and grains for the horses, along with small chores to keep the stables tidy. He cut the twine on a hay bale of mixed grass and alfalfa and forked it over the doors into each stall. Jeffrey came behind him with a small scoop of oats, just the way Michael had taught him, and dumped one into each horse's bucket.

They went about their work and after a few minutes, Jeffrey's eyes lit up. "Listen," he said. The sound of faint hoof beats reached them. "Hurry, Mikey. She's coming." They rushed through the rest of the hay and oats and went outside to wait. Michael picked Jeffrey up and perched him on the top rail of the corral fence and then climbed up beside him.

The hoof beats got louder, and the big chestnut emerged from the woods.

"There she is," Jeffrey shouted. He stood and waved excitedly.

"Careful, Jeffrey. You don't want her to have to fish you out of the corral the minute she gets here, do you?"

But Jeffrey ignored him and shouted to his mother.

13

The boys watched as horse and rider edged closer. Michael's heart swelled with his teenage crush on the mistress of the mansion—his vision of the most perfect woman in the world. In his eyes, the horse was beautiful and the woman even more so. They moved together perfectly.

"Watch, Mikey," Jeffrey said. "Watch her. She's going to jump. Watch."

Michael watched, but something else caught his attention. A timber rattlesnake was coiled in Prince's path. Alarm filled Michael's face and fear gripped his heart. As Prince drew close, Michael stood to shout a warning to Miss Lily, but she only smiled and waved, her eyes fixed on her son.

In the next instant, Prince reared and with only one hand on the reins, Jeffrey's mother was caught off guard and tumbled from the stallion's back. Prince bent his head low and the snake struck his nose. He screamed and reared again, then brought his hooves down, catching the snake under them. Over and over his hooves struck, crushing the snake. But by then, Miss Lily had rolled into his path and one of his hooves caught her head.

Michael jumped from the fence. "Stay here," he called to Jeffrey. "Don't move."

Prince had killed the snake, but continued to buck and rear, only calming slightly when Michael grabbed his reins.

"No!" Despite what Michael had told him, Jeffrey ran across the corral and threw himself on his mother's body. "Mommy! Wake up! Mommy! Mommy! Please wake up." He shook her shoulders, and then collapsed against her chest, sobbing into her hair.

"Come on, Jeffrey." Michael pulled at him, trying to dislodge him from his mother's still form. "Let go. You have to come with me. We need to get our fathers." Michael hoisted Jeffrey onto his shoulders, and they sprinted for the house.

Michael's father, Melvin, ran toward them. "I heard screaming," he said. "What's happened?"

"Miss Lily's horse got bit by a snake," Michael panted out. "Prince reared and she fell … she's hurt bad."

Cook Carson appeared in the kitchen door and Melvin hollered to her, "Send Mr. Sinclair. Miss Lily's had an accident."

Michael jogged to the kitchen and eased Jeffrey to the floor where Cook Carson enfolded him in her arms. "Come here, child," she said. She rocked him back and forth to soothe him. But he continued to sob.

Michael turned back to the stables and Mr. Sinclair passed him in his car, speeding toward the corral. He scooped up his wife and placed her gently in the front seat while Melvin hopped in the back. They roared off across the fields.

At the corral, Prince paced restlessly. Anthony, the groom, approached the horse, but Prince backed away and continued to snort and rear. "Michael," Anthony yelled. "Will you have someone call Doc Hardy? Prince's nose is already swelling where the snake bit him."

Michael returned to the kitchen and found Cook Carson. "Anthony said to call Doc Hardy for Prince's snake bite," he told her. She left the kitchen and returned a few moments later. She poured glasses of milk for the boys. "The doctor will be here within an hour," she told Michael.

Michael took a seat at the table and Cook Carson joined him there with Jeffrey on her lap. He buried his head in the cook's shoulder and continued to sob.

"I tried to warn her," Michael said. "But she didn't see me. She only waved at Jeffrey." His voice broke. "What will we do if ..."

Cook Carson freed one of her hands from around Jeffrey to rub Michael's shoulder. "We need to pray, son," she said. "That's the most important thing we can do now."

And together, they bowed their heads.

Henry Sinclair paced the empty waiting room, his hands tearing through his hair. Had it only been mere hours since he watched his beautiful Lily out his office window? He felt like the black cloud surrounding him had hovered for days.

"Please God ... please ..." The words formed a steady stream, punctuating his every step around the small room. Dark stains covered his shirt and tie, and his hands bore the rusty crust of his wife's blood.

In desperation, he fell to his knees and Melvin knelt beside him. "Please God ... please," Henry continued his prayer. His mind searched for words but came up short. Finally, without conscious thought, his voice took over. "There's nothing more I can do, Lord. This is in your hands. Please help my darling Lily. Help me to be strong for her. Help—"

The door from the emergency room swung open and Dr. Elliott stood there, his surgical mask limp around his neck. "Henry ..."

Henry rose. "Bob ... please ... please tell me."

"Henry, I'm so sorry."

"No!" he screamed. He fell to his knees and Melvin moved beside him. "Don't say it," Henry continued. His voice rose. "She can't be dead. She can't be." He beat the floor with his fists, then turned to Melvin and shook his shoulders. "She's full of life, Melvin. You know that. Her son is only six. Tell him! Tell Bob she can't be dead. Tell—" Henry's words stopped and guttural wails filled the room, followed by body-racking sobs for several long minutes. Melvin held him tight, tears streaming down his face as well.

"There was nothing we could do," the doctor said gently. He knelt beside Henry and Melvin. "She was gone when she got here, but we tried to revive her anyway. We tried everything ..." His voice trailed off at his friend's distress. "The damage from the horse's hooves was too great. She had extensive brain injuries." The doctor could no longer make himself heard over Henry's anguish. He turned to Melvin and said, "I am so, so sorry."

The three of them sat in the middle of the floor, huddled together in a pile. Then Henry spoke again. "I want to see her," he managed to choke out.

"I strongly advise against that," the doctor said. "We had to—"

"I want to see my wife." He said it quietly, but with authority.

"As you wish." Dr. Elliott led the way and accompanied Henry into the room where his wife lay with a sheet over her face. Fresh sobs erupted, but Henry remained firm. "Pull the sheet down."

The doctor did as asked and the left side of Lily's face appeared, untouched except for a few bruises. But a large bandage covered the right side of her face. Henry fell to his knees again. "No," he repeated. "My beautiful Lily ... my love." He turned tortured eyes to the doctor. "We need her," he whimpered. "Her son is only six. We need ..."

No more words came. Only raw pain. Melvin helped him to his feet and the doctor gave him a sedative.

The following morning Melvin told Mr. Sinclair that despite Doc Hardy's best efforts, Prince died late in the afternoon, as well.

A dark sadness hovered over the mansion.

The flowers in Lily's gardens bobbed bright in the sunlight, despite the gaping hole left in the family by her death.

It was the first of many such tragedies that would face them.

CHAPTER FOUR

2017

"Gramps told me about Cook Carson," Mattie said to Bill as they settled at Henry's desk. "That you both lived here," she added. "No wonder you love this house so much. How is your mother?"

"She died last year."

"Oh, Bill, I'm so sorry."

"She loved this place," Bill said. "She was pregnant with me when Mr. Sinclair was murdered—told me many times how horrible it was. And a shock to the entire household."

"I can imagine."

"My mother always considered herself lucky that Mrs. Sinclair kept her on for several years—until she moved the family to Greece full time. You don't know what it means to be back here. It's very special to me."

"Oh, I'll bet I do. I feel the same way about this place."

"I was so young when we left, I didn't remember much about it. My mother's description of this house and her stories about the people who lived here kept it alive for me."

"I understand that, too," Mattie said. "When Gramps tells me stories, I can imagine myself right there beside him as events happen." She reached for a stack of documents. "I tried to arrange these chronologically, but this is as far as I got." She shuffled through the first few. "We won't need all of these, but honestly, this place fascinates me so much, I have trouble putting documents aside without reading every word. I mean, look at this," she said, "here's a newspaper clipping that includes a picture of Lily and Prince, along with the details of her death. I didn't need this for the summit application, and I doubt I'll need it for the restoration grant, but it's obvious that Lily's portrait was painted from this same picture. In fact, earlier I found both the invoice and the ledger entry for a check made out to the artist who created the painting. The dates coincided with Lily's twenty-fifth birthday. It just breaks my heart."

"That was one of my mother's stories to me," Bill said. "She told me the party for Miss Lily's birthday was the last happy celebration this house saw. Miss Lily died the following year and Mother always said the house was never the same after that."

"Really?" Mattie asked. "Even after Mr. Sinclair married again?"

Bill shrugged.

"Although Gramps told me that Constance was very different from Lily. I mean, it's easy to see how beautiful Lily was. And well-loved in the community. Look at all these notes attached to this article. It must have warmed Mr. Sinclair's heart to know how many lives she touched."

The opening notes of "Sweet Dreams," a song by the Eurythmics, a band from the eighties, filled the room. "Oh," she said. "Sorry … that's my phone. Hey, Simone," she said, addressing her assistant at the bureau. "What's up?"

Mattie finished her call and turned to Bill. "I'm really sorry. I'm needed in the event tent. I probably won't have much time to meet with you again until our Halloween Gala is over. May we get back together next week?"

"I would love that," he answered. "And your grandfather said he'd join me later to fill me in on more of the details of my job. In the meantime, I'll poke around and continue putting things together to archive."

Mattie headed to the event tent and passed the small family cemetery on her way.

A breeze stirred the trees and leaves floated slowly down, kissing the ground. The dim light faded to semi-darkness as the sun hid behind a cloud, and the breeze on her face chilled.

She shuddered.

Leaves crunched behind her in stealthy footsteps, and she whipped her head around. "Hello?" she called. "Is someone there?"

CHAPTER FIVE

Silence greeted her and a trickle of fear touched her heart.

She took several deep breaths and one more step when loudspeakers to her right roared into life and music from Taylor Swift's newest album blasted around her.

"Damnation," she shouted. Then she looked around sheepishly, hoping no one had heard her swear. Or witnessed how high she jumped.

She took one more deep breath and continued to the event tent where her assistant, Simone Rousseau, stood in the middle of the sound technicians, her hands covering her ears.

"Turn it down," Simone shouted. Abruptly, the music stopped.

"So … that works," Mattie said in the sudden quiet.

Simone flashed her a grin and then, along with the sound technicians, checked every microphone, from the dais to the band set-up. Mattie surveyed the room.

Round tables already occupied their spots, each with eight chairs—about half of which sported crisp white covers with orange and black bows decorating their backs. Small dried fall arrangements nestled in the bow's loops and matched the foliage she'd selected to surround the large candle centerpieces. The electricians from the day before hung crystal chandeliers on the overhead electric cables.

"Mattie," Simone called, "are the words on the screen clear?"

"Nope … a little fuzzy," she answered. "You might want to sharpen them up."

"Sure thing."

She checked some items off her list and turned toward Simone.

Muscular arms encased her from behind in a big bear hug, and a strong

20

chin plopped down on top of her head. She jumped and then recognized the source.

"Sir," she said sternly, "if you don't unhand me immediately, I will have my grandfather bodily remove you from the premises."

He laughed from behind her and gave her an extra squeeze. It was a game they had played since Mattie's childhood—her grandfather sneaking up behind her and Mattie pretending to be afraid. Since her return to Sinclair Station after the upheaval in her life, however, her grandfather's big hugs were especially meaningful to her.

She stood on her toes and kissed his cheek.

"I'm glad to see you, Gramps. In fact, finding you was next on my list."

"I'll bet it had something to do with the fact that the flagstone walk from the parking lot still has some lawn debris on it. Am I right?"

"As rain," she answered.

It was another of their games ... Mattie's standard response to his "Am I right?" question.

"I know you so well," he said. "Ninety-nine people out of a hundred would have looked at that walkway and pronounced it perfectly presentable. But I knew my little Mattie Mat wouldn't be pleased." His gray eyes twinkled, and he pinched her cheek. "Listen."

A motor buzzed.

"A leaf blower, huh?" She turned her list so he could see it and made an exaggerated check mark next to *Get the walk cleaned*. He chuckled.

"Thanks, Gramps." She hesitated a moment. "Gramps ... have you noticed any activity that doesn't belong? Like, people here who aren't supposed to be?"

"Good heavens, girl, how could you tell?" he asked. "Look at this place. It's a hive of activity. What's the matter, Mattie Mat?"

"I'm not sure. A feeling ... something ... I don't know. I thought I saw somebody duck behind a tree yesterday, and just now I thought I heard someone walking through the leaves by the cemetery. Both things seemed ... stealthy, furtive ... like they didn't belong. Oh, Gramps. We can't have anything go wrong. It's too important now that—"

"We've been chosen for the summit," he finished. "I know. When are Bryan's guys supposed to arrive?"

Mattie had arranged for Sheriff Bryan Bennett and his deputies to provide security at the gala, but he told her earlier he would need to hire additional temporary staff from the Pinkerton Agency to secure the entire area.

"Around five-thirty," she said.

"That's only five hours from now," her grandfather said. "Don't worry, honey. In the meantime, I'll have my crew keep a look out."

Mattie kissed her grandfather one more time before he left and then walked over to Simone who worked on sharpening the image from the projector.

"So the florist told you they would be late delivering the centerpieces?" she asked.

"Yes," Simone answered. "Of all the nerve ... after you gave them a chance to prove themselves, too. I can't imagine what they're thinking."

Mattie gave her assistant a quick hug. "What time did they tell you they'd be here?"

"Four or four-thirty," Simone answered. She snorted in disgust and Mattie couldn't help but smile. Simone's ownership of event details—and her personal affront if things didn't go as promised—was one of the reasons Mattie hired her. That and the fact that she had such a creative flair that blended well with Mattie's nuts-and-bolts approach.

"That will be a little tight," Mattie said, "but it will still work." She hesitated another minute and said, "Is everything else okay?"

Simone stopped working on the projector and looked up. "Uh-oh," she said. "I know that voice. What are you worried about? Did one of the speakers cancel? Or the band? What's wrong?"

"Neither of those things, I hope," Mattie said with a laugh. "No, as far as I know, our program is still on track. But I've seen ... no, that's not right. I've felt ..."

"What?" Simone said. "My goodness, tell me."

Mattie shook her head. "It's just a feeling. A sense of foreboding. I honestly don't know why." She shrugged. "I'm sure it's just me being silly," she added. "It's nothing. Still ..."

"Okay, now I'm officially freaked," Simone said.

Mattie hugged her again. "I'm sorry, kiddo. That wasn't my intention. Look, I've got to go back to the office and pick up a few last-minute things for tonight. Are you okay with everything here?"

"I thought I was."

"You are," Mattie assured her. "I'll see you back here around five."

Mattie headed to the parking lot, avoiding the dense canopy of the arbor after her fall the previous day, and hopped into her car.

She started to back out but saw movement from the arbor's dense foliage. There was no wind and nothing else moved. She fixed her gaze on the arbor's entrance.

No one was there.

She opened her door and stuck her head out. "Hello?" she called, as she had earlier in the day.

Silence.

She repositioned herself at the wheel and closed her door but took one long last look. Nothing moved, but she knew she hadn't imagined it.

The small cloud of unease that had hovered around her all day mushroomed into full-blown fear.

CHAPTER SIX

1945

Washington, DC

"I don't know, Richard," Henry Sinclair said. "I don't think I'm ready yet. Lily's only been gone a few months."

"It's been almost a year and a half, man—and your place needs a woman," Richard Baldwin countered. "How's your little boy doing?"

"Oh, some days are good. But some days he just hangs his little head. He keeps to himself a lot."

Henry downed his bourbon and water in a single swallow. It burned his throat all the way down and then churned in his stomach, empty from skipping dinner the previous day and breakfast that morning.

He frowned. His mood should have been joyous. His meeting with the government procurement agent at the Capitol had resulted in a new purchase agreement for every bolt of fabric produced in Henry's textile mill for the next year. Primarily wool for fresh soldier uniforms now that the war was over, but also thinner fabrics for parachutes and duffel bags. Even with the healthy discount he gave, Henry's profit would still be substantial.

But he didn't like the turn the conversation with Richard, one of the mill's attorneys, had taken. Since Lily's death, he had steadfastly refused to discuss his love life with anyone.

"Thank you for your concern, Richard," Henry said, "but I don't want to discuss it."

"Well that's a shame," Richard said. "Because I think you'd really enjoy spending time with my daughter, Constance. And her son, Robert, would be a great playmate for your little boy—what's his name again?"

"Jeffrey."

"Yes ... Jeffrey."

"Besides ... I don't even know your daughter."

"You met her at Lily's funeral."

"My goodness, man. I was beside myself that day. I hardly remember anything about it. Other than Jeffrey sobbing uncontrollably as his mother's coffin was lowered into the gr—" Henry's voice broke and he stopped talking. Several minutes passed before he could speak again. "I had to hold onto him," Henry continued after a moment, his voice no more than a whisper, "to keep him from hurling himself in after her."

"Sorry, my friend. I know that was a hard day for you. I'm only trying to look out for your well-being, Henry. I hope you know that."

Henry signaled the waiter for another drink.

"You'll be attending the Biltmore Christmas Eve party, won't you?" Richard asked.

Henry didn't answer. His father had attended the first Christmas Eve celebration as part of the family's long history with the Vanderbilts. It was George who'd purchased the Western North Carolina Railroad, co-owned by Henry's father and William Best, to ship in building materials. While that transaction created the beginning of Henry's family wealth, it also introduced Henry's father to Richard Morris Hunt, George's architect and personal friend. Henry became such good friends with both men that even before Biltmore was complete, Mr. Hunt designed Henry's home, Clairmont Place, as well. Then when George died suddenly in 1914, Henry's father helped George's widow, Edith, fulfill his wishes by selling thousands of acres of managed forestland.

Once his father retired and Henry, Jr. assumed his role in the family companies, the Vanderbilts had been good friends to him as well. During the war, Biltmore had been closed, for the most part, but George's grandson, George Vanderbilt Cecil, recently opened it again to celebrate the fiftieth anniversary of the first Christmas Eve celebration. There was no way Henry could miss it after all the families had done for each other. And it was heralded to be quite the event. So, yes, he decided, he would certainly go to the Christmas Eve party at Biltmore.

But Henry wasn't ready for Richard Baldwin's clumsy attempts at matchmaking. So he decided Richard didn't need to know his plans.

A jackhammer pounded Henry's skull and a nest of worms writhed in his stomach. Worse, the room flew around the edges of his vision, refusing to settle down and let him catch his breath.

He focused on the portrait over the fireplace and realized he didn't know who it was. Neither had he ever seen the coverlet over him or the chair in the corner. He had no idea, in fact, *where* he was nor how he got there.

But he did know he had to move. And fast. The worms wanted fresh air. He heaved the covers and made a beeline for the basin on the washstand. He emptied his stomach and then stood there, dry heaving for long minutes. He wiped his mouth and made his way back to the bed and fell into it, gulping deep breaths. He still didn't know where he was, but he felt slightly better.

The door opened and a woman in a dressing gown stood there, a tray balanced in her hands. Henry frowned at her.

"Well," she said. "You're awake. I brought you some breakfast. Merry Christmas."

The aromas of bacon and sausage washed over him, and he ran for the basin again. When he finished, he returned to the bed. But the woman was still there. Something about her was familiar. He just couldn't remember what.

"My goodness, Henry," she said. "I had no idea you'd had so much to drink."

"Where am I?" he managed to ask. The room started to spin again.

She laughed. "Are you serious? You really don't remember?"

He shook his head and instantly regretted it.

"I must say, the fact that you don't remember being at the Biltmore Christmas party makes me wonder what else you may have forgotten about last night."

He tried to focus. Her voice sounded familiar. Annoying … but familiar. If he could only remember. He closed his eyes. Little snatches of memory poked at him, then scurried away to return again seconds later. Biltmore … yes, he remembered arriving and receiving a flute of champagne. More and more champagne. But he'd neglected to eat dinner. He hadn't had any food at all, he finally remembered, since the previous morning. And a lot to drink.

"Oh my goodness," she said. "I was kidding. But you really don't remember, do you?"

He filtered through the memories floating by. Ordering a double bourbon after the champagne when he first arrived. Someone handing him another one not long after that. Richard Baldwin slapping him on the back. Handing him champagne. And then more champagne. And more and more. Dancing with a woman … the woman in the door. Being swept under a sprig of mistletoe … kissing. Lots of kissing.

"It was you," he said. "I kissed you."

She snorted. "Yes, you certainly did." She put the tray down on the chaise lounge by the window and approached him, hands on her hips. He studied her through eyes open only as wide as swollen slits allowed. She leaned her face in close and her perfume threatened his stomach again. "And then you did a lot more than that," she added. "Almost ruined my new dress in your haste to get it off me."

"I … I … what? I'm so sorry. That is not like me at all. I can't believe—"

"It's okay, Henry," she said. "Because all of that happened after you took my hand at midnight and said, 'Constance, will you marry me?'"

He bolted upright in bed. "I did what?" His stomach heaved with the sudden movement.

"That's right, Henry. You proposed. In front of witnesses. Including my father. Your attorney." She studied him, her mouth turned down at the edges.

Then she moved to the bed and sat beside him. She took his hand and raised it to her lips. "I said 'yes,' by the way."

CHAPTER SEVEN

2017

Sinclair Station, North Carolina

Mattie was certain her eyes hadn't played tricks on her, and her fear still plagued her. She was almost at the ramp for the highway, but at the last second, she jerked her wheel into the police station parking lot instead.

She entered Bryan's office from the lobby, a sheepish expression on her face.

"Thanks for making time for me today, Bryan," she said. "I'm sure you're really busy."

"It comes with the territory." He checked his watch. "Did you want to grab a quick bite?"

"Thanks, but I don't have time right now. I just wanted to talk to you about—"

Mattie stopped talking and Bryan waited.

"About ..." he prompted her.

"Look, I feel silly even talking about this, but I keep seeing—hearing—things at Clairmont Place. Movements ... things that don't belong."

"With all those people there getting ready for your event, how can you tell what does or doesn't belong?"

"That's what Gramps said."

"A wise man." Bryan smiled.

"I just wanted to make certain you have enough coverage ... and to let you know I really feel like somebody who's not supposed to be there is prowling around. Hiding in shadows."

"Are you seeing ghosts now, Mattie?" he asked. His eyes twinkled.

She shook her head. "Wow, you're right. That sounded really lame, huh?" Without waiting for him to answer, she added, "But Bryan, you know how important it is that everything goes perfectly now."

"Yes, I do. And it will. In fact, hold on a minute … let me check the number of Pinkertons we have coming. The list is on my secretary's desk."

He left the room and Mattie stood to look at the pictures covering his wall. Bryan holding a trophy for winning the decathlon at state. Throwing the winning pitch in the regional finals. Posing with the basketball team during his senior year—the "High Scorer" plaque in front of him.

Mixed in were more formal pictures, too, where he wore a suit. He'd been a year ahead of her in school, but she remembered he was chosen as "Mr. School Spirit," president of both the Student Government and the Honor Society, and *both* Homecoming and Prom King. In fact, there were very few titles up for grabs that Bryan Bennett hadn't won.

Plus, he was a really nice guy. She had even gone out with him a time or two … never anything serious. During his senior year, he was recruited by every college on the East Coast. But he turned them all down and entered the service just a month after graduation, telling everyone that the terrorist bombings of September 11, 2001 had affected him profoundly. So he planned to do something about it.

She lost track of him when she went to college, but heard he did several tours in the Middle East—Iran, Afghanistan, and Pakistan, for certain. Probably others, as some of the pictures indicated.

The last picture was more recent—his graduation from the police academy, where he finished at the top of his class. *Naturally.* And he was elected sheriff of Sinclair Station by a landslide six months after that.

At his swearing in ceremony, both of Mattie's grandparents hinted strongly that he would be a great catch for her.

But she wasn't ready.

They could be friends, she had decided, but that was it.

"See anything you like?"

Mattie jumped.

"Oh … sorry," Bryan said. "I didn't mean to startle you." He laughed.

She smiled sheepishly. "I'm very skittish these days," she said. "I have been ever since …"

Her voice trailed off and Bryan dropped his gaze to his shoes. Everyone knew the horror she had experienced and tried to keep her from dwelling on it.

"So … will you have enough officers?"

"Oh. Yes. Ten are coming from Pinkerton. And the five of us will be there. Trust me, Mattie. I don't want anything to happen while your event takes place, either. And I certainly don't want you taking any unnecessary risks."

"Believe me, Bryan, I'm such a chicken, that's the last thing you'll have to worry about from me."

She stood, and Bryan came around his desk. She held out her hand, but he pulled her into a quick hug instead.

"Okay. Thanks," she said and pulled away. She avoided his eyes and made a hasty retreat to the door.

But seeing him hadn't dispelled the fear that clung to her. It settled in the pit of her stomach and then spread.

Mattie tied her shoe again when she reached the parking lot, then slid into her car.

Her nerves jangled from the fear that refused to leave her. But worse, Bryan's hug made her heart thump erratically. *I have to keep that from happening. Bryan will have to keep his arms to himself if we're to work on projects together in this small town.*

She couldn't open herself up again. It was still too soon. She couldn't— wouldn't—allow herself to become involved, to become vulnerable. She wasn't sure she would recover a second time.

No, better to never get involved than to risk the loss of a loved one.

Another loved one.

Thoughts of that loss had flitted around her brain since mid-morning and refused to be ignored any longer. She steeled herself for the pain and let the memory flow.

His name was Paul Reynolds and they were juniors at Wake Forest when they met. By the time they were seniors, he had asked her to marry him.

Their wedding took place on the grounds of Clairmont Place the week after their graduation, and to Mattie, it was the most beautiful service she'd ever seen.

He'd been accepted at the University of Baltimore Law School, so earning her advanced degree at Stratford University's Baltimore campus made perfect sense. Mattie's parents and grandparents hated to see her leave the state but recognized the great opportunity for the young people.

Their life together couldn't have been better. Mattie worked for IBM where she designed front end systems for Phillips Seafood Restaurant.

Paul finished his law degree the following year and joined one of Baltimore's most prestigious firms. He and Mattie spent their days working at their dream jobs and their nights in each other's arms.

At the end of their first year together they had paid off their student loans and saved enough money to start getting ahead. And six months later, Mattie learned she was pregnant ... a little sooner than they planned. But they were thrilled, regardless.

The dinner at the Phillips Restaurant was a congratulatory gift from her friends there. She planned to fly to North Carolina the following day to tell her parents and grandparents about the baby.

Neither Mattie nor Paul saw it coming.

The man stepped out from behind one of the pillars on the fifth floor of the parking garage, close to Paul's new BMW. A bandana-like mask covered the bottom part of his face. But not his eyes. Mattie's fleeting thought when she saw them was that they appeared to be almost gold— feral—animal-like in the low light.

He flashed a gun, but Paul was turned away to unlock Mattie's door and didn't see it. The man grabbed her around the throat and pulled her back, cutting off her air. She couldn't scream ... couldn't even breathe. So, she raised her hands and clawed his face, pulling his bandana mask down around his chin. Startled, the mugger threw Mattie from him and she slammed into the next car, the wind knocked out of her.

He shoved his pistol into Paul's back.

"What the hell?" Paul whipped around and recognized what was happening. He raised his arms. "Okay, buddy, just tell me what you want."

"Money and car keys," the man said in a raspy voice that held a distinct accent ... a voice Mattie knew she would never forget.

"Okay, you can have them, but please let me make sure my wife is okay."

"No." The man motioned with his gun for him to stay back. "Hurry it up ... keys ... wallet."

Paul pulled his wallet from his pocket and, in a single motion, threw it at the man's face. A corner of it hit his eye and in that second of distraction,

31

Paul threw a punch to his head. But the blow skidded off his cheek and the man lunged at him. They rolled around on the garage floor.

Able to breathe again, Mattie stood.

Just as the gun fired.

She whirled in time to see Paul's body go slack. His killer rose, ran to the other side of the car and took off.

"No!" Mattie knew the sound came from her, but she didn't recognize the high-pitched scream filled with misery. The security guard found her and tried to help her stand, but her stomach twisted in pain and she blacked out.

She woke to sirens screeching all around her. EMTs lifted her onto a stretcher, but she motioned at them to save Paul. Flashes of sympathy filled their eyes and when she turned to look at her husband, a white sheet covered him all the way to the top of his head.

She screamed again and then sobbed, raw pain tearing from her throat and shaking her body. One of the technicians gave her a sedative and the cool sensation of it traveled the length of her arm. Before she lost consciousness, her stomach cramped and a whoosh of sticky liquid gushed from between her legs.

She woke in the hospital to find her parents standing over her. One of them stayed with her every minute, through her recovery from her miscarriage, through Paul's funeral, and the mountains of paperwork from his law firm that followed.

When she was well enough to leave the hospital, the police asked her to come to their office to identify Paul's killer. She expected to spend grueling hours going through police photos, but after only twenty minutes, his face stared up at her from the desk. She fought hysteria and pointed to him, then learned he was a well-known hit man for hire ... a member of the Greek mafia that operated close to the Inner Harbor ... who had eluded capture for years.

She also learned the police found Paul's BMW in the warehouse district the morning following his death, with the body of a rival gang member stuffed in the trunk. The police speculated the hit man simply seized an opportunity to make a quick buck and pick up a car on his way to do a job, an MO associated with him.

Mattie chose to go home to North Carolina with her parents, promising to return to Baltimore for a trial, if necessary. But it hadn't come to that.

Paul's killer was never found.

She settled back into her former life and at her family's insistence, reverted to her maiden name. They convinced her it reduced the risk, somewhat, of the killer finding her and eliminating his final witness.

But he was never found. Never arrested. Never brought to justice. Even with the DNA samples of his skin taken from under her fingernails.

So her family insisted she take a weaponry course—Gun Training for Women. She found the length and intensity of the course shocking, but she kept at it. Every time she aimed at a target, she pictured the face of Paul's killer. She didn't like firing a gun—even after her training—but she knew in her heart that if necessary, she could shoot quickly, and she could shoot straight. And if, God forbid, she ever found herself face to face with the man who had deprived her of her beloved husband, she believed she would gladly pull the trigger.

She didn't think she would ever stop missing him or their baby. But eventually, time allowed her to think about them without the sharp, wrenching pain that had characterized that first year after he was gone. The insurance from Paul's company ensured she could live comfortably for a while, but when the position with the Visitors and Conventions Bureau presented itself, she jumped at it. Not for the job itself as much as the need to think about something else, a reason to get up in the morning.

She was thankful to be back with her family. They had been her best therapy. And they were all she needed.

So, she simply wouldn't open herself up to that kind of pain again. She *couldn't.*

Her head fell back against the neck rest.

She had so much to do … a ton of things that demanded her attention.

She started the car and drove to her office in Asheville.

She had to think of something else for a while. Her mind needed to rest.

And her heart needed more time to heal.

CHAPTER EIGHT

1946

"Is this really what you want, Henry?"

"I'm not sure it even matters what I want, Arnold," Henry said. "Especially since I asked her to marry me in front of people. I'd look like a pretty big cad to go back on a proposal when there were witnesses to it."

The two men had gone to Henry's office after drinking on the patio for hours. Michael Maguire, the groundskeeper's son, had hovered around them, trimming bushes, filling fountains, fetching drinks, and, Henry was certain, eavesdropping. The boy seemed to be enamored with Henry's uncle Arnold, an airline pilot for Pan Am.

To many people in town and at Clairmont Place, Arnold Sinclair, the much younger brother of Henry's father, was somewhat of a legend. Only three years older than his nephew, Arnold had accepted Henry's invitation to be the best man at his marriage to Constance Baldwin at the end of the week. The men had considered themselves best friends for most of their lives and with Henry's companies demanding less of his time, Arnold—who constantly tinkered with various investments—delighted in floating new business deals in front of him.

"Besides," Henry added, "I'm not sure it makes a lot of difference. I had the love of my life and I'll never find another Lily. My poor little Jeffrey can't seem to get over his grief ... spends all his time with Cook Carson in the kitchen or alone in his room. Drawing. Always drawing. He's pretty good, too."

"So you're lonely? Is that it?"

"Not really. But I do like the thought of a woman in the house again to handle day-to-day issues. She has a son just a couple of years younger than Jeffrey. Funny … they even favor each other—same coloring, same build." Henry gazed out the window at the beech trees that lined the driveway. "So Constance will be as good a wife as any. Her father is one of my attorneys, so he'll look out for us." Henry filled their glasses from the bourbon decanter in the corner.

"He'll look out for *her*, you mean."

"Yes, okay. But look, Arnold, why do I care? I have enough money. So what if she wants to spend some?"

"Well, I'll tell you why you should care. What if you die? Who gets Clairmont Place? What if she sold it out from under Jeffrey, and he didn't get anything from it? Or suppose you had an accident and couldn't run your businesses any longer. Do you really want her father to step in and take over? Do you want them to sell *your* father's priceless art collection? Or what if—"

"But they're good people. They wouldn't do any of that."

"Do I need to cite instances of other men who uttered those exact words only to have their children end up with nothing?"

"Okay, okay," Henry said. "I still don't think we have to worry about it, but I see your point. What should I do?"

"You have her sign a prenuptial agreement. And spell everything out—what happens if you die, if you're incapacitated … even if you get divorced. Since she has a son, she'll understand. You can even throw in a multi-million-dollar insurance policy—a lump sum payment to her if you die. Enough to make her one of the wealthiest women in the country."

"I suppose it's the right thing to do. Of course, I can't really ask her father to draft it."

"Remember, Henry, I earned my law degree in North Carolina, so even though I live in Maine now, I'm still licensed to practice in this state. We can draw it up together, tonight. I'll take care of the legal mumbo-jumbo in the morning. Why don't you get Charles in here? He can type it as we go."

Henry pushed a button under his desk and in minutes his secretary, Charles Hudson, showed up at the door.

"How can I help you, sir?" He addressed Henry, then saw Arnold leaning against the window. "Oh, Mr. Arnold. How nice to see you again."

Arnold drained his glass and headed to the decanter to refill it. He picked up Henry's empty glass on his way. "Thanks, Charles, same to you.

Join us in a drink?"

Charles smiled at him. "Thank you, sir, but no." He turned back to Henry. "Do you need my services this evening, sir?"

"Yes," Henry said. "My uncle here"—he indicated Arnold with a vague wave and then accepted the full glass of bourbon—"thinks I need to have my fiancée sign a prenuptial agreement. Personally, I think it's silly, but he insists. Will you type it as we draft it?"

"It would be my great pleasure, sir."

Charles's response was enthusiastic, and Arnold lifted his head toward him, a quizzical expression on his face. "Interesting, Charles," he said. "Your voice sounds like you think it's a good idea, too."

"I do, sir. A very good idea."

"Really," Henry said. "For any special reason?"

"No sir, just a feeling. But it never hurts to protect yourself and Master Jeffrey."

Constance's personality was reserved, Henry knew. Not outgoing like Lily's was. And she wasn't outdoorsy, either. She had told him the Maguires would go back to handling all the landscaping—she wanted no parts of planting flowers the way Lily had. And she was afraid of horses— Lily's other passion. Which was fine with him. Lily was gone and he didn't want a pale imitation of her. But he believed Constance would make a fine wife and represent him well at social gatherings and with the wives of his business associates. That was really all he needed these days.

"Okay, then, let's get started," Arnold said. He rolled up his sleeves and Charles left the office to return a few minutes later with his typewriter and a ream of paper. "We'll dictate while Charles types," Arnold said. He took a big swallow from his drink. "And then, my dear nephew, you just have to get Constance to sign the damn thing by Saturday."

"Fine," Henry said. "Maybe I'll even sweeten the pot with a shopping spree in Greece when we're on our honeymoon."

"Good idea," Arnold said. "So, let's begin. By the way, why does she go by her maiden name of Baldwin rather than her married name, whatever that was?"

"Oh," Henry said, "some vague reason about being married to a man who died suddenly after engaging in questionable business practices. Her father believed it would be better for her and her son to resume the Baldwin name rather than being associated with her deceased husband's."

Arnold shrugged. "That's as good a reason as any," he said.

The men spent the next couple of hours drafting the prenuptial agreement while Charles typed. Henry was amazed at all the situations Arnold thought of. The property did, and always would, belong to Jeffrey in the event of Henry's death, so several provisions dealt with the fact that Constance couldn't sell the land, the mansion, or any of its contents, even if she moved away from it. She could, the document stated, lease the grounds prior to Jeffrey's twenty-first birthday and keep whatever payments ensued. If the property remained on lease after Jeffrey turned twenty-one, he would first have to agree to it. Then half the lease payments would be hers and the other half would go into an account for him that he could access on his thirtieth birthday.

The last few sections dealt with "Termination Events." Or divorce, in plain language. Henry didn't like this section because he didn't see the need for it. He would never initiate such a thing.

When the document was finished, Henry re-read it and shook his head. "Arnold, I don't know about this."

But Arnold insisted, convincing Henry that he never knew what might happen. He needed to be prepared.

"Well, this document will certainly leave me prepared." He picked up the sheets Charles had typed. "My goodness—twenty pages? Is all that really necessary?"

"Believe me," Arnold said. "There may come a day when you will thank me for this. I sincerely hope not … but, if so, I'll be glad we took care of you and Jeffrey."

The following day Arnold dictated a few corrections to Charles and then Henry invited Constance and her father to breakfast on Friday—the day before the wedding.

Henry heard Constance coming before he saw her—the click-clack of her heels on the marble floor announcing her presence. He wondered if he'd ever get used to the sound.

She bustled into the room with her father trailing along behind her. "I don't know why we have to do this now, Henry," she said. "We still have a million things to do." She flounced into the chair he held for her and whipped her napkin into her lap. "I need coffee," she barked to Cook

Carson, who laid a tray of pastries on the buffet.

Filling Constance's cup was not the cook's job, Henry knew. Lily would never have been so brusque with her. He shot the cook an apologetic look, but she simply smiled and filled Constance's cup. "Coffee, sir?" she asked Constance's father. The cook filled all the cups and then retreated to the kitchen.

Constance kept up a steady stream of chatter, mostly about details for the wedding, but also complaints about Henry's staff. "My goodness, Henry," she said. "You give that Charles person too much latitude. Why, he has the run of the house, seems to hang around the kitchen way too much. Doesn't know his place, if you ask me."

"I don't think he did ask you, Constance," her father said. She snorted.

"Constance," Henry said. "There is something we have to discuss. And I'm glad your father is here to advise you."

She set her cup down with a bang and fixed him with a stare. "Well, what is it? I don't have time to waste here."

Henry reached into the chair beside him and brought out the document he and Arnold put together. "Since this property has been in my family for years and since Jeffrey is so young, I need you to sign a prenuptial agreement."

Constance's father gave a little gasp and Constance's eyes widened. She half rose from her chair. Anticipating a bad reaction, Henry had fortified himself since dawn with hefty doses of Irish whiskey in his coffee. He was prepared to stand firm.

"I beg your pardon?" Constance said. "You want me to what?"

"To sign a prenuptial agreement. Today. Right now."

"How dare you. I've never—"

"Calm down, Constance," her father said. "Let's read it first." He turned to Henry and held out his hand. "May I?" Henry handed him the document and he flipped through the first few pages, slowing down when he reached the section about not selling the property.

Constance sat back in her chair, her arms folded. "Well?" she spat out at her father.

"It's very fair, Constance," her father said. "It basically says that as Henry's wife you may do as you wish as long as the two of you are married. If he dies, you receive a lump-sum settlement via an insurance policy, plus a monthly allowance of one thousand dollars. But you may not sell the land, the house, or any of the contents."

Constance remained quiet so Richard continued. "If the marriage dissolves prior to two years, you keep the property you brought into the marriage, plus a thousand dollars monthly."

"But no lump sum?"

"Not if you divorce prior to two years." Constance's father looked at Henry. "Pretty powerful incentive to stay married."

"What a stupid thing to say," Constance said. "Of course we'll stay married. Why else would we do it if we didn't intend it to last?"

Henry handed her a pen, and she grabbed it from his hand. "So?" she asked her father. "Do I sign this?"

Her father smiled. "Only if you really want to marry Henry."

She bent her head over the paper and added her signature in angry strokes, then threw the pages at Henry. "There," she said. "I hope you're happy. Your precious little Jeffrey is protected from the big, bad stepmother." She rose, spilling the remainder of her coffee as she did. "I'm leaving. I have things to do. I'll see you at tonight's rehearsal and dinner."

Constance swept out of the room. She knocked into Charles Hudson on her way, growled out an expletive and then shoved him into the door jamb. He looked after her as she left, then ducked his head into the room.

"Good morning, sir. Is everything okay? Do you need—"

"No, Charles. Thank you. We're good here."

Henry drained his coffee cup ... almost pure whiskey by then.

CHAPTER NINE

1946

Hundreds of candles glowed bright in All Souls Cathedral near Biltmore in Asheville. Henry's son, Jeffrey, and Constance's son, Robert, walked slowly down the aisle along with Cook Carson, Charles Hudson, and the Maguire family. One by one, they slid into a front pew to await the ceremony.

"Really, Henry," Constance had said earlier, "you're inviting your servants? To our wedding? Will they even know how to act in that kind of social circle?"

Henry's temper flared, but he kept it in check. He had known the extent of Constance's haughtiness from the beginning, so he reminded himself to simply ignore her inappropriate remarks. "Most of those folks have been with me all my life, Constance," he said in a controlled voice. "And with my father before that. They're like family to me. They will have places of honor at such an important occasion."

Constance had frowned but refrained from saying more.

Arnold studied Henry in the low light of the groom's chamber. "It's not too late, you know," he said. "You don't have to go through with this."

Henry flashed his uncle a grin. "Give it up, Arnold. I'm going to marry her. Besides, what are you worried about? She signed the prenup."

"Okay, man. It's your funeral. Don't say I didn't warn you."

The music changed and the two men made their way to the altar. They took their places and Henry winked at his son, snuggled close to Rachel Carson, the family cook. Jeffrey appeared to be miserable, but Charles Hudson and Cook Carson had brought hard candy and small books to keep him entertained. Robert and Michael Maguire even benefitted from Jeffrey's bounty.

The first notes of the wedding march played and Henry, along with everyone else, turned his attention to the back of the church. The doors parted and Constance stood there, leaning into her father's arm, a huge smile filling her face. They moved down the aisle and the yards of cream-colored lace on Constance's floor-length gown gave her the appearance of floating.

It will be fine, Henry told himself. *This will all work out. And it will be better for Jeffrey. I'm sure of it.*

The ceremony went off without a hitch and the congregation traveled the short distance to the Biltmore Estate for a sumptuous reception dinner, offered as a wedding gift by George Vanderbilt's grandsons. The Clairmont Place staff, along with Jeffrey and Robert, celebrated in the Biltmore kitchens before heading home early. Arnold and Constance's father rode back to Clairmont Place with Henry and his bride and they all adjourned to the parlor for nightcaps.

"Well, my dear," Henry said to Constance after an hour, "shall we adjourn to our room?"

She drained her glass and accompanied him up the stairs but stopped in the hallway before they reached the door that led to his room. She laid her hand on his arm. "I'm really tired, Henry," she told him. "And we have an early morning to catch our flight to Greece. I'll sleep in the next room tonight."

She entered and closed the door firmly behind her. The lock clicked.

Fury flew into him. In two angry steps he reached her door, intent on breaking it down and confronting her about her attitude. But in seconds, his own fatigue washed over him, so he changed his mind and went into his room instead. They would have a serious talk when they reached Corfu. It could wait until then.

The sun rose brilliantly over the Ionian Sea and Henry breathed in the fresh sea air. Terra-cotta pots lined the balcony wall and a profusion of blooms in all colors spilled over their tops. Henry leaned out over the railing and saw bougainvillea tumbling around rocks and down the hillside all the way to the sea.

Lily would have loved this. What a shame we never got here together.

He straightened up and looked around, guilt filling his face. He had a new wife now. His thoughts should be about her.

As if on cue, Constance's voice reached him from the interior of their rooms. "My goodness, Henry, what are you doing out there in that glare?"

"It's beautiful out here, Constance. Why don't you join me? I have fresh coffee."

"No," she said. "Too much sun. I'm going to take a bath."

"Fine," he said, heading toward the door. "I'll wash your back."

"No," she said again. "Just let me be. It won't take me long and then we can go to lunch and shopping. As you promised." She left him without another word and closed the bathroom door firmly.

The days had been like that. With very little physical contact. Some days it appeared to be all Constance could do to be civil to him. He had no idea what he had done to bring about the change in attitude, but he didn't like it. So far, his marriage did not fulfill his idea of what it ought to be.

But whenever he brought it up, her anger erupted and then hovered, ready to explode again at any minute throughout the remainder of the day. Their time together had been miserable. So he approached her less and less and allowed her to dictate the terms of their relationship. He found it very unsatisfying but there were fewer knots in his stomach that way.

At least, his mind told him, it can't get worse.

He would later remember that thought and wonder how he could have been so naive.

CHAPTER TEN

2017

Corfu, Greece

Stavros filled the glass to the precise measurements his employer had drilled into him for the past ten years. A scoop of crushed ice—a rare commodity on the island—then ouzo to the halfway mark and bottled water to reach an inch from the top. A sprig of fresh mint from the window box completed the milky white concoction.

He presented the glass on a small teak tray.

"Will you require anything else this evening, sir?"

"No. You may go."

Stavros closed the door behind him, and his employer shuffled out to the balcony. He slumped into his overstuffed chair, its crevices the exact shape of his body. The last rays of sun slid under the awning, warming his face and transforming the surface of the Ionian Sea into millions of blinking diamonds.

He drained his glass—so carefully prepared to his exact specifications—in one swallow and reached for the ouzo bottle. He expected the night would be long and lonely.

"Will you be okay?" the priest had asked him earlier that day.

He knew the holy man referred to his emotional state.

He scoffed. *As if that would be an issue.*

His emotional state was fine. Good, in fact. Better than that ... great, actually.

The real problem centered on his financial state.

For years, her illness eroded their reserves, removing bits and pieces of their way of life. But last week when he tried to increase her morphine, the nurses refused. He owed too much money, they told him. No more credit, they said.

He chugged straight from the bottle.

He missed the early days. When they'd first moved to the idyllic island.

She was healthy then and vibrant. And happy. She treated him kindly … none of that constant stream of angry sniping. They spent their days walking the streets, going to the markets, and discovering restaurants. When she napped, he languished on the beach.

The difference in her manner once they reached Greece was both dramatic and welcome. Especially after moving from that mausoleum they called home in North Carolina—the one where her heels click-clacked across the marble floor, announcing her anger to everyone in her path.

Her father got sick first, and with few doctors on the island and no health insurance, the money dwindled. He refused to return to the States for treatment, so she took care of him, the costs of his nursing and medication bordering on the outrageous.

He'd been oblivious to their financial plight until her father died. After all the years of costly medical care.

Which ate into their remaining funds even further.

And more recently, inflation and the ensuing issues around Greece becoming part of the Eurozone heralded the end of their easy life. Every day their dwindling resources paid for less.

So her anger returned. With him as her sole focus for it.

Never would he forget the venom that erupted from her mouth all those years earlier.

"Look at you," she spat at him when they returned from her father's funeral. *"What have you done with your life? I'll tell you what,"* she screamed, without giving him time to answer. *"You've become a fat, lazy slug. A parasite living off me and my generosity."*

He couldn't argue. She had taken care of him ever since they moved there.

She homeschooled him, but she hadn't seen any point in his attending college.

Neither had he.

So he spent his days lounging at home or sunning on the beach. They kept to themselves because she considered herself superior to "these foreigners," as she referred to them—good enough to be her servants, but not her friends, and certainly not potential romantic interests. For either of them, she said.

He took another long drink from the bottle. The first stars dotted the evening sky, and a slight breeze cooled his face. He tried to relax the knot in his stomach.

She wrote letters. Mostly to the attorneys who managed her late husband's estate. Ten years ago, he found them. They were all the same. She wanted more money—first she pleaded, then she berated and finally demanded. But the attorneys either turned her down cold—reminding her of the prenuptial agreement she had signed—or on rare occasions, sent her small stipends.

"Who do they think they are?" she screamed to no one in particular. "They work for me. They can't treat me this way."

Her anger became rage and her rage rose to all out fury.

And he was the one in her path. Her only outlet for all that wrath.

He spent nights on the beach to escape it.

Her anger took its toll. On him, of course, but even worse on her. It ate at her insides, shutting down first one organ and then another. For a while she pretended nothing was wrong and compensated for her physical problems in other ways. Until it was too late. Until she passed out one day and he couldn't revive her. Until her only choice was an existence on life support.

Very expensive life support.

With no insurance.

And no advance directive or medical power of attorney. Which meant that legally no one could pull the plug.

For the past year she lay still, her heart and lungs artificially manipulated to pump up and down, in and out.

Her body shriveled away to nothing. And even life support could no longer force her organs to move.

Her medical bills and cremation expenses depleted the very last of their funds. He wasn't sure how he would survive.

Until this afternoon.

When a miracle happened.

He'd returned from her service—her urn under his arm—to find a letter at his door. A permission letter to allow the house in North Carolina to be used for some kind of international meeting. And he figured it would pay. Big money.

He took one more drink, pulled himself out of his chair and shambled unsteadily to her desk. He scratched a quick note on the bottom of the letter and stated that they would be happy to sign for a fee—half a million dollars seemed about right. He added his name—Jeffrey Sinclair—to the bottom of the note. Tomorrow he'd find someone to fax it back to Sinclair Bank & Trust.

Then he returned to the balcony with her urn.

A Grecian urn, he thought with a small smile. He continued to stare at it, and the smile bubbled into uncontrollable laughter.

Perhaps I should say an Ode. She would have loved that. Keats was one of her favorites.

He removed the urn's top and stared inside. He'd never seen the results of a crematory process before. The ash wasn't as fine as he'd expected. It had bits and pieces of ... he wasn't sure what. And decided not to dwell on figuring it out.

He held the urn way out over the stone wall of the terrace and slowly sifted its contents into the night air. The breeze caught the ashes and swirled them down to the sea, some falling on the bougainvillea that climbed the wall to the balcony, some falling on the rocks below.

He replaced the urn's top, set it down on the glass table and picked up his bottle. He drained it and threw the empty container out after her ashes.

His stomach relaxed slightly. And his shoulders lifted. He even managed a small smile.

He returned to the kitchen in search of a full bottle of ouzo and found a cold one. He opened it and held it high over his head in a silent toast before taking a long, slow drink.

The small smile spread until it filled his whole face.

His nightmare was finally over.

Constance Sinclair was dead.

CHAPTER ELEVEN

1947

New York City, New York

"You're right," Arnold Sinclair answered in response to the question on his nephew's face. "We're headed to the edge of the city. The Upper East Side, to be exact."

When he'd arrived at the New York airport, Henry Sinclair, Jr. jumped into his uncle's limousine, anticipating a very short ride to the financial district, his heavy briefcase balanced on his lap. That was the reason, he believed, he had come to New York instead of Arnold's estate in Maine—to sign papers of incorporation for a new private airline they planned to begin together—aptly named *Sinclair Air*.

But to Henry's bewilderment, the limo bypassed every downtown exit and motored, instead, toward Central Park and Manhattan.

"Because?" Henry questioned. He worked hard to keep his annoyance from showing.

"Because …" Arnold hesitated, "we're meeting a distant relative. One who asked to meet you specifically."

"Good heavens, Arnold. Do I have to guess?"

"No," Arnold answered. "I'll tell you. We're meeting with Harry Sinclair."

Henry struggled to remember a relative by that name, but a newspaper headline popped into his memory.

"Wait a minute," he said slowly. "Harry Sinclair, the *oilman*—the one who got in trouble with the government twenty-some years ago? The one accused of trying to steal the country right out from under the people? *That* Harry Sinclair? We're related to him?" Henry asked.

"We are," Arnold told him. "You see, he and I are second cousins," Arnold continued, "which makes you a second cousin once—"

Henry held up his hand. "Please don't try to explain all that distant relation stuff," Henry said. "I don't care enough." He stopped talking, still trying to rein in his aggravation. "How did you meet him? And why does he want to see us?"

"I know I never told you outright, Henry—and I certainly never told your father—but do you remember our conversation last year, before you and Constance married?"

"You mean the night we had too many cocktails on the garden patio?" Henry smiled. "I remember *some* of it. Why?"

"You asked me why I went to work for Pan Am, and I told you that my former business deals had soured. Which was true. But I also told you I enjoyed my time in Europe and the Far East so much, I had to figure out another way to get there. Which was also true ... and my way of alluding to what I'm about to tell you now."

"The main thing I remember," Henry said with a small laugh, "is that Michael Maguire—our groundskeeper's son—almost fell out of a tree he pretended to be trimming so he could eavesdrop on us." Henry smiled. "He was quite taken with you, Arnold."

"Yes, I remember him. Seemed like a bright lad." Arnold shifted in his seat before continuing. "What I didn't tell you that night in the garden was that I joined Pan Am when I quit my former job."

"Which was?"

"I used to work for Harry Sinclair."

Henry's gasp was genuine. "Are you kidding? You worked for the person who almost single-handedly brought down the Warren Harding administration? Who was the center of one of the worst scandals in the country's history—the, um, what did they call it again?"

"Teapot Dome."

"Oh right ... Teapot Dome." Henry frowned. "But I can't remember what that name had to do with anything."

"It was from a rock formation sitting on top of the oil fields ... shaped like—"

"Oh yeah, like a teapot. In Wyoming, right? My goodness ... he was in trouble for years, Arnold. What did you do for him, anyway?"

"I handled his Russian deals."

Henry gasped again. "His—good grief, man, you *are* full of surprises."

"Right. In fact, I was in Russia almost full time before Harry was on

48

trial."

"I can't get over it, Arnold … Russia? What if you're in trouble with the government? Wasn't it only a couple of weeks ago that Truman signed some foreign policy thing against geopolitical expansion of the Soviet Union and communism?"

Arnold shrugged before speaking again. "I'm no threat to the government, Henry. And remember, the Russians still wanted to be friends back then. They were even our allies during the war that just ended. And that worked great for Harry and his global ambitions. There he was, pumping oil from the Wyoming fields—hundreds of millions of dollars' worth of oil, by the way, but—"

"Let me guess," Henry said. "That wasn't enough for him, right?"

"Right. He also tried to make a deal with the Russians for oil reserves over there."

"I still can't picture you working for one of the most flamboyant men in the country's history," Henry said. "What did my father say about it?"

"I already told you, I never mentioned it to him. You know how low-key he was. I think he always suspected I was involved in something he wouldn't like, and he was right. But he never asked, so we never had to have the discussion."

"Did you get the Russian oil deal?"

"Almost. The Russians wanted it. They had just consolidated their loose federation of allies into the Union of Soviet Socialist Republics in 1923. But their condition to sell the rights to Harry—along with millions of dollars, of course—was for President Harding to recognize them by their new name—as a world power."

"My … Arnold, you … you met the president, too?"

"Once," Arnold said. "And Vladimir Lenin. Even stayed in a former czar's palace while we were there for the negotiations meeting. And the deal was done. All that remained was the president's signature." Arnold wiped his brow.

"So, what happened?"

"We found out on our return journey from Russia that Harding had died. Suddenly. And unfortunately," he continued, "Harry had already made millions of dollars worth of commitments and Lenin insisted he keep his part of the bargain."

"Even though Harry's only presidential leverage was dead?" Henry shook his head.

"As you can imagine, the Russians were angry. And the angrier they got, the more aggressive they became, exerting more and more—sometimes violent—pressure on Harry and those close to him ... claimed they had documentation that he owed them money. And forgiveness was not one of their strong suits. Neither was—is—forgetting. That's when I pulled out of the business."

Henry's amusement at his uncle's story vanished at the mention of violence and a finger of fear traced a track down his spine.

"Okay," he said slowly, "that helps me understand why he wants to see you. But ... what does Harry Sinclair want with me?"

Arnold wiped his brow again. "I'd rather he tell you himself." He looked out the limousine window. "Come on. We're here."

They had arrived at Seventy-Ninth Street and Fifth Avenue, site of the Sinclair mansion. Arnold led the way and Henry followed him into the spacious foyer, his palms damp with nerves.

"Arnold! Great to see you again," a voice boomed from the door. "Come in. Have a seat."

While shorter than Henry had envisioned, Harry Sinclair's bigger-than-life personality filled the room and commanded attention. Henry didn't want to warm up to him, but the man exuded such an optimistic outlook and zest for life, he found it impossible not to.

"Henry," Harry Sinclair said, "it's a pleasure to meet you. Arnold has told me so much about you."

"The pleasure is mine, Mr. Sinclair."

"Please, call me Harry. We're all friends here. And related, too, I understand. Did Arnold explain?"

"Yes sir, he did," Henry said. He accepted a drink from the butler even though it was scarcely past noon. When the three men had settled comfortably, Harry turned his full attention to Henry. "I guess your uncle has filled you in somewhat."

"He told me he used to work for you, Mr.—Harry—but not why you wanted to see me."

"Well then, I'll get right to the point."

Henry remained silent.

Arnold studied his shoes.

"You see, Henry, I'm getting ready to retire in a year or so ... just don't have the energy required to keep up with the day-to-day exertion all my holdings require. So, I'm tying up loose ends and selling off some of my foreign interests." He hesitated and cleared his throat. "I've come across some information that I felt compelled to share with you. Unfortunately, while it originated from my former Russian, um … 'friends,' it affects you directly."

Harry retrieved a single sheet of paper from a small rectangular metal box on a table beside him. "I concluded the bulk of my business dealings in Russia right after President Harding died, since I no longer had the … connections … the Russians sought."

"Yes," Henry said. "Arnold told me that."

"Since then," Harry continued, "it's no secret that the Russian economy has weakened—which means, of course, their determination to get money from me—from anywhere they can, I suppose—has strengthened. Every few years, some new Russian zealot—a peon in the government trying to make a name for himself with Moscow—discovers our near-miss of a deal and takes it on himself to come after me with whatever means he has at his disposal."

"Including violence?" Henry asked.

"Sometimes," Harry said. "But here's my point. With the Russians needing money, and frictions between them and the United States intensifying with Truman's new foreign policy, his 'doctrine' I think he called it, they've begun activating some of their hidden resources."

"Hidden resources? I don't understand."

"There's no reason you should," Harry said. "So, let me explain. Some years ago," he added, "the Russians began planting their people—trained agents, actually—into various locations in the United States. Other countries, too, I assume, but that's not what concerns us here."

"You mean spies?" Henry asked.

"Yes," Harry said. "But, more subtle than that. Entire families were given new identities, came to America, and assimilated into their communities for generations—simply living as Americans, not acknowledging their origin, and having no overt contact with Russia. Until, at some point— and once the families are here it may take twenty years or more—the Russian government reaches out to them—or sometimes even their grown children—and gives them an assignment. Normally to gather information. But I can't lie to you, son, sometimes their missions are more sinister."

Henry's stomach tightened.

"Most assignments involve infiltrating our government, or the military, or a financial system. But sometimes, the assignment is to become part of a family the Russian government believes will benefit them. I've uncovered several such foreign plants along the East Coast, and I have reason to believe their mission is to get to me through my family—however distant—since they still think I owe them money. And, Henry ..." The older man hesitated for a moment before continuing. "I'm so sorry to tell you this ... but one of the Russian plants exists in your household." He handed the single sheet of paper to Henry. "We have this name, but we understand there could be others ... others that may have been recruited."

Henry's vision swam when he saw the name on the paper. His throat constricted, and he took a large swallow of his drink, then remained silent, his hands clenched into fists at his side.

"I am really sorry you were dragged into this, Henry," Harry Sinclair said gently. "You have my word that I will help you in any way I can to rid yourself of this plant. And I will provide you with substantial resources for your trouble." Harry put the small lockbox from the table beside him into Henry's lap.

Henry looked inside. "Bonds?" he asked.

"Yes, war bonds. I've found them very effective forms of payment. And Henry, the Russians would dearly love to get their hands on these. If you won't be offended, I'd like to outline a plan for you that should both remove the infiltrator from your midst and protect you and your little boy in the process. I've never known a Russian plant to refuse a bribe. Are you interested?"

Henry nodded. He welcomed Harry Sinclair's plan.

He could no longer think. His world toppled around him and fear overtook all other functions. A spy ran free within his household. Someone he'd trusted completely. And his only child was still there ... without Henry's protection.

He had to act quickly. His son was in danger as long as the Russian influence remained.

CHAPTER TWELVE

2017

Sinclair Station, North Carolina

At a very young age, "The Operative"—TheO—had learned his history. He was one of a select group secreted out of his homeland as a tiny child and raised with a new family to be American.

He'd also learned his mission: to assimilate totally into his new life so those around him never knew he hadn't been born there. And to be ready when the order came.

He was one of the lucky ones.

His order had reached him nine months earlier and since that time, updates found him in various places. All contained vital information about what he was supposed to do.

He had worked hard to position himself correctly, to be ready when he was needed.

And he was.

He was a difference maker, one of the few who would not only give valuable information to the motherland, but who would also be instrumental in restoring his country to the respected position it deserved in the world.

His first test would take place soon. Right here in Sinclair Station, the town he had called home for decades. Among people who'd been his friends since childhood. But he was ready.

He dressed carefully and left his home after combing the small house to make certain no telltale information—anything that might arouse suspicion—could be found.

Just in case he was unable to return.

His training had been thorough.

He parked his car, zipped his jacket, and casually strolled to the middle of the waiting group.

CHAPTER THIRTEEN

1947

New York City, New York

Henry Sinclair put the small gold lockbox key into his jacket pocket and climbed into the waiting limousine. His heavy briefcase rested on his lap and the lockbox Harry Sinclair had given him—stuffed with more than two million dollars in war bonds—sat at his feet.

"Back to La Guardia," Arnold said. "By the way," he leaned forward to speak directly to the driver. "I forgot to ask you about Stanley, my regular driver. I was a little distracted when we first got in. But how's he doing? His wife is pregnant, and I know she was having some trouble. Did she go into labor?"

"Yes, sir," the driver said. "I believe she did."

At the airport, Henry and Arnold stepped out of the limo only a few feet from Arnold's new Beechcraft Bonanza, and Arnold began his flight check prior to departure.

The limo driver left the area, headed for a small, remote park in Queens. As dusk gave way to darkness, he opened his trunk and in the cover of thick trees, dumped the chain-wrapped body of Stanley, Arnold Sinclair's regular limo driver, into the edge of the swampy lake.

Apprehension filled Henry's head and fear knotted his stomach. If not for Jeffrey, he would never have agreed to fly at night. Especially after this long day where his world had crashed down around him.

He hated to fly at all, preferring to schedule his meetings within easy driving distance and boarding a plane only when absolutely necessary—

when his business interests demanded it. But he'd *always* avoided flying at night—even on large, commercial planes. Yet, here he was preparing to board a small Beechcraft Bonanza, where night flying was a relatively new occurrence.

But Arnold had insisted that flying at night was perfectly safe and climbed confidently into the pilot's seat. He adjusted the custom controls, installed to accommodate his left leg, crushed in a tarmac accident during his tenure at Pan Am six months earlier. He used the settlement he received from the airline to buy his Beechcraft.

Reluctantly, Henry followed him and slid into the passenger's seat. He worried that the stress and fatigue from the day might hasten the onslaught of the migraine he'd held at bay all afternoon.

But Arnold exuded confidence and when he began humming "Stairway to the Stars"—a song popular from a decade earlier—Henry relaxed his neck against the leather headrest. He was exhausted. And talked out. He didn't even want to think. Within minutes, sleep overtook him.

The first rays of sun kissed the morning, and Arnold nudged Henry awake at the Asheville airport. "See?" Arnold said. "I told you I'd get you home in time for Jeffrey's birthday."

The two men embraced, and Arnold disappeared into the small airport's interior. Henry drove himself straight to his attorney's office to inaugurate the plan created the day before in Harry Sinclair's parlor.

CHAPTER FOURTEEN

2017

Mexico City, Mexico

The morning sun found his feet and then slowly expanded until it engulfed the entire courtyard at *La Mascota*, his favorite cantina in the heart of *El Centro*. He leaned back and closed his eyes, allowing the warmth to radiate through his body. He remained motionless, luxuriating in the sultry feeling.

But then his small metal table shook slightly and rattled the shot of *mezcal* in front of him. He opened his eyes far enough to squint at the large man who settled himself in the opposite chair.

"You are *El Gringo*?" the man asked. He was dressed stylishly in an expensive-looking navy suit, obviously tailored to fit his bulk.

"Who's asking?"

The man produced a card and slid it across the table. "I am told you have relative in location called Sinclair Station. In States. Is true?" The accent was strong … heavy … possibly eastern European. Definitely not Mexican.

"Again," the other man said, "who's asking?"

"You will want to speak with my employer. Important job at location of next U.S. G7 Summit. Could be yours. Pay is big."

The other man picked up the card and read the company name: *Universal Security and Surveillance*.

"And what is it that Universal Security and Surveillance would want El Gringo to do for 'big' money?"

The large man stood, almost overturning the table and spilling the shot of *mezcal*. "Come with me to office. Find out." Without waiting for an answer, he strode toward the courtyard gate.

The other man jumped up and scrambled to follow.

Their journey terminated abruptly, and El Gringo looked around with amazement. Then he climbed the stairs to the fourth-floor meeting room at the Russian Embassy.

The large man escorted him inside to a plush office where a tall gentleman faced wall-to-wall windows that overlooked the city. He turned to them as they entered.

"Ah, El Gringo. You come. Good." The gentleman, as stylishly dressed as his colleague, walked toward them and indicated a large leather chair. "Please, sit." He stared intently. "So, we meet. I am Hektor Orlov and my companion is Yakov Borodin. El Gringo is your given name?"

"Look," El Gringo said. "I'm the one who will ask the questions here." He remained standing.

Hektor nodded and sat down.

"No, El Gringo is not my given name. It's not even one I gave myself. It's what my Mexican friends call me. I'll be happy to give you my name," he continued, "as soon as you tell me about this so-called job and how much it pays. And what, exactly, you want from me."

"Of course," Hektor said. He rose and went to his desk. "This," he said, holding a piece of paper, "is copy of telegram our government received in nineteen forty-seven. Have you ever heard of Henry Sinclair?"

"I guess ... in a roundabout way. Isn't he the dude Sinclair Station is named for?"

"For his father, actually, but yes, you have correct family. This telegram," Hektor said, handing it to El Gringo, "was sent by limousine driver, who worked for our government. He sent it the same day he delivered Henry Sinclair to relative's house in New York City—a *Harry* Sinclair who made millions in oil. And after that visit, limo driver took Henry Sinclair back to LaGuardia Airport."

The words on the telegram, blurred with age, read *Twenty-nine March, nineteen forty-seven STOP Payment given and accepted STOP Lockbox with Henry Sinclair when he got on plane STOP.*

"Okay. So?" El Gringo asked.

"So," Hektor continued, "Harry Sinclair made deal with my government in nineteen twenty-three for millions of dollars. Never paid. My government still wants money. And limo driver reported that Harry gave large sum—in war bonds, he learned—still worth lot of money—to relative, Henry. Limo driver saw Henry put key to lockbox in pocket."

"That was a long time ago. Anybody could have gotten to those bonds by now."

"My government," Hektor said, "monitored conversations in Sinclair household at the time. We know Henry had bonds at house."

"Wait a minute. Henry Sinclair ... isn't that the dude who got himself killed?"

"You are correct. Henry Sinclair returned to Sinclair Station, and was murdered same day. Widow moved family to Greece. From communications we intercepted, we know she never found bonds. So, Henry must have hidden lockbox—and key—somewhere in house ... same day he got home. Before he was killed."

"And you want me to get it for you, right?"

Hektor nodded. "You get key for us, we do the rest. Perfect opportunity. Big international meeting being held there. We set up company chosen for surveillance equipment. You install. With relative in town, will be easy for you."

"Sure, no problem," El Gringo said. "But what's in it for me?"

Hektor leaned back in his chair and formed a tent with his fingers. "Five percent of whatever we find in lockbox. We believe is worth more than twenty million dollars."

El Gringo sucked in a quick breath. Five percent of twenty million dollars meant a million dollars for him. In fact, "more than" a million dollars, the way Hektor described it.

His ticket to the big time.

He smiled broadly and extended his hand. "My given name is David. David Rousseau. Nice to meet you."

CHAPTER FIFTEEN

Sinclair Station, North Carolina

The Chamber Quartet from the University of North Carolina, Asheville—courtesy of Mattie's mother, Adelaide, as Chair of the UNCA Classics Department—provided the perfect background music to the sold-out crowd at the Visitors and Conventions Bureau Halloween Gala on the grounds of Clairmont Place.

Mattie meandered to the back of the tent, weaving carefully among the tables and stopping occasionally to speak to some of the younger guests. Her assistant, Simone Rousseau, seven years her junior, did the same. They made a good team.

At the back of the huge tent, Mattie surveyed the room. Boasting its highest attendance in its history, every chair—all three hundred of them at two hundred fifty dollars per plate—was filled and the air buzzed with happy conversation as guests enjoyed every last morsel of their gourmet meals. The event had exceeded all expectations.

Simone came up beside Mattie and leaned on a silent auction table. "Whew," she said. "I've been on my feet for most of the evening. These new heels have pinched my toes unmercifully the entire time."

"Well, they certainly are beautiful," Mattie said, admiring their teal color, obviously dyed to match Simone's dress—and to highlight her eyes.

Simone reached up and twisted a blond curl around her index finger—a habit, Mattie knew, since childhood. She stopped when Mattie grinned at her.

"Okay, okay," Simone said. "I know I need to stop that." She sighed. "But it's kind of like my security blanket."

"No problem, kiddo," Mattie said. "Do what you have to." Mattie winked at her.

Dignitaries from the area—including mayors from both Sinclair Station and Asheville, along with federal and state senators and representatives from the local districts—occupied places of honor on the dais. Cameras flashed and recorders rolled as local reporters captured every second of the evening.

Most of the guests finished their dinners and only one speaker remained on the agenda. Outside, the night had chilled, but the tent heaters hummed along quietly, bringing the inside temperature up to a comfortable seventy-two degrees. Servers whisked away empty dishes and refilled wine glasses.

"We're closing in on the finish," Mattie said, standing next to Simone. "Thank goodness. Once the senator announced us as the venue for the summit, I've been obsessed with putting this event behind us and getting on with that one. It will be the largest thing we've ever done, you know."

"Yes, I do know," Simone replied. "And I'm right there with you about getting started on it."

Mattie took a deep breath and a small shudder shook her body.

"What's wrong?" Simone asked.

Mattie hesitated and then said, "I still have an uneasy feeling. As if somebody were here to make trouble."

Simone laughed. "Are you paranoid that the other summit venues—the ones that *weren't* chosen—are out to get us?"

"Well no," Mattie said. "At least I wasn't ... until now." They both laughed. "I'm sure it's nothing. I'll feel better once we get through dessert. You'll give me the word when it's time, right?" Simone gave her a mock salute and Mattie worked her way through the tables to the front of the tent. A murmur of anticipation rippled through the crowd.

Within minutes, Simone's voice sounded in Mattie's earpiece. "Everything's ready. You can cue your dad any time."

"Thanks," Mattie said and then wove a path to her father. When she reached him, Mattie's father stood and bent his head toward her. As president of the Sinclair Bank & Trust Company—the premier sponsor of the gala—Matt Maguire had executed the role of emcee for the past five years.

Announcing dessert was one element of that role. And he performed it flawlessly.

Dessert, Mattie knew, had become a grand tradition at the Halloween Gala and corporate guests renewed their ticket purchases and sponsorships year after year based solely on the theatrical display.

Matt Maguire stepped up to the microphone.

"Ladies and gentlemen!" His voice boomed deep and rich. "Please take your seats and make certain the space around your chairs is clear and free from obstacles."

The majority of the guests knew what was coming, so they tidied up their areas quickly. Guests new to the event followed suit.

When the shuffling subsided, Mattie's father spoke again.

"Lights, please!"

That was Simone's cue. The lighting technicians had rigged a button for her so she could plunge the tent's interior into semi-darkness with just one click. Members of the event staff held tent flaps open wide on all four corners.

"Ladies and gentlemen," Mattie's father said again, "dessert is served!"

The clear trumpet notes that heralded the beginning of Johnny Cash's "Ring of Fire" sounded over the speakers and the audience broke into wild applause. Waiters entered the tent from each corner, swaying in time to the music and balancing trays of flaming Baked Alaskas high above their heads. Light from the flames danced on the waiters' sharp red coats and crisp white gloves.

Through the first two verses, they moved slowly through the crowd with choreographed twists and turns that allowed each guest to see them up close and hear the sizzle of the fiery confections. By the time the music swelled to the chorus, the waiters met in the middle of the tent. They formed a big circle and sashayed around it, flames still high, creating their own ring of fire as The Man in Black sang about it. For almost three minutes, the intricate routine wound its way through the tables while each chorus added new movements to make the ring of fire increasingly spectacular. The crowd's applause almost drowned out the famous voice.

The waiters, part of a seasoned group from Asheville, specialized in such lavish displays and Mattie knew they could be counted on to avoid losing their balance or tipping their trays and sending brandy-fired meringue into hairspray-stiff coiffures or expensive toupees.

The song finished and the regular wait staff stepped in to serve the desserts. The Asheville team danced its way out of the tent to a standing ovation.

Mattie approached Simone with her hand held high and Simone

slapped it. Only one speech remained, followed by an hour or so of dancing to a local rock band.

"So," Simone said. "As long as the sound system continues to work and the video presentation equipment doesn't break down in the middle of the last speaker's slides, we can mark this one as successful and move on, right?"

"You got it, kiddo," Mattie answered. "Next stop—G7 Summit Engagement Groups."

After the final speaker wrapped up, Mattie and Simone strode toward the front of the tent, ready to supervise the band set up.

It happened so fast. Neither of them saw it coming. Flames licked up the back wall. Ten seconds later, they jumped to a waiter's sleeve when he rushed over to help. One of the band members grabbed a pitcher of clear liquid and threw it at the blaze.

The fire flared even higher.

"That was white Sangria, you idiot," the bartender screamed. He pointed a small fire extinguisher at the flames and within seconds another bartender joined him.

The band member just stood by watching, a look of horror on his face.

Mattie ducked out the back of the tent and heard shouts erupt from the crowd. Her grandfather held a hose and aimed a stream of water at the back wall of the tent, dousing the flames that had burned through the heavy fabric. Mattie picked up a second hose and joined him. Sirens wailed in the distance.

The fire was out by the time the fire department arrived, but a heater-sized section of the tent was missing, its edges scorched and ragged. Only a slight odor of smoke hung in the air, accompanied by the aroma of scorched fabric.

"Oh my goodness," Mattie said when she came back in. "Is anybody hurt?" She unzipped several of the surrounding panels and pushed them aside, so fresh air could remove the smoky smell.

"No—the waiter got out of his jacket before being burned. And the bartenders acted so quickly, no one else was even close to the fire," Simone said.

"I didn't see how it happened," Mattie said. "Did you?"

"It was my fault." They both turned toward the voice … the band member who threw the Sangria. "That heater was right where my drums needed to go. I thought I could slide it enough to make room, but it caught on an uneven floor panel and fell backward. It happened so fast." He put his hand on his forehead. "I can't believe it. I'm just … I'm so sorry." The other band members crowded around him.

Mattie's grandfather, flanked by volunteer firemen, appeared beside the distraught young man. "Accidents happen, son," Michael Maguire said. "That's why we try to plan for every possibility … and why we have hoses close by."

"That's right," Mattie said. "Every time we have a tent here. Especially," she said, addressing the firemen, "if there are heaters … or flaming desserts. We've just never had to use them before."

"Thank goodness for that." Mattie and Simone turned toward the new voice, Mattie's boss from the bureau. The Asheville Chamber's board chair and the owner of the tent company stood on either side of him.

"I'm really sorry this happened, Morgan," Mattie said to her boss. "I take full responsibility."

"I heard what this young man said," he responded. "And … Jerry," he added, turning to the tent company owner, "aren't these things supposed to be fireproof?"

"They are," the owner said. "Under normal circumstances. But when a heater gets tipped directly onto the fabric, it's no longer working as designed. At that point, all bets are off. You can't guarantee the outcome."

Senator Reginald Bradley appeared at Mattie's elbow and said quietly, "It's a good thing the G7 Selection Committee already awarded the venue to us." He frowned. "What do we say to them if they hear about this?"

"We tell them exactly what Jerry just told us," Mattie's boss spoke before she could answer. "Not much can be done if a fire comes into direct contact with fabric. Our focus should be on Mattie's quick action with her hose." He put a hand on her shoulder in support. "Besides, Reggie," he said, "the events for the summit will take place inside the house. I doubt we'll even have any of these heaters on the premises. I'm just glad the fire didn't start from one of those flaming desserts slipping off a tray."

"We'll still want to do some investigating," the fire chief said. "But it seems pretty straightforward to me."

"Good," Mattie's father said when he joined the group. "We have a celebration to finish here." He turned to the fire chief. "Why don't you take off that heavy coat, Tom, and join in the dancing?"

The band finished setting up, and Mattie's father stepped back to the microphone.

"Folks," he said, "we apologize for that bit of drama. Please come back inside the tent. The little fire is totally out and these fine young people"—he gestured toward the band—"are all set up and ready to go. I've instructed our bartenders to open more champagne—courtesy of Sinclair Bank & Trust," he added quickly at the distressed look Mattie shot him, "and to keep it free-flowing for the rest of the evening. Come on back in and enjoy this beautiful night."

Mattie relaxed. "Good ol' Dad," she said and smiled at the group. "What a party-saver."

"Right," Simone said. "Maybe even a *job* saver."

The band played the first few notes of "The Air That I Breathe," a song by The Hollies, a group popular in the nineteen-seventies.

Mattie drew in her breath. "That's my mother's favorite song," she said softly. "Dad must have made a deal with the band."

Matt Maguire held out his hand to his wife and the two of them whirled around the floor like a bride and groom at their first dance. Their movements were so beautiful, the crowd not only returned, but also formed a hushed circle around them...the fire temporarily forgotten.

An hour and a half later, Mattie and Simone shed their shoes and dove into the middle of clean-up with the rest of the staff. Mattie's arms ached from stacking chairs, so she was glad for the break when her grandfather came up beside her.

"Will you come with me, Mattie Mat?" he asked quietly. "We have a ... situation."

She fumbled with her shoes as the vague unease that had plagued her all afternoon returned and blossomed into full-blown dread. Her grandfather led the way to the patio in Clairmont Place's formal gardens. They neared a group of people, and Sheriff Bryan Bennett was the first person she recognized.

"Mattie," Bryan said as she approached. "Will you tell me again what you thought you saw and heard earlier that made you nervous?"

"Of course," she said. "But first, please tell me what's happened."

"One of my men—from the temporary force I told you about—was attacked."

"Oh no," she said. "How badly is he hurt?"

"Hit on the head with a blunt instrument—probably the butt of a gun. He's been in and out of consciousness, and I'm figuring he has a concussion. An ambulance is on its way."

"A gun? Here? With all these people around?"

"So, what did you see?" Bryan pulled out his notebook.

"I told you … a movement out of the corner of my eye—a blur." Mattie shook her head. "And then this afternoon, footsteps in the leaves. Stealthy, furtive. But apparently, my feelings were right, huh? Somebody *was* here. Was your man able to describe his attacker?"

They had moved to the man on the patio, covered with a blanket. He was awake.

Bryan knelt beside the bleeding man. "Jorge," he said, "can you tell me again what happened?"

"Sure," the man answered. He spoke haltingly. "I headed back to my post … East Portico … after the fire. I rounded the corner and saw someone at the door. I beamed my light and yelled at him to state his business." The man's eyes closed, and Bryan shook him slightly.

"Is that all?" Bryan prodded.

"The fool rushed me. I turned to call for back-up—we don't carry weapons," he said to Mattie. He shrugged. "That's all I remember until you shook me."

"Did you see his face?" Mattie asked. "Or how tall he was?"

"Oh … probably not quite six feet," Jorge answered. "Kind of thin, dark hair."

"Would you recognize him in a line-up?" Bryan asked.

"Nah … too dar—" The man called Jorge passed out again and tires crunched in the drive. Within minutes, two ambulance attendants loaded him onto a stretcher and sped off.

"Oh, Gramps," Mattie said. "Maybe the fire wasn't an accident after all."

"I had that same thought," her grandfather said. "What do we need to do now, Bryan?"

"We'll comb the grounds for anything the attacker might have dropped. Look for footprints, car tracks—all the usual stuff. But honestly, unless we get lucky, there's very little chance of figuring out—quickly anyway—

who it might have been. Or why he was here. I'm sorry, but that's the way it goes. Not as cut and dried as it is on television."

"Is there any way we can keep this out of the news?" Mattie asked.

"Probably not," Bryan answered.

"Then we need to have a meeting with the senator and my boss, Gramps," Mattie said. "I'd really prefer we sit on this, but if we can't, we have to bring them into the loop. Will you call me on my cell, Bryan—day or night—if you have anything to report? Or if there's anything we can do to help?"

"Of course. And I'd be interested to hear from you if you can think of a reason someone would try to break into the house. Could it have anything to do with being the venue for the upcoming Summit?"

"That was my first thought," Michael Maguire said. "And you're right, Mattie Mat, about bringing the senator into this. He might know how upset the other venues in the final three were. It's possible someone from one of those cities is trying to discredit us. Regardless, Bryan, while you're investigating, I'll have my crew install additional lights at all the entrances—motion activated. That should help."

Mattie's earlier unease crept up her back again. She put an arm around her grandfather's waist. "My goodness, Gramps," she said with a small shiver. "I can't believe this is the first time it occurred to me, but if someone *is* trying to mess with us because we were chosen for the venue, it could be dangerous for you and Nana, too, here on the grounds all by yourselves. Maybe you should—"

"Mattie Mat," he said, giving her a squeeze. "You have enough to worry about. Nobody's going to mess with a couple of old coots like us."

But that worry wormed its way into Mattie's thoughts more often in the days that followed.

CHAPTER SIXTEEN

The Operative, or TheO as he was called, was surrounded by fools. All of whom stood to get in the way of his mission ... his assignment.

Word reached him the previous afternoon about another operative—also from his homeland, but with a different mission. A very different mission, as evident from his briefing. And the damn fool had shown up last night in the middle of a big event.

Even if both groups could fulfill their assignments—without compromising the other—the timing was wrong. Too early. Anything at this point would only arouse suspicion.

But that's just what the moron did ... showed up in the daylight when the grounds were swarming with people and prowled around.

And then, of all things, he came back at night and tried to get into the house. TheO's briefing had warned him that the other operative was armed, so when one of the idiot security guards at the Halloween event spotted him, TheO had no choice but to knock the guard out and chase the armed operative off the grounds. It wouldn't do for an unarmed guard to be shot by some psycho who couldn't follow orders. Heaven only knew how a shooting would look to the people who chose the site for the upcoming summit. That stupid fire was bad enough.

But a shooting. That could easily have been the end of it with the summit reverting to one of the other sites.

TheO couldn't let that happen. This mission was far too important, and he'd been preparing for it—they'd all been preparing for it—far too long.

His superior, The Vysokom, called him right away. They only communicated through voice-altering communication devices, so neither knew the identity of the other. The homeland wanted it that way for added protection.

TheO replayed the conversation in his mind.

"What the hell, TheO? How did that imbecile get into the middle of things? I didn't think we had to worry about him for another few months."

"I didn't, either. Do we need to take him out?"

"No ... not yet. I warned those other guys to stay away from here, but that ass, Hektor—bored with his little embassy in Mexico—is out to make a name for himself with the big boys in Moscow ... wants to go back to the motherland and thinks he's found the way. I'll approach him one more time, but if that doesn't work, I'll get someone from headquarters to have him back off or—"

"Or we handle it ourselves," TheO said, his lips spreading into a grin. "Trust me, that would be my pleasure."

"Sit on that one for now. And good job handling the situation so quickly last night. I'm doing what I can to keep any mention of it out of the papers."

"Any new orders in the meantime?"

"Just stay alert. They promised that half-wit who showed up last night big money to complete his part of the job, so I'm sure he won't back off. We'll talk again soon."

TheO inspected the rooms of his little house again before going out. He had to do whatever was necessary to see that his mission stayed on track. Nothing must stand in the way of the International G7 Summit being held right here in Sinclair Station so he and The Vysokom could report every nuance to Russia.

CHAPTER SEVENTEEN

The savory aroma of frying bacon floated into Mattie's room at her grandparents' house and forced her decision from indulging in another five-minute snooze to bounding out of bed, ready for breakfast.

She threw on jeans and a tee shirt—part of the clothes stash she kept there—and twisted her hair into a ponytail before joining her grandfather at the kitchen table. Mattie slid into the chair next to him and pecked her grandmother's cheek after accepting the mug of steaming black coffee from her.

"Fried or scrambled?" Mattie's nana asked.

"Fried," Mattie answered, helping herself to several pieces of bacon.

"One or two?"

"Two," she answered. "So ..." she said to her grandfather, "anything in the paper about the fire? Or the attack?"

Her grandfather handed her the metro section.

She grinned at the image of her parents, whirling solo around the dance floor.

Front page, above the fold, a coveted placement as long as the news was good and not full of fires or attacks on security guards.

The picture's caption read "Sinclair Bank & Trust president, Matthew Maguire, sweeps Chair of the UNCA Classics Department, Adelaide Maguire, off her feet." Both of the local mayors—from Sinclair Station and Asheville—along with Senator Bradley and two representatives, applauded in the background.

The reporter did mention the fire, tucked on an inside page, along with a picture and apology from the band member who had knocked into the heater.

"That's good," Mattie said. "Did you see anything about the attack?"

"I'm sure this section was printed by the time that happened. We'll want to check with Bryan today and see if he's found anything. And whether any reporters have contacted him."

"Right," Mattie said. "And I'll need to contact Senator Bradley's office. I'll start with his aide ... um ... phooey, I can't remember his name. But Simone will know—he chatted her up most of the night. And Morgan. I'll need to call him, too. I'll offer to meet with them today." Mattie sighed. "But I hope they turn me down."

She pulled out her phone and sent a text to her boss, asking him to call her when he had time. After breakfast, her grandmother relieved her from kitchen clean-up, so she put on a light jacket and walked over to the event tent, where company employees dismantled the structure, section by section. Her grandfather followed her out and spoke with the fireman from the previous night, who studied the section of slightly charred ground.

When everyone left, Mattie searched for her grandfather and found him on his knees in the small family cemetery, brushing leaves from some of the graves.

His parents' graves, she saw. *Bless his heart.*

"All done, Gramps," she said. "I'm anxious to hear what the fireman told you."

"He said there was no evidence of arson. But even if there had been, it would probably have gotten wiped out from all the traffic back and forth."

"That's what I figured."

"Me too. He really thought it was as simple as what that young man said ... that he bumped the heater and it tipped."

"So he hadn't changed his mind after the attack?"

Her grandfather shrugged. "I'm not sure he knew about that. And I'd rather wait to hear what Bryan has to say before talking to anyone else about it."

"Yeah, I'm with you. But I'll let Senator Bradley's office know what the fireman said."

Mattie knelt beside her grandfather. When he didn't look at her, she put an arm around his shoulder. "You okay, Gramps?"

"I'm fine, honey." He put his large hand on top of hers. "Every once in a while, I come here for a visit with these souls who will be my neighbors

71

a few years from now."

A little chill rippled down Mattie's spine. She knew her grandfather, at eighty-five, was in perfect health. But she also knew that didn't necessarily mean anything.

Henry Sinclair had been in perfect health, too. Prior to his murder.

"I can't remember the last time *I* came in here," she said. "And I hadn't realized there were so few graves. Only seven. Did I count right?"

"Seven," he said. "That's right."

Mattie looked at each grave. "I see your parents and four Sinclair graves," she said. "How many of the Sinclairs did you actually know, Gramps?"

"All of them, some better than others. I was around ten when the first Mr. Sinclair died. But my father worked for him almost twenty years before that and brought me here often … from the time I was three or four. So, yes, I spoke with him a few times. I also remember his wife very well. Miss Evelyn." He turned and gave Mattie a half smile. "She always made sure I was given ginger snaps and milk when she saw me."

"Aww, I would have loved to see your little three-year-old self with your cookies and milk," Mattie said. "I'll bet you were the cutest thing." She pinched his cheek and he snickered. "But didn't you and your family live here then?"

"No. Miss Evelyn's mother lived in the house where your grandmother and I live. Back then, we lived several blocks away. My father walked here every morning and home again every night. The old man—Mr. Sinclair, Sr.—had retired by the time I started coming here regularly and Henry, Jr."—he indicated the grave to the left of the first Mr. Sinclair—"managed the businesses."

"How well did you know Henry, Jr.?"

"Very well. I started working here—small chores, mostly, whatever my father thought I could handle—from the time I was eight. By then, Henry, Jr. and Miss Lily lived here, too, with little Jeffrey. He was a really sweet little guy. We even hung out some before his parents died. His mother died first."

"Did you know her, Gramps?"

"Yes, I did. She was a beautiful woman, Mattie Mat. With a good soul. Always smiling. Or singing. She wasn't very tall … could stand completely under Henry, Jr.'s chin. And I saw them stand like that a lot. I think I must have had a crush on her." He gave Mattie a sideways look and smiled. A small, sad smile.

"Oh, Gramps, how sweet."

"I used to love helping her in her flower gardens. It was my favorite job on the place. When she worked in the soil with the beautiful colors all around her, I thought she looked like an angel and smelled like sunshine."

"Gramps, I've never heard you so poetic before."

"She was really something. And as a twelve-year-old, I couldn't imagine finding a more perfect woman." Again, he cast a sideways glance at Mattie. "Until I met your grandmother, of course."

"Of course," she said with a smile.

Mattie's grandfather stopped talking and a cloud of sadness seemed to surround him.

"This last grave shocks me," Mattie said to change the subject.

"Yes," her grandfather answered. "Charles Hudson. Mr. Sinclair's secretary."

"And the man who killed him," Mattie added. "Isn't that weird? I mean … that Mr. Sinclair's killer would be buried in the same cemetery, only three graves away from his? How'd that happen, Gramps?"

Mattie's grandfather shrugged. "I'm not really sure. If I remember correctly, when he died, Charles no longer had any family to claim his body." He shrugged. "I remember Charles, though. He always seemed like a nice enough fellow."

"Until he snapped, I guess," Mattie said.

CHAPTER EIGHTEEN

1947

Henry spent time with his Asheville attorneys, then, satisfied that his plan rested in good hands, drove the twenty-two miles east to Sinclair Station, the town his father created half a century earlier. Normally, he enjoyed the drive—he had loved the North Carolina landscape all his life—but this morning he couldn't focus on anything other than figuring out how he could have been so blind.

He entered the grand foyer at Clairmont Place, the family mansion built on the property in nineteen hundred, and rested at the bottom step of the magnificent marble staircase. Exhaustion claimed his limbs, and the stairs appeared to stretch up forever. Worse, the migraine that taunted him earlier exploded and filled his entire head.

If he could just make it to the next floor ... to lie down ... he was certain he'd feel better.

But that had to wait. A few things demanded his attention first.

With a heavy sigh, he bypassed the large staircase and headed instead to the smaller one at the back of the house that took him to the floors below. He hid the lockbox Harry Sinclair gave him and returned to his office on the main floor.

He had to rid himself of the cloud that consumed him. But he also had to act with caution. Harry had advised him to conceal his knowledge from the Russian infiltrator, fearing that information might hasten the Russian's timeline and put him, and others, in immediate danger.

He sank heavily in his large leather chair. Items on his desk vied for his attention, but the portrait over the fireplace claimed it. Lily smiled out at him, her eyes reflecting love and happiness.

She looked angelic, ethereal.

Which certainly fit.

He drank in every feature of her beautiful face and his heart ached with the emptiness left by her death—the pain still sharp after almost three years. He had truly believed that once he and Constance married, the agony caused by Lily's death would dull and that his life with his new wife would be full and rich. But he'd been wrong about that. He remembered thinking during his honeymoon in Greece that his and Constance's relationship couldn't get worse. Unfortunately, he'd been wrong about that, too. Their separate rooms were bad enough, but their paths hardly ever crossed, unless a social event demanded they both attend. That wasn't the kind of marriage he'd had with Lily, and it wasn't what he'd had in mind when he married Constance.

Henry's stomach tightened again with the news Harry Sinclair had given him. He worried about others in his employ. Could they be in danger, too? Or, worse, were they among the people recruited to plot against him?

Henry reached into his top drawer and took out an album—a gift he'd put together for his father's eightieth birthday, five years earlier— only months before Henry, Sr. died. The album chronicled his father's success—his business deals with George Vanderbilt, of course—but mostly the businesses begun in Sinclair Station, the town that bore his name. Henry's father began the area's first textile mill, a bank for the mill's employees, and then extended his railroad holdings from Sinclair Station to Mobile to open trade routes for his textiles through the newly-opened Panama Canal.

Almost everyone in town worked for the mill when it began in 1900, including the parents and sisters of Melvin Maguire, Clairmont Place's current lead agronomist. Henry thumbed through the pages of his father's album and found the article he sought about the accident that resulted in the Maguire family becoming close to the Sinclairs.

SINCLAIR STATION, NC. Saturday, May 9, 1903:

Screams broke out in the cotton warehouse at the Sinclair Textile Mill on Saturday when several cotton bales tumbled from their stack, pinning twelve-year-old twins, Mary and Martha Maguire, beneath them. They died on the spot from the massive weight of the five-hundred-pound bales on top of them. The girls were the daughters of Morris and Millie Maguire, both of whom also worked in the mill.

> *In addition to their parents, the twins are survived by a younger brother, Melvin, two years old.*
>
> *Mr. Henry Sinclair, owner of the mill, told this reporter his heart went out to the Maguires and he would take steps to ensure an accident like that never happened again.*

And that, Henry knew, is exactly what his father did—although he never talked about it. But Henry, Jr. had found the ledger entries that detailed the level of his father's distress about the accident—a check to Melvin Maguire's parents for one thousand dollars—the equivalent of a year's wages for the entire family at the time of the accident. And later ledger entries to North Carolina State College in Raleigh with the notation *For Melvin Maguire.*

Henry Sinclair, Sr. paid all the expenses for Melvin Maguire's four-year college degree.

After Melvin completed his studies, Henry, Sr. hired him as caretaker and head agronomist for Clairmont Place.

Entry after entry in his father's calendar and appointment books noted suggestions Melvin had made and, for the most part, implemented—new plant species he introduced for better cross-pollination, names of suggested thoroughbreds to breed with the Sinclair mares, drawings that laid out some of the ornamental gardens—done in Melvin's own hand—along with an addition to the stables that was never built.

And now his son, Michael, works here as well. They're such great people. I can't believe I could have let this happen. Or that I might now have to worry about one or more of the Maguires being involved in this horrible plot.

But Harry had told him it was normal for the infiltrators to recruit others—those close to him—with promises of large sums of money.

"Oh, Mr. Sinclair. What a surprise. I hadn't expected you back so early."

Charles Hudson, Henry's secretary for more than ten years, hovered inside the office door.

Is Charles part of the scheme to betray me? We've been together so long ... and like the Maguires, Charles's father worked for my father. I've always trusted him with everything.

Henry shook his head to clear it.

76

Kaye D. Schmitz

"Arnold flew me back last night, so I could be here for Jeffrey's birthday," Henry said. "We landed this morning."

Charles' eyebrows shot up. "*You* flew at night? The way you feel about flying?"

"It isn't something I would like to do again anytime soon, believe me. Do you need me for something, Charles?"

"No, sir. We received a letter from the Internal Revenue Service that questioned a donation to a charity ... one that Mrs. Sinclair and her father worked on. I've been putting together documentation to answer the inquiry. But I can come back later."

It wasn't lost on Henry that Charles used the term "we" when referring to the Internal Revenue Service communication. Henry appreciated the fact that Charles kept as tight a rein on the family money as he did.

Henry shoved the album to the corner of his desk and the pages flipped randomly. He laughed softly when he saw the picture that stared up at him.

"Look at this, Charles," Henry said. "You'll get a kick out of it."

The album page lay open to a faded sepia-toned picture of a young, dark-haired man with intense eyes and a disarming grin. He leaned on what appeared to be a large sledgehammer.

Henry loosened the picture from its corner brackets and handed it to Charles. "Have you ever seen the back of this?" he asked.

Charles read the caption aloud. "'Little Billy Hudson drives the last spike on the Sinclair Railroad to Mobile. August 1, 1914.' My father," he added in a hushed voice.

"Funny how our family histories are entwined, don't you think?" Henry asked him. "Did you know that your father was accused by some of the mill workers of starting the avalanche of cotton bales that killed Melvin Maguire's sisters forty-five years ago?"

"No," Charles said softly, "I didn't." He stared at the image in his hand.

"But Melvin's parents assured my father it was simply an accident. They never pressed charges and convinced my father not to fire him. And then years later, he led the installation of the railroad to Mobile. He got that last spike in place just two weeks before the Panama Canal opened."

"And then died the next day, right? The day after this picture was taken?"

"That's right," Henry said. "When the stack of extra railroad ties

77

tumbled down on top of him."

"When I was little, my mother told me your dad sent her a check after he was killed."

"I've heard the story a number of times, myself," Henry said. "From my father. And I've seen the ledger entry for the check. It read: *Burial expenses for Billy and a scholarship fund for his little boy.* My father really liked him, Charles."

"Your father was very generous, Mr. Sinclair. As are you." Charles replaced the picture and looked Henry in the eyes. "I know I don't tell you very often, sir, but I hope you understand how much I love working here … working for you."

Henry's stomach knotted. He wished he could tell Charles about the Russian plant in their midst. There was just too much history between Charles' family and his.

Charles can't possibly be part of it. He just can't. But, how would I know? I suppose if the spy job is done correctly, the spy's target never knows. Until it's too late.

Henry's head throbbed and sweat dotted his forehead.

"Thank you, Charles," he said. "I appreciate hearing that."

Charles headed toward the door. When he reached it, he turned around and bowed to Henry. "Yes sir. I'll come back later, Mr. Sinclair." He hesitated for a moment before continuing. "Thank you for showing me the picture of my father."

Charles left and Henry heard him say, "Oh, pardon me, ma'am."

Henry heard his wife's high heels clicking across the marble foyer and figured she was headed out. He really needed sleep, so he decided not to detain her, knowing he could see her after his nap.

He placed several calls, tidied up some papers on his desk and stood.

"Excuse me, Mr. Sinclair."

Rachel Carson, the family cook, stood in his doorway, a coffee tray balanced in her hands. "Mr. Hudson told me you were home, sir, so I brought you coffee and pastries."

Henry smiled. "Thank you, Cook Carson."

She placed the items on his desk, and he welcomed the caffeine, hoping for relief from his migraine. He drained the cup, without even considering that the cook could be in on the plot … could have poisoned his coffee. With that thought, his chest remained tight and his breath restricted.

Still, he had to navigate the stairs, to see Jeffrey—the one person he knew he could trust completely.

And it was Jeffrey's birthday. His eighth.

His mother would have loved seeing him now. She would have been so proud ... as I am.

CHAPTER NINETEEN

2017

Corfu, Greece

He woke abruptly to pounding on the door and eased his swollen eyelids up far enough to confirm the sun shone.

Both of which brought considerable pain to his throbbing head.

He attempted to raise himself from his balcony chair and then fell back, exhausted. His right hand reached up to rub his forehead but smacked it instead with the neck of a bottle. One eye cracked open a little wider. An ouzo bottle. His second one from the night before. Empty.

The bottle slipped from his grasp, and he winced at the sound as it crashed to the stone floor.

The heat was unbearable. Sweat poured from him and drenched his silk shirt. It clung to him, and his linen pants bunched around his legs, limp and wrinkled.

A shower would feel really good. If he could just rise …

He closed his eyes again and drifted off. Only to be roused by a new wave of pounding. Louder … more insistent.

He heaved himself to a sitting position and regretted it immediately as bright bursts flashed in his blackened vision.

Pounding … pounding … pounding.

He made it to a standing position. Unstable, but upright.

He took one tentative step. And then another, headed for the door.

"Yes?" he said when he reached it. "Who is it?"

No answer. He swore under his breath.

But at least he was up. He headed for the bathroom, relishing the thought of cool water on his burning body. It cascaded over him until his legs could no longer support his massive weight. For the next few minutes he stood directly in front of the fan and then stepped into a light terry robe and tumbled onto his rumpled sheets. Sleep overtook him.

But it wasn't restful. Time and again, he thrashed around the bed and then woke himself as he jumped suddenly to avoid the demons pursuing him. After the fifth time his dreams jolted him awake, he gave up and painfully rose from the bed, clad only in his lightweight robe. It barely closed around his middle.

He was still hot. And parched.

Ouzo would help, he decided, so he left his bedroom in search of a fresh bottle. *Maybe one of the cold ones, in the fridge.*

He lumbered through the foyer on his path to the kitchen and saw the envelope sticking out from under his door. Stiffly, he bent and picked it up. The return address was from Sinclair Bank & Trust.

He ripped it open and read:

Memo to: Mr. Jeffrey Sinclair, Corfu, Greece

Re: Signature for Clairmont Place, property in Sinclair Station, North Carolina

Mr. Sinclair,

Thank you for your note regarding the signature to allow The Sinclair Estate to be used as the site for the International G7 Summit.

I must inform you, however, that any money received in conjunction with the international meeting on the property can only be used for the property in question, with no money available for your living expenses in Greece.

We have enclosed a duplicate copy of the permission letter. Since Constance Sinclair is the family contact of record, the letter must contain her signature, notarized and dated, to confirm its authenticity. If there is a problem with her ability to sign it, please send documentation, also notarized, describing such problem.

Time is of the essence. Feel free to call me at the number below my name. Thank you for your prompt attention to this matter.

Signed: Matthew Maguire

President, Sinclair Bank & Trust

1-828-100-1000

He read the letter. And then read it again. Precious time would be wasted finding a notary and having Constance's death certificate copied.

And notarized. And sent.

More time. More costs.

Regardless of his irritation, his brain grudgingly grasped the fact that no more money would come his way until he complied with the bank's request.

At that thought, a worse one seized him. Once the bank found out that Constance was dead, the monthly stipend she had received for as long as he could remember would cease. For good.

Sweat trickled down his back and white-hot fury flew into him.

Followed by cold black fear.

Creditors continuing to hound him.

More time before he had the money he'd counted on from the original letter.

No money. No ouzo.

He balled the letter up and threw it. It trickled to a stop by the front door.

When he reached the refrigerator, he drained half the ouzo from the cold bottle—his last—in one swallow.

CHAPTER TWENTY

Sinclair Station, North Carolina

Mattie was glad to see her father's car in The Cottage's driveway when she and her grandfather returned from the cemetery on Clairmont Place. She was certain her father's upbeat humor would bring her grandfather out of his melancholy.

They joined her father at the kitchen table, and she studied the two men. They were both very handsome, she decided ... despite the fact that one was in his eighties and the other in his sixties. Still fit and strong, their hair, once coal black like hers, had turned snow white and salt and pepper, respectively. *If I age half as well, I'll call it a success.*

"There you are," Mattie's grandmother said. She set down bowls of beef stew and slid into a seat at the table. "Here, honey, I've saved you a seat by me." She patted the space beside her. "Come on over here, my little Matilda Matson."

Mattie slid beside her grandmother and planted a quick kiss among the wrinkles on her cheek.

Most people, Mattie knew, assumed her name was simply the female version of her father's name, Matthew. But her given name, Matilda Matson, and the reason her grandfather always called her "Mattie Mat" actually honored her grandmother's Aunt Matilda Matson, the former vaudeville star.

When Mattie was little, her grandmother thrilled her with stories about the first Matilda and the lavish, feathery outfits worn by the stage legend before she retired—remnants of which remained in her grandmother's chest of vaudeville memorabilia.

"You know what, Nana?" Mattie said. "Someday I'd like to go through Great-Aunt Matilda's trunk with you again. I always thought everything in it sparkled and glittered."

"I thought so too, honey. What made you think of that?"

"Oh, hearing you call me 'Matilda Matson.' It made me feel a little nostalgic."

Mattie's grandmother laughed. "We'll get that trunk out again. I would like that, too."

"There's something we need to talk about, little one," her father said after a minute. "And I wanted to talk to you first before your boss—or the senator—hears about it."

"Okay," Mattie said. "I'm sitting down. What is it?"

"I probably should have told you sooner, but you had so much going on—"

"Come on, Dad. You're scaring me. Is Mom okay?"

"Good heavens, yes. She's fine. Right as rain," he said. "No, this is business. And I don't know yet how serious it is."

"You're making me nuts," Mattie said. "Will you just tell me?"

"Yesterday, we received the signature letter from Greece."

"Oh," she said, heaving a sigh of relief. "But that's great. In fact, checking on that was at the top of my list. Why is that a problem?"

"Because we sent the letter to the family member of record."

"Okay, and …"

"And we filled out all the paperwork listing Constance Sinclair as the main contact, but the letter came back with a note on the bottom signed by Jeffrey Sinclair. And he demanded a fee of half a million dollars for his signature."

"Is that all?" Mattie asked. "Can't we just call and tell them to have her sign it? And that any money that might come in has to go toward expenses for the meeting itself?"

"Gee, little one, what a great idea. I wonder why I didn't think of that."

Mattie's grandparents chuckled and Mattie ruffled her dad's hair.

"Okay, smarty pants, you thought of that. So what happened?"

"The first couple of times we called, no one answered. The last couple, we got a recording that said the phone was disconnected."

"Oh. That *is* more of a problem."

"We sent another letter and arranged to have it delivered by a courier service," Matt said. "One that requires a signature. If that works, we're good. If it doesn't, we'll have to figure out our next steps. And who we'll need to get involved. And soon."

"Darn," Mattie said. "I wish that part had gone smoothly. I just hate for something so important to be left hanging," she added. "I know the selection committee picked us, but I had the impression they could change their minds at the drop of a hat. Plus, I know you're on the hook with the senator to get that signature." She stopped talking for a moment and shook her head. "I've been so nervous the last couple of days with ..."

Her father looked at her sharply.

"With what?" he asked.

"Oh, it sounds silly, but ..."

"Mattie Mat thinks she saw someone duck behind one of the trees in the drive and that she heard someone walking through the leaves in the family cemetery," her grandfather said.

"Well," she answered. "I must have been right. Look at what happened to Bryan's Pinkerton guy. Obviously, somebody who doesn't belong has been sneaking around. It probably has nothing to do with this signature situation, but we need to get it resolved. There's just too much at stake."

Mattie's father leaned back in his chair. "I agree, little one. I just wish Constance Sinclair would sign the letter and be done with it. Without any stupid demands."

"When do you think you'll hear from the courier company?" Mattie asked.

"I'm expecting a call from them any minute."

They all jumped when the ringtone on Matt's cell phone broke the silence.

"Hello?" he said. She couldn't hear the other end of the conversation, but from her father's end, it didn't sound promising.

"Well?" she asked when he disconnected the call. "What did they say?"

"That they went to the address, but no one answered the door."

"So?"

"They shoved the letter under it."

"Are you kidding me?" Mattie said. "They didn't wait for a signature? Wasn't that the whole point?"

"Yes, it was. But maybe delivery people on a remote island in Greece aren't as concerned with what's *supposed* to happen as we are in this country," Matt Maguire said. "The courier did say trash was piled up outside the door, so they figured someone still lived there."

"I know we confirmed the address," Mattie said.

"Of course we did," Mattie's father answered. "And the bank still sends a monthly stipend to that address for Constance Sinclair. It's never been an issue. That's why I felt comfortable assuring the senator that getting a signature wouldn't be a problem."

"Maybe Mrs. Sinclair died," Mattie said. "How old would she be now, Gramps?"

"She was probably in her late twenties," Mattie's grandfather said, "when she closed up the house and took the boys to Greece. So that would put her in her nineties now."

"Wait ... boys?" Mattie's father asked. "Plural? I thought there was only one boy. And he was mean. He used to throw stones at me."

"*That* boy *was* mean," Mattie's grandfather agreed. "But there were two boys. Jeffrey and Robert."

CHAPTER TWENTY-ONE

1947

Jeffrey Sinclair's heart filled with joy at the sight of his father's frame filling his door. In three long strides, his father stood beside him, kissed the top of his head, and then settled into one of the child-size chairs at his drawing table. His father folded his long legs under him, his knees pointed to the ceiling.

"It's your mom and Prince, isn't it?" his father asked. He held the drawing of a yellow-haired woman sitting astride a brown horse. At Jeffrey's nod, his father smiled again—bright blue eyes crinkling around the edges, resembling mere slits of sky in his face.

"Son, this is very good. You have a real talent." Jeffrey saw the pride on his father's face and heard it in his voice. "But," his father continued, "your mother's hair was red. Why did you make it yellow?"

"I didn't have the right color," Jeffrey answered. His hand swept the pile of multi-hued charcoals and crayons in front of him—most worn down to small nubs.

"Maybe we can fix that," Jeffrey's father said, his smile widening. He reached around behind him to produce a package wrapped in brown paper and tied with red ribbon. "Happy birthday, Son."

Again, Jeffrey's heart filled with joy and his eyes filled with tears. He thought no one had remembered his birthday. He left his chair and threw himself into his father's arms, leaving his package untouched. His father hugged him back and then placed his hands on Jeffrey's shoulders. "Come on, big guy," he said, his eyes crinkling once again with his smile. "Let's open your present."

Jeffrey tugged at the bow and the brown paper fell away to reveal a long box of new charcoals—chalk in every color imaginable. A tin of watercolor paints with twenty colors and five different brushes rested beside it.

But it was the Crayola crayon box that made his eyes bulge. Row after row after row of crayons. Forty-eight of them ... more than he had ever seen in one place. And every color, some of them in six different shades. The exact color for his mother's hair. And for her horse, Prince's, chestnut coat. And that perfect shade of green—new-leaf green, he called it in his head—for the first little spring leaves on the trees outside his window.

Speechless, Jeffrey brought his eyes up to meet his father's.

"That box is a prototype," his father said, "a model," he added at Jeffrey's confused expression. "It's a design the company is testing on artists—like you—and won't even be available to the rest of the world for almost two more years. But I was able to get it for you from a friend in Pennsylvania. Do you like it?"

Jeffrey's eyes filled once more. "I love it. Thank you, Father."

Jeffrey's father moved the remaining brown wrapper to reveal drawing tablets—heavy cream-colored paper, parchment, and bright white sheets— in three different sizes. Jeffrey's mind raced at the possibilities, and he selected a crayon from the box. His hands moved across the paper as if on their own, at work on a picture of the new foal Michael Maguire showed him the previous day. Its little legs looked like match sticks, and he was certain he could capture their spindly quality. His father watched the scene unfold in bright colors.

Despite his focus on the picture, Jeffrey saw his father fumble with the knob on the table drawer closest to him and then reach into his pocket. He placed a small gold object in the drawer and then closed it. Jeffrey looked up, a question in his eyes. Beads of sweat stood out on his father's forehead.

"Son," his father said in a low voice, "I'd like to keep that little key there for a while. But let's make it our secret. I'll come back and get it from you in a couple of days." His father closed his eyes and swallowed hard. "But if anything should ... should happen to me, even then, don't tell anyone about it until you see your Great-Uncle Arnold. You remember him, right? You saw him at your grandfather's funeral and again at my wedding to your stepmother."

Alarmed, Jeffrey stood and covered his father's large hand with his small one. His father managed a half smile and took Jeffrey's hand in both of his. "It will be fine, son. I'm sure of it. I'm just being cautious. But remember, no one is to know about this except your Uncle Arnold. He'll know what to do with it. It's really important." His father squeezed his hand one last time, then rose stiffly and kissed the top of his son's head again. "I'm going to lie down for a while in the next room. Maybe you'll have some new pictures ready for me when I wake up. What do you think?"

Jeffrey watched him go. He loved it when his father slept in the room next door, the one where his mother used to do her correspondence. His father had done that a lot lately and it always made Jeffrey feel safe.

But when his father left his table, worry gripped his heart and shudders shook his body.

He tiptoed to his closet and went straight to its back wall—the wall that separated him from the bedroom next door. He put his eye up to a small hole—one his mother had made the year she gave him the toy telephones. She had hooked wire to his telephone and ran it through his closet wall to the bedroom on its other side. Then she connected the wire to the other telephone on the desk she used for her correspondence. They had enjoyed marvelous conversations on them.

His stepmother, Constance, removed the phones when she came to live with them.

His body shook again at the thought of his stepmother. His father told him it would be great having a mother again, after his own mother died. His father also told him he would love having a brother to play with.

But none of that had been true.

None.

Having a stepmother hadn't been great. It had been awful. And he could hardly stand to be in the same room with her son, Robert. Every time they were together, Robert did something naughty and blamed it on Jeffrey. And his stepmother always believed her son.

So, Jeffrey was punished while Robert laughed at him or made faces when his mother wasn't looking. It had happened that way so often, Jeffrey no longer bothered to tell his father.

Still, he hated it.

Most of all, he hated the sound her high heels made on the long marble staircase—click-clack, click-clack, click-clack.

He had hated that sound every day for the entire year and a half she and her son had lived there.

Click-clack. Click-clack.

She walked fast. The click-clack of her footsteps sounded like she was always angry.

So, he simply removed himself. And spent most of his time in the kitchen with Cook Carson. Or in his room. Life was easier that way.

Lonely, maybe. But easier.

The small hole gave him the perfect view of the room next to his, and he saw his father stretched out on the bed. A soft cocoon of safety and love wrapped around Jeffrey and he smiled, satisfied that his father slept. A small sigh escaped him, and he let go of his worry.

Back at his table, he finished the picture of the foal and quickly drew two more—one of him with Michael as they replaced a bird's nest that had fallen from the wisteria bush outside his father's office and another of the row of trees that lined the long drive leading to the house. A blank sheet of paper beckoned, and he chose a bright color from his new crayon box.

But his hand froze in mid-air at the sound of hurried footsteps coming up the hallway. He held his breath.

The footsteps continued past his door.

He let out his breath and then took another one—deep and ragged—before he relaxed completely. He knew the footsteps didn't belong to his father and there were very few others in the household who would treat him kindly.

His hand fell to the page in front of him, and he made the first few strokes of a new picture. His mother's flower gardens. He intended to use every bright color in his new crayon box. And he was determined to have a large stack of pictures waiting for his father when he woke up.

But another sound claimed his attention.

A second set of footsteps. They too, approached his room. And kept on going.

He smiled. The two of them would certainly stay next door with his father for quite some time. They wouldn't bother him.

He returned to his drawing, and his picture came to life on the blank page.

CHAPTER TWENTY-TWO

2017

The gala was easily the most successful in the bureau's history, but Simone worried its success might be overshadowed by the other incidents of the evening—the fire and the attack on the security guard. Mattie told her the story as they finished the clean-up.

"I have no idea what this will mean to the Summit Selection Committee, but I really hope it isn't enough for them to reverse their decision," Mattie said. "Of course," she added, "if that happens, I'm probably out of a job."

That conversation preyed on Simone's mind. She returned home from the gala, unlocked her door and freed her sore feet from the tight, teal shoes.

But her heart leapt to high alert when a noise sounded from her den.

She whirled toward it and held her breath before working up the nerve to investigate. She grabbed her high school field hockey stick—tucked into a small niche by her front door—and tiptoed toward the sound, hockey stick held high.

Before she reached the hallway, the light blinked on and a man blocked her path.

She screamed. And jumped.

Then lowered the stick.

"David," she said. A sense of impending doom invaded her space. "You scared me to death. What are you doing here?"

Simone slept fitfully and woke early.

Normally she cherished her time in her own little place with her first mug of steaming coffee. But finding David in her apartment after the gala erased her joy. Even her favorite aromatic brew failed to soothe her.

He hadn't explained why he was there, and she was still upset, her stomach knotted so tight, her breath came in short, unsatisfying spurts.

Worse, anger built on distress as she surveyed her kitchen and her inner neat freak surfaced. Slight differences jarred her sense of order ... a canister turned so the palm tree faced a different direction from the way she lined it up with the others, the pantry door slightly ajar, and the dishtowel she kept draped over the sink caught in the lower cabinet door rather than falling free the way she left it.

Her mood darkened. Five years had passed since David last stepped foot in her apartment—since she had seen or heard from him, in fact. So, it was bad enough he was there at all. Really bad he'd been there long enough to mess with her stuff.

Regardless of her irritation the night before at his dropping in without notice, she had pushed herself to make up the bed in the spare room rather than have the fight she knew would eventually follow.

In the cold light of dawn, however, she wished she had just gotten it over with.

She picked up David's jacket where he'd slung it over the back of a kitchen chair.

It clunked against the aluminum frame.

She froze and stared at the jacket for a full minute.

Simone knew what she would find but eased her fingers into the pocket anyway. Then she pulled back as if she had touched a scorpion.

A gun.

In her apartment.

That he even had a gun bothered her almost as much as the fact that he brought it into her home. She took several deep breaths, pulled the dishtowel from the cabinet door and wrapped it around her hand. Cautiously, she wiggled the gun out of his pocket and covered it with the towel.

She'd never held a gun before, so she prayed the safety was on. Although, she realized, she didn't know if it even had a safety. Or how to tell.

Grateful it hadn't gone off and killed her, she took the towel-wrapped gun to the freezer and hid it behind the boxes of Girl Scout cookies she'd stored there for more than a year.

The freezer door slammed from the force of her anger and she turned back toward the sink. But her toe skidded a few inches, and she saw the scrap of paper under her shoe.

She picked it up, and the hair on her neck rose as she read: *One Hundred Clairmont Place, Sinclair Station, North Carolina*—the address for the Halloween Gala the previous night.

The paper shook in her hand as she sank into the nearest chair.

"Morning, Sis." David bounced into the kitchen and headed for the coffeepot. "Boy, the coffee sure smells g—"

He stopped short and studied her face. "What gives?" he asked. "Did somebody die?"

"Well, we're not sure yet, are we? Is that what you intended?"

"Huh? What the hell are you talking about?"

"Where were you last night?" She held the small paper up to him. "And what is this? Why was it in your pocket? And why"—she tried to control her shaking voice—"did you bring a gun here?"

He put the coffeepot down, his cup still empty, and turned toward her, anger darkening his features. His hands balled into fists. "You went through my pockets?"

Simone recognized his intimidation posture. He leaned in, using his size to threaten her.

It had always worked. Her whole life.

Until now.

Years of counseling for dealing with abusers kicked in.

Slowly she rose and looked him in the eye. He didn't back off, but she held her ground even though she was almost a foot shorter than he was.

She raised her hands and held them out in front of her, palms almost touching his chest. The scrap of paper fluttered to the floor.

As had always happened—he still towered over her and she was still afraid. That had been their dynamic ever since their parents died together seventeen years earlier in a car accident.

But this time was different. This time she knew what to do.

With her hands still out in front of her and her voice low, she adopted a commanding tone. "Hold it right there." She saw the flicker of uncertainty in his eyes and knew he hadn't expected her to stand up to him. "You can't get away with this any longer," she continued. "I will not be intimidated in my own home."

She didn't raise her voice. She didn't cry. She didn't scream.

But her knees shook. And her heart knocked against her ribs.

She held his eyes with hers, however, and never let him see her fear.

Slowly, he relaxed his fists and took a step back. He rearranged the scowl on his face until his features became almost pleasant. While he took his time speaking to her, she saw that his brain chugged into overdrive.

"Come on, Sis. We haven't seen each other for years. You don't have to pick a fight with me first thing." His voice wheedled to the point of whining. Another of his tactics ... to try and turn the situation around so whatever happened appeared to be her fault.

She continued to look deeply into his eyes but said nothing.

"And as far as the address, when I got to town, I wanted to see you right away."

She knew it was a lie and was fairly certain he knew she knew. Still she said nothing.

"Yeah," he continued, plowing ahead, "when I got off the bus, I asked the guy at the station if he could help me find your address. Real talkative fellow. He gave it to me but told me I wouldn't find you here ... that everybody for three counties was up at the big house on the hill for some kind of shindig."

"So you went there? And, for heaven's sake, how did you get in here?"

"Oh, getting in here was easy. Your building manager must not get paid much. He let me in for twenty bucks once he confirmed the last name on my ID matched yours."

Simone grimaced.

"David," she said quietly, "did you start the fire? Or attack the security guard?"

In an instant he closed the gap between them, his face millimeters from hers. "I don't know what you're talking about. A fire ... attack. And," he said, "I don't appreciate your accusations. How dare you? I can't believe you have the audacity to—"

"Give it a rest, David. Your bullying won't work on me anymore."

Again, he backed off slightly. "I did go to your fancy shmancy party. For about five minutes. I don't know how you stand hanging around with all those stuffed shirts in their monkey suits. That place was so crowded I decided to wait for you here where I could have you all to myself. But I sure as hell didn't do anything in that short time that you seem to want to accuse me of."

She wasn't convinced but decided against questioning him further without others present. He stepped toward her again.

"Come on, Mony Mony," he said, holding out his arms. "Don't you want to give your big brother a hug?"

She hated that nickname.

He was five when she was born, and he couldn't say "Simone." So he called her "Mony." Then when he heard the Billy Idol remake of the nineteen sixties song, it became "Mony Mony."

And after he found out she hated it, that's all he ever called her.

"Don't try to pretend we're friends, David. The last I heard you had escaped to Mexico to stay out of jail. What happened? Why did you come back?" Her impatience intensified. "And most of all, why did you come here with a gun?"

A flash of anger lit his eyes for just a second. She saw it because she knew him so well. She recognized it because it was all part of his routine. He wanted something and it wasn't sisterly love. He had shown up unexpectedly for a reason and she had to find out what it was.

"That's a lot of questions all at once." He eased back to the counter and filled his coffee cup, turning his back to her. Another technique, designed to make her feel insignificant and unimportant. She refused to give in to his mind games.

"Fine," she responded. "Pick one."

"Well, first," he said, "I came back because I got a job here in the States."

"Delivering drugs, no doubt. Are you still selling pot, or have you graduated to the harder stuff?"

He whirled around and started toward her with his fist drawn back. She stood still.

"David," she said quietly. "You'd better think about that long and hard." He stopped moving toward her, but his fist hung menacingly in the air. "The next time you hit me," she added in the same quiet voice, "you'd better kill me. Because if you don't, I will have you locked up so tight, you will never again see the light of day."

"That's mighty big talk for such a little girl." He backed off slightly.

Simone shrugged. "You don't have to believe me. But trust me, it's a sacred promise."

He turned his back and said, "What did you do with it, anyway?" He swung his head around and stared intently into her eyes.

"What?" She frowned. "With what?"

A look of disgust filled his face. "Now *you're* playing games. You know what I'm talking about. The gun."

"Oh. That. I've hidden it. I'll give it back to you when you leave. Which, by the way, will be very soon."

"That's where you're wrong. I told you, I have a job. Right here in Sinclair Station."

Cold dread surrounded her heart.

"And it pays big money," he continued. "Something that could benefit you, too. If you'd just work with me."

"Have you lost your mind?"

"You don't have to be mean. I'm serious. You're going to want to hear what I have to say."

"I can't imagine what you could say that would possibly interest me."

"How about that I've been hired to do a job for the big meeting that's coming here?"

Her former dread spread to her stomach, then gripped her throat. "What ..." she said. Her voice faltered. "What are you talking about?"

"Oh please," he snapped at her. "Don't pretend. The summit thing. I know all about it."

"How did you find out about the summit? You've been in Mexico."

"You think news doesn't reach that part of the world? Let's just say I've been hired to represent some special interests for my employers."

"Your employers? Who are they? And *what* do they want?"

"There you go again, asking a lot of questions. If you're not willing to help, then none of that concerns you, now does it?"

But Simone had stopped listening.

"David, look ..." Heat rose in her cheeks, but left her hands. They felt like ice. "I don't know what you're planning with this employer of yours, but you have to stay out of this. It's too important to the state—the country. To me," she finished weakly.

A wicked smile played with his mouth. "And you think that concerns me ... why?"

"You know what, David? Just stop. I don't want to hear any more. You need to stay out of this."

"Too late, little sis. I'm already in. And I stand to make big money from it. *Very* big. You just stay out of *my* way and let me do my job."

She handed him his jacket. "Get out of my house."

"Give me my gun."

"No. Not now. Meet me at the diner on Main Street in an hour. I'll bring it to you there."

He stood there looking at her, working the muscles in his jaw. His hand clenched and unclenched. She stood her ground.

He snatched his jacket and stormed out the door, slamming it so hard the screws from the top hinge flew out and clinked against her refrigerator.

She let out the breath she'd been holding and slumped down in the closest chair, totally drained.

First order of business, change lock. Second, swear at building manager.

Chapter Twenty-Three

David reached the diner first and sat sprawled at a corner table, dominating the space around him. His dark expression told Simone everything she needed to know about the direction their conversation would take.

She drew a deep breath, squared her shoulders and pointed herself in his direction, filling her face with false bravado and nodding to several people on her way. But every step that closed the distance between them added tighter knots to her stomach.

He didn't bother to stand when she reached him. Or to help with her chair, which was tangled with those from neighboring tables. She held her oversize purse tight to her shoulder as she wrestled to free the snarled mass of legs, a frustrating exercise that did nothing to improve her mood. He just sat there and watched her struggle, his scowl magically converted to a mocking smirk. It took every ounce of her strength not to turn around and walk out.

But she had to get rid of his gun. She didn't want it—or any reminder of him—in her apartment.

She jerked her chair loose and sat across from him, her back to the rest of the restaurant. She reached into her purse but stopped in mid-motion as the waitress appeared at her elbow.

"Hey, Simone. Why didn't you tell me you had such a good-looking brother?"

"We ... he—"

"My business keeps me out of the country for long stretches at a time," David said smoothly. He looked pointedly at the waitress's name tag. "My sweet sister never knows when I might pop up, Sally." He put his hand on the waitress's arm and rubbed it seductively. The scene disgusted Simone to the point that she had to physically restrain herself from batting his hand away.

"Well, while you're here, don't be a stranger, handsome. More coffee? Simone, you ready for a cup?"

Simone nodded.

When the waitress left, David's face returned to its surly expression.

"Well? Do you have it?"

"Yes. It's in my bag. I'll give it to you when we go. Or sooner if you assure me you're leaving town."

"I already told you. That's not gonna happen. I have a job here."

"David, you can't—"

"Simone? Tony Adkins," a voice said beside her. And then a hand shot out in front of her. "We met last night. I just started working with Senator Bradley."

"Yes, Tony." Simone shook his hand. "I remember. How are you?"

"Good. Really good. Thank you. Um … I'm sorry to interrupt, but I was afraid I might miss you and I wanted to invite you … both of you," he added, looking at David, "to a reception tomorrow night at Asheville City Hall. I left a message for Mattie, but I was hoping you could come, too."

"I can't speak for my sister," David said. He stood and offered his hand. "But I would love to be there. Thank you for the invitation."

"Oh? You're Simone's brother?" She couldn't help but notice that the aide's expression lightened, and his smile broadened.

"David Rousseau," David said, shaking the other man's hand.

"Tony, as I said, Tony Adkins. Simone and I met last night at the Halloween Gala. It was a wonderful event," he added, looking at her. "The senator has some legislation pending," he said, turning back to David, "and enjoys sharing his ideas with people in the community. Especially people connected to the Visitors Bureau and the Chamber of Commerce. Do you have a card?"

"Sorry, not with me," David answered. "Sis, will you give him one of yours? You can let Simone know the details, Tony, and she'll make sure I get them, too."

Simone's stomach rolled. Of all the things she *didn't* want to happen, having David at an important event topped the list. She wanted to remove her brother from her life, not embed him deeper into it.

"Wonderful," Tony said. "Senator Bradley will mention the upcoming summit, too, and I'm sure he'll want to introduce Morgan as head of the organization leading the effort. And Mattie and you, too, of course," he added, looking into Simone's eyes.

He stood there expectantly.

She dreaded reaching into her purse. She didn't want to risk anyone seeing David's gun. But she did want the handsome man beside her to have her contact information.

She placed the bag in her lap and opened the top flap an inch or so ... just wide enough to access her little card compartment. She drew one out and attempted a smile as she handed it to Tony. "Thank you," she said. "I'll look forward to getting the details from you."

"Right. I'll email you later this evening. Nice to meet you, David."

With that, he was gone, and Simone fixed her brother with a venomous stare.

"Why did you do that?" she hissed. "You can't come to that reception."

Lazily, he leaned his chair back until it rested against the wall, his features arranged in a wicked smile. "I most certainly can, sis. I was invited. And I'll be there to hobnob with all those important people. You forget, I'm part of the team, now. Maybe your friend will want to introduce me, too."

She opened her mouth to respond angrily, but a full mug of coffee slid in front of her. "Here you go, hon. Do you want to order?" The waitress filled David's cup. "Breakfast?"

"Sure," he said. "I'll have the special."

"Simone?"

She shook her head. "Nothing, thank you."

The waitress left and Simone stood to leave.

"Hey," David said, his hand on her wrist. "Aren't you forgetting something?"

"You think I'm going to give it to you now? After you accepted an invitation to attend a reception for a senator? No way."

"You don't want to make me mad, Simone." His voice held barely controlled fury.

"I told you. I'll give it to you when you promise me you're leaving town." His grip on her wrist tightened. "David, you need to trust me on this. There are two plainclothes policemen sitting at the table by the window. I know them both. One scream from me and they'll be over here in a heartbeat. So. You'd. Better. Let. Me. Go."

Gradually, he released his hold.

"I'll make a deal with you," she said. "You get a bus ticket, and I'll meet you at the station and hand you your ... package just before you board. Forget about staying here and all the other ridiculous notions you have about a job for the summit. Just go back to whatever life you had before and leave me alone."

The last thing Simone wanted was to have his gun in her possession. She knew it put her in danger. But neither did she want *him* to have it when he might show up where she was and put other people in danger as well. She didn't think he had ever shot anyone. But then she hadn't seen him in five years. Who knew what might have happened in all that time?

His jaw muscles tightened. He appeared ready to blow. Rather than wait for it, she turned to leave and almost knocked Sally down in her haste.

"Did you want more—"

"No," Simone said over her shoulder. "And he'll pay for my coffee."

Before leaving the diner, Simone made a point to speak to the police officers she'd mentioned earlier. David needed to know she was serious and his days of bullying her into submission were over.

Once outside, she leaned against the wall and gulped deep breaths of crisp air until her legs stopped shaking. Then she got in her car and drove directly to the hardware store where she bought new locks and a deadbolt.

At her apartment complex she stopped in to see Ryan, the building manager, on her way to her apartment. To give him a piece of her mind.

No more surprises, she decided. No more vulnerability.

CHAPTER TWENTY-FOUR

1947

Jeffrey sang while he worked—a song his mother had taught him when he helped with her flower gardens.

"You are my sunshine, my only sunshine. You make me happy—"

Sounds of a scuffle reached him from the room next door and the song flew from his lips. Something wasn't right.

He left his picture and started across his bedroom floor but stopped after only a couple of steps. Papers covered his drawing table and he knew from experience that his stepmother would be angry if she saw them scattered there. So he returned, shoved his charcoals and paints into one of the table drawers and most of his paper into another one. He took the crayons and a small stack of paper with him, and at the last second, grabbed the little gold key from the drawer where his father had put it.

The bumps and thumps from the next room grew louder, and he heard shouting. He hurried across his bedroom and positioned his eye to the small hole, again.

The room came into view, and he saw his father on the bed.

Within seconds, a gun fired.

His head jerked in shock, but the sound from the blast swallowed his scream.

A smell—like blown out candles—touched his nostrils and he stifled a sneeze.

But his view of the room remained intact.

His father still lay on the bed.

But his face—the face Jeffrey loved—was gone. The new face was different. Covered with blood. A huge hole shattered its forehead. And the bedspread under it—and the wall behind it—wore feathery patterns of red that hadn't been there the last time Jeffrey looked.

He sucked in his breath sharply but didn't allow himself to scream again.

The struggle continued with shouting and furniture falling. He wanted to stop watching, but he couldn't force himself to leave.

He saw the entire room and everyone in it.

He saw the second shot. And its devastation.

Somehow, he knew the horror he'd witnessed extended to him. He couldn't let anyone know what he had seen or that he had even been in his room when it happened.

His heart slammed into his throat. He had to protect himself.

He decided to hide in the space his mother had called *"the safe room"*—built right into his closet floor. He remembered the story she told him about a baby. Lind … something … who was stolen right out of his bedroom a few years before Jeffrey was born. And never returned. His mother hadn't wanted that to happen to him.

So she taught him how to hide in the small space if he ever felt threatened.

They even practiced.

But he'd never before used it for real danger.

He eased his closet door closed, kicked back the rug that covered the safe room door and yanked the cover up … heavier than he remembered. He tossed in his paper and crayons and then heaved himself in behind them.

Quietly, he pulled the cover down, careful to catch the rug with it so the door's outline remained hidden.

Just before the little door closed completely, he heard more footsteps. They ran from the next room, paused at his door, and then ran again.

But he stayed put. His instincts forced him to stay hidden. And quiet.

Droplets of sweat coated his upper lip and his damp forehead captured limp bangs, imprisoning them in large, sticky clumps.

But no moisture reached his dry mouth.

Terrified he would be found, he pulled his knees to his chest and huddled against them, sucking in air with short, shallow breaths. His small body shook uncontrollably, and he compressed himself tighter against the rough walls of the tiny dark room, obsessed with avoiding discovery. Even at his young age, he knew that continued silence was his only option.

Fat tears trickled down his little cheeks and his throat burned raw from choking back his screams.

But fear outweighed everything else. The smallest sound might give him away.

He held his breath until his vision blurred and little fireworks danced around the dark edges of his reality.

His heart roared in his ears and he struggled to calm it, to push the horrible scene from his head, to think of something else ... anything else. Sights and sounds flew by like leaves in the wind and then tumbled, end over end, just out of his grasp.

He lost track of time until one by one, his senses clicked off. And he just sat, aware of nothing. He didn't know how much time had passed. He took a few quiet breaths.

But the air was so stuffy, even shallow breathing was difficult in his cramped space. His lungs, starved for a long deep breath, invited a new wave of panic.

He had to move. Even if that meant leaving his hiding place.

He *had* to.

Slowly, carefully, he raised the heavy wooden cover above his head far enough for a quick peek under his closet door. A horizontal beam of bright light greeted him—wide enough to see that no shadows lurked there. Fresh air rushed in and cooled his face.

He pushed the cover wider and guided it carefully so it didn't thump his closet's back wall. Then he climbed out and sat cross-legged on the floor, dropping his head to his hands and gulping deep breaths.

His emotion had spent his last spark of energy, and exhaustion crept over him. He had to think, to figure out what to do.

But his mind refused to focus.

His brain replayed the nightmare of crashes and shouts—gunshots and screams.

Over and over and over.

He pushed against his temples, willing his ears to stop hearing the noise.

But the memory he'd been holding back slammed into his head and he shuddered so violently he threw up.

He was helpless to stop it. No longer could he push the horrible sights and sounds away. They washed over him, robbed him of his breath, and sucked him down into misery and hopelessness.

He didn't want to remember, but he couldn't stop.

His shoulders shook with silent sobs.

And the little gold key—the one his father had said was their secret—cut into his damp palm from the force of his clenched fist.

CHAPTER TWENTY-FIVE

2017

"Two boys?" Mattie's father asked again. "I never knew that. The only one I ever heard of was Jeffrey."

"That makes sense, son. Jeffrey was Mr. Henry's son by his first wife, Miss Lily, and Robert was the second Mrs. Sinclair's son from her first marriage. He was a couple of years younger than Jeffrey. And he came with her, of course, when she and Mr. Henry married."

"And that little devil was the mean one," Mattie's grandmother said. "I remember clearly. I was pregnant with you, Matthew, and I saw that little boy collect rocks and throw them at the birdhouses on the property. He even hit some of the little wrens. The spoiled brat."

"He also messed with the animals on Clairmont Place," Mattie's grandfather said. "He thought it was great fun to swat the horses on their rumps. Until he did it to Lucifer—beautiful big, black stallion. Lucifer reared and broke down his stall door. If I hadn't pulled Robert out of the way, he would have been trampled. After that, my father had a stern talk with his mother. I'm not sure what she threatened Robert with, but they left for Europe again not long after that."

"So the other boy ... Jeffrey ... was the one you told me about who used to hang out with you, Gramps?" Mattie asked. "You say he was a sweet little kid?"

"Yes. He was. But after his father was killed," Mattie's grandfather told the group, "he withdrew, didn't say a word. Kept to himself. It was my understanding that he went to Greece with his stepmother, but on their last several return trips, there was only one boy. And Mrs. Sinclair called him Jeffrey. No one ever knew what happened to Robert. Anyway, that's why it's not surprising you never heard of him, Matt."

CHAPTER TWENTY-SIX

1950

Michael Maguire noticed the extra activity around Clairmont Place the morning after the family's latest return from Greece. Lights dotted the upper rooms of the mansion and Cook Carson stood at the back door to welcome Johnny, the delivery boy from the greengrocer. The cook's son, little Billy, not quite three years old, peeked around her skirt, holding tight to one of her legs.

Michael's father, Melvin, had gone to the big house extra early to meet with Richard Baldwin, who had moved into the mansion with his daughter after her husband's death. The two men sat in chairs in the ornamental gardens on the patio closest to the East Portico. Mr. Baldwin held a sheaf of papers and handed them, one by one, to Michael's father, who listened attentively, occasionally making notes on them.

Watching them as he trimmed hedges, Michael heaved a heavy sigh. Those chairs had been the favorite meeting places for Henry Sinclair and his uncle Arnold. He had hung around the last time they were there—only five short years earlier. Just before Mr. Sinclair married Miss Constance.

So much has changed. And not for the better.

Not since Miss Lily died had the property been engulfed in such overwhelming sadness.

And darkness. Almost three years had passed since Mr. Sinclair was killed. But even with the family traveling to Greece on a regular basis—their return to the property did nothing to dispel the black shroud of grief that pervaded Clairmont Place.

Michael missed the old way of life. And the happiness he'd known when Miss Lily was still alive. But even after that, even after Mr. Sinclair's second marriage, the atmosphere surrounding Clairmont Place was still alive with activity.

Now, the air itself feels dead to me ... as if every spark of life was sucked right out of it. He raked his hedge trimmings and bent to put them in his basket when he caught a movement from the corner of his eye. A curtain fluttered back into place in one of the upstairs bedrooms. A few minutes later, there was another movement and this time, a small face appeared at the window.

Michael straightened quickly and stared. He tried to determine the owner of the face and hoped it belonged to Jeffrey. One of the strangest changes since the family began going to Greece was the loss of one of the boys. At Henry Sinclair's funeral, two boys accompanied Constance and her father to the graveside. But after the family's third trip overseas, only one boy was ever seen, and Mrs. Sinclair called him Jeffrey.

Michael finished the hedge, stored the clippings behind the garden shed and washed his hands at the hose. He walked back toward the house and saw that the patio chairs where Mr. Baldwin and his father had sat were empty. He continued to the kitchen door and knocked.

"Hello, Michael," Cook Carson said. "What can I do for you?" Her son sat in his highchair close to the table.

"Cook Carson, could you ask Jeffrey to come outside and see me?"

Cook Carson appeared nervous. "Why, Michael?" she asked. "What do you need?"

Her reaction shocked him. He shrugged. "It's been a long time since we talked and there are new baby goats in the barn. And some rabbits. I thought he would enjoy seeing them."

Cook Carson came out onto the stoop and closed the door behind her. "I'd be happy to ask, Michael," she said softly. "But I know what the answer will be." She bit her lip. "Mrs. Sinclair instructed me to let her know whenever anyone asked to see Jeffrey. The few times it's happened, she wouldn't let him even go to the door. He never comes to the kitchen anymore. In fact, I haven't seen him since the first time the family returned from Greece. I don't know why she's keeping him away from everyone. She says it's because he's still so upset about his father dying. That he doesn't talk any more. But ..."

"But what?" Michael said. "What?"

"I don't know," she answered. "He was such a sweet little boy, I would just feel better if I could see him myself. Maybe he would talk to me."

"Or to me," Michael said. "We used to have great conversations." He shoved his hands in his pockets. "Well, thanks for letting me know. If you do get to see him, please tell him that I'd love to see him again, too." He turned to go and then stopped. "What about the other boy ... Robert?"

Cook Carson spread her hands out at her sides, palms up. "I have no idea," she said. "After one of the trips, I asked if he would be joining the family for dinner and Mrs. Sinclair screamed at me to never mention his name again."

"Really?"

"Yes. I don't know if he died in Greece and it's too painful for her to talk about. Or if he ran away. Or ... I can't even think what else might have happened. And I don't dare ask her father. So Jeffrey is the only boy here now. And as instructed, I'll never ask about the other one again."

CHAPTER TWENTY-SEVEN

2017

"And Mrs. Sinclair never gave an explanation about being down to one little boy?" Mattie asked.

"I'm sure she didn't feel she owed any of us an explanation. She treated us very differently from the way the other Sinclairs had. After Cook Carson told me Mrs. Sinclair screamed at her for asking about the other boy, I certainly didn't want to approach her."

"Losing your husband is very traumatic," Mattie said quietly. Her father squeezed her hand. "If something did happen to her son, too, it may have just been too much for her."

"Regardless," her grandfather said. "She never talked about what happened to Robert. At least not to anyone I knew. I even asked my father if Mr. Baldwin ever mentioned him, but he didn't. Mr. Baldwin wasn't very approachable either. My father's conversations with him centered on the business end of running the property and what needed to happen when the house was closed. Nothing about family." He shrugged. "I suppose Robert could have died in Greece. He certainly got into enough trouble while he was here, so heaven knows what might have happened to him in a foreign country."

"But," Mattie said, "from some of the things you've said about the family, once they returned from Greece, you make it sound like you weren't sure the boy she called Jeffrey really was."

"I had no reason to doubt her," he said. "But she never let anyone get close to him. I think I would have known if I could have talked with him, but Mrs. Sinclair never allowed that." Mattie's grandfather shrugged. "Of course, little Billy was born by then, so you'd think we could ask him, but I can't imagine Mrs. Sinclair let them hang out together, either. And then, after a few years, they were gone for good. Apparently, Mrs. Sinclair inherited a lump sum at Mr. Henry's death. Gossip was that she signed a prenuptial agreement so she couldn't sell the property. But I don't know any details."

"This talk is all well and good," Matt Maguire said. "But my major concern right now is for someone to answer the freaking door in Greece. And to sign the document we sent. If that doesn't happen soon, I'm up to my neck in hot water. The Board of Governors won't like a scandal swirling around their bank president."

"Could it really be that bad for you, Dad?" Mattie asked. She rubbed his shoulders.

"Yes, it could. Bad for me for guaranteeing permission to use a property I hadn't secured first. Bad for Senator Bradley who told the president everything was taken care of and bad for the town if we lose the venue over something so minor. Especially now that it's been touted all over creation. If all of that happens, the bank's board of trustees will waste no time in finding a new bank president. I'm sure of it."

Mattie's head fell to her hands. "Whew. If the selection committee hears about this—on top of the things that happened the night of the gala—I wonder how long Senator Bradley can keep them from changing their minds?"

"It doesn't make sense to me," Matt said. "I can't imagine what motivation Mrs. Sinclair would have for ignoring communications. Our next step will be to hire someone to go there and bang on the door until it's opened." He shook his head. "Don't they realize we could hold the stipends until we hear from them? And will, if something doesn't happen soon."

"I know we figured out how old Constance would be," Mattie said. "But how about Jeffrey? How old would he be now?"

"Well, let's see, he was eleven or twelve when Matt was born," Mattie's grandfather said.

"So that means he would be seventy-six or seventy-seven," Mattie's father finished.

"Gramps," Mattie said, "can we go through it one more time?"

"Of course, Mattie Mat. But I'm not sure what else I can tell you," Michael Maguire said.

"Okay, Mrs. Sinclair received a settlement when Henry died and probably just decided to get away from everything that reminded her of the horrible ordeal she'd endured," Mattie said. "Right?" Her grandfather nodded. "And as far as you know, Gramps, they *all* went to Greece. Including Jeffrey?"

"As far as I know."

"And how long after that did she come back and close up the house?"

"They came back every six to twelve months for the first six or seven years ... never stayed very long. And then Mrs. Sinclair closed up the house for good—oh—in the early nineteen-fifties."

"And for how much of that time was there only one little boy?"

"Oh, maybe the last four years or so. I never saw any of them after the mid-fifties."

Mattie stood and kissed her grandfather on top of his head. "Well, Gramps, I think it's time."

"Time? Time for what?"

"That you see some of them again."

"Now how would I do that?"

"Come to Greece with me. If Dad has to hire somebody to go to the door in Corfu anyway, it might as well be us. I'll do the business end of things and record the meeting." She laid her hand on her grandfather's arm. "We can't mess around any longer, waiting for that signature. You heard what Dad said. More delays will only make things worse. And if Mrs. Sinclair did die, we could confirm it while we're there and witness Jeffrey's signature on the document. You're the only one still alive who can verify it's really him, Gramps. You could ask him questions that only the real Jeffrey would know—things that happened when just the two of you were there. If he gives you the right answers, we're done. We get the signature and relieve my dear father of his worry." She leaned across to her father and kissed the top of his head, too. "Then, we're free to move ahead with preparations for the Summit Engagement Groups. What do you say?"

"I guess I could consider it. When are you thinking of going?"

"Tomorrow," she said. "Or the next day. I'll take care of the tickets."

Her ringtone sounded and Simone's name lit up her screen.

"Hi," Mattie said. "I'm glad you called. Do you remember the name of Senator Bradley's aide? The one who chatted you up most of last night?" Mattie smiled into the phone.

"Mattie ..." Simone said.

Mattie's smile faded at the sound of her friend's voice. "I need to talk to you," Simone said. "Right away. May I come over?"

"Sure. I'm at my grandparents' house. Why don't you come here? Are you okay?"

"Yes ... no ... not really. Look, I'll be there in ten minutes."

Chapter Twenty-Eight

"I had to let you know," Simone said. She wrapped one of her blond curls around her index finger up to the second knuckle. "I'm just not sure what he's capable of anymore." A single tear trickled down her cheek. "He had a gun," she whispered.

Mattie had hugged her friend and then seated her at The Cottage's dining room table with Mattie's father and grandfather on the other side.

"A gun?" Mattie glanced at her father anxiously. "Do you think we should get Bryan involved?" She slipped into the chair next to Simone.

"Not yet, little one," Matt Maguire answered. "Let's talk before we bring the sheriff in. Can you start at the beginning, Simone? Tell us exactly what he said that's got you so worried."

"Well, to begin with, he knew about the summit."

"That's not exactly a secret," Matt said. "There's been pretty good news coverage that we won the venue."

"But he's been in Mexico for the past five years," Simone answered, reaching for another curl. "And he said he's been hired to … I'm trying to remember his exact words." She took a deep breath. Her hands shook. "His words were something like he's been hired 'to represent some special interests for his employers.' It sounded … well, like a threat the way he said it. Like he'd be willing to sabotage the summit as long as 'his employers' got what they wanted. Whatever that is."

"His employers—did he say who they are?" Matt asked.

"No." Simone was visibly distressed. "And honestly, I didn't ask him. I just wanted him out of my apartment. But the more I thought about it, the more worried I got. He said it pays 'big money. Very big.' Those were his exact words. And at first, he told me it could benefit me, too, but I said

114

'no' and threw him out of my house. Why on earth does anyone think there could be that kind of money to be made on an international meeting?"

"Did he tell you what your part would have been if you'd agreed?" Mattie's grandfather asked.

"No, and again, I didn't ask him. I just turned him down cold and sent him packing. From what I know about his character—or lack of it—I can pretty much guarantee that neither he nor the group that hired him has the world's best interest at heart."

"It would be really helpful to know what—and who—we're dealing with here," Matt said.

"I haven't even told you the worst part," Simone said, twisting the new curl around a second finger. "He was with me when Tony Adkins— you remember him, right, Mattie? Senator Bradley's aide—"

"Oh right," Mattie said. "Tony, that's his name. We'll definitely need to talk to him tomorrow."

"At the diner, Tony invited me to the senator's press conference and David was there. Now he's planning to come, too. I know he'll make trouble. I just know it. And Mattie, everybody will know he's my brother and it will look bad on the bureau, and ..."

Twisted curls webbed Simone's fingers together in a blond tangle.

"Okay, kiddo," Mattie said. "We can fix this. Just stay calm." She patted Simone's untangled hand and then turned to her father. "What do you think we should do?"

"You're probably not going to like what I think we should do," Matt answered.

"Well ... what?" Mattie asked.

Matt picked up Simone's hand. "Simone, I hate to have to ask you this, but will you meet with him again? Maybe even tell him you've changed your mind and that you *will* help him after all?"

"Oh my goodness," she said, her eyes filling. "Why would I do that?"

"If we could find out who he's working for, what he's supposed to do, and more importantly what he wants you to do, we'd have something to go on. We'd know if he's just full of himself or if there's a real threat that the authorities need to know about."

"I could be there with you," Mattie suggested.

"No," Simone said. "I'm sure he wouldn't be honest in front of anyone else. I'm not sure he'll even tell me the truth."

"But we have a much better chance of that with you than with anyone else," Matt said. "Right? Don't you agree?"

Simone nodded, freeing the curls from her fingers.

"How about this," Matt continued, "you see if he'll meet you for lunch at the diner, tomorrow, if you can. I'll arrange to be there and sit close to your table. You can give me some kind of sign if you need help."

"And I'll join you," Mattie's grandfather added.

"But he'll expect me to give him his gun back. I can't do that when I know he's planning to be around Senator Bradley."

"What if you told him you simply forgot to bring it? Where is it anyway?"

"In my freezer. Behind the Girl Scout cookies."

"Do you know if he has a permit?"

She shook her head. Blond curls bounced.

"If you can do this, Simone," Matt said, "when your meeting is over, you can bring his gun to the bank and we'll lock it up in the vault. At least until you find out if he's carrying it legally."

Simone looked at him, worry filling her eyes.

"It will be fine," Matt said. "What do you say?"

Simone sat silently twisting her curls. "Okay," she said. She let her curls go and clutched Matt's hand. "But please, you *have* to be there. I'm really afraid of him ... of what he might do."

"I won't let you down."

Simone punched in David's number and made plans to meet him the following day.

While the two of them talked, the three Maguires listed questions Simone could ask her brother without arousing David's suspicions.

Mattie looked up as Simone ended her call. But before Mattie could ask her about it, Simone ran to the bathroom.

"Oh dear," Mattie said. "That must have been harder on her than I thought it would be. It sounds like she's throwing up." She looked toward the bathroom door. "Poor kid," she added.

CHAPTER TWENTY-NINE

D avid sauntered to the back of the diner where Simone waited. His face wore a smug expression and fury shot through her veins.

"So … the little sister wants to lean on the big, strong brother after all," he said. "I'm glad you came to your senses."

He pulled out a chair and flopped into it—his back to Matt and Michael Maguire's table. Matt faced Simone and gave her a slight nod. She knew he was ready if she needed him.

This whole role-play thing was distasteful to her. Simone wanted nothing more than to reach over and slap the holier-than-thou look off his stupid face. Instead, she smiled sweetly and said, "I couldn't stop thinking about what you said yesterday. I love what I do, but nonprofits don't pay very well, you know. So I'm willing to talk. What's the job? And you said big money. What, exactly, does that translate to? How big?"

"Not so fast," he said. "I believe you have something that belongs to me?"

Simone allowed distress to fill her face. She put both hands up to her head. "Oh no," she said. "Oh my goodness, David, I was so anxious to get here, I totally forgot it."

David's face darkened.

"Look," she added. "As long as we're here, we might as well talk, right? Since you're in town for a while, we can take care of … your package … any time." She watched his face carefully. "Come on, David. I bought you a beer." She pushed it toward him.

Sally, the waitress from the previous morning, appeared at his elbow. "Welcome back, handsome. Your sister here sure is sweet to buy you a beer, huh?"

"She sure is," David answered with a smile. "And because she's buying, you just keep 'em coming, right? You can bring us two more any time. And hey, why don't you join us?" David's hand slid around her waist.

"I'd love to, sugar, but I'm the only one on duty right now. Maybe I'll catch you later tonight?"

"I have an important meeting tonight," he said. His hand rubbed her back. "But I'll be sure and look you up when I'm free."

Simone closed her eyes in disgust at the exchange between them. She saw Matt Maguire shake his head slightly. She caught his meaning. She needed to see this through.

Her phone rested in her lap and she hit the "record" button.

"I'll have an iced tea to go along with my beer, Sally," Simone said. "And we'll be ordering soon."

Slowly, David released the waitress and turned back to Simone, his smile still in place.

"So," Simone said, holding up her beer, "a toast to working together." He tipped his bottle to hers and took a long swallow. Simone barely touched the bottle to her lips and set it down again. "How about filling me in? Who's this wonderful company you work for and why are they planning to pay you big money?"

The smile left his face and he leaned toward her, his voice low. "I'm not crazy about your attitude, Sis. You need to know, I can do this without you. I only invited you in because we're related."

"And the fact that we're related, that I have access to all of the information about the summit, doesn't have anything to do with why this mysterious company hired you in the first place?"

He leaned back in his chair just as Sally set two more beers on the table. He smiled at her. When she left, he leaned back in toward Simone. "It might," he said. "It just might." He took another long swig. "Look, Mony—" Simone stiffened and David held up his hands. "Okay, okay, sorry. Look, *Simone*, let's do this. It will be good for both of us—maybe even make us closer. Come on, Sis, we're the only family we have left. Let's work together." With his next drink, he drained his bottle and reached for a new one.

"Fine," she said. She took a deep breath. "You're right. We're family. Will you give me the details?"

"I don't have them all yet, but they hired me as soon as this place was announced as the summit winner." The second beer was half gone as Sally showed up to take their orders. "A burger for me and a salad for my sister," David said.

He slid his arm around Sally's waist again. "And you can bring us two more beers."

"I'll have the fish," Simone told her. "And maybe you should bring a pitcher of beer."

Simone saw the question on Matt Maguire's face when she ordered the pitcher, but she ignored it. David laughed and finished the second beer.

"I think we got sidetracked," Simone said.

"About?" he asked, reaching for the second of the new beers Sally had brought.

"Who your employer is and what they want you to do. And how you found them."

"Oh yeah. They found me, actually."

"In Mexico?"

"That's right. I was working security at a bar and this fella in a real nice suit—stuck out like a sore thumb in that crowd—said I'd been recommended to him for a job back in the States. Imagine how surprised I was when I found out it was here. And you're right, he knew I had family here. I had to go with him to talk to his boss, but they hired me on the spot."

"To …"

"To," he took a long swallow from the new beer before continuing, "install surveillance equipment for this summit thing you've got going on here." His voice sounded hollow. He was lying. Or at least not telling her the whole truth.

The waitress set a pitcher of beer in front of David and several minutes later delivered their food.

Simone tasted her fish. "Why would they pay you big money to do that?"

"There will be other stuff," David said. "They called it, um, oh yeah, 'tasks as needed.'" He took another long drink.

"And you don't know what that consists of? Or how I could help?"

"He did say I'll need to go into the house and survey all the rooms— they plan to install cameras, motion sensors—you know—all the bells and whistles."

"And I can help how?" she prompted.

"I'll need to figure out where all the equipment will go and, you know, build a list of materials. That's where you come in. To get me inside. We may need to go through things inside the house," David added.

Simone's radar shot up. "That sounds really interesting. Did he mention what we'd be looking for?"

"Nah. Wait a minute. That was the part where he talked about a key and 'millions of dollars.' Yeah ... that the thing we look for is what would lead to millions of dollars. See, Sis? You'll be a whole lot better at that part than I will."

David filled his glass from the pitcher.

"David, do you remember the name of the company? Or where they're located?"

"Sure, uh ..." His voice trailed off while he fished in his shirt pocket. "I have a card here somewhere. Here it is." He held up a small stained rectangle.

She took it from him and held it at the edge of the table, then positioned her phone so she could snap a picture of it. "Great job, David. This sounds impressive. Universal, huh? I guess it must be a global company."

He nodded and poured his second glass of beer from the pitcher—bringing his total to five beers in less than thirty minutes. Simone looked at his eyes. Glassy. She smiled at him.

"Sally," Simone signaled the waitress. "Will you bring me the check—and when he finishes this one, please add another pitcher of beer to the bill."

She saw the question in Matt Maguire's eyes again.

"Thanksh, Sis. Tha's good of you."

Simone slid her chair back, and Sally handed her the check. She paid it and met the Maguires outside.

"I think you got what we needed," Matt said.

"Right," Simone answered.

"I'll do an Internet check on this company and see what I can find," Matt said. "And if you don't mind," he added, "I'll have my secretary check its financials and affiliations. For a company called 'Universal,' their parent company could be anywhere."

"I thought the part about 'going through stuff inside the house that will lead to millions' was the most interesting part. I can't imagine what that means. But honestly, if he is authorized to go inside the house, it will be a lot better to have me—or someone—with him. He's a bit of a bull in a china shop, if you know what I mean. He's not careful about keeping things in order when he searches for something."

"Until we get that letter signed by Mrs. Sinclair, he won't be authorized to do anything." Matt frowned. "I know Reggie—Senator Bradley—worked it out with the selection committee somehow, since I promised him—and he promised the president—that getting a signature wouldn't be a problem. I hope I didn't lie to him."

"There's something else that worries me about this meeting, Mr. Maguire. David is lying. Or at least he hasn't told me everything. He's holding something back. Something he decided not to tell me. But I don't know why. Normally, when he drinks that fast, he spills his guts."

"Oh, okay, now I understand," Matt said, "I was really surprised when you kept buying him beer. He was pretty slurry by the time you left."

"Yes, to get him to tell me everything—which didn't work. Yet, anyway. But mostly, I'm hoping," Simone answered, "that he'll keep drinking and forget about coming to the press conference tonight."

"Oh. Well, I hope so, too," he answered. "For your sake. I'm sure it would make you feel better if he didn't show." He patted her on the shoulder. "Do you have the … item … you would like to store at the vault with you, or will you need to get it?"

"I have to get it. I really hate having it with me when I go places. I'm always worried someone will discover it and think it's mine. I can be at your office in half an hour."

Matt Maguire met Simone in the spacious lobby of the Sinclair Bank & Trust. "I'll be really glad to get rid of this," she said. She patted the small box she held.

"Is it unloaded?" Matt asked.

"I have no idea. I've been afraid to touch it."

"Okay," Matt said. He motioned to a guard, and the three of them entered a conference room with a massive table and leather chairs. "Sidney is my most trusted security guard," Matt told Simone. "He's been with the bank for thirty years. If you'll give him your brother's gun, he'll unload it, and then wrap it in what we call a *gun rug.*"

"Gun rug?" Simone asked.

"It's a little pouch used to store and transport firearms. Then we can lock it in one of the cages in the vault so there won't be any danger of someone else stumbling across it. Are you okay with that?"

"Yes. Very okay," Simone said. "Thank you."

"But please understand," Matt said, "that while it's in the vault, you can't simply come in anytime you want and pick it up. And of course, neither can your brother. You'll have to get my permission to retrieve it. Which could translate to a substantial wait. Is that still okay with you?"

"Yes. I honestly don't know why I didn't just throw it in the garbage." She opened the box and handed the towel-wrapped gun to the security guard.

"It's a good thing you didn't," Matt said. "Somebody else might have found it, and we'd still have the problem of dealing with it."

The guard set the gun on the conference table, carefully unloaded it and encased it within the heavy bag he carried, then zipped it. He handed the gun rug to Simone and said, "Please keep this in your possession until we reach the vault." She put it back in her box and held it tight.

"Simone," Matt said, "will you accompany us to the vault? You can hand the gun over to him when you get there and see exactly where it will be stored. That should relieve your mind. When I have my secretary check out his company's credentials, I'll also see if she can find a permit in his name."

"I can't thank you enough, Mr. Maguire."

"No problem. I'll be in touch."

They left the conference room and wound their way through the lobby, crowded with afternoon business. Simone almost collided with a grizzled man watering plants.

"Your brother will probably get more aggressive about trying to get this back," Matt told her. He inserted his key into the lock and Sidney did the same with his key. "I'm going to leave you with Sidney now," Matt said.

Simone entered the vault with Sidney, then handed him her box. He removed the gun rug and placed it in one of the vault's wire containers.

"Maybe I can keep my brother drunk to take his mind off this." Simone grinned. "Thanks, Sidney. I appreciate your help. It's a huge relief to be rid of that thing."

They left the vault and again, Simone almost knocked into the man watering plants.

"Oh, excuse me," she said. "I'm so clumsy sometimes."

"No problem, miss." The man smiled at her, revealing only a few teeth—three on the bottom and two on top—all of which were yellowed with rotting roots. He smelled of kerosene and gave her the creeps.

She hurried away, rushed outside, and drew her first deep breath since finding David's gun in her apartment.

Two problems fixed, she thought. At least temporarily. David's gun was safely away from him, and he would be too drunk to show up later at Senator Bradley's reception. She allowed herself to relax. Then she thought of seeing the senator's handsome aide later that evening and excitement surrounded her heart.

CHAPTER THIRTY

While Simone disposed of David's gun, Mattie sat in a conference room at the Sinclair Bank & Trust with a box of documents from Henry Sinclair's estate in front of her. She'd arranged to fly to Greece with her grandfather the following day but wanted to see if she could find anything in the bank's files that might save them time when they got there. Getting the family contact signature on the summit letter demanded her focus—both for her father's sake and for the town's reputation.

She unpacked the first stack of papers, consisting mostly of newspaper clippings.

The account of Lily Sinclair's death—a duplicate of the one she'd seen—rested on top. Under that was a clipping about Henry, Jr.'s marriage to Constance Baldwin—also with a picture—Henry, Constance, and two little boys—just as her grandfather had said—identified as Jeffrey and Robert. Constance's father, Richard, even appeared in the picture.

She thumbed through several other clippings that included; celebrations at the textile mill, the retirement of a long-term bank employee, and surprisingly, an obituary for her great-grandfather, Melvin Maguire. The resemblance to her own gramps was unmistakable.

Under that, she found a front-page article dated March 31, 1947, detailing Henry Jr.'s murder the previous day. His face smiled at her from the black-and-white photograph, so faded his eyes took on a sepia hue. Curiously, there was no picture of Henry's killer, Charles Hudson, who died on the same day from a self-inflicted gunshot wound.

Since the accused murderer was also dead, the article reported, there was no speculation, no question about the necessity of a trial, and nothing

124

about testimony except that of Constance Sinclair, Henry's widow. Mrs. Sinclair told the police she chased Charles Hudson up the stairs to the room where her husband slept and fought with him to get the gun. According to her testimony, the secretary pushed her down, shot her husband and then held the gun on her. But at the last second, he moved the gun to his own head and pulled the trigger.

Oh, the poor woman. Other than the murderer turning the gun on himself, I know exactly how that feels. You've already suffered the shock of seeing the person you love most in the world killed right in front of you, but then you're fearful for your own life. How awful for her. How utterly awful.

Tears trickled down her face. She hoped Constance Sinclair was still alive. She wanted to tell her that she understood how horrible it was for her. She pushed her feelings away. She didn't have time to wallow in her own grief.

The one new thing Mattie learned was that the murder weapon was a Smith & Wesson Model Ten handgun—the article called it a Victory Model—and it was actually registered to Henry Sinclair himself. The paper gave quite a detailed description of it.

She added the newspaper to her pile of clippings and pulled out several more documents, including a stack of letters and some invoices. She began with the invoices.

The first two, marked "Paid," were from attorney Richard Baldwin, Constance Sinclair's father. She remembered his name from one of the clippings. They dealt with various situations for the Sinclair Textile Mill, notably filing government forms.

The next three were from an attorney's office, Lawrence & Higgins, in Asheville.

They're still in business ... we even got a donation from them for the Halloween Gala.

Two of the invoices dealt with the sale of some property Henry Sinclair, Jr. had owned in conjunction with an Arnold Sinclair—a name Mattie had never heard before—in Rogue Bluffs, Maine, and were both also stamped with the "Paid" symbol.

The third invoice was slightly different. For one thing, there was nothing to indicate it had been paid. Even more curious, she thought, was the fact that it was dated March 30, 1947—the day Henry Sinclair, Jr. was killed. And the notation on it read "New Will."

Bingo. That will tell us if there are any additional heirs. She put the unpaid invoice aside and dug into the box for the next stack of documents. Her fingers closed around a bulky packet wrapped in a large legal-sized document with the blue backing used by attorneys years earlier. She removed the heavy rubber bands, discolored and brittle with age, and unfolded the legal document. Tucked inside it was a leather-bound appointment book with the year 1947 embossed on the cover.

She turned the pages in the book and her fingers trembled at the feel of the history she held in her hands. Not surprisingly, the pages from March thirtieth and on remained blank. The hair on the back of her neck rose, however, when she read the final entry: *8:00 a.m.—Appt. with Lonnie Lawrence, Asheville office.*

That makes sense, given the earlier invoice I found from that office dated the same day. So Henry Sinclair saw his attorneys the morning he died and apparently talked to them about a new will. That's something I will definitely check out. I could even ask Mrs. Sinclair about it if she's still alive.

She put the book aside and opened the legal document. Right away, she saw it was the prenuptial agreement between Constance and Henry Sinclair prior to their wedding. The one her grandfather had mentioned. The document was lengthy at nineteen pages and covered the fact that Mrs. Sinclair could not sell the family property—just as her gramps had said—and then a myriad of circumstances Mattie had never even thought of. She quickly scanned the sections, skipping over great chunks of legal language until one section caught her eye: Termination of the Agreement. *Or, in today's terms, divorce.*

Mattie had no experience with divorce language, but the terms seemed fair to her. If the Sinclairs divorced, Constance Sinclair would receive alimony of one thousand dollars per month. And if Mr. Sinclair died prior to a divorce, she would receive a lump sum of five million dollars *plus* one thousand dollars per month. With no end date.

She did a quick Google search. *Wow. Five million dollars in 1947 would have ranked Constance Sinclair among the top ten percent of wealthy women in the world. Of course, I'm sure she would still rather have had her husband with her.*

The agreement didn't specify who would inherit Clairmont Place, so

Mattie figured that was spelled out in his regular will and would certainly be Jeffrey.

But she was out of time. She'd have to find that document another time. Or, if things went the way she hoped once she and her grandfather arrived in Greece, she wouldn't need to find it at all.

She replaced the documents in the box but put the unpaid invoice and the appointment book aside. She re-folded the legal-sized pages of the prenuptial agreement and saw that they skewed unevenly. A staple fell onto the table from under the top blue tab bent down over the first page—standard in legal documents of the time. A small ragged triangle of paper floated down after it. She lifted the top flap of the blue backing. The other two staples were stretched out and loose in the binding. She knew she had only counted nineteen pages, but the numbers on the first page, previously hidden by the blue binding, read *Page One of Twenty*. So, the words on the final sheet, *Page Nineteen of Twenty*, came as no surprise. Two more small ragged scraps of paper remained attached to the staples under the last sheet where page twenty should have been.

Ripped out—obviously.

The missing page must be further down in the box of documents, she figured, but she didn't have time to look for it right then. The file carton's top rested in the chair next to her and when she picked it up, a piece of crumpled paper floated to the floor. She retrieved it and then smoothed it to reveal a receipt for a draft from the Sinclair Bank & Trust to The Machias Savings Bank in a place called Rogue Bluffs, Maine. The draft was for ten thousand dollars and was dated August 5, 1950.

Rogue Bluffs ... the name was familiar.

She shuffled through the invoices and found it ... the location of the property jointly owned by Henry and Arnold Sinclair. That had to be significant. And might lead to an additional heir.

She added the bank draft to the documents she'd set aside and went down the hall to her father's office.

"Dad," she said, "do you know anything about a bank in Rogue Bluffs, Maine?" She handed the receipt to her father. "A Machias Savings Bank?"

"I think I've seen that name on the list of banks in our electronic funds transfer database." He looked at the draft she handed him and then frowned. "Where'd you get this?"

"It was stuck in the seam of the Sinclair file carton's top," Mattie said.

"I'm betting it falls into the confidential category, huh?"

Matt ignored her question and punched numbers from the draft into his computer. He studied the image, switched screens a time or two and then frowned. He leaned back in his chair. "Why do you think this draft is related to Clairmont Place?"

"Well, the location caught my eye." She pulled the paid invoice out of her portfolio. "Especially after I found this … a paid invoice for a company that dealt with the sale of property in Rogue Bluffs, Maine—the same town name as the one on that draft. And it looks like somebody named Arnold Sinclair was partners in this property with Henry prior to his murder."

"According to what I'm seeing here, Henry's murder didn't end whatever the relationship was with Maine. For one thing, this initial deposit took place after he was killed. And the same account number that received that first ten thousand dollars has been automatically receiving the sum of one thousand dollars a month ever since. Right up to and including this month."

"Really? Is there a name on the account?"

"Oh, sure there is … somewhere … but it doesn't show up in my records."

"It has to be related to that Arnold Sinclair name I found, don't you think? Have you ever heard of him?"

"Nope, can't say that I have. But I'll bet—"

"Gramps can tell us," they said in unison.

CHAPTER THIRTY-ONE

Mattie turned into the long drive leading to Clairmont Place. She wanted to check with Bill to see whether he had found anything else among the documents still at the mansion that would provide a clue as to additional heirs.

Sun filtered through the fall leaves of the beech trees that lined the lane, forming shadowy patterns on the ground and glowing golden overhead. Squirrels scurried across the path, their little cheeks filled with fallen nuts from the low branches. The scene, she decided, for the thousandth time, was striking enough to grace the October page on a calendar. Or a Thomas Kinkade painting.

She entered the front door and as always, her breath caught at the magnificence of the foyer. She stood at the bottom of the beautiful staircase and looked up. A decorative railing that matched the balustrade graced the top of the staircase and protected the landing between the two floors, forming a perfect balcony overlooking the marble steps. Behind the balcony, stairs to the floors above rose at right angles on both the left and right.

Her hand rested on the newel post, the end cap wobbly beneath her fingers.

Bill appeared from around the corner. "Miss Matilda," he said. "How nice to see you."

"Hi," she said. "I came to see how things are going for you. And whether you've found anything that might lead us to additional heirs."

"Not yet," he said, "but I'm making progress."

"Me too," Mattie said. "In fact, I found a copy of the prenuptial agreement Constance Sinclair signed—one of those legal-size documents with the blue binding lawyers used years ago. But the last page was ripped out. Maybe you can be on the lookout for it. There would be a notation at the top that reads 'Page Twenty of Twenty.'"

"Certainly," he said. "Your grandfather told me you two are going to Greece. He also asked if I'd come across anything that might help with your search. But I haven't."

"Well, hopefully, we'll get lucky with whoever we find there. Were you headed somewhere?"

"Yes." He smiled at her again. "I needed a break, so I thought I'd go upstairs and look around. I accompanied my mother up there once when the family was in Greece. I remember she seemed nervous ... as if she was worried about being discovered upstairs. She said Mrs. Sinclair treated the staff very differently from the way the other Sinclairs had."

"My gramps said exactly the same thing, almost word for word. If you don't mind, I'll join you."

They climbed the steps and entered a large room. Heavy green velvet drapes covered the windows and hung from the sturdy four poster bed. The valet chair, the pictures, the carpets ... everything screamed masculinity. "I'm guessing this must have been Henry Sinclair's room," she said.

In the middle of the right wall, an open door led to another room.

"Oh," Mattie added, "I remember reading that men and women—even kings and queens—had separate rooms with a common room between them. I'll bet that's what this is." Mattie entered through the open door and looked around.

The mixture of furniture, mostly covered against dust, appeared vastly different in size. One large chair with sturdy legs peeked out from a dust cover and another smaller one with only its dainty legs showing. Mattie wandered the room and stopped below a portrait over the large fireplace. "I'm figuring this must be the second Mrs. Sinclair," she said.

"Yes," Bill answered. "Although I only saw her a couple of times."

"Hmm, she certainly wasn't the beauty the first Mrs. Sinclair was, huh?"

They continued through a door on the opposite wall and entered the room Mattie thought to be Mrs. Sinclair's bedroom. Drapes, fluffy and floral, adorned the windows and matched the few patterns visible under the covers on the ornate furniture.

They went back into the hallway and peeked into other doors—

guest rooms, each with a different color scheme and theme—and then continued down the hallway until they reached the second from the last room. Mattie opened the door and drew in her breath. The enchanting room was decorated with fairy tale pictures embellishing the walls, one of which featured every animal she could think of entering Noah's ark, two by two. Letters of the alphabet, sporting happy little faces, marched between the windows on stick legs while rowboats, sailboats and pirate ships—complete with chests of gold—sailed the empty spaces beneath them.

The furniture was small, and Mattie could see that the bed, even though covered, was child-size. By the window a low round oak table with four little chairs rested in the middle of a wide sunbeam.

"Jeffrey's room," she breathed. "It must be. I love it."

They left that room and entered the last door on that hallway. A delicate writing desk stood against the wall that backed up to Jeffrey's room and a large bed, bare to the frame stood in the center. The air seemed different and she felt a chill.

"Oh," Mattie said. "Is this where…"

"I believe it is," Bill said.

"Creepy," Mattie said. "Even after all these years."

They walked back toward the stairs. "Before we go down," she said, "I'd like to see the second Mrs. Sinclair's portrait again."

They entered through Mrs. Sinclair's room and continued into the connecting parlor.

"There's something about her I find intriguing," Mattie said. She walked toward the portrait and stopped under it. "Oh, what a shame," she said when she reached it. "It looks like a piece of the frame is chipped." She stood on a footstool and reached out to touch it. Dust flew and swirled around her, but she batted it away.

"Wait a minute." Something crinkled in her fingers. "This isn't chipped wood. It's … paper." She held it up to show him. "Folded a bunch of times." The frame banged softly against the wall when she removed it, and the portrait skewed slightly.

"Oh. I guess it was there to help keep the picture straight." She chuckled. "That strikes me as funny. My view of the people who lived in this house is that everything was always perfect." She turned her comments directly to Bill. "You know … if something was dirty, it got cleaned right away, or if it broke it got fixed right away, or faded it got painted right away. It never occurred to me that they may have lived exactly as we do … well, as I do. Like holding up a bra strap with a safety pin rather than sewing it immediately." She saw Bill's face go red. "Or using a bobby pin to unlock a door." She held up the folded paper. "Or using folded paper to prop things up or help them hang straight."

She studied Constance Sinclair's portrait again and decided that the face was not so much intriguing as unsettling.

They went back downstairs and entered Henry Sinclair's office. She absently set the piece of folded paper on the edge of the desk and told Bill about finding an invoice with the notation "New Will."

"Of course, if all goes the way we hope it does in Greece," she said, "that won't matter anymore." She closed her eyes and shook her head. "Oh, my goodness," she said, "we have to find either Constance or Jeffrey tomorrow. We just *have to*. Lots of reputations depend on it."

CHAPTER THIRTY-TWO

Asheville City Hall

Mattie waved to Simone and then walked in her direction, shaking hands with several acquaintances in her path.

Within minutes, Tony Adkins, the senator's aide, greeted them. "I'm so glad you came," he said to Simone. "Both of you," he added. Mattie saw that he glanced briefly at her, but most of his attention centered on Simone. "Will your brother be joining you?"

"I doubt it," Simone said. "I think he was rather ... indisposed this afternoon."

"Oh. That's too bad," Tony said. "I wanted to get to know him better." Someone on the makeshift stage motioned to him. "Excuse me," he added. "I have to go now, but I'll talk to you after the senator speaks."

Simone's hand shot up to her blond curls and wrapped one around her finger. Mattie caught her eye and Simone let it go.

"I know, I know," she said. "I'm trying to stop. But right now, I'm really stressed."

Mattie put her arm around the younger woman's shoulder. "I know you are, kiddo. Don't worry about it."

Tony stepped up to the microphone.

"Ladies and gentlemen, thank you so much for coming this evening. The senator wanted you to be the first to hear about the new legislation he's introducing for our state. Please join me in welcoming the Honorable Reginald Bradley, State Senator for District Forty-eight."

"Dad said you got a lot of information from your brother," Mattie whispered. "Have you had time to check any of it out yet?"

"No," Simone whispered back. "After I met with David, I went to the bank with your father and we put the you-know-what in the vault."

"Right. So why don't you think he'll be here tonight?"

Simone giggled. "I bought him a lot of beer at lunch. I mean a *lot* of beer. I'm hoping he's still sleeping it off."

"—significant tax incentives for the Chinese manufacturer who will relocate its weaving business to North Carolina!" The senator finished speaking—his voice triumphant—to rousing applause.

"Oops," Mattie said. "You might need to pump your buddy, Tony, for details of the senator's speech. I've never known him to be so brief."

Simone giggled again, and they both clapped politely along with the others.

Several other people spoke and while information sheets about the new legislation were passed around, the senator introduced Mattie's boss, Morgan, along with Mattie and Simone. He congratulated them all on Sinclair Station winning the venue for the G7 Summit.

Seconds after the wine and hors d'oeuvres appeared, Tony joined them with two filled glasses.

"Here you go, ladies," he said. "It was great of you to come, and I hope you'll talk this up within the bureau and the chamber. Won't it be great for Asheville? And Sinclair Station, too." He grinned.

"We certainly will," Mattie said. She sipped her wine to avoid further discussion.

"Simone," Tony added, "I'd love to discuss this with you over lunch ... or dinner, if you have the time, of course."

"I'm sure she would love to."

Simone choked on her wine, her face ashen.

"Oh, Mr. Rousseau," Tony said, offering his hand. "I thought maybe you left town. It was good of you to come. Please help yourself to ... oh ... I see you already have wine."

Simone's brother nodded and then held out his free hand to Mattie. "I'm Simone's brother, David," he said. "I don't believe we've met."

"Mattie Maguire," she said, shaking his hand and doing her best to sound pleasant.

"Maguire, huh? Any relation to the Maguires who are caretakers at the big house in Sinclair Station?"

Simone's eyes widened.

"Yes," Mattie said. "My grandfather, Michael, is head caretaker at Clairmont Place."

134

"Interesting," he said. He drained his glass. "Anybody need more wine?" Without waiting for an answer, he turned and strode back to the bar table.

The silence was sudden and uncomfortable.

"So ..." Tony said to Simone. "How about if I call you to arrange something?"

"Huh?" she said. "Oh. Sure. That would be great."

As soon as he left, Simone twirled a blond curl all the way to her second knuckle.

"Okay, so not enough booze," Mattie said.

"What do you girls have your heads together about?" David held a full glass of wine. Only one.

"Simone was just telling me she was surprised to see you ... that she didn't know you were coming into town," Mattie said. "Your business brought you here suddenly?"

Mattie saw the flicker in his eyes—not anger exactly—but heavy-duty irritation certainly.

"Something like that," he said. "I just finished up some old business and have a new deal in the works. Did she tell you about it?" The smile left his face with the question, and he turned a stony expression on his sister.

"Something about surveillance equipment for the summit. So I guess we'll be working together," Mattie responded. "Of course, I'm certain your company told you that time at the mansion needs to be scheduled through the committee. And we're not quite ready yet—"

"I know how it works, lady. Don't get in my face about it." He drained his wineglass in one swallow, turned abruptly and headed back to the bar.

"Well, that was rude," Mattie said.

"Oh, Mattie. Don't provoke him." Mattie watched Simone wrap her curls so tight around her fingers, she struggled to remove them.

"Simone," Mattie hesitated. "That simple statement shouldn't have been enough to 'provoke him,' as you say." She looked intently at her friend. "Has he ever hurt you?"

"Not much since we were teenagers." Her voice was a mere whisper, and her eyes revealed misery.

"Not much? Oh, my goodness. We definitely need to get Bryan in the loop."

"No, Mattie," Simone said. "Not yet anyway." She cocked her head in

135

David's direction. "He can certainly turn on the charm when he wants to though, huh?" she added.

"Charm, maybe," Mattie said. "But if you watch closely, you see a handshake that gets a little too familiar. A polite laugh that turns loud. And I just noticed that he nearly lost his balance a minute ago and had to take a few steps backward to compensate. He almost bumped into a waiter. Honestly, I'm torn between trying to rescue him and letting him fall on his own sword. What's your vote?"

"We should probably rescue him," Simone said. "He's told too many people he's my brother, and I don't like being embarrassed like this. He doesn't deserve to have his butt saved, but it's more about keeping the bureau out of any kind of scandal." Simone turned sad eyes toward Mattie. "But I could use your help."

"You got it, kiddo. What's the plan? Manhandle him to a car and drive him to a hotel? Or is he staying with you?"

"No. I let him stay the first night he was in town. But once I discovered the gun, I made him leave."

"We'd better go get him, then. I'm figuring he's not a happy drunk, right?"

"Uh, no, he's not. Thanks, Mattie."

The two walked over to the bar where David's hands appeared ready to touch one of the female wait staff inappropriately. Simone put her arm around her brother and pulled him back slightly, out of the way of his target. "David, I'd like to show you something outside."

He turned toward her and shook her arm off. "Get your hands off me."

Mattie stepped in. "Then maybe you'll accompany me to my car. I don't like walking in the dark by myself." The female waiter mouthed a silent thank you to her.

His eyes had glazed over and he reeled, apparently struggling to maintain his balance.

A building security guard—one of Mattie's friends—followed them to the exit. "Anything I can do, Mattie?" he asked quietly.

"Maybe watch to make certain we get to my car safely," she said. "That would help."

David stumbled down the stairs, with Mattie and Simone on either side to keep him upright.

"David," Mattie asked, "are you staying at the inn?"

He nodded.

Mattie guided him toward her car and through the door Simone had opened. They stuffed him into the passenger's side and buckled his seat belt. He passed out.

"Now all we have to do is get him out again once we get to the hotel. I'll bring you back here afterward."

They had driven about fifteen minutes when David woke up. "What're you doin'?" he growled, his words slurred. "Stop the car ... washn't ready to leave." He lunged for the steering wheel and jerked it to the right, out of Mattie's hands.

The car skidded onto the shoulder in loose gravel.

Mattie wrestled the wheel and turned into the skid but overcompensated, and the back of the car fishtailed. Several seconds of out-of-control-swerving passed before she straightened the tires and braked to a complete stop.

"What the hell were you thinking?" Her voice was harsh. "Oh great. Now look what you've done."

Red and blue flashing lights reflected in the side mirrors and cast eerie patterns across the road.

"Please just sit still and be quiet," Mattie told David. She found her license and registration and hopped out of the car before the policeman approached.

"Are you all right, ma'am?" the policeman asked. "It looked like you lost control there."

"Yes, officer, I'm sorry. I—"

"Will you step this way, ma'am?"

Mattie followed the policeman a few steps from her car. "Ma'am, I'm Officer Daniel Scott, North Carolina Highway Patrol. You are Mattie Maguire, right?"

Mattie nodded.

"Your security friend at Asheville City Hall called me. He said you had an inebriated passenger and was afraid you might have trouble. Do you need help?"

Mattie smiled. "That was very kind of him. And he was right. My front seat passenger has had way too much to drink, and I'm taking him to the inn in Sinclair Station. He grabbed the wheel when he came to and that's what caused my skid."

"How about if I come talk to him and then follow you the rest of the way?"

"That would be great."

The officer approached the passenger side of Mattie's car, and she lowered the automatic window.

"Hey, buddy," the officer said to David. "I hear you've been partying. Had a little too much to drink, maybe?"

"I'm fine."

"Well, that's good to hear. You're pretty lucky, too, that this lady is driving you to your hotel. If you'd been in your own car, I'd be taking you to jail now."

"Don't have a car."

"Even better. She saved you from a long walk."

"Mmph."

"So I'm going to follow you the rest of the way. How about if you don't give her any more trouble?"

"Mmph."

"Thank you, officer," Mattie said.

Mattie climbed into the driver's seat, and the policeman returned to his own vehicle. But before she could buckle her seatbelt, David unbuckled his, flung his door open and jumped out. He ran across the field that bordered the highway.

"What the …?" Mattie said.

"Oh no," Simone wailed from the backseat.

Mattie got out of the car again and met the policeman as he headed her way. David continued to run. His steps were unsteady, but he remained upright for as long as they could see him in the pale moonlight.

"What do you suggest, officer?" she asked. "And please know that I'm not inclined to run after anybody in these shoes."

Simone joined them.

"Technically," the officer said, "he hasn't committed a crime."

"Unless you consider stupidity a crime," Simone said. "Sorry you got pulled into this, officer. That drunken fool is my brother. Mattie was just helping me out."

"As I said, he hasn't committed a crime in this county so there's nothing I can do. Is this normal behavior for him?"

Simone shrugged. "This is the first time I've seen him in five years. I don't know what's normal anymore."

"What do you want to do, Simone?" Mattie asked her. "Do *you* want to take off across the field after him?"

"No way. If he's stupid enough to do that, let him fend for himself. Why don't you just take me back to my car?"

They followed the policeman and headed back toward Asheville.

"That might give us another chance to find him," Mattie told Simone. "Maybe he'll have worked his way back to the highway and we'll see him on our return to Sinclair Station."

Simone was silent.

"Will you pick him up if you see him on the road?" Mattie asked.

"No. And I don't want you to either. And ... oh my goodness ... I am so glad he doesn't have his gun. Heaven knows what he might have done."

They reached the parking lot at Asheville City Hall.

"Stay safe, Simone," Mattie said.

Mattie waited until Simone got in her car and started it, then they both turned back toward Sinclair Station. She followed Simone on the drive home but saw no sign of David. At the turn to her apartment, Mattie gave a quick tap of her horn and drove off.

Simone turned the opposite direction to her own place. She pulled up to her building and turned off her car. But before she opened her door, movement in the tall bushes by the stairs caught her attention. She sat perfectly still, watching. In a few seconds, a gust of wind rippled through the shrubbery and the streetlight shone bright on a man's face. He crouched close to the sidewalk, as if he were ready to spring.

She restarted her car and punched Mattie's number into her cell phone.

"I just found David," she said. "May I stay at your place tonight?"

CHAPTER THIRTY-THREE

Sinclair Station, North Carolina

The morning following the senator's reception, Simone drove slowly through the parking lot of her apartment complex. Lawn maintenance crews performed their morning clean-up routine and a number of delivery trucks blocked several parking spaces close to the building. She eased her car into a slot well away from her normal spot.

She scanned the faces of those around her. No David. She punched in the number for her building's manager, who lived on the premises. No sense in taking chances, she decided.

He answered right away.

"Ryan, it's Simone Rousseau. Are you in your apartment?" She heard the nervousness in her voice and hated that David's presence brought that out in her. "I had an issue last night with my brother showing up and waiting for me outside, so I would really appreciate it if you could accompany me to my apartment. Just in case. Will you do that? Please?"

"Yes, certainly. Give me a minute and I'll meet you outside your building."

She waited in her car, and her anger built by the second. Something had to give. She could not allow David to continue to produce such strong reactions in her. If he really was planning to stay in town for a while, they would have to have a come-to-Jesus meeting. She couldn't—*wouldn't*—live her life afraid to enter her own apartment.

Ryan walked toward her, so she gathered her things, locked her car door, and met him at the bottom of the stairs.

"I'm really sorry for letting your brother in," he told her for the tenth time. "He seemed like such a nice fellow."

"I understand. But I know you won't ever do a thing like that again.

You just never—"

She left her sentence hanging. Splintered wood littered the floor outside her door. Which tilted open at an odd angle.

"Oh, my goodness," Ryan said. "I can't believe no one reported that."

"Well," Simone said, "I guess I would have been the one to report it, but I didn't stay here last night after I saw David hanging around in the parking lot."

"We need to call the police before you even go in," he told her. He entered the number in his cell phone and waited.

She selected one of her curls and twirled it while her anger expanded.

Within minutes, two uniformed policemen rounded the corridor toward them. State troopers, Simone saw, rather than officers from the Sinclair Station sheriff's office.

"Thank you for coming," Ryan told them.

The officers nodded. "Let us go in first. It's unlikely the intruder is still there, but we don't need to take chances." They entered the apartment, their guns drawn. Simone and Ryan heard them moving through the rooms.

Several minutes passed and then one of them stuck his head out. "It's clear. You can come in, now. We'll need to get some information from you."

The policemen made notes as Simone walked slowly from room to room, her anger dissolving to heartbreak. Nothing appeared to be missing. Her television, her computer … even her jewelry and her mother's Department 56 collection of Snowbabies were all still there.

But everything was broken and the whole place trashed.

David. Mean, angry David.

"Do you have any idea who might have done this, ma'am?" one of the officers asked.

"You bet I do."

"Will you give us a name? We'll want to apprehend that person for questioning."

"It was my brother, David Rousseau."

"How can you be so certain it was him?"

"Because we had … an incident last night after a reception in Asheville. And I saw him hanging around the parking lot when I got home. Luckily, I didn't stay here."

"Do you know where we might find him?"

"No. Not really. He came in town earlier in the week. But I haven't seen him since last night. He may be staying at the inn."

"You think he's been at the inn all week?"

"No. Actually, he spent his first night here. But then I told him he had to leave. I don't know where he went after that."

"But you saw him last night?"

"Yes. I told you. He showed up at a reception I attended in Asheville. He had way too much to drink and my friend offered to give him a ride home. But he jumped out of her car—it was stopped," she added quickly when the policeman's eyes widened.

"So that was the last time you saw him? When he jumped out of her car?"

"No. I just told you ..." Her patience was razor thin, and she took a breath to calm herself. "When he jumped out of the car, my friend took me back to Asheville to get my car. When I got back here, that's when I saw him waiting outside my building. Hiding in the bushes. So I spent the night with my friend."

"Thank you, ma'am. We may want to speak with your friend, too."

"Fine." Simone stopped talking. She was livid. She took another deep breath.

"So," she said after a minute, "what do I do now? I need to change clothes. Do I have to wait for something else?"

"I know you have renter's insurance, Simone, since it's a requirement of the lease," Ryan said. "You probably should call your company before you do anything else. They'll want to take pictures for your claim."

"He's right, ma'am. And we'll need to dust for prints. I would suggest you find somewhere else to stay for the next day or so since this is a crime scene. But first, we need your contact information. Cell phone, email address." She handed him one of her cards. "That should do it for now. But when we find your brother, we'll want you to come to the station to identify him."

"It will be my immense pleasure," she ground out between clenched teeth.

She was ready to blow.

She turned and stormed off down the hall.

"Simone?" Ryan said.

She stopped but didn't turn. Part of this was his fault. He should never have let David in her apartment the first time.

He caught up with her and she turned toward him, her face like granite.

"Look, Simone, I feel like this is at least partly my fault."

She said nothing, but her face told him she agreed.

"So since you've always been really good about paying on time, even ahead sometimes, I'd like to offer you a few nights in one of the weekly suites. To help compensate for your trouble."

Her face softened and she even managed a small smile. "Thank you," she said. "I accept your generosity." She reached out her hand and he shook it. "I'll call my insurance company and then come see you for a key."

She left the building and climbed back into her car.

Her whole body shook from shock and rage.

But one thing was certain. If David had vented his anger on her the way he had on her possessions, she could easily have lost a lot more.

Like her life.

She continued to tremble.

And without warning, tears started to flow. Within seconds, her body shook with choking sobs.

CHAPTER THIRTY-FOUR

"Pardon me, ma'am."

Mattie's grandmother knelt beside her stack of freshly picked zucchini and wiped her brow with the back of her gloved hand. She looked up to see a young man watching her. "Yes?" she asked. "How can I help you?" She prepared to rise.

"Please," he said, "let me help you." He put a hand under her elbow and stabilized her as she stood.

"Thank you, young man," she said. "Getting off the ground used to be a lot easier than it is these days." She smiled at him. "Now that I can see you properly, what can I do for you?"

"I'm new in town and was hoping someone could tell me the hours that big house is open." He pointed to Clairmont Place.

"Oh, it's not ever open. Been closed up tight for more than sixty-five years. You must be from far away. Even people in Asheville know that."

"Yes, ma'am. I'm from up north, but I've actually been out of the country the past few years. I met a couple of fellas who told me about it and said it was really beautiful inside."

"Well, like I told you, the house has been closed for a long time. Those guys you met must have been pretty old to remember what the inside looked like. Or ghosts." She laughed at her own joke, but he didn't appear to be amused. She bent and picked up the cut zucchini and stacked the vegetables in her apron. "Sorry I couldn't help you."

She turned toward her house.

"I've come a really long way to look at it," he said. His voice trembled. "You see, it reminds me a lot of my grandparents' home. Where I was raised. I just came into some money and am building a house to honor them. Up north. And wanted to incorporate some features from that mansion into the one I'm building. Are you sure there's no one who could let me go in? Or go in with me? It's so important to me, and I've come such a long way."

"Honey, I wish I could help you. My husband's head caretaker here, so he's the only one who ever goes in—to perform maintenance, you know. Although, there's a big meeting coming, and the house will be open in a few months. You're welcome to come back then."

"I'm sorry," he said and put his hand on her arm. "I didn't mean to impose. You've been most helpful. May I carry your vegetables for you?"

"No, I live in the house right here. I can manage that far. Why don't you give me your name in case my husband has any other ideas? And let me know where you're staying."

"Oh, that's okay. I probably won't be here that much longer."

David left the woman he knew to be Mattie Maguire's grandmother. Seeing and talking with her had been a stroke of luck.

And he found out everything he needed to know.

No one goes inside the house. Nobody around except for a few maintenance people. And only an old couple on the premises.

He walked down the flagstone path toward the empty parking lot, but once out of the old lady's line of vision, he cut across the lawn. He ducked under some low-hanging trees and crept along a path of dense shrubs to the east side of the building. Lights, mounted above the door, clicked on when he got close.

Motion detectors. Good to know.

He tried the knob. Nothing moved. But he studied the locking mechanism to determine what he would need to pick it if that became necessary. Fairly old lock, he saw. Should be easy.

And no security to get in his way.

A broad smile filled his face and he left the cover of the trees, skirted around a long arbor of canopied locust trees and headed to the parking lot.

Mattie drove to her grandparents' house to have lunch with them and then catch an Uber ride to the airport with her grandfather. Once there, her grandmother told her about meeting a young man, who didn't give his name, but wanted to get into the house. Worry crawled up the back of her neck.

"I'm going to just do a quick check of the grounds," she told her grandparents. She made a mental note to alert Bryan that her grandmother would be at the house by herself for a couple of days.

She pulled her jacket tight around her in the chilly afternoon wind and walked toward the East Portico. Before the trees cleared enough for her to see the door, she saw movement to her right and swung her head in that direction. The same feeling of unease she had experienced the day of the gala gripped her again and her heartbeat quickened.

A man stood at the door with his hand on the knob. It wasn't Bill. The man at the door was about the same height, but his hair was the wrong color. He looked around. As if he knew he shouldn't be there.

Oh no. David.

He must have been the man who spoke with her grandmother. She shivered at the thought. He was bad news, and she didn't want him anywhere near the people she loved.

She backtracked and hid behind some heavy shrubs, then watched as he fiddled with the door a few moments longer. She stayed hidden until he took the path to the parking lot, then returned to her grandparents' house.

Quickly, she punched in Simone's number. "Simone," Mattie said, "I have to talk to you right—oh my goodness. What's wrong?"

"Oh Mattie," Simone said, her voice breaking at the last syllable. "It was awful—"

"Hey, kiddo," Mattie said softly, "you know you can talk to me. What was awful and how can I help? Are you hurt?"

"No. I'm not hurt." Mattie heard Simone sniffle. "Not physically anyway. But when I went home after I left you, my door was broken, and my apartment completely trashed."

"Oh, my goodness. I am so glad you didn't stay there last night. I'm assuming it was David. Is that what you think?"

"Yes." Her voice was only a whisper.

"So, where are you now? Do I need to come and get you?"

"No. My building manager is letting me stay in one of the weekly rentals in another section of my complex. And we called the police. They're dusting my apartment for fingerprints. I can't even get my clothes out."

"Did he steal stuff?"

"I don't think so. It didn't look like anything was missing. But everything was smashed. It looked like he broke in to search for his gun and when he didn't find it, went on a rampage. I'd bet a million dollars that's what happened."

"Yeah, it sure sounds like it. Has he contacted you?"

"No. I don't have a clue where he is."

"Well, brace yourself," Mattie told her. "I saw him just a few minutes ago. That's why I called you. He came to my grandparents' house and actually spoke with my grandmother while she was in her garden."

"Oh no! I can't believe he bothered your sweet little grandmother. Did he hurt her?"

"No, but he did badger her to let him in the house—Clairmont Place, I mean. Of course she told him it was closed. But then I saw him shortly after that, fiddling with the doorknob, so he probably plans to come back. Honestly, after what you've just told me, I'm betting he's primed to go on the same kind of rampage here. And then trash these beautiful rooms, too, if he doesn't find what he's looking for. Whatever the heck that is. I wish we knew why he's in such a hurry to get in."

"I don't care any longer, Mattie. I'm through with him. After we tried to help him last night and he repaid me by breaking in and trashing my place, I would love to see him in jail."

"Well, my next call is to Bryan to let him know what I saw. And that my grandmother will be here by herself for a couple of days. Gramps and I are flying to Greece tonight to find either Constance or Jeffrey Sinclair and get the summit letter signed once and for all." Mattie hesitated. "Are you really okay, Simone?"

"Yes," she answered. "When you let Bryan know about seeing David there, please also tell him what happened at my apartment. David is obviously more dangerous than I originally thought."

"Yeah," Mattie said. "He sure is."

"If Bryan needs to talk to me," Simone continued, "I'll be available. And good luck, Mattie," she added. "I really hope you can find one of the Sinclairs so we can get the signature piece resolved. It will be good for us to concentrate on the summit meetings."

"Take care of yourself, kiddo. I'll be back in a couple of days. With good news, I hope."

CHAPTER THIRTY-FIVE

Corfu, Greece

The afternoon stretched before him.

Stavros failed to show up for work. For the third day in a row.

Money. It had to be because Stavros hadn't been paid in almost a month. No one, in fact, had been paid since well before Constance died.

Responding to the letter about the signature held risks for his future. And whatever he decided to do would take time—a commodity that further complicated his lack of money.

But he had to do something. Several times a day, fists pounded on his door. Creditors. He refused to answer. But he was out of food. And his normal restaurants—even the ones he and Constance had supported for more than fifty years—no longer delivered to him.

He crafted a plan. He stuffed all of Constance's jewelry in one of her ornate boxes to take to the pawn shop on the corner. Maybe he could get enough to pay off his most urgent bills. He re-showered, dressed, and snuck out of his villa, wearing a hat and dark glasses. He hoped his disguise was sufficient to avoid the thugs who sought to take their money from his hide.

He made it to the street without incident, then ducked into the cool, dark interior of the shop. It was empty except for the owner, who frowned at seeing him.

"*Kaliméra* … good morning." He knew the owner well. He'd been there before.

The owner nodded, wary.

Carefully, he poured the jewelry on the glass counter. The owner's eyes widened.

"Pawn or sell?" the owner asked.

"Sell." It was all hers. He never wanted to see it again.

"American dollars?"

"Yes, please."

He watched the owner pick up a diamond and emerald ring that he knew had cost more than three thousand dollars fifty years earlier. The owner cleaned the stones and checked them with a jeweler's loupe.

"Five hundred," the owner said.

The offer angered him, but he controlled it.

"Make it fifteen hundred," he responded. He really needed to get a thousand dollars per piece—at a minimum—in order to make a dent in what he owed.

"Eight hundred."

His anger burned hotter. But he pushed it away.

"Twelve."

"One thousand." Success. He handed the ring over and the owner counted out ten dog-eared and dirty one hundred-dollar bills into his pudgy fingers.

They continued their negotiation ritual through the remainder of the pieces. When he left, a little more than fifty thousand dollars in crumpled bills rested in the ornate box where the jewels had been. He visited the people who were after him and one by one, paid them off. At least the ones he'd owed the longest. He didn't bother to find Stavros. He probably had another job at this point anyway.

He checked his remaining cash. Just enough for a few days' meals.

At the corner market, he bought food. And ouzo. A case of ouzo.

He slipped through his door and locked it behind him. He should be okay for a while. His most aggressive creditors had been paid.

He would figure out what to do about the bank paperwork tomorrow. No offices were open right now, anyway.

He made a sandwich, opened a bottle of ouzo, and settled in his favorite chair on the balcony, enjoying the scant breeze that reached him.

CHAPTER THIRTY-SIX

Fewer than forty-eight hours after Mattie convinced her grandfather to accompany her to Greece, they settled comfortably in their business class seats on the last leg of their trip—Paris to Athens and then a quick hop to Corfu.

Mattie tilted her champagne glass toward her grandfather's.

"Here's to getting the Sinclair signature," she said.

"And to moving on with international meetings," he responded, clinking her glass with his.

They were scheduled to arrive in Corfu shortly after noon and planned to go straight to the address Mattie's father had given her for Constance Sinclair.

Her stomach rolled and her mind jumped from one thought to another, flitting between anxiety and anticipation with lightning speed.

"What if they refuse to see us?" Mattie asked.

"We're pretty persuasive, the two of us," her grandfather responded. "Besides, we only have good news for them. They have no reason to refuse."

"It will be great to have this part behind us," Mattie said. "I've never seen Dad so worried. And this meeting is really important, Gramps. To Sinclair Station, yes, but to the world as well. We have to make this work."

"No use in worrying about it ahead of time," her grandfather said. "We'll know for certain in a few hours, anyway. Why don't you sleep?"

"Great idea." She retrieved her pillow and blanket and eased her seat back. Her eyes fluttered shut and in no time at all, she awoke to sun streaming through the cabin windows.

With only carry-on bags, they made it out of the airport quickly and found a cab.

Despite her worry about the coming meeting, Mattie loved the feel of the small island town. Lush greenery hung from balconies, and the architecture delighted her senses.

"Oh, Gramps, look at that cathedral." She pointed to a large white stone building to their left, the front of which sported rows of columns topped by a high domed roof. "That looks almost exactly like the Greek Orthodox Cathedral of the Annunciation in Baltimore. I passed it every day on my way to the Phillips restaurant. Baltimore had quite a large Greek community, you know."

Before he could respond, the cab pulled up in front of the address they had given the driver. Mattie was amazed that in just two short blocks, the buildings morphed from public structures into spacious villas. Although she couldn't help but notice that the small patch of grass in front of the one they sought was uncut and full of weeds.

"This is it, Gramps," she said softly. "You're about to see Constance or Jeffrey Sinclair—maybe both—after all these years."

"I'm ready, Mattie Mat."

They climbed the few steps to the enclosed foyer. Trash remained piled outside the front door, just as the courier had reported earlier. More than a week's worth, by its appearance. She took a deep breath and knocked.

Several minutes passed. No response.

Mattie knocked again. Louder. After several more minutes, sounds of shuffling feet reached them, followed by deep coughing.

"Who is it?" a voice from the other side of the door called. "What do you want?"

Mattie frowned. That wasn't the greeting she had expected. She signaled for her grandfather to speak.

"Jeffrey, it's Michael Maguire from Clairmont Place in North Carolina."

They heard a gasp, crystal clear through the heavy wooden door.

"Why are you here?"

Mattie frowned again. "I wanted to check on you and your stepmother," Michael said, "and see if you were all right. You haven't responded to letters sent from the bank about Clairmont Place. Please let me come in. I would really like to talk to you ... to see you again."

Several more seconds passed, then they heard locks click and scrape.

Mattie steeled herself for the appearance of an eight-year-old after seventy years.

He was not very tall, but he *was* wide. His light terry robe barely closed around his waist and a fat roll peeked out above the loosely tied sash. His eyes, mere bloodshot slits, squinted at them from an alcohol-bloated face. Thin gray hair revealed a lot of forehead, neither of which appeared to have been washed for days.

An odor assaulted Mattie's senses as soon as the door opened. Rotten food was part of it, she could tell, along with stale body and breath.

"Michael, is that really you? You look different."

"I could return the compliment," Mattie's grandfather replied. "But I'm surprised to hear you call me 'Michael.' Do you remember what you called me when we were both younger?"

The man hesitated and then said, "Of course. I called you 'Mike.'"

He moved aside and let them enter.

"So, Mike, why are you here? And who is this?" He leered at Mattie.

"This is Matilda Maguire, my granddaughter. She's the event director for the North Carolina Visitors and Conventions Bureau and she will be leading the preparation for the international meeting to take place in Sinclair Station. But we need Mrs. Sinclair's signature. Is your stepmother here?"

"She's dead."

"Oh my goodness, I'm so sorry," Michael said. "When did it happen?"

"Couple of days ago."

"Jeffrey, please accept our condolences."

"Sure," he said. He shrugged.

"Since she's listed as the family contact of record, it would be helpful to have a copy of her death certificate."

Jeffrey shuffled to the desk and returned with an official-looking document. Mattie snapped a picture of it with her phone.

"All we need, now that Constance Sinclair is deceased, is proof of your identity."

"I'm Jeffrey."

"And I'm here to help you prove it," Mattie's grandfather said.

"Why is that necessary? I just told you who I am."

"True. But when Mrs. Sinclair left the United States, she took two boys with her—Jeffrey and Robert. I'm here to confirm that you are Jeffrey, the rightful heir and property owner, rather than Robert."

"Are you saying I'm lying?"

Mattie couldn't believe the hostility radiating from the unkempt person in front of her. If it really was Jeffrey, the traumas he suffered in his early life must have turned him sour for the rest of it. She longed to break into the conversation and yell at him for speaking to her grandfather that way. But she remained quiet.

"You mistake me, Jeffrey," Mattie's grandfather said calmly. "I'm not accusing you of anything. I'm simply here as a witness since I am probably the only person still alive who can confirm your true identity. As I told you before, we just need to make an official identification in order to keep the monthly lease payments coming to you."

Mattie saw the change in his eyes and realized her grandfather had hit his mark. Money motivated the man in front of them.

"May we sit down and talk for a few minutes?" Mattie's grandfather continued. "I know Mrs. Sinclair's father moved here with you, but I'm figuring he passed away some time ago. What about Robert? Is he here?"

"You're right. Constance's father died several years ago. And I don't know where Robert is. He hasn't been with us for years."

"I'm very sorry to hear that," Mattie's grandfather said.

The man in front of them shrugged again. But he indicated with his flabby, outstretched arm that they should sit in two large chairs. With much heavy breathing, he settled himself on the couch opposite them. The cluttered room, with empty bottles, papers strewn about, and garbage on almost every surface, mirrored their host's appearance exactly.

"Constance and her father were both sick for a long time," he said. "And doctors come at a premium here. Most of Constance's inheritance is gone. So I'm very willing to do whatever is necessary to keep money coming in. I need it."

"Have you ever considered going back to Clairmont Place to live?" Mattie asked. She hoped she knew the answer.

"No way," he said. "I hated that place."

"Really?" Mattie's grandfather asked. "During the time we spent together, I thought you loved it … coming to the stables with me and wandering through the boxwood gardens. You wanted to know the names of all the plants and trees so you could go back to your room and draw pictures of them. Do you still draw?"

The man shook his head. "No. No more stupid pictures—they were so childish. But no, I won't go back. I like it here."

Mattie didn't understand how anyone could be happy to live in the clutter that surrounded them.

"Do you realize, Jeffrey, that with Constance Sinclair gone, you are the sole heir of any proceeds from Clairmont Place?" Michael Maguire asked.

The eyes of the overweight man glittered, and he smiled for the first time. "You're right, Mike. That means," he said and clapped his hands, "that I could sell it. He took a deep breath. "Let's do it. Whatever you need so they know I'm Jeffrey."

"Good. That's good," Mattie's grandfather said. "We just want you to answer some simple questions. And my granddaughter will record this meeting to make our identification statement official. I assume you have no objections?"

His gleeful expression flickered, but he shook his head and answered, "Of course not."

Mattie clicked the record button on her phone. "Just for the record, Mr. Sinclair, will you state your name, address, and birth date?"

He swallowed hard. "Certainly. Jeffrey Sinclair ... owner of Clairmont Place, Sinclair Station, North Carolina."

"And your current address?"

"1950 Bougainvillea Drive, Corfu Island, Greece."

"Birth date?" Mattie prompted.

"February twenty-eighth, nineteen forty-one."

"Thank you," Mattie's grandfather said. "And will you tell me the date your father, Henry Sinclair, Jr., was killed?"

"How do you expect me to remember a thing like that? I was just a kid."

"Oh," Mattie's grandfather said. "The newspaper accounts said he died on your eighth birthday."

The overweight man's expression flickered again.

"That's right. Of course. Forgive me. Since Constance died, I've had trouble remembering things. Yes, it was my eighth birthday."

"What would that date have been?" Mattie asked. "For the record."

"Uh, well, I guess it would have been nineteen forty-nine. On my eighth birthday."

"Thank you, Jeffrey," Michael said. "Just a few more questions. What was your mother's name?"

"Co—wait a minute. I spent most of my life with Constance, so I naturally came to think of her as my mother. My mother was, um, Lucy. Yes, that was it … Lucy."

A chill traveled the length of Mattie's spine. Her grandfather continued as if the man had been correct.

"And the name of her horse?"

"Her horse? Why would I know that?"

"Because that's how she died. I assumed you would remember the name of the horse that threw her, causing her death. You and I watched the whole thing. You don't remember?"

"Of course I remember that. But I must have blocked the name of her stupid horse."

"Certainly," Mattie's grandfather said. "Perfectly understandable, given the circumstances."

The large man visibly relaxed.

"One last question," Mattie's grandfather said. "You and I had found something that morning … the morning your mother died. And you were excited to tell her about it. That's why we were sitting on the fence waiting for her to return from her ride. What was it we found?"

This time fear filled his whole face.

"I … I must have blocked out that whole day. I don't, um, a pretty stone? Was that it? I know I was always looking for stones."

Mattie's grandfather leaned forward in his chair, and Mattie watched his eyes harden.

"Yes, Robert," Mattie's grandfather said. "You were. You liked to throw them at the birdhouses on Clairmont Place. You even hit them from time to time."

The man in front of them tried to rise from the couch. His eyes grew large and protruded from his head while his breath shortened. He clutched his chest.

Oh my goodness. He's going to have a heart attack and die right here in front of us.

"You're wrong! I'm Jeffrey. How dare you?" He struggled to rise and then lunged for Mattie's grandfather, hands outstretched, reaching to seize his throat. But Mattie's grandfather, in much better shape physically, rose swiftly, caught both of the shorter man's wrists with his hands, and towered over him.

"I know the truth, Robert. You are not Jeffrey. You are not heir to Clairmont Place. Jeffrey's mother's name was Lily, not Lucy. I guarantee the real Jeffrey wouldn't have forgotten that. And Lily's horse's name was Prince. And Jeffrey and I found a bird's nest that he was excited to tell her about. And he always called me 'Mikey'—never 'Mike.' You're not Jeffrey," Mattie's grandfather repeated. "You can no longer lie your way into getting any more money from his estate."

Mattie rose, too, her phone still recording. Her grandfather held tight to Robert, who writhed under the rock-hard grip.

"So, where is Jeffrey? What did your mother do with him?" her grandfather demanded.

Robert struggled to get away, but Mattie's grandfather held tight.

"Where is he?" Her grandfather's voice rose.

"I don't know. He hasn't been with us since the first few years we were here."

"For seventy years?" Mattie's grandfather almost shouted. "What would she have done with him?"

"I told you. I. Don't. Know. But he isn't here. Hasn't been for decades."

"So your mother, Constance, got rid of Jeffrey and tried to make it look like you were the rightful heir. Is that correct?" Mattie's grandfather still held Robert's wrists. Robert continued to struggle.

"I don't know." Robert whined and appeared to be close to tears. "I was just a kid. I don't know what she did. Let me go. You're hurting me."

Mattie's grandfather released him and pushed him roughly back to the couch. Robert rubbed his wrists and started whimpering.

"Let's go, Mattie," her grandfather said. "We're done here."

Robert continued to cry softly, rocking back and forth on his couch.

He had never seen it coming. That someone from his past, his mother's past—Jeffrey's past—would show up at his door and call him out. He had lived as Jeffrey Sinclair for so long, he believed it.

He truly didn't know where the real Jeffrey was. Nor did he care.

He hadn't thought about Jeffrey for years. Even now, he had no regrets about the millions of dollars from Jeffrey's estate that had supported his lifestyle. And his mother's and grandfather's. He felt they were entitled to share in that.

Slowly, the truth wormed its way into his brain.

It was over. Michael Maguire would see to it that he didn't get another dime from the North Carolina estate. Life as he knew it was finished. No stipend. No money from the sale of the property. He had no means of support. He would have to move. He would have to sell whatever he had left. He would have to find a way to make money.

No, his brain countered. *You will do none of that. You will not give up. Nobody knows the truth except those two Maguires—servants of the Sinclairs, for heaven's sake. They're nobodies. Michael said he was the only one left alive who could identify Jeffrey.*

So once he and his granddaughter are no longer alive ... business as usual.

He reached for his phone and called the number of the pawn broker who had bought his mother's jewelry. "I need to hire somebody," he said, "to do a job. Two people." Sweat dripped from his temples and ran down his body. He wiped his face with an oversized handkerchief, then continued in a rush. "They're only here through tomorrow. But the job needs to be done quickly. It will have to look like an accident. A hit and run ... something like that. If it doesn't happen here, take care of them as soon as they get back to the States. I'm sure you have connections there, too. Right?"

"Most certainly, my friend, in many American cities. Do you know where in that country your subjects live?"

"The south. North Carolina. You have contacts there?"

"Hmm, no. Closest resource is Baltimore."

"Why the hell are you telling me that? What do I care where they come from? The less I know the better."

"I tell you, my friend, because someone having to travel like that will cost you extra. A lot extra. May I assume you have the proper down payment?"

"I will have plenty of money when those two people are taken care of—an estate worth ten to twelve million dollars. I'll have the money as soon as the job is done and I sell Clairmont Place. I'll pay one quarter of the proceeds for the job."

"As I said, my friend, I will need down payment."

His mother's jewelry was gone. His furniture was worthless and there was no art to speak of. But there must be something he could promise—something that would work.

An inspiration hit.

"My villa," he said. "I'll give you the deed to my villa here. It's easily worth half a million dollars. Maybe more."

The voice on the other end paused and clicking sounds filled the silence. *He's checking the property value.*

"That will work," the pawn broker said after a minute. "Bring me deed and I will find you resource."

"I'll be there in fifteen minutes."

CHAPTER THIRTY-SEVEN

M attie and her grandfather hurried out through the enclosed foyer and down the few stairs to the weed-infested lawn.

"Good thing we got out of there when we did, Mattie Mat," her grandfather said. "That man is in a rage and desperate to boot. He might follow us with a baseball bat."

"Or a gun," Mattie said. She shivered.

Mattie took a deep breath when they reached the street. "Ah, fresh air. Everything in there smelled disgusting." She hailed a cab and gave the driver their local address.

"So, Gramps, what do you—?" He held up his hand.

"Let's wait until we get to our room before we talk," he said quietly.

"Oh. Right."

They reached Mattie's room and she pulled up the recording on her phone, then opened her laptop to note the inconsistencies between the facts and the answers the man who called himself Jeffrey had given them.

They went through the recording line by line. Every time Jeffrey gave an incorrect answer, her grandfather told her to stop and make a note.

"And remember," her grandfather said, "he didn't know the real Jeffrey called me 'Mikey.' You weren't recording when that came up."

When Mattie finished her list, it consisted of five outright lies in addition to the birth date that didn't fit with the death of Jeffrey's father.

"Well," Mattie's grandfather said, "unfortunately, this trip didn't clear up the problem of getting a signature on the summit letter."

"Yeah, and we still don't have a clue where the real Jeffrey is. Or if he's still alive." Her eyes filled. "Poor Dad. This will devastate him. We're starting at square one again."

"It's hard for me to believe Robert doesn't know where Jeffrey is," her grandfather said. "Could Jeffrey really have been missing for almost seventy years? Could Constance have gotten rid of him?"

"You mean killed him?" Mattie asked, her eyes wide. "What on earth would make you think that about a poor woman who watched her husband get murdered?"

"You're right, Mattie Mat. I guess that's unfair. And true, I didn't know her very well. But I didn't like what I did know about her. She was just so standoffish with the whole town. Still, I can't believe she would have resorted to something that drastic. I don't think her father would have gone along with it, either." He leaned back in his chair.

"Okay, Gramps, don't get upset with me," Mattie said, "but could the way you felt about Lily when you were a teenager have colored your opinion of Constance? That, you know, nobody else could ever live up to your angelic ideal?"

"I don't know, Mattie Mat. I just don't know."

"Look, there are still a lot of documents at the bank I haven't gotten to yet," Mattie said. "And Bill's making great progress in sorting out the ones left at the mansion. Surely something in one of those places will provide a clue. I'll start there first thing when we get back."

Her grandfather rose. "*I* think we need to start—first thing—with a cocktail. What do you say to that, my little Mattie Mat? Am I right?"

"As rain," she answered.

She shrugged into her sweater on their way to the outdoor lounge that overlooked the Ionian Sea. They ordered drinks and Mattie opened her wallet to get her credit card.

"Oh yeah," she said. "I put these here so I wouldn't forget to ask you about them." She brought out two pieces of paper. "This first one is an invoice from a company that handled the sale of some property jointly owned by Henry, Jr. and somebody named Arnold Sinclair in Rogue Bluffs, Maine. And this one," she said smoothing the wrinkled paper out, "is a transfer draft for ten thousand dollars to a bank that's also in Rogue Bluffs. Dad looked it up while I was there and—" Mattie paused when she saw her grandfather's face. "Oh, my goodness. What is it? Do you know him? Arnold?"

"Yes," her grandfather said. "I even met him, several times. He came for the first Mr. Sinclair's funeral and some years later for Henry and

Constance's wedding. And then of course for the younger Mr. Sinclair's funeral almost two years after that."

"Really? Who is he?"

"I doubt he's still alive, but he was a brother to Henry, Sr. He was much younger, I remember. Like thirty years or so. I think the elder Mr. Sinclair's father married a younger woman when his first wife died—so Arnold was only a few years older than his nephew."

"That makes sense. I think the invoice I found was for a deal between Henry, Jr. and Arnold. Impressive that you remember him."

"Oh yes," her grandfather said. "I remember him very well."

"Because ..."

"Because he was an extremely interesting man. An airline pilot. Flew for Pan Am and operated out of New York City. Just imagine, Mattie Mat, a young country bumpkin like me, being in the presence of someone with a job I considered bigger than life. I'd never even been to Asheville or ridden on a train, and then I found myself in the presence of a man who not only flew airplanes but had also been all over the world. My goodness, I haven't thought about him for years."

"What else do you remember?"

"That Arnold and the younger Henry seemed to really enjoy each other's company. When Arnold came to the first Henry's funeral, he must have stayed for a couple of weeks. He and Henry spent most of their evenings having whiskey highballs in the gardens by the East Portico after the sun went down. That's how I learned so much about him."

"They let you have highballs?"

Mattie's grandfather laughed. "No, of course not. But I convinced my father that yard work needed to be done—weeding or trimming or some such thing—even after sunset. Just so I could be in Arnold's presence."

"These days they'd call that a 'man crush,' Gramps," Mattie said with a small laugh. "Or a 'bro-mance.' Was he married?"

"Not that I remember. But I was ten, so that wouldn't have been important—or even interesting—to me at the time. The thing I remember most was the difference in him from the first Henry's funeral to the second Henry's funeral."

"Different how?"

"Well ... only five years had passed, but when I saw Arnold the last time, he looked as if he had aged twenty years. He had the limp, for one thing. And he no longer flew for Pan Am."

"What happened? And how did you get information with no opportunity to eavesdrop?"

"I was fifteen by then and bolder. Plus, I had seen him a couple of years earlier, when he was best man at Mr. Henry and Constance's wedding. So I worked up my nerve and just went up to him. And he was willing to talk to me. He didn't even mind telling me how he got his bum leg. So bizarre. He was on one of the little shuttles that took people out to their flights and it was hit by a gasoline truck on its way to refuel one of the planes. Apparently, the gasoline truck driver was drunk and came around the corner too fast. It turned the shuttle onto its side and Arnold's leg was pinned underneath. He made it sound like he was lucky he didn't lose it. Anyway, he couldn't fly commercially after that. He got a huge settlement from Pan Am."

"So did he live in Maine by then, or did he move there after his accident?"

"I'm not sure when he moved there, but he did come from Maine for the second Henry's funeral. I remember that because he told me he left the snow in Maine to come to balmy North Carolina. So he was there by the late nineteen forties, for sure."

"So, technically, he would be an heir, too, huh?"

"Well I guess so. If he were still alive. But that would make him more than a hundred twenty by now. Of course, if he married or had children, they would be heirs, too." Mattie's grandfather studied her face. "I see how your little mind is working. You're already planning on contingencies if we can't find Jeffrey, right?"

She grinned at him. "As rain, Gramps. Plus, I didn't tell you everything before. The Sinclair Bank & Trust sends a thousand dollars every month to a household account in Rogue Bluffs, Maine. That tells me that *somebody* associated with the property still lives there. It could be Jeffrey, couldn't it? I mean, that would make sense, right? Obviously, Constance was hoping her son would inherit Henry's estate. That must be why she called him Jeffrey."

"But," her grandfather said, "we just proved it was Robert, not Jeffrey."

"So if she really did want to keep all the money for herself, Constance may have simply sent Jeffrey to live with his uncle rather than have him with her. And then set up a monthly stipend to keep his uncle quiet about it." She stopped talking and her eyes widened. "Oh my goodness, Gramps. That could be it."

"It certainly could," her grandfather said. "It makes sense to me."

"And if we can just find him, we can still get our signature and get Dad off the hook." The worry surrounding Mattie's heart lifted a little. "Gramps, I have to find him. I *have* to."

"I agree, Mattie Mat."

"Okay, so, how about if I change our tickets to fly from here to Maine instead of North Carolina? What do you think? Will you come with me?"

He shook his head and laughed. Then he raised his glass and clinked it with hers.

"Sure," he said. "Why not?"

They signaled the waitress to bring the dessert menu and Mattie visited the ladies' room. On her return, she passed the entrance to the street and saw a very large man wearing a wrinkled white suit, a white hat with a narrow brim, and large sunglasses.

Robert. She watched him lumber along the street with a portfolio clutched to his chest, his steps uneasy, his head swiveling in every direction. She moved into the shadows and watched him until he disappeared around the corner.

"I just saw our imposter," she said when she returned to the table. "He was wearing sunglasses and a hat and looked really nervous. He's probably trying to figure out what new angle he can take to get money from the Sinclair Estate."

"Let him try, Mattie Mat. Let him try."

CHAPTER THIRTY-EIGHT

1950

Rogue Bluffs, Maine

His clothes had been packed. But not one toy accompanied them. Nor anything connected with his few hobbies. And only two pairs of shoes. Not even a coat. He had shivered in the corner of the train car for the entire two-day trip.

At the station, his uncle took off his own coat and wrapped it around his small shoulders.

He learned quickly that his uncle didn't talk much. But then, neither did he. At all, in fact. He hadn't said a single word for almost three years. So a note had been pinned to his shirt to inform the various train conductors of his final destination.

He'd only been in Maine a few days when his uncle took him to the boarding school. Straight to the office. Up two flights of stairs. Difficult with his uncle's bad leg.

The headmistress was stern, but she didn't try to make him talk. Which was fine with him.

She took him to a classroom and dumped him there. All boys. Mostly mean. At the end of the school day, the headmistress found him again and took him to his room—one he shared with three other boys. *All* mean. They ganged up on him that very first night.

He went to breakfast the next morning with two black eyes.

Not one person asked him why.

He kept to himself. But it didn't matter. They found a way to torment him. For days his eyes were swollen shut—partly from crying when he was certain everyone else was asleep, but mostly from their constant beatings. He couldn't read his assignments, so he fell behind in class. Daily, a thick wooden paddle took its toll on the palm of his hand because he wasn't prepared.

And still he didn't talk.

At the end of the first full week, he woke to see two of his three roommates leaning over him, their eyes wide. Within seconds, the third burst through the door, leading the headmistress in her robe and nightcap. She did not look happy.

"What's going on here?" she demanded.

"He was screaming," one of the other boys said. "I never heard anything like it. I don't think he was even saying words—just grunts and shrieks. It scared us."

"Did you beat him this evening?" she asked. She looked at each of them in turn, her face like a thundercloud.

"No, ma'am," one of the other boys answered. "He never cried or hollered. We got tired of it."

He lay there, trying to shake the nightmare. But its hold on him remained, strangling him.

He sobbed. He couldn't stop. Even when the headmistress shook him by his shoulders and commanded him to. She led him out of the room with his pillow and blanket and made him sleep on a hard bench in the hallway.

He never closed his eyes again that night.

The next day, he was forced to attend classes. He felt detached from his body. With no sound penetrating his consciousness except the roaring in his ears—regardless of who spoke to him. And he couldn't connect that with anything going on around him. So, his teacher made him stand in the corner for being impertinent. He stayed there through lunch and the rest of the day. Until he passed out.

Someone took him back to his room. But he was afraid to sleep … afraid of the nightmare that might follow.

Again, he was shaken awake and suffered through a repeat performance of the previous night.

But at dawn the next morning, he snuck into his room and got his coat and slippers. Still clad in his pajamas, he left through the front door and ran. He ran until he fell down when his legs failed him. He didn't know where he was going. Just away. Away from everything.

He finally slept.

And woke to a dog licking his face. A collie. A man knelt beside the dog. A man with a good face. A friendly face. A caring face.

"Hold on, son," the man said when he tried to sit up. "Just take it easy for a few minutes. You got a couple of really nice shiners there."

He stayed still. The man continued to talk but his words edged in and out of the roar in his ears.

The man pulled him to his feet. His coat fell away from his pajamas and revealed the school emblem embroidered on his shirt pocket.

"Come on, little fellow. I'll take you back."

He pulled away and started to run again but the man caught up with him.

"Don't want to go back, huh?" the man said.

He said nothing. He stood still but hung his head.

"Well, we have to start there. I don't know where else to take you. And I'm sure someone must be frantic by now. It's almost noon."

He tried to run again but the man caught him and put him in the car. They pulled up in front of the school and without warning, fat tears trickled down his face. The man saw them.

But he picked him up and carried him up the front steps. When they entered the building, they were taken to the headmistress's office.

"Oh, my goodness, thanks be to God," she said as she took him from the man's arms. "We've been looking everywhere since breakfast. Thank you for bringing him back."

The man hesitated, but he was ushered out the door. As soon as the man was gone, the headmistress hit the boy in the head.

"What were you thinking, running away like that? We don't tolerate that kind of behavior here. You will not be allowed to have dinner for the next three nights. Now go get dressed and get to class."

He was only eleven years old. It was more than he could handle.

As soon as she was gone, he found a way to get outside again and ran, just as he had earlier.

He had only gone a short distance when he heard barking and the same collie, along with his nice man, stopped him.

"I was afraid of this," the nice man said. "They don't treat you very well there, do they?"

He said nothing and stood still, silent tears falling onto his coat collar.

"Can you tell me your name?" Still, he said nothing, his head low. "Okay, look, I'm going to take you back there and find out who your family is. Then I'll take you to them. If you're this set on running away, we have to get you somewhere you'll be safe."

The next two hours were awful. The nice man took him back to see the headmistress, but that time, he didn't leave. The nice man insisted on getting the family name.

He tuned everything out, listening only to the roaring in his ears.

At some point, the nice man put him in the car and the next thing he knew, they walked up the steps to his uncle's house. The butler answered the door and then his uncle limped into the foyer. The nice man explained what had happened. His uncle thanked the man and the man left. Then his uncle stared at him and tried again to get him to talk.

But he didn't. He couldn't. He hung his head and swiped at tears that insisted on flowing.

His uncle called the butler to get him something to eat.

He was ravenous. The butler smiled at him and gave him a grilled cheese sandwich and a steaming bowl of tomato soup. And then later, a cookie. A chocolate chip cookie, warm from the oven. A sweet memory floated around the edges of his brain, just out of reach.

He relaxed slightly. The butler ran warm water in the tub and bathed him, then found him clean pajamas and put him to bed.

He slept. Soundly. For the first time in almost three years.

It wasn't home, he decided, but maybe the next best thing.

CHAPTER THIRTY-NINE

2017

Sinclair Station, North Carolina

David tipped the half-liter bottle to his open mouth and welcomed the sensation of the gin burning all the way down. He liked that. The burning meant it was working, doing its job for his nerves.

"Liquid courage" he called it ever since the first time he tried it. When he had sex with Samantha Spiegel in the empty music room during his free period in high school.

It had worked then, and it hadn't let him down since.

Another long swallow. A half-empty bottle. He'd have to pace himself.

He lay down on top of the coverlet and closed his eyes. His plan was simple. Go back to Clairmont Place after dark, pick the lock, and look for hiding places.

His employers at the Russian embassy had texted with a new timeline—an urgent one. He didn't understand their wording, but his orders were clear.

Complications from rival group ... pressure on us to cease our search. Can't wait for summit ... find object NOW. Timing critical. Hundred-thousand-dollar bonus when you bring us key.

He had no idea who or where the rival group was. And he didn't care. He focused on getting into the house, finding the small key the Russians sought, and receiving an additional hundred thousand dollars. He couldn't be bothered to wait for the paperwork rigmarole everybody talked about before getting inside the house.

The smile on his face faded with sleep and within seconds, he snored.

The morning sun slammed into his room and jolted him awake. Pain shot through his head and settled behind his eyes—a sure sign of a massive hangover. He lifted his hand and squinted at the empty gin bottle still clutched tight.

Nausea hit his stomach. He groaned. Then he cursed, using every swear word he had ever learned, including some in foreign languages.

He barely made it to the bathroom before he threw up.

A lukewarm shower refreshed his spirit and he headed for the diner.

Simone ducked into the entryway of the newspaper office beside the diner and watched David navigate tables. He chose the one in the corner. The minute he sat, the waitress appeared to take his order.

She called Bryan Bennett.

"Bryan? Simone. I was told to call you if I saw my brother again so he could be picked up for questioning. Well, I'm looking at him right now. He's here in the diner at a corner table. Twins baseball cap. Please hurry."

Within minutes she heard sirens, and a local police car screeched to a stop in front of the diner. The sheriff and one of his deputies entered and made a beeline for David's table. When he realized he was their target, David rose and accompanied them without a struggle.

Just before he entered the back seat of the patrol car, Simone stepped from the shadows and faced him, a satisfied smile filling her face.

His face hardened. He glared at her until the car turned the corner and disappeared.

At the jail, David was booked for destruction of property and escorted to a cell. He retreated as far into the corner as possible, planning to keep to himself and speak to no one.

But his cellmate, very drunk and reeking of body odor, staggered into his space.

"Hey, buddy. You're new here, huh?" The man wobbled a few steps and then said, "Wait a minute. I know you. I seen you with that cute little blond woman in the diner a couple days ago. The one with the curls. Yeah. That's where."

The man frowned. "And then I seen her again … yesterday, I think."

He stopped talking and appeared to focus on staying upright. "No … wait a minute … the day before. In the bank."

"Why were you there?" David asked. "Withdrawing your cash so you could drink it up?"

"S'funny," the man answered. He brushed his unkempt hair out of his eyes. "No," he continued. "Had a job. Watering plants. I did the job first"—he punctuated his words with a finger jab to David's chest—"An' *then* I got drunk." He laughed at his own joke.

"So, what was she doing there … the blond woman?"

"I dunno. Looked around like she was nervous. Then a guard come over to her and they went to the vault." He laughed again. Empty spaces appeared where most of his teeth should have been. "When I see somebody head for the vault," he continued, "I always find a job close to it. So I can look inside and maybe see some of that money," he confided conspiratorially.

David turned his head away, but the man kept talking.

"The woman and the guard went right into the vault. Right inside, I tell ya. She was carrying a box. I figured it must'a had lots of money or jewels in it. She held it really close to her, like she was afraid somebody'd take it away."

The man had David's attention.

"Yessir. Money or jewels, that's what I figure it must'a been."

Or my gun.

No wonder he hadn't found it in her apartment. His hands clenched and unclenched, but his new plan formed quickly in his head.

Later that day, Simone called Bryan again.

"Bennett," he said.

"Bryan, it's Simone, again. I wanted to thank you for arresting my brother. I feel much better having him off the streets. And I'm ready to testify, if you'll tell me what to do."

"It's my job to bring people in, Simone. But I'm glad you called. Look, I'm no attorney—and I suggest you speak to one—but the way North Carolina law reads, it will be tough to make a case that's airtight enough to keep him here for very long."

"After all the damage he did?"

"He'll get a considerable fine, that's for sure. But his sworn statement is that he knew you weren't there when he broke in and that he was looking for his own property. And he insisted you had taken it from him."

"Did his statement include the fact that his property was a gun?"

"No, but I checked, and he does have a license. It's not a concealed weapons permit, but it is legal for him to have it. So even if you testify—and I'm not trying to discourage you—the charge against him will probably remain no more serious than a misdemeanor. The punishment for that, more than likely, would be community service."

"Here in Sinclair Station?"

"Right. If your goal is to get rid of him, that's probably not the way to do it."

"Good grief."

"So," he continued, "you can still testify if you want, but unless you can prove that he's lying—that you were home, that he knew you would be home, that you didn't have anything that belonged to him—it could be over pretty quickly and not to your liking. You could always initiate a civil suit, but that also means he'd be hanging around town until the case is settled."

"Bryan, he did so much damage. It will take me days to get it all cleaned up. Insurance will cover the cost of replacing most of the stuff, but, oh my goodness. I'm so mad."

"I understand. And rest assured, the insurance company will probably go after him to pay them back for the things they covered. But you shouldn't have to be bothered with that since you've already given them your statement." He hesitated. "Again, Simone, I'm not an attorney. And I'm not trying to tell you what to do. I'm simply trying to give you the facts of how this could play out, even if you do testify."

She ended the call and paced her small kitchen. The police and insurance company had finished their investigation, so she had returned to her own place to begin the cleanup before moving back in. The amount of work she faced seemed overwhelming. She picked up items from her counters and then put them back down. The results of his senseless, rage-filled destruction fired her anger all over again.

But she had learned from experience to avoid making decisions in the throes of emotion.

She plopped into a kitchen chair and poured herself a glass of wine.

David and his public defender appeared before the judge and bail was set. He convinced his attorney to retrieve the money from his hotel room and by early afternoon he was a free man.

He headed to the discount department store at the edge of town, where he purchased a very realistic-looking toy pellet gun and a large, wide blade knife. He threw in some wrapping paper, a couple of dish towels, and a few candy bars so the cashier wouldn't be suspicious.

He needn't have bothered. The person at the register didn't blink an eye and he sailed through checkout with record speed.

He hid the gun and knife in his pockets, ate a couple of the candy bars and trashed everything else. The first step of his plan was complete.

It was a good plan.

He smiled and turned into the long lane leading to Clairmont Place.

Things were definitely looking up.

CHAPTER FORTY

D avid stopped a young man with a hedge trimmer in his hands. "Can you tell me where I can find Mr. Maguire? Is he on the premises?"

"No, sir. He's out of the country." The young man poked out his chest. "He left me in charge. How can I help you?"

"Thank you, but this is a family matter. Personal. Do you know if Mrs. Maguire is around?"

"The last time I saw her, she was in her garden," the young man told him.

"Thanks." David gave him a mock salute and continued to the small patch of land where he had seen Mattie Maguire's grandmother earlier. At the edge of her garden, she leaned on her hoe and removed her gardening gloves.

"Hello."

She jumped.

"Sorry, ma'am," David said. "I didn't mean to startle you."

"Oh, hello," she said. "You're the young man who was here yesterday. Nice to see you again. I thought you'd be gone by now."

"I had a change of plans," he said. "I'm really sorry to bother you, but I wonder if I could trouble you for a glass of water. I've done a lot of walking today and I'm really thirsty."

"Of course," she answered. "I was just headed into the house anyway. Come on." She gathered up her tools and the few vegetables she had picked and led the way.

"Please, let me help you with that," he said. He took the hoe and rake from her full hands and propped them up by the porch. They climbed the few stairs to the back door, and David followed Mattie's grandmother into her kitchen.

With her back to him, she reached up to get a glass, and David pulled the pellet gun from his pocket. Mattie's grandmother turned toward the refrigerator.

"Never mind, Mrs. Maguire," he told her. "I didn't really come here for water. I came for you."

Her eyes widened when she saw the gun, but she didn't scream. Or move. "Whatever could you want with me?"

"You're a means to an end, ma'am. I need something your son has at his bank."

"You mean money?"

"Well, no, at least … yeah, now that you mention it, that's a great idea. But he also has something of mine that my sister gave him. And I need it back."

"Do we know you? Or your sister?"

"That's not important now. I need you to call your son."

She didn't move, and her eyes never left his face.

"Look, Mrs. Maguire, I don't want to hurt you. I really don't. But you need to do what I'm telling you."

Slowly, she put the glass on the counter. "Fine," she said. "My phone is in the den."

"I'll go with you." He followed her into the den and stood at the door. A small trickle of sweat slid from behind his ear to his collar. "And you need to show me the number you call," David told her. "I really hope you won't try anything stupid, like calling the police."

She selected the number and turned the phone around so he could see the name she punched. *Matt—office.* He nodded and she put the phone up to her ear.

"Hello, Maryanne. This is Marilyn Maguire. Is my son in? This is pretty important."

David watched her intently. She stood still and waited.

"Hi, honey," she said after a minute. "I have a situation here—"

David motioned for her to give the phone to him. He put it to his ear and heard Matt Maguire talking. "Has something happened to Dad or Mattie?"

"I don't know," David said to him. "But that's not what this call is about."

"Who is this?" Matt's voice was sharp. "What are you doing there with my mother?"

"I just needed her help to get to you."

"Tell me who the hell you are and what you want."

"Who I am isn't important. But what I want is. You have something of mine in your vault, and I want it back."

Matt Maguire hesitated on the other end.

"Is this Simone's brother?"

"Very perceptive. Yes—and I will trade your mother for my gun."

Another moment of silence greeted him. "Of course," Matt said quietly. "Come and see me at the bank and I will be happy to give you your gun back. Just leave my mother alone."

"I'm not stupid, Mr. Maguire. There's no way I will show up there so you can have me arrested the minute I step through the door. No. You bring my gun, and fifty thousand dollars in cash, to your mother's house. We'll make the trade here."

"You'll have to give me a few minutes."

"Sure, Mr. Maguire. No problem. You should be able to do all that in fifteen minutes, I would think. We'll wait here."

"That won't work. It's David, isn't it? Look, I'll need more time. It will take me ten minutes to get into the vault—we have procedures we have to follow, or alarms go off and the police come automatically. And then it will take me another ten minutes to get to my mother's house."

"Fine. Twenty minutes. But Mr. Maguire, I need to tell you … I don't want to hurt your mother—she seems like a very nice lady. But if you double cross me or even think about bringing the police into this, I can't promise that your mother will stay alive. You really don't want to mess with me right now."

"Fine, son, fine. Stay calm. I'll get everything together and be there within twenty minutes. But David, I need to tell you, if anything happens to my mother, all bets are off. I will hunt you down and kill you myself. You can count on that."

During the conversation, the position of David's gun never wavered—lightly touching the back of Marilyn Maguire's head.

He disconnected the call and threw the phone on the desk. "I need something to tie you up with," he told Marilyn. "Nylon rope or bungee cords. Something like that."

"You really don't need to do that, young man. I won't try to go anywhere. Is my son coming here?"

"Look, ma'am, I'm really sorry you got dragged into this. It's my sister's fault. If she had just stayed out of my business, I'd have what I need and wouldn't be bothering you. But when your son gets here, he has to know I'm not fooling around. Now please, get me some rope."

"It's in the laundry room."

"Lead the way. I'll follow."

Marilyn rummaged through several drawers. "Will this do?" She held a long section of clothesline, still wound on its spindle. "I can't find anything else."

David glanced in the open drawer. "Sure," he said. "And bring the duct tape."

Marilyn gathered the items and closed the drawer.

He motioned with his gun. "Back to the kitchen. Put the rope and tape on the table."

David pulled out a chair and moved it to the middle of the room, facing the door. "Here. Sit."

She hesitated for an instant and he shoved her roughly. "You don't want to cross me, Mrs. Maguire. I'm not in the mood. Now sit down."

He pulled her hands behind her and wrapped her wrists with the clothesline rope, weaving the ends in and out for maximum strength. Then he wrapped duct tape around her wrists and after a few seconds, from her midriff around the back of the chair. She winced.

"That's very tight, young man. I promise you, I won't try to escape. Please loosen that. I'm having trouble breathing."

He remained silent and bent to tie her feet in a similar fashion.

"I think I heard my son call you David. Is that right?"

"Please stop talking, ma'am."

"Look, David. It sounds like your sister has made you angry, but you don't need to be angry with all of us. We haven't done anything to hurt you."

He continued to work on her feet, first with the rope and then the duct tape, wrapping both around and around so her legs were bonded to the chair.

"You're really hurting me, David. I don't know why you're doing this. My son will certainly get the idea. You don't have to do any more. You can just—"

"Shut up! Just stop talking." He hopped to his feet, tore off a long piece of duct tape and wrapped it around her head, covering her mouth. Carefully, he moved the tape so it didn't block her nose. His eyes bore into hers. "I told you to stop talking. You should have listened."

Tears welled in Marilyn's eyes, but she remained still. Silence filled the room.

David strode to the window and then back to the table.

To the window and then the table. Window. Table.

He was ready to blow.

Matt Maguire buzzed for his secretary. "Maryanne, please have Sidney come and see me right away."

"I'm sorry, Mr. Maguire, but Sidney is off today. He took his wife for a CAT scan."

"Damn. Okay, who's on duty?"

"Russell, sir. Russell White."

"How long has he worked for us?"

"Thirteen years, Mr. Maguire." She hesitated. "Is something wrong? Is there any way I can help?"

"No. Thank you, Maryanne. Have Russell meet me at the door to the vault. Immediately."

"Yes, sir. Is there anything else?"

"No."

Matt picked up his cell and punched in his wife's number. She didn't pick up. He entered her number again and texted her. *Situation with Mom. If you haven't heard from me in forty minutes, call my cell first. If I don't answer, send the police to The Cottage. TELL NO ONE ELSE.*

He threw on his suit coat. Then he emptied the contents of his briefcase onto his chair and shoved it under his desk. He picked up his keys and sunglasses and walked out his door. Maryanne's eyes followed him, but she remained silent.

Russell waited at the vault.

"How can I help you, sir?"

"It takes two keys to open the vault. Do you have yours?"

"Yes, sir."

"Okay, I'll go first."

Matt inserted his key and waited while Russell did the same. A series of clicks followed, deep within the heavy metal doors. In seconds, they popped open.

"Come with me." The two men entered the vault. Matt turned to the bank guard as soon as they cleared the door. "Russell, I'm certain when you trained as a guard, the occasional need for confidentiality was impressed upon you. Am I correct?"

"Yes, sir. That was emphasized."

"That's good. This is one of those times. Until I personally tell you differently, you are never to tell anyone what has happened within this vault today. Not even your wife. Do you understand?"

"Yes, sir."

"Fine. Come with me." They entered the section of the vault that housed the special bins. Matt hadn't accompanied Simone and Sidney when they took the gun into the vault, so he didn't know which bin held it. He opened three of the steel mesh containers, dug through them and found what he sought in the fourth—the gun rug Sidney had used.

He didn't bother to open it.

"One more thing," Matt said. "Do you know where we keep the marked bills?"

Russell nodded and pulled out a drawer. Matt reached in and found bills in several denominations, banded in fifty bill stacks. He selected several—five stacks of twenties, six stacks of fifties, and six stacks of hundred-dollar bills. He filled in the log for the amounts he took and asked Russell to confirm the total.

"Yes, sir," Russell said. "Fifty thousand dollars."

Matt stuffed the gun rug and money into his briefcase.

"Russell, I can't tell you how important it is that you continue on your day as if this never happened. We'll discuss our next steps tomorrow. But right now, I have to leave, and you have to maintain your sworn silence. Are we clear?"

"Yes, sir."

Matt walked to his car and called his mother's phone.

No answer. He sent a text. *On my way ... have everything. Be patient. And don't hurt my mother.*

Gravel crunched as tires braked in the driveway.

David watched Matt Maguire emerge and then retrieve a briefcase from his black Lincoln Navigator.

He moved into position behind Matt's mother, his gun snug up against her skull.

His chest tightened in anticipation.

The kitchen door opened, and Matt Maguire filled its frame. He just stood there and looked at David.

"Good heavens, man," he said. "My mother is in her eighties. Why did you think you needed to restrain her like that?"

"No small talk," David said. "Just hand it over."

"I'm not giving you a damned thing until you get that tape off her mouth, at least. Mother, did he hurt you?"

Marilyn shook her head.

David's eyes narrowed, but he moved to Marilyn and unwound the tape from her head. She jumped and whimpered with each tug as the tape caught on her hair and pulled. Once her hair was clear, David lost patience and snatched the rest of the tape from her mouth. Marilyn cried out.

"You son of a—"

"Look, mister," David interrupted. "I did what you said. Now hand it over. Just lay it on the table. Nice and easy."

Matt put the briefcase on the edge of the kitchen table.

"Now back off." David moved the weapon in his hand from Marilyn's head and waved it at Matt. "You stay there. Don't come any closer."

Matt didn't move, but David eased toward the briefcase, still waving the gun he held.

"Just stay calm, David. You have what you want, so just leave us alone."

David opened the briefcase and flipped through the stack of bills.

"It is very interesting, though," Matt said, "that you went to all this trouble to get your gun back when you already had another one. Why, I wonder, would you do that? Why would you risk creating all this drama if you didn't really need another gun?"

David stopped flipping bills and looked up as Matt rushed him, knocking the gun out of his hand. Matt kicked it across the room and drew back his arm to land a punch in the younger man's stomach. But before he connected a second time, David whipped out a knife with a wide blade and held it to Marilyn's throat. Her eyes widened in terror.

"Not smart, Mr. Maguire," David said. "Not smart at all."

"Okay, son. Okay," Matt said, holding his hands up, palms toward David. "I'm sorry. You win. Let's put that behind us and finish this trade. Just take the briefcase and go."

David pulled out a chair opposite Matt's mother. "Sit," he commanded.

Matt slid into the chair, his hands still in the air.

His cell phone rang in his pocket.

"Don't answer that," David warned. His knife point indented the tender skin on Marilyn's neck. "Unless you want to watch your mother bleed to death."

Marilyn let out a small sob.

Matt's hands stayed in the air. "No problem. Look, my hands are right here. Please, David, just take your things and go. We won't try to follow you."

"Cell phone on the table," David commanded. "And don't get funny taking it out of your pocket." Carefully, with one hand still in the air, Matt reached into his pocket for his phone and put it on the table. David knocked it out of his reach.

He picked up the duct tape and tossed it to Matt. "Tape your feet to the chair. And again, Mr. Maguire, don't try anything funny because I'm going to inspect your job before I leave. Make it tight."

Matt bent and did as he was told.

"Fine," David said. "Now shove the duct tape back over here and then cross your arms over your chest. And no other moves."

Again, Matt followed directions exactly.

"You have tried my patience, Mr. Maguire," David said. "And I suggest you don't do it again." He felt the sweat pour down his face and pool below his collar.

David left Marilyn and moved quickly to Matt, wrapping the duct tape around his middle and then all the way around the rest of the chair. He made four rotations. Then he taped Matt's mouth and put a new piece of tape across Marilyn's mouth. Blood from the small puncture David had made on her neck reached the white collar of her blouse.

David went back to the briefcase and pulled out the stacks of money. He fondled the bundles, one by one.

Then David dragged out the gun rug and opened it. He smiled. "Good,

Mr. Maguire. You did just fine." He pulled the gun from its cover along with the cartridge magazine—fully loaded with eight bullets.

He snapped it dramatically into place and chambered a round.

His eyes bore into Matt's with each movement.

Slowly, he pointed his fully loaded gun at Matt Maguire's head.

Marilyn's eyes filled with fear and she rocked back and forth in her chair, guttural noises rumbling from her throat.

David cocked the gun.

A muffled scream sounded from Marilyn's direction.

"Are these bills marked?" David asked.

Matt shook his head violently.

"You'd better not be lying to me, Mr. Maguire. Because I know where your mother lives. And guess what else? I know where your daughter lives. Oh yes," he said at Matt's startled expression. "You didn't expect that, did you? If you're lying, you and your whole family will be sorry."

David gathered his things to leave. But the memory of his sister's smug smile as he rode away in the back of the police car popped into his head. Along with sudden fury.

Blind, unreasonable fury.

She took his gun and hid it from him. And then the bitch had him arrested just because he went to look for it.

He waved the cocked gun wildly around the room. "I've been betrayed enough," he screamed. "I'm sick of it. If it happens again—"

A shot rang out. Chunks of crystal flew from the dining room chandelier, and another muffled scream sounded from behind Marilyn's taped mouth.

David stopped talking and stared at the gun as if seeing it for the first time.

Matt grunted and David looked up to see the bound man nod his head toward the money and then the door.

Without another word, David stuffed the money in his jacket and then released the ammunition from the gun's stock, pocketing the magazine in his pants. He took one last look around and headed toward the door. But he stopped mid-stride and hit Matt in the forehead with the butt of the gun he still held. Then he shoved it in the waistband of his pants and ran out the door.

Marilyn Maguire sobbed behind her tape.

Matt's head hung, his chin on his chest. Blood oozed down his face and pooled on the front of his starched shirt.

His mother bounced her chair to get closer to him. She tried to stand but the binding held her legs tight. She rocked her chair in an effort to propel her upright.

She got close and tried again.

But the front legs of the chair slipped out from under her and she cracked her jaw and then her head against the edge of the table on her way to the floor. Blood flowed from gashes on her chin and temple.

She lay unconscious beside her son.

Adelaide Maguire burst into the kitchen of The Cottage with two uniformed policemen right behind her. She felt her husband's pulse first and then bent to her mother-in-law.

"They're alive, but Marilyn's pulse is very faint. Call an ambulance. Hurry."

CHAPTER FORTY-ONE

Corfu, Greece

Mattie slammed against her grandfather's side as their cab driver squealed around the third intersection in a row on their way to the airport.

"What is going on?" she asked the driver. "Do you always take corners this way?"

"We are followed," he said. His eyes darted to the rearview mirror, and he jerked the car into the adjacent lane. "Ever since your hotel."

"Oh." Mattie turned around in her seat. The street was clogged with bumper-to-bumper traffic. "How can you tell?"

"Dark blue sedan. Watch."

The driver careened around another corner and shot down a narrow alleyway. Without slowing, he blasted out of the alley onto a new street.

"Oh my goodness," Mattie moaned. She covered her eyes. Her grandfather sat beside her, his knuckles white from his vice-like grip on the armrest.

"See, miss? Look behind. Dark blue car."

Mattie twisted toward the rear window again. He was right. The same sedan from the previous street hugged their bumper.

"Is there any chance they're following you?" Mattie's grandfather asked.

The driver shrugged. "I'm driving since middle of night. No blue sedan until you get in."

The car behind them struck their bumper. Hard. Mattie's neck jolted forward.

"Ow. Gramps, are you okay?"

His hand found hers. "Fine. Hang in there, Mattie Mat. Driver, how much longer to the airport?"

"Ten blocks. Is okay. I fix."

The driver pulled hard to the left and skimmed by the tables of an outdoor café, sending menus flying. The blue car followed.

The driver tugged the wheel left again, through a bazaar and a red light, barely escaping a direct hit from a garbage truck. He zigzagged through one back street after another for the next few blocks, while Mattie and her grandfather flew into each other with every turn.

"Finally," Mattie breathed as the cab sped onto a wide street and zoomed the length of it. The airport control tower appeared in full view at its end. She threw a handful of euros at the driver, tossed her bag over her shoulder, and hopped out of the car. In an instant, she tugged her grandfather's door open and helped him out, his bag tight to his chest. The driver skidded off and Mattie guided her grandfather into the middle of a large group of people headed for the airport's interior.

"Do you think …" Mattie's question hung unanswered as a huge explosion, followed by a giant orange fireball, commanded their attention in the street they just left.

"Oh." Mattie's voice was soft. "That was our cab. And it could have been—"

"Us," her grandfather finished for her.

"Oh, my goodness. My goodness," Mattie said. She stifled a sob. "Oh, that poor guy. After he did such a great job to get us here."

She and her grandfather stood, staring down the street at the resulting chaos from the explosion.

"That poor man," Mattie said again, her voice low. "I just can't believe it."

Her grandfather put an arm around her and hugged her close. Silence engulfed them for several minutes before they turned toward the check-in counter.

"Gramps," Mattie said as they waited, "do you think that was a coincidence? I mean, could Robert …" She took a breath. "Does he really have it in him to do such a thing?"

"I don't know," her grandfather said. "But we need to be cautious from now on, regardless. He must be a lot more desperate than we figured."

"Are you really okay, Gramps? I would never forgive myself if something had happened to you back there." She hugged into him as they walked.

"I'm fine, Mattie Mat. But I must confess, my legs are a little rubbery. I haven't been thrown around like that since my last jeep ride in the Korean War."

She had used her laptop to change their return destination from Raleigh to Bar Harbor, Maine, the previous evening, so she scanned the board for departing flight gates and ushered her grandfather toward the one they needed. She settled him into a chair and went to check them in.

But before she reached the gate, "Sweet Dreams" sounded on her phone.

"Hi, Mom," she said. "Boy, you can't imagine what we've just been through. We—"

"Mattie," her mother interrupted. "Are you on your way home?"

Mattie stopped walking. Her mother's tone alarmed her.

"Yes ... well, no, but ... what's happened?"

"Your father and grandmother are in the hospital. They were both held at gunpoint."

Mattie gasped in a deep breath, and her vision blurred. "How badly are they hurt?" she managed to croak out.

Her mother hesitated.

"Mom! Oh my goodness, talk to me. You have to tell me. How bad—" She stopped talking as tears took control of her voice. Her grandfather appeared at her side, his ear up to her phone. "How bad ..." she tried again.

"Your dad was just banged up. He has a constant headache, but he'll probably be released later today. Your grandmother—"

"Just a minute, Mom," Mattie interrupted. "I'm putting you on speaker. Gramps is here."

"Adelaide," Mattie's grandfather said into the phone's speaker, "it's Michael. What's happened?"

"Oh, Mike, Marilyn is in a coma. I can give you details now or when you get here."

"Start talking," he said. "Good heavens ... we've only been away overnight. What the hell happened?"

"Simone's brother held Marilyn at knifepoint and forced her to call Matt to bring him the gun Simone had hidden in the bank vault. Fortunately, he sent me a text before he went so I knew what was going on and was able to get there quickly with the police. But Marilyn—" They heard a dry sob from the other end of the phone and then Adelaide cleared her throat. "He bound them into chairs before he left and then hit Matt on the head. With his gun, we think. Matt figures his mother tried to rock her chair closer to him after the guy left, and she hit her head on the table somehow. Her blood pressure was really low by the time they got her to the hospital."

Mattie saw her grandfather's hand shake and a tear trickle down his cheek.

"How is she now?" he asked.

"She's stable. But still in a coma. She needs you, Mike. We all need you. Are you leaving soon?"

"I'll change our tickets back, Gramps," Mattie said. "Mom, I'll let you know what time we'll land. Can someone pick us up?"

"Of course," Marilyn said. "I'll talk to you later."

"If anything changes, Addy," Michael added, "please let us know."

Mattie clicked her phone off and made a beeline for the counter to change their tickets back to Asheville. She explained the family emergency, and the agent agreed that she and her grandfather could fly standby on their original flight back. The agent even called an airport shuttle to take them to their new gate.

Mattie reported their arrival time to her mother, who promised to have someone at the airport to pick them up and take them directly to the hospital.

"Oh, Gramps," Mattie said. They held onto each other for a long time. "I'm so sorry. I feel like it's all my fault. I should never have taken you away. I can't believe it. I just can't believe it."

"You had no way of knowing that young man was so disturbed," he told her. He patted her back with one hand and held her tight with the other. "It will all be fine, Mattie Mat. I'm sure it will." He buried his face in her hair, and she felt his body shake. "It has to be," he said squeezing her harder. "It just has to be."

CHAPTER FORTY-TWO

Sinclair Station, North Carolina

Mattie and Michael Maguire stepped off the small plane at the Asheville Regional Airport to see Simone's tear-stained face shining at them from the group of people waiting to pick up passengers. She waved and instantly burst into fresh tears.

Michael reached her first and she threw herself into his arms, sobbing harder.

"I'm so sorry," she said. "I'm so, so sorry. I can't believe that even David would have sunk so low. I never knew him to hurt people before. Well, except the times he beat me up when we were teenagers."

Michael released Simone, and Mattie hugged her and patted her back. Simone continued to shake.

"Come on, kiddo," Mattie said to her. "Get yourself together so you can take us to the hospital. What car are you in?"

"Your mother's. I convinced her to let me be the one to pick you up since this is all my fault. But she insisted I bring her car." A new set of tears streaked down Simone's face.

They walked to the car, but Mattie convinced Simone to let her drive.

"So," Michael asked from the backseat. "How are they doing? When I talked to Addy the last time, she told me Marilyn's blood pressure had improved somewhat. Has there been any change since then?"

Simone blew her nose. "Yes, she's improving, and her doctors believe that having you there will be just what she needs to come out of it."

"What I want to know," Mattie said, "is where your brother is right now. I thought he was in jail. How'd he get out?"

"Bryan told me there wasn't a strong enough case to hold him. David convinced them he knew I wasn't there and that he was searching for his own property. Which he said I stole from him. And apparently, he does have a permit for his gun. So he made bail. They let him go and haven't found him again. None of the marked bills have shown up, so they can't track him that way, either." She wiped her eyes again. "I've been so afraid he'd come to my place to make more trouble. Now I wish he had instead of … oh, I can't believe I let this happen." She lowered her head and sobbed quietly.

"I'm surprised he didn't come for you, too," Mattie said. "What are you doing to protect yourself?"

"I convinced Morgan to let me work remotely this week," Simone answered. "I've mostly been working from the hospital, and their security has escorted me each time I come or go. There's been extra security on the floor where your dad and grandmother are."

Mattie pulled up to the hospital doors. "Gramps, I know how anxious you are. You go on in. I'll be there shortly."

Mattie parked and walked toward the building with Simone beside her. They had almost reached the sidewalk when a black car rushed at them, screeching around the corner. Mattie jumped back and pulled Simone with her.

"Please tell me I'm being paranoid," Mattie said, "and that car wasn't really trying to hit us. Did you see who was driving?"

"No. The windows were tinted," she said. "And I don't see how it could have been David. As far as I know, he doesn't have a car, or a valid driver's license to rent one."

"I wasn't worried about him. Someone followed us in Greece on our way to the airport. It was like a scene from a mob movie. The cab blew up the minute we got out." Her voice broke. "With the cab driver still inside," she said. Her voice shook and it was a minute before she could talk again. "I guess that's why I'm so skittish." She looked behind her, but the car had disappeared. "That driver probably just took the corner too fast."

Michael Maguire walked into his wife's hospital room and his daughter-in-law rushed over to hug him. His son sat in a chair at the end of the bed.

"Oh, Mike, I'm so glad you're here," Adelaide said.

"Me, too, Dad." Matt stood to greet his father but sat down fast and put his hand to his bandaged head. "Whew. Got up too fast."

Michael went over to Matt and hugged him around the shoulders. "Maybe you should stay put then." Michael looked at Adelaide. "Has there been any change?"

"Not since we talked the last time."

Adelaide pulled her chair closer to the bed and held it for her father-in-law. He sat and picked up one of his wife's hands, rubbing the back of it with his thumb. He raised it and kissed it, then held it against his cheek. His wife showed no reaction.

Mattie entered the room after dropping Simone at the cafeteria. She couldn't conceal the shock in her eyes when she saw the bandage on her father's head and her grandmother's bruised face. She rushed over to Matt.

"No," she told him. "Please don't get up. I love hugging you like this." She stood there for a moment with her eyes closed. "How are you feeling, Dad?"

"I'm much better today, especially now that Mom's more stable."

"Is she?" Mattie left her father and stood beside her grandmother's bed. "Any reaction yet, Gramps?"

He shook his head.

"Mattie," her father said, "in all the hubbub, I've forgotten to ask what you found out in Greece. Which one of the boys is it?"

"It's Robert. And you were right, Dad. He *is* mean." Mattie shook her head. "Actually, way worse than that. Horrible. Wicked. Nuts. He tried to choke Gramps!"

"To choke—"

"And," Michael picked up the story, "we believe he was responsible for hiring the man who followed us to the airport and tried to run our cab off the road and then blew it up. Poor cab driver didn't make it," he added in a quiet voice.

"Run your … good heavens. Why would Robert want to hurt you?" Matt asked. "Especially after all these years?"

"Oh. We forgot to tell you the other part," Mattie said. "Constance is dead, which means his source of income has stopped. So he needed to keep posing as Jeffrey to try and bleed every cent from Clairmont Place he could. But now that Gramps has identified who he really is, my guess is he's desperate. And probably thinks that if the two people who can identify him are out of the picture, he can continue to leech money from the estate."

"Do you think he was actually trying to kill you?" Mattie's mother asked. "Or simply trying to scare you into forgetting what you found out?"

"It doesn't matter now," Michael said. "We're away from there. I'd be surprised if his reach could extend to Sinclair Station after having been away for so long."

"I hope you're right, Dad." Matt shook his head and grinned. "Wow," he said. "Here's something funny. I thought you two were having the time of your lives over there while we were here being assaulted. Who knew you were in the middle of the same kind of mess?"

"At least our mess didn't land us in a hospital." Mattie rubbed her father's shoulders.

Simone walked in, her eyes large. "I spoke with one of the security guards," she said. "A man fitting David's description was seen hanging around the staff entrance. But he ran when the guard asked him for his ID. My goodness," she said, her eyes filling. "How does he have the nerve to show himself? He must have snapped."

CHAPTER FORTY-THREE

"So, now he's armed again. And I'm considering him dangerous," TheO told The Vysokom. "Did you make any progress with Hektor to have this guy back off?"

"No, not yet. If I knew what they wanted, I'd be inclined to let him go ahead and have the run of the place to find it and get the hell out of our way, but that ass, Hektor, holds everything tight to his chest. He's not talking."

"Can't we just eliminate this bumbler? What do we care?"

"No, we can't. Hektor has convinced Moscow that his project is necessary and will yield very satisfying results. I found out that much even though no one would tell me what those results were supposed to be. No," The Vysokom said again. "We have to sit tight for now. You'll know if he shows up at the house to try and break in, right?"

"Right. My contacts there will tell me."

"Let's go with that for now. If we actually get our hands on him, we can make him talk. And then we can decide if we help him, or if we buy him off and take the project ourselves."

"Sure," TheO said. "Whatever you say."

TheO disconnected from The Vysokom and simply sat for a minute.

Fine. He couldn't eliminate the nuisance, but he had an idea to help keep a sharper eye on him. He decided to act on it right away.

No need to ask for permission first.

CHAPTER FORTY-FOUR

Her name was Sally, David remembered. He didn't know her last name but that didn't matter.

He had few places left to hide. Visiting his sister was certainly out of the question. He also felt certain the police had searched his room at the inn. So he came up with a plan.

A brilliant one. He was sure of it.

He hid in the shade of the trees across the street from the diner and watched the place clear out. Not long after that, the man he recognized as the cook left through the front door and the waitress—the one who flirted with him each time he'd seen her—locked the door behind him.

No one was visible on either end of the street, so he crossed the road and sauntered up to the door as if expecting it to be open. When it wasn't, he rattled it.

He had just turned, pretending to go, when the door opened behind him.

"Well, hello, handsome," she greeted him.

"Oh, no," he said as he pointedly looked at the diner hours posted beside the door. "I'm so sorry. I didn't realize you were closing. I thought I could get a quick ... but," he stopped and turned sad eyes toward her. "I'm sorry, Sally," he said. "Never mind." He turned to go. "I'll let you close up. Sorry to bother you."

"Wait, wait, wait." She linked her arm through his and drew him into the diner. "The cook just left, but I can whip something up for you. I'll be happy to do that. Besides, that will give us a chance to get better acquainted." He dragged his feet, but she led him to a table and pulled out a chair for him. "You come on and sit down right here and don't worry about a thing." He slumped into the chair and her hand lingered on his shoulder. "So, we'll start with drinks. Hot or cold?"

He looked up at her, gratitude plainly showing. "I can't believe you would do this for me, Sally. It's been a really crappy day and honestly, I could use a friendly face." He reached up, put his hand on top of hers and gave it a little squeeze.

"It's my pleasure. David, right?"

"Right." He smiled at her, but purposely kept his eyes sad.

"I can't make you a cocktail. The cook and I lock up the liquor together before he leaves. But I can get you a beer. How's that sound?"

"It sounds perfect."

"And I was actually going to make myself a bacon, lettuce, and tomato sandwich on toast. You interested in having one of those with me? I can rustle us up some chips, too."

He forced his eyes to tear, careful not to let them spill over. "It sounds like heaven." He leaned back and closed his eyes. "You have no idea what you've done for me this evening. Maybe I can think of a way to repay you … sometime."

"I'm happy to do it." She pulled the shades down on every window, brought him his beer, and opened one for herself. "Now you work on this and I'll be right back with the sandwiches. Wheat or white?"

"Wheat. Look … can I help?"

"No way. It won't take but a minute." She walked toward the kitchen but turned before going through the door. "And then we'll work on making your crappy day a whole lot better."

It had almost been too easy.

He spent the night at her place on the edge of town. She left him there the next day when she went to work at noon. He stretched luxuriously in her bed and smiled at the ceiling through the perfect smoke ring that had just left his lips.

His strategy had worked beautifully. No one would ever think of looking for him at Sally's place. He could stay as long as he wanted. He was certain of it.

He decided to lay low for a couple of days and enjoy the benefits of his ingenious plan, build up Sally's trust and gain information from her.

Then he would go into the mansion and complete his mission—find the little key the Russians sought.

And after that, his heart swelled at the thought. He'd collect his million dollars, plus his bonus, and leave the country. Never to return.

He rolled over, stubbed out his cigarette and took a nap.

CHAPTER FORTY-FIVE

Mattie snatched a few hours' sleep, then returned to the hospital for a visit with her family. She reached her grandmother's room and almost collided with Bryan Bennett leaving it. His smile was warm.

"Welcome home," he said, pulling her into a quick hug. "Your grandfather told me about your adventure. I'm thinking I'll need to hire several more people just to keep the Maguire family safe."

She forced a smile. "Or you could find one lunatic and put him in jail," she said. Tears threatened and Bryan rubbed her arm. She shot him a grateful smile. "Any leads on David's whereabouts?" she asked.

"Not since security reported him lurking around here last night. I was able to check on the people who hired him, though," he added. "You're not going to like this, but from what I can tell, the company has Russian roots."

"Oh good heavens," Mattie said. "They warned me about that ... the selection committee. Remember?" He nodded. "But like an idiot, I didn't believe them. Are you sure? Can there be a mistake?"

"I don't think so. It was pretty clear."

"But we haven't even started anything yet. We still need the Sinclair signature on the summit letter. What would the Russians want at this point?"

"I don't know that answer," Bryan said. "But you have to trust me, Mattie. We're doing everything we can to find David and put him away for good."

"Have you told my father any of this?" she asked.

"No, not yet."

"Could you wait, then? He's so stressed about the lack of a signature, I don't want to give him anything else to worry about. I'm planning to go to an attorney's office in Asheville this afternoon and see if I can find any additional Sinclair heirs. And then tomorrow I fly to Maine to check out a lead there. We have to find a person who is qualified to sign that letter."

"I understand," Bryan said. "You're right. He doesn't need anything else on his plate right now."

"Thanks, Bryan."

Mattie stuck her head into her grandmother's room. Her parents looked up, but her grandfather's head rested on the bed where her grandmother lay, absolutely still.

"Any change?" she asked.

"No, little one," her father answered. "But at least she's no worse." He rose and joined her in the hallway. "I guess you saw Bryan," Matt said. She nodded. "And he told you there hasn't been any sign of David?" She nodded again. "So, maybe he left town now that he has his gun. You think?"

"I might think that, if he hadn't said he'd been hired to do a job for the summit. Of course, his plans might have changed since he beat you and Nana up. How's Gramps doing?"

"He hasn't left her side. Your mother brings his meals. She even brought him a fresh set of clothes. He showers right here in her room so he doesn't have to leave her."

"And you? How are you?" she asked. His forehead still sported a large white bandage, centered in a field of black and blue bruises.

"I'm okay."

"I wanted to tell you … I'm going to visit an attorney in Asheville today to see if I can find a copy of Henry Sinclair's new will. Remember the invoice I showed you from the file box? Anyway, maybe it will give us a clue as to another heir we can contact."

"Maybe Bryan should go with you, little one. We have no idea where David might be. Who knows what he'll think of next?"

"It's only a half hour drive, Dad," Mattie answered. "I'd hate to pull Bryan away from whatever he's doing to find David," she added. "Just to babysit me." She reached up and kissed her father's cheek. "I'll be careful. I promise. I'll call you as soon as I leave the attorney's office."

She left the hospital with a security guard who stayed with her until she reached her car.

"Thanks," she said with a wave.

She pulled out of the hospital's parking lot as a cloud hid the sun. She shivered and her father's words, warning her about David, flew back into her head. She felt her stomach clench and a tiny trickle of fear worked its way in and settled. With a clunk.

Her dad was right. She had to be more aware.

Who knew what lay around the next bend?

CHAPTER FORTY-SIX

Asheville, North Carolina

"Miss Maguire, how nice to see you again. Mr. Higgins told me your event last week was wonderful. He always brags about your flaming Baked Alaskas."

"Thanks, Sarah. That display really is spectacular. You should convince Mr. Higgins that you need to come next year."

"Great idea. In the meantime, what can I do for you?"

"I was hoping to talk with Mr. Lawrence. I heard he still comes to the office every day."

"That's right," she said. "Every day for the past seventy years. We celebrated his anniversary with the company just two weeks ago."

"Wow. Seventy years. He's been an attorney that long?"

"Not quite. He worked with his father—the first Mr. Lawrence—as an intern while he finished his schooling. But he always said sitting in on meetings with his dad was the most valuable training he received."

"I can appreciate that," Mattie said. "And that's why I wanted to speak with him. I'm sure you know that Sinclair Station was chosen as the venue for the next G7 Summit in the United States." Sarah nodded. "Well, we need to get a signature from a Sinclair heir, and we've found out there's no longer any Sinclair family living in Greece, so we're looking for others. As a place to start, I'm hoping to find out if Mr. Lawrence sat in on any meetings between his father and Henry Sinclair, Jr."

"Oh, the gentleman who was killed."

It always happens. The murder is the first thing people think of.

"Right," Mattie said. "Would you ask him if he could see me?"

"Sure. Hold on a second." Sarah left her desk and disappeared behind a thick teak door. Within minutes, she was back and held the door open for Mattie.

"He said he'd be glad to see you. I'll take you to his office."

Mattie entered and the attorney rose and came around his desk, radiating vitality with every step. He stood straight, despite his age, and his appearance was flawless. His starched white shirt complemented his crisp white hair. Even the knot in his tie squared up perfectly.

Mattie responded warmly to the genuine smile that lit up his clear blue eyes.

"Come in, young lady. How nice to see you. I'm sorry I missed your big shindig on Halloween. Heard you had more fire than just the flaming dessert. Ever find out who was responsible?"

Mattie shook hands with the elderly man, enclosing his in both of hers. "Nice to see you, too, sir. And in answer to your question, the fire was simply an accident. The heater tipped when one of the band members shoved it aside to set up his drums. Fortunately," Mattie continued, "it was over quickly, and no one was hurt. So it was still a very successful event. I'm hoping we'll see you there next year."

His smile broadened and he squeezed her hands. "These days, my girl, I don't make plans much past lunch. We'll see … we'll see." He moved toward the conference table by his window and gestured for Mattie to follow.

"Now then, tell me how I can help you."

Mattie repeated her purpose about searching for additional Sinclairs in conjunction with the upcoming summit. "I've found a couple of documents that I'm hoping you'll look at. I figured you would be the only one who could shed light on them."

"Let's see what you've got."

Mattie pulled out several documents from her portfolio. "I've spent some time going through the Sinclair estate files at the bank and found a couple of things directly related to your firm." She flipped the pages in Henry Sinclair's appointment book to the last entry. "Look at this, Mr. Lawrence. This entry shows that Mr. Sinclair had an appointment with your father at eight o'clock in the morning on the day he died." She turned the book so he could see it. "And this," she said, pulling out the invoice, "is dated the same day and has a notation that reads 'New Will.'" She laid the paper out in front of him. "But this invoice doesn't show it was paid, so I'm assuming there's no copy of the new will in the files I'm going through. At least I haven't found it yet." She sighed. "And honestly, Mr. Lawrence, as I told you, since there are no Sinclairs left in Greece, I really hoped I could find information in the will Mr. Sinclair *intended* to leave rather than the one that was actually executed after his death."

"Let me get Sarah in here," the attorney said. "We digitized everything some years back ... whatever that means." He grinned. "But Sarah oversaw all that, so if it can be found, she's the one to do it."

He called his executive assistant and explained what he needed. She made a notation of the date and took the invoice so she could make a copy.

"Is there any chance, Mr. Lawrence, that you remember sitting in on that meeting with Mr. Sinclair on the day he was killed?"

"Oh, I remember it, all right. And yes, I did sit in on that meeting. Part of it anyway."

Mattie's breath quickened. "Can you tell me anything about it? What Mr. Sinclair's attitude was ... why he may have wanted to change his will? Anything at all?"

Mr. Lawrence smiled. "Normally, I would cite attorney/client privilege. Since I sat in on that meeting, the confidentiality rules applied to me, too." He chuckled. "But since both the lead attorney and the client at the meeting in question have passed away, I won't be breaking any ethics laws to talk to you about it."

"Thank you. Do you mind if I record you?"

"Not at all. What's the worst that could happen? Disbarment at ninety years old?"

Mattie hit record and Mr. Lawrence began speaking.

"I remember Mr. Sinclair was very agitated when he came in that day. He had flown all night from New York to get here. I remember that clearly because it really impressed me. Understand, I was very young at the time. I'd never even been on an airplane, and I'd certainly never met anyone who had flown at night before." He stopped talking for a minute and leaned back in his chair. "It's funny," he said, "how I can clearly remember things from that long ago, but I couldn't begin to tell you what I had for breakfast." Mattie smiled at him. He sat forward again and continued. "Anyway, Mr. Sinclair had met with a distant relative in New York and was really upset about something he'd found out there."

"That might be helpful to know," Mattie said.

"I'll bet it would," he responded. "But unfortunately, I can't tell you what it was because the other thing I remember about that day is that Mr. Sinclair got off the airplane with a really bad headache—a migraine would be my guess. So my father sent me to the drugstore around the corner to get medicine for him. As a result, I missed a lot of their conversation. But," he continued after a minute, "when I returned, they were talking about a large sum of money. I got the impression that the funds in question came from the relative in New York. In fact, I assumed that was the main focus of the new will."

"Oh," Mattie said. "So, you don't know if there was a new heir?"

"No, I don't. But to my knowledge, we made the changes he'd requested that afternoon." His chin dropped to his chest. "And then we found out he'd been killed. So, I honestly don't remember what happened to the paperwork. If it's still with us, Sarah will tell us."

Mattie turned off her recorder and Mr. Lawrence leaned back in his chair again. "Such a sad situation," he added. "Losing his first wife had been so hard on him and his son. What was his name?"

"Jeffrey," Mattie said.

"Oh yes. Cute little guy. Went through a horrible trauma when his mother died." He stopped talking and shook his head. "I remember meetings Mr. Sinclair had with my father before he remarried. He told us the little boy was so distraught, he thought the only way to pull him out of it was to bring another woman into the house. And when he met a woman with a son of her own, that seemed like the perfect solution. The little guy would have someone to play with. You say he—what did you call him, Jeffrey—wasn't in Greece?"

"No, sir," she said. "I'm taking a trip tomorrow to try and find him."

Sarah entered the room. "I found it," she told them. "And I also pulled a copy of Mr. Sinclair's previous will—the one the new will would have replaced—so you'll have something to compare it with. Here are copies of both. And Mr. Lawrence, your next appointment is here."

She handed the copies to Mr. Lawrence, along with a memo, which he signed. Then he handed the copies to Mattie. "Here you are, young lady. We'll put this signed memo in the file to show that I allowed you to take copies from the office."

Mattie accepted the documents, stuffed them in her portfolio, and stood. She held out her hand to the gentleman in front of her. "Thank you so much, Mr. Lawrence, for your time," she said with a smile, "and your memory. You've been a big help. I'll look at the new will and see if it gives me any other leads. Especially if I run into a dead end with Jeffrey Sinclair tomorrow." Mattie turned toward the door.

"There was one more thing," Sarah said, holding out another sheet of paper. "This document was digitized and attached to the new will. It's a brochure about illegal immigration and deportation procedures."

Chapter Forty-Seven

Sinclair Station, North Carolina

"That's right, Dad," Mattie said into her speaker phone on her return trip from Asheville. "According to Mr. Lawrence, Henry, Jr. dictated a new will the morning he was killed. And the law firm made the changes that afternoon. But he died before he had the opportunity to sign it. They also gave me a copy of his original will that was executed when he died, so I can find the differences. Not that the new one matters much at this point, unless it indicates a new heir."

"Interesting how a few hours changed everything. Timing has a funny way of working, doesn't it?"

"Sure does," Mattie replied. "And, oh, I forgot to tell you. There was one interesting development. Attached to the copy of the new will was a brochure about illegal immigration and deportation proceedings. Why on earth do you think he would have wanted that?"

"I can't imagine. Did they have any clue about it?"

"Not really," Mattie said. "But Mr. Lawrence did tell me that Henry Sinclair came straight to the office from the airport, after visiting a relative in New York. That he was very agitated. Unfortunately, Mr. Lawrence didn't know why. Regardless, it will be really interesting to see what changed. Whatever it was," Mattie added with a sigh, "My heart still goes out to his poor wife ... widow. I feel so sorry for her, standing right there when he was killed. And then having to fight for her own life." Thoughts of her own husband, dead on the concrete, blurred her vision.

Then she caught her breath as she remembered her dad's struggle with David. "Oh, Dad, I'm so sorry. You kind of had to go through that yourself, huh? I didn't mean to be insensitive."

"No problem, little one. And you've been through it, too. Plus, there was only an instant when I believed he might actually shoot me. I was more worried about your grandmother."

"Any change with her yet?"

"No. Your grandfather hasn't left her side."

"How are you doing? Headaches?"

"No. In fact, I'm back in my office today. For a little while anyway."

"I'm going to see Nana now and I'm planning to go to Maine first thing in the morning."

"Good heavens, little one. Do you have to go this soon? I really think you should stay put for a while until we get to the bottom of what's going on."

Mattie's stomach tightened again, and worry surrounded her.

"Dad," she said. "I *have* to go. To get to the bottom of the Clairmont Place heir. To find out if Jeffrey is still alive." She heard her voice rising and took several deep breaths. "We have to get through this," she added quietly. "To get a signature so we can proceed with planning for the summit." She didn't add, "To get you off the hook and save your job." But she thought it.

Her father was silent for a moment. "My goodness, you are a stubborn woman. If you're this determined, will you at least take someone with you? Your grandfather won't go, you know."

"Yes, I do know that. I'm hoping I can Skype with him." She hesitated. "Dad, thank you for your concern, but honestly, I already have all my plans made, and I can move really quickly by myself. Besides," she added, "if there is any danger, I'm not going to want to involve anyone else at this point. Please understand."

"You're a grown woman," he said. "I guess I can't keep you from doing what you've decided to do. But I'm begging you to always be aware of your surroundings. And for goodness sake, little one, you must be careful. I couldn't stand it if anything happened to you."

"Okay, Dad. You have my word. I'll be extra careful. Love you."

Mattie disengaged her Bluetooth from her father's call and then used voice commands to dial Simone.

"I'm checking in to see if you're okay," Mattie said. "Has your brother shown up anywhere?"

"No, thank goodness. It's almost time for me to move back into my own apartment, but I hesitate to do that with him still out there."

"Hard to believe he beat up my family and then went into hiding. I would have expected him to show up at the mansion."

"Me, too. But I know extra security has been there every night with no sign of him. How's your grandmother?"

"I'm on my way to see her n—what the hell?"

A black car zoomed up behind Mattie, swerving erratically. Again, her father's words flew into her head. To be aware of her surroundings. She had been alone on the road. Until the big black car appeared from nowhere.

"What?" Simone said.

The car edged into Mattie's bumper, nudging her forward. She gripped the wheel, intent on maintaining control.

"Mattie, talk to me! What's that noise? Please ... what's happening?"

"Car behind me. Hit my bumper—"

The next hit was harder. Mattie flew forward and she skidded off the highway onto the shoulder. She tapped on the brake, but every time she did, the car behind her hit her again. One of her tires slid into the loose gravel at the edge of the shoulder and the steering wheel jerked out of her hands.

She was vaguely aware of Simone's voice screaming at her through the still connected phone. But her total focus tunneled in on keeping her car from spinning into the steep ditch and then plowing into the dense row of pine trees just beyond it.

The car behind her smashed into her at full speed.

She lost the battle and her tires lifted from the pavement, propelling her headfirst into the side of the ditch she'd worked to avoid. Her brain froze that moment in time, and she lost awareness of anything other than the looming bank. She traveled through a soundless vacuum until the last instant before impact when the explosion of the air bag filled her ears. Then for another instant ... nothingness.

Sticky moisture drenched her face and her eyes clouded.

Awareness slowly returned, and she saw a dark figure moving outside her window.

Help.

She thought she screamed. But she heard nothing.

Help, she screamed again.

Still no sound.

She moved her mouth. "Help." But even to her still roaring ears, the word sounded like a croak.

With effort, she turned her head to look for the dark figure she had seen seconds earlier. *He must be here to help.*

She fumbled with the buckle on her seatbelt to free herself in anticipation of the door flying open and waited expectantly for helping hands to reach in and gently pull her from her car.

But when she found the figure in her blurred vision, it just stood there, pointing at her.

Her brain cleared.

A gun—he's pointing a gun!

She squeezed her eyes shut and heaved herself down across the seats. A split second later, an explosion of glass erupted around her and the bullet bore straight through the car, shattering both windows in its path.

She heard a grunt.

And then something else. Sirens. Getting louder.

Followed by running footsteps. Then the sound of an engine revving and tires squealing.

She opened her eyes carefully and shook her body slightly to slough off the glass shards. She heard more footsteps and heavy breathing. Her brain worked feverishly to formulate an escape plan.

She inched her way to the passenger's door, planning to open it and let herself fall out. Then she could run to the cover of the woods.

But everything hurt. And before she cleared the driver's seat, her door jerked open a few inches.

She closed her eyes again, waiting for the final gunshot that would end her life.

"Miss Maguire! Can you hear me? Try not to move too much until we determine how badly you're hurt."

Her eyes flew open and painfully, she turned her head toward the voice. It belonged to a familiar face. The name didn't come to her, but she knew the face.

"I'm Officer Scott," he told her when he saw her confusion. "We met on this same road the night you had a drunken passenger."

Mattie closed her eyes and nodded slightly.

"How…?"

"Your friend, Miss Rousseau, called nine-one-one and I happened to be cruising close by. Can you tell if anything is broken? Have you tried moving your arms and legs?"

Cautiously, Mattie sat up. She raised each arm and then each leg.

"Excellent," he said, watching her. "You have a nasty gash on your forehead and another one on your left arm. And you'll probably have two black eyes. I've called for an ambulance and a tow truck. I'm going to see if I can open your door wide enough to get you out. Just stay still."

The driver's door refused to open so the officer left for a minute and returned with a long rod. A crowbar, Mattie figured. More sirens sounded.

Officer Scott pried her door open far enough that she could slide through.

"But don't try it yet," he warned. "The paramedics are pulling up now. It's best to let them assess the situation before we pull you out of there."

Within seconds, two more people appeared in her window. Hands reached in through the half open door and explored her limbs and torso. She answered their quiet questions. Satisfied, the paramedics and the officer pulled the door open and one of the men squatted beside her.

"We'll get you out of the car now. I'm going to swing your legs to the door. Okay?"

Mattie nodded.

"Good ... that's good. Now, can you put your arms around my neck so I can lift you out?"

Mattie was shocked at how easily she was removed from the car. Once on the ground, the paramedic cleaned her face and studied it intently. "We'll want to do tests, of course, but that cut on your head doesn't look nearly as bad as we originally thought."

"Good," Mattie said. She struggled to stand. "Because I need to—"

"Just a minute, ma'am," the paramedic interrupted. "Please let me check your legs again." The paramedic poked and prodded the entire length of both legs.

"I'm fine," she said. "Really, I am. But I need to get back to Sinclair Station."

Officer Scott spoke. "These gentlemen have to take you to the hospital first," he said. "Standard procedure after an accident. And then I'm going to want to talk to you about what happened."

One paramedic helped Mattie stand and then the two of them lifted her the few steps up the bank to the road. They sat her gently on a stretcher.

"Oh please," she said, strong enough now to be annoyed. "I really don't need this. All I need is a ride. I was headed to the hospital anyway to see my grandmother."

"Now, ma'am," the shorter paramedic said to her, "I know you wouldn't want us to get in trouble for not doing our jobs properly." He gently pushed her down on the stretcher and snapped the strap around her middle.

Officer Scott appeared by her side. "I'll accompany the ambulance," he said. "I got your purse, cell phone, and portfolio from the front seat. Is there anything else you'll need?"

"No. Thank you. Well, yes. Could you call my father and let him know where I'll be?"

"Miss Maguire," the paramedic broke in, "I'm giving you a mild sedative to relax you for your ride."

Mattie quickly gave the officer her father's phone number. Within seconds, the cooling sensation of the sedative traveled up her arm and settled in behind her eyes.

Then everything went black.

CHAPTER FORTY-EIGHT

Mattie's eyes eased open. But before she was fully aware, several voices drifted over her at once.

"Hello, little one." Mattie's father grinned at her. "I've asked the hospital administrator for a family discount. They've had more than their share of our business lately."

On the opposite side of her bed, Mattie's mother reached over and kissed her on the side of her forehead without a bandage. "Honey, we've been so worried about you."

"Oh, Mattie," Simone said from the end of her bed. "You scared me to death. What happened anyway?" She wrung her hands and then raised them to twist one of her blond curls.

"Yes, I'd like to know that, too." Mattie saw Officer Scott enter her room. "I just came from the lot where the tow truck took your car. There are big smudges of black paint all over your back bumper."

"I told you that's what was happening, officer," Simone said. "Oh, my goodness, Mattie, what you must have gone through. It sounded awful over the phone." Without any hesitation, Simone wound a second curl around her index finger.

"All of a sudden, the car was just there," Mattie said. "The whole trip from Asheville, I pretty much had the road to myself until this big black car showed up in my rear-view mirror."

"Did you lose control because it was so close to you?" Officer Scott asked her.

"It actually hit me—several times. You said yourself you saw black paint on my bumper. It was only a nudge at first, and then it sped up and pushed me into the ditch. And then the driver shot at me."

Mattie's father sucked in his breath. "Somebody shot at you?"

"Yeah," she answered. "If I hadn't ducked down into the seat at the last second ... well, who knows?"

"Do you have any idea why anyone would want to hurt you?" Before Mattie could answer, the officer turned to Mattie's father. "I heard what happened to you and your mother, Mr. Maguire," he said. "Could this incident be related to that?"

"I don't know," Matt Maguire said. "Ladies, any insight?"

Simone sank into a chair. "I know David doesn't have a car," she said.

"Simone," Matt said, "I know you love your brother, but considering some of the stunts he's pulled lately, I don't think obtaining a car would be much of a problem for him. He could easily have stolen one. Especially now that he has his gun back."

"I guess you're right."

"There's one other thing I can think of," Mattie said. "But it seems too ridiculous to even talk about."

"Go on—" Officer Scott told her. He opened a small notebook.

"My grandfather and I just got back from Greece. We proved that someone who claimed to be the owner of Clairmont Place was lying. He was very upset about it because he was trying to use his false identity to get money. He even tried to choke my grandfather. And then on our way to the airport, a car tried to run our taxi off the road. And then ... and then, as soon as we left it, the taxi exploded." A small shiver seized her. "And the driver ..." Mattie couldn't finish.

"And Mattie," Simone said, "don't forget that a black car almost hit you—us—in the hospital parking lot the night you got home."

"Oh yeah. I thought maybe I was imagining things, but you're right. It looked like the same kind of car."

"So are you saying you think someone put a contract out on you?" Officer Scott's eyes widened as he said the words.

"Good grief, that sounds so incredible. How could I be important enough for anyone to try and get rid of?" Mattie asked.

"Money—or lack of it," Officer Scott said, "is powerful motivation for some people." He looked down at his notes. "I have to ask this question. Is it possible it could have been a simple case of road rage? And a coincidence with the other things you've told me about?"

"Normally, I would shrug it off and say 'yes.' But I don't believe the driver who hit me simply had road rage. I told you, I had the road to myself, so I couldn't have cut anyone off or passed too closely or any of the reasons you normally hear about for road rage. Plus, I mean, forcing me off the road was one thing, but for him to get out of his car and shoot out my windows ..."

Mattie's mother shivered. "So, what can we do about this, officer?" she asked.

"I'll definitely do more investigation at the scene," Officer Scott said. "But depending on what we find, if the problem does turn out to be international, there's not much I can do until we get the proper agency involved."

"Regardless," Mattie said. "I'm ready to go home. Actually, I want to go see Nana first. Any change?"

"No," her mother said quietly. "Your grandfather's still with her."

Simone twirled her blond curls and bit her lower lip.

A nurse strode briskly into the room. "How are we doing?" she asked Mattie.

Mattie suppressed a small smile. "I don't know about everybody else. But I'm doing fine. In fact, I'm ready to go home. When can I leave?"

"That's what I came to tell you," the nurse said. "Your doctor has released you. Someone will bring your paperwork shortly and then you're free to go."

"Great," Mattie said. "I still need to see Nana. And then get ready to go to Maine."

"I wish you wouldn't go," Matt Maguire told his daughter. "Too much has happened. It's just too dangerous right now."

"Dad, I told you before. I *have* to. We have to get that letter signed. You said yourself—"

"Fine," he said. "I really wish you wouldn't drive yourself to the airport, though."

"Not a problem since I no longer have a car." She managed a grin. "I planned to Uber to the airport anyway, Dad," she said. "Don't worry."

She completed her release paperwork and then followed her parents to her grandmother's room. "Gramps," Mattie whispered, "how's she doing?"

Her grandfather jumped up and hugged her hard. "Oh, my goodness, my little Mattie Mat. Are you really okay?"

"I'm fine, Gramps. But I'm worried about Nana. Is she going to be all right?"

"As rain." It was only a whisper, but they all jumped.

"Marilyn," Mattie's grandfather said. He took her in his arms. "Oh, thank the good Lord." He lowered his head to her chest, and she caressed his neck.

A nurse rushed into the room but waited until Mattie's grandfather broke away from his embrace to take his wife's vital signs.

"Mrs. Maguire, you're doing fine. Are you hungry?"

Mattie's grandmother shook her head.

When the nurse left the room, Matt took her other hand. "Mom. Welcome back. We were all so worried about you. How are you feeling? Can you tell yet?"

"I can tell," she said with a slight nod. "I feel like hell."

It felt good to laugh after so many days of worry. The family hovered around her bed until she drifted off again.

Mattie heaved a sigh of relief and hoped the worst was over.

She would find out sooner than she expected.

Chapter Forty-Nine

With Sally at work for long stretches at a time, David bored easily. Daytime television held no interest for him, and each passing minute moved him one tick closer to coming unglued. Texts reached him daily from his Russian employers, the urgency of completing his mission mounting by the hour.

They didn't understand. Security was too tight. And he was their target. After what happened with the Maguires, he couldn't risk being seen.

But he had to figure out something. He'd almost worn a hole in the threadbare carpet with his pacing.

He hated the way he felt. Trapped. Like a caged animal.

At the edge of dusk, he left Sally's apartment, his gun tucked into the back of his pants, and took the stairs to the ground floor. Outside, the crisp air improved his mood slightly and he filled his lungs. He adjusted his new baseball cap, put on yellow-lens sunglasses, and zipped his jacket. Nondescript brown. If he kept to the shadows, he could probably go unnoticed.

He avoided the main streets and adopted a circuitous route, walking slowly as if he were simply out to get exercise. Very few people appeared in his path that time of day, so he moved steadily toward Clairmont Place. When he reached the beech-lined drive, he resisted the temptation to take it, choosing instead the dense patch of woods just beyond it. After several minutes of wading through the undergrowth, the house came into view. He slowed his progress and stepped lighter to lessen the crunching sound from each footfall on the thick, autumn ground cover. Then he zig-zagged from tree to tree, maintaining visual contact with windows and doors on the old mansion.

So far, so good. No lookouts.

But he needed to check out the entire perimeter. He couldn't risk capture and jail time.

He angled toward the back of the house with the formal gardens to his right, stables to his left, and paused beside the garden shed for a better view. He stood still.

But the sound of footsteps swishing through leaves ... stealthy ... hesitant ... reached him.

He whipped around and looked behind him. Nothing. The sound got louder. He moved to the edge of the small building and carefully positioned himself at the corner. He stuck his head out for a better view.

Still nothing in sight, but louder sound.

His heart beat faster and he pressed himself against the shed, moving slowly to the next corner. He reached it as a small doe caught his scent and bounded away from him out into the open yard surrounding the gardens.

He heard a shout from somewhere close to the house and within seconds, the deer ran his way again and shot past him deeper into the woods. He turned and saw a deputy running toward him, gun drawn. He hefted himself up and silently eased through the slightly open window in the back of the shed, pulled his gun out, and then pressed against the inner wall. The deputy ran to the corner of the shed.

Several seconds passed before David realized he wasn't the deputy's target. He relaxed and stayed hidden but kept the deputy in his line of vision. He saw the officer walk a little further into the woods, turn in several directions, and then head back toward the house, holstering his gun as he walked. Static from a walkie-talkie reached David's ears and he heard, "Nah, just a deer. No sign of him from the north lookout." More static crackled and then a muffled, "No sign from the east, either." The conversation continued, too far away for David to catch the words.

But he'd found out what he needed to know. Lookouts posted at the house. Waiting for him to show up. He slumped against the wall, careful to avoid the tangle of rakes close by.

He waited another fifteen minutes, put his gun away, and removed his glasses before easing back out of the shed window. He'd been lucky. It was the perfect hiding place. And who knew, it might come in handy in the future. He hurried away from the property and returned to Sally's place by a different route.

He needed a new plan. And he needed it fast.

CHAPTER FIFTY

D r. Joseph Harrington studied Marilyn Maguire's chart while her family watched anxiously. "Mrs. Maguire," Dr. Harrington said, "if you can correctly give me family birthdates and a few other simple things, I'll agree to let you go home as early as tomorrow. As long as you promise me you will rest when you get there. No working in your garden the rest of the week, understand?"

"I understand," she said. "And you have my word. Let's just get this question foolishness over with."

The family gathered at the foot of her bed.

"Now, no help from any of you," Dr. Harrington said, turning toward them. "It's important to determine that her brain is completely awake before we release her to the world. Got it?"

They all agreed.

The doctor fired questions at her, some in really quick succession. But Mattie's grandmother didn't hesitate and answered all his questions quickly and correctly. "That's fine, Mrs. Maguire," he said. "Really good. Much better than I expected."

Mattie and her father high-fived and Michael squeezed his wife's hand. Mattie's mother wiped her eyes.

"Okay, Mrs. Maguire. I'll want to continue to monitor you tonight, pump some more antibiotics and fluids into you. But you should be good to go by early tomorrow afternoon."

"That's great news," Michael said. He bent to kiss his wife's cheek.

The doctor left and Mattie's mother rubbed her father-in-law's shoulders. "Why don't you spend the night in a real bed, Mike?" she asked. "I can stay here with Marilyn tonight."

"No, Addy. Thanks. I appreciate the offer, but I would really rather stay here. I can sleep in a real bed when I have her beside me again." He smiled at his wife. "But I do think I'll leave for a little while early tomorrow morning … go back to the house, take a shower in my own place, check on things. I'll also pick up some fresh clothes for Marilyn to wear home. So, if one of you would leave me a car, that would be great."

"You can use mine," Mattie's mother said. She handed him the keys.

Marilyn Maguire drifted off again and the rest of the family left for the night. Mattie's parents offered her a lift since her car was totaled. They emerged from the hospital and started toward the parking lot when Mattie's mother said, "Oh for heaven's sake—I forgot to give Mike the ticket to get out of here tomorrow. I'll be right back." She re-entered the hospital and Mattie's father went to get the car. Mattie stood by the door, waiting for her mother when "Sweet Dreams" sounded from her jacket pocket.

"Bryan," she said.

"I'm calling to check on you. How are you doing? I understand you had another scare this afternoon."

"Right," she said. "But I'm okay. Just a little rattled. Do you have news?"

"No, and we're beginning to think David might have skipped out. He hasn't shown up at the inn. The owner said all of his stuff is still there, just like he left it. And nobody has seen hide nor hair of him around town. It wouldn't have been that hard for him to walk to the edge of town at night and hitch a ride with a semi-driver."

"My dad thought the same thing," Mattie said, "although I'm not buying it yet. So, does that mean you're closing the case?"

"No, of course not. But I wanted you to know that either he's gone or a lot more clever than I originally gave him credit for."

"Who knows? By the way … how's your guy … Jorge, was it?"

"Yes. That was his name."

"Oh dear … *was?*"

"Yes. He died yesterday. So if we ever find this guy, David, we'll take him in on manslaughter rather than trespassing."

Mattie shivered. "I'm really sorry you lost a man, Bryan."

"I am, too." He hesitated. "What did you find out at the attorney's office?"

"Not as much as I had hoped, so I'm still going to Maine in the morning. Finding Jeffrey Sinclair is our last hope. And I truly believe he's in Maine."

"I hope you're right," Bryan said. "It would be great for all of us if this issue were resolved and put to bed."

"I agree. And finding Jeffrey is finding the key—the one that will unlock everything."

"I think you're right. How's your grandmother?" he asked.

"She's really good ... coming home tomorrow. My mother tried to get my grandfather to leave the hospital tonight for a while, but he said he'll wait until very early tomorrow morning while Nana's still sleeping."

"That's great, Mattie," Bryan answered. "Tomorrow around noon, I'll move my men to guard your grandparents' house instead of the big house. You know, just in case."

"Sounds good, Bryan. Good night."

Mattie's father pulled up as her mother walked out the door. Without warning, sudden shudders traveled Mattie's spine and the same disquiet—the unease that had plagued her the night of the gala—surrounded her again. She couldn't get in the car fast enough.

She hated being such a chicken, but she resolved herself to the fact that cowardice would probably taunt her for the rest of her life.

Matt Maguire pulled out of the hospital parking lot onto the main road, and David Rousseau stepped from behind a large ornamental shrub. He had heard Mattie's end of her phone conversation, and he smiled into the darkness. Her side of the conversation sounded like the sheriff was ready to give up on trying to find him. Good.

Her words also sounded like she knows about the key. And she's going to get it.

He smiled again. Mattie's side of her conversation with the sheriff fed into his new plan. Given the number of guards at the mansion, he had figured out that any attempt to get into the house on his own was a foolish waste of time. But from what he'd just heard, Mattie Maguire was all set to do his job for him. She'd do the work. He'd swoop in at the end and take the key.

Then once the Russians retrieved the contents of the lockbox, he'd collect his million dollars. Plus, his hundred-thousand-dollar bonus.

He walked back across the parking lot into the dense woods and laughed out loud. He actually skipped for a few steps and clicked his heels in the air.

He made a stealthy stop at the inn and snuck into his room unobserved where he gathered a few things and voice-texted his contacts to let them know he would have the key by the end of the next day.

When he reached Sally's place, his heart overflowed with happiness.

The Maguire woman was going to Maine.

The job was almost done.

The money was almost his.

All he had to do was carry out his part in the morning.

CHAPTER FIFTY-ONE

Michael Maguire lost track of the number of hours he'd spent at his wife's bedside. But it had all, thank goodness, been worth it. She'd been very fortunate in the scheme of things. Her jaw hadn't been broken, and her coma lasted only long enough to give her a good rest. Her face still sported battle scars, but even her bruises had morphed from deep indigo to light purple with yellow edges—"the color of my spring irises"—she'd said when she saw them.

"What time is it?" The room was dark, but her voice was strong, alert.

"Oh no, did I wake you?" He stood by her bed and took her hand. "It's almost five. I'm going to make a quick trip to the house to check on things and get you fresh clothes for your homecoming." He put her hand to his lips. "I'll probably take a shower before coming back, too. There's just something about your own space," he said.

"Tell me about it," she answered. "At least you haven't had to go to the bathroom in a bedpan." Her lips lifted in a small smile, barely visible in the low light.

"Well, not much longer for you, either," he said. He kissed her hand again. "Since you're awake, do you have any preference for what clothes I should bring you?"

"Something bright—red—I'm pretty tired of these drab hospital colors."

"I know just the thing." He put on his jacket. "Will you try and sleep a little more? The nurses will be in to bathe you in a couple of hours, but I hope you can rest until then. And I'll be back shortly after that." He picked up her hand again and brought it to his lips.

"Okay. I think I can do that." She squeezed the hand that held hers.

"Be careful. They haven't found that young man yet. He may be getting desperate by now for whatever it is he's looking for."

"I'll be fine, Marilyn. In fact, guards are still stationed outside the door. I'll even ask one of them to accompany me to Addy's car. How's that sound?"

"That sounds good, my darling." She squeezed his hand again. "Do you have any idea how much I love you?"

He bent down and kissed her lips. "Yes," he said, kissing her again. "I do. A mere fraction of the amount I love you."

They laughed together softly.

His heart was light, and he left her to return to the home he hadn't seen for days. He closed her door behind him and was joined within seconds by a man wearing a dark hat and a navy-blue jacket. The familiar emblem of the Sinclair Station Sheriff's Office was prominent on his sleeve.

"If you're leaving the building, sir," the man said, "I've been instructed to accompany you to your car. Can't be too careful, you know." The man fell into step beside him.

"I do know that, young man, and I appreciate it. Having you with me will make my wife feel a lot better."

They walked along in silence through the almost empty halls. Nurses chatted at their desks but didn't look up as the men passed. They reached the door and headed outside to the parking lot. Addy had told Michael where her car was parked, and he indicated the direction to the guard. The gray sky wore the first pink rays of morning as they turned toward a far corner of the lot. Michael Maguire breathed deeply, happy that his family's ordeal was almost over.

He reached the car, which Adelaide had backed into the space for ease of driving right out. He clicked the button on the key fob and unlocked the doors. "Thanks so much, officer," he said. "I can take it from here." He opened the door.

"I don't think so, sir."

Startled, Michael looked up over the top of the car.

And stared into the barrel of a gun.

"What the hell?"

"I'm sorry, Mr. Maguire," the guard said, "but you will go where I tell you to. Get in."

Slowly, Michael eased into the front seat. The guard climbed in beside

221

him from the passenger's side, the gun aimed at Michael's heart. "So," Michael said, "obviously you don't work with Bryan."

"That's right. I have my own agenda. But you're going to help me." He motioned with his gun. "Start the car. Let's go."

"You must be David," Michael said. His heart thumped in his chest, but his hands held steady on the wheel. "I haven't had the previous ... *pleasure* of meeting you as the rest of my family has."

"Drive."

"Sure, son, sure. Where are we going?"

"Your place."

"David, I beg you to leave me be. You're only going to make this worse for yourself."

"Please stop talking, Mr. Maguire." The gun snugged up to Michael's chest.

He drove in silence and turned into the long lane leading to Clairmont Place. They passed the large house and saw a guard turn the corner toward the front. He waved a greeting to Michael.

"Good, Mr. Maguire," David said. "You did well not to attract the attention of the guard. Now slow down and turn here." David motioned for him to take a path to the left of The Cottage. "We're going to the shed at the edge of the gardens."

Michael took the path. With the gun pressing into him, he decided to simply follow orders.

"Okay, now pull around back and park."

Again, Michael did as he was told. Light from the early morning sky disappeared, blotted out by the thick tree cover that surrounded the shed. The dashboard clock read five forty-five.

"Out," David said, poking the gun deeper into Michael's chest. "And I warn you, Mr. Maguire ... don't try anything. I don't want to shoot you. But I will."

They walked around to the door. "We keep this shed locked, son. Lots of valuable tools in here," Michael said. "And I left the keys for the foreman. I don't have a set with me."

"No problem." David fished in his pocket and brought out small metal rods. "Move over here by the door, Mr. Maguire, so I can keep an eye on you. I'm warning you again not to try and run or shout out. It wouldn't go well for you." David picked the lock quickly and forced Michael into the dark interior ahead of him. "I was here the other day," David said. "It's not a bad place to hang out." He indicated a lawn chair with his gun. "Sit."

Again, Michael did as he was told.

"Now give me your cell phone. Slowly. I can't emphasize strongly enough that you shouldn't try anything." Michael reached slowly into his pocket and produced his phone. David snatched it out of his hand and then removed plastic cable ties from his jacket pocket. "Hands on the chair arms."

He bound Michael's hands and legs to the chair.

"That's awfully tight, young man," Michael said.

"Quiet." He punched buttons on Michael's phone. "Okay, Mr. Maguire. Here's what we're going to do. We're going to call your granddaughter and you're going to tell her you're with me. You will not tell her where you are, and you will not say anything else. I'll have my gun in your gut the entire time. Just say you're with me and that you're fine. I'll talk to her after that. Do you understand?"

"Yes."

"I mean this, Mr. Maguire. Your son tried to be a hero. I suggest you don't."

"Fine. Whatever you say. Just please—"

"Quiet. I'll tell you when it's time to talk."

CHAPTER FIFTY-TWO

Mattie waited with the other passengers at the Asheville airport for her six o'clock flight. The plane was small, so boarding happened quickly. She closed her eyes, her insides quivering in anticipation of finding Jeffrey Sinclair. He had to be there. He *had* to be. She had told Bryan the truth the previous evening. She believed that finding Jeffrey held the key to scaling the last hurdle in the summit process. Now that she and her grandfather had verified the death of Constance Sinclair, Jeffrey's signature on the letter, a copy of which rested safely in her portfolio, would complete the last of the preliminary steps. They could move forward. Her father could rest easy.

She had secured a room at the only bed-and-breakfast in Rogue Bluffs and a rental car at the Bar Harbor airport where she'd be landing. She'd even obtained driving directions for the forty-five miles that separated the two towns. Her flight landed early enough that she should easily be able to make it to her destination and back to the bed-and-breakfast well before dark.

She had also done a search for Arnold Sinclair ... a simple one. She entered *address Arnold Sinclair Rogue Bluffs Maine*. And there he was. With a street address—no phone number—but enough to locate him. So she was set.

And now she was about to take off to find him. And, she hoped, Jeffrey as well.

She believed this would be a good day, a lucky day. Nana would be home from the hospital and Mattie would, hopefully, solve the last of the issues holding up the summit.

Well, almost the last. Simone's brother, the idiot, was still on the loose.

Maybe this day would be lucky for Bryan, too. She willed it to happen and smiled as she imagined her father giving her the good news that David was in jail when she called to give *him* the good news that she had Jeffrey Sinclair's signature on the letter.

Yes, she decided. This was going to be a good day.

The flight attendant called for the passengers to board the plane and Mattie buckled herself in. She reached for her phone to turn it off as "Sweet Dreams" sounded in her hand. Her grandfather. Not like him to make phone calls so early in the day. She answered immediately.

"Gramps," she said. "What's wrong? Has Nana relapsed?"

"Mattie …" he said. His voice sounded weird … strained. Her heartbeat escalated and fear filled her.

"What? Gramps? What is it? What's wrong?"

"David …"

"What? What's he done now?"

"I'm with him."

"What? Why?"

She heard shuffling on the other end and an unfamiliar voice sounded in her ear.

"I have your grandfather," he said. "He's fine, but he will stay with me until you return from your trip to Maine."

"How did you know?"

"Stop talking, Miss Maguire," he interrupted. "And listen. Carefully. I know where you're going, and I know why. And as it turns out, you and I are after the same thing."

"Turn off your cell phone, miss," the flight attendant told her.

Mattie turned wild eyes to the attendant and shook her head vehemently.

"I don't know what you're—"

"I told you," he hollered into her ear. "I will do the talking. You will go to Maine, you will find a relative of Henry Sinclair's, and you will get the little key to the lockbox."

Tears stained Mattie's cheeks. Mattie saw the flight attendant hovering and knew that any second she would insist again that Mattie stop talking and turn off her phone.

"David," Mattie said, "I don't know what you're talking about. I'm trying to find Jeffrey Sinclair to get him to sign the summit letter. I don't know anything about a key or a lockbox."

"Stop lying," he thundered. "If you ever want to see your grandfather again, you will do as you're told. Find the key and bring it to me. I'll meet you inside the house tonight at nine o'clock. Don't tell anyone else. And. Don't. Involve. The. Police. I mean what I say. Your grandfather's life depends on you following my orders."

"Please, you have to tell me what—"

The line went dead. He was gone.

Mattie looked at the flight attendant, tears streaming steadily now.

"Miss, please. I'm sorry if you've received bad news, but we've begun our taxi and will take off in minutes. You must turn your phone off."

Mattie clicked her phone off and threw it on the seat beside her. She sobbed into her hands. Seconds later, the flight attendant was back with a package of tissues. "I'm really sorry, miss. Is there anything we can do for you?"

Mattie shook her head but accepted the tissues. From what had happened to her father and grandmother, she had no doubt David would carry out his threat. She didn't understand what he wanted, but knew she had to continue with her journey and hope that someone in Maine would understand. And help.

Chapter Fifty-Three

Rogue Bluffs, Maine

The sun peeked above the water and crept slowly up the cliffs that protected the old estate. He loved the house, loved the Tudor lines of it, the dormer windows, and the jasmine that wound thickly around the columns supporting the wraparound porch's roof.

The house sat on one of the United States' easternmost promontories, encircled by the small Englishman Bay that flowed eventually into the North Atlantic. The unique location allowed the man everyone called Robert to be among the first in the whole country to witness the birth of each new dawn.

As this day began, he was ready, ensconced in his favorite chair in the east conservatory, his lap robe tucked snugly around his legs against the morning chill.

Sunrise was his favorite time of day, when the world held promise and the air glowed fresh with the new morning. He had begun more than twenty-four thousand new days in exactly this way.

He hadn't always believed the world held promise. At first, after the tragedies of his early life, he'd often wished the night would take him with it when it blinked out and faded into daylight.

But gradually, his sadness lessened, and he appreciated the freedom from anxiety and constant worry that had occupied every waking moment all those years ago.

As a child, he'd studied the waterways surrounding the house and loved looking out over the water, imagining the lands that same water touched on the other side, and fantasizing about the people who lived on its far shore. He longed to communicate with them and tossed empty soda bottles, corked to hold the message and pictures he sent to children in

England, Spain, even Africa, he hoped. Once, a bottle actually came back to him, but, disappointingly, his own message nestled inside.

Yes, it had taken a while to be comfortable here, but once the butler saw him sketching on a scrap of paper, everything changed. His uncle bought him art supplies, and he attacked them with the same gusto as he had the grilled cheese sandwich when he first came back to the house after leaving the school.

His uncle came to see him every day and sometimes they took short walks together—a form of therapy for the bum leg, his uncle explained to him. After a while, his uncle took him to the beautiful little church in town every Sunday, where he met other boys his age. Friendly boys. Boys he came to like. Slowly, he came out of his shell. He still didn't speak, but he found other ways to communicate.

In the fall, a nice lady from town showed up at the house to give him his lessons.

And every day he drew. Or painted. Or sketched.

After about a year, his uncle complimented him on a picture of a dog. A collie. He looked up and smiled.

"Thank you," he said.

His uncle's eyes filled with tears and his face with joy. He reached down and hugged the boy he called Robert.

He drank the last of his tea, the delicate china cradled in his hands. Orange Blossom Mint—his Tuesday tea. He had filled his hours around his artwork by creating routine—teaching art classes to children in town during his twenties and thirties—and in more mundane ways later in his life, like choosing a different tea for each day of the week.

The light was almost perfect. He rose and padded over to his easel, taking the basket of charcoals with him. He always began with charcoal sketches and sometimes painted over them with oils. Or watercolors. And sometimes he felt the charcoal sketches were complete on their own. Each day was different, and he welcomed the whim that helped him decide.

Stacks of canvases surrounded him, many of them sporting the same scene—some with different light, some with experimental colors.

He never ran out of supplies. They appeared as if by magic. The same way food came to him. And clothes. Although he had worn the same size and many of the same things for decades. His painter's smock, for example. His uncle gave it to him, along with three others exactly like it, on his fortieth birthday. They all still fit perfectly.

"More tea, sir?" Bailey, his butler, materialized—ghost-like—in the doorway bearing a teapot that matched the delicate cup the man called Robert held. A small plate of biscuits rested beside it on his tray.

"Yes, thank you, Bailey."

Bailey poured and the morning sun, having risen above the bluffs, streamed through the floor-to-ceiling windows.

Bailey cleared his throat. "Excuse me, Mr. Robert, sir."

"Yes?"

"I wonder if I could have a few words with you?"

"Of course." He indicated the chair he had vacated. "Please. Have a seat."

"That won't be necessary." Bailey cleared his throat again. "Sir, it happens that my birthday is next month."

He was surprised. Bailey never talked about himself. "Well … Happy Birthday … uh … in advance."

Bailey bowed from the waist. "Thank you, sir. But that's not why I told you. I will turn ninety on that birthday, sir, and I plan to retire."

He put down his basket of charcoals. "Bailey, I had no idea. You've just always been here."

"Yes, sir."

"But, well, of course you must retire. I will, hmm, I'm not sure what I will do. But it will be fine. I'll figure out something."

"If it presents a burden, sir, I could stay another couple of months, but—"

"No, no, of course not. It's a surprise, that's all. It's not your problem, Bailey. I'll take care of it. I'm very happy for you."

"Yes, sir."

"I will speak with someone from town tomorrow and begin interviewing for your replacement. Please don't worry."

"Yes, sir. Thank you, sir."

"So, what will you do? Do you have family close by?"

"No, sir. But my youngest sister lives in North Carolina. She wants me to come and live with her."

"North Carolina?" The words emerged as a whisper. Foggy memories flirted with his brain. A beautiful woman—someone he had loved—riding a horse. A wonderful man, whom he had also loved, smiling at him and bringing him art supplies.

"Yes, sir," Bailey said, "North Carolina. She said their winters are normally mild ... milder than here with very little snow."

"Yes," he said softly. "I remember."

"I beg your pardon, sir?"

"Nothing," he answered. "Sorry. It was nothing."

Bailey bowed and left the room.

The man called Robert retrieved his basket of charcoals and resumed his position in front of the canvas. But his mind was far away—running through beautiful flower gardens and watching the birth of a foal.

He knew—way back in his head—that bad things had happened in North Carolina.

But there had been good memories, too.

He allowed them to come. A smile. A touch. A feeling of warmth and love. It had all been so long ago. After his uncle died, he couldn't remember the last time he'd been touched by another human being. Other than Bailey accidentally brushing into him when serving his tea.

But that didn't count.

He stared out the windows, across the sea grass and over the bluffs. The bay was calm, and the sun formed diamond sparkles on the gentle ripples. But they disappeared from his sight as, for the first time in many years, he let the memories have their way.

Without conscious thought, his hand moved, and lines appeared. More lines. But they were different from what he'd expected. It happened that way sometimes. His head's idea of the picture he would draw competing with the image his heart dictated.

His hand continued to move.

The lines formed a face. A face he had loved. A face he hadn't seen for decades.

He stared at it. Familiar memories and long dormant feelings tugged at his insides.

And for the first time in many years, thoughts of his past warmed his heart.

CHAPTER FIFTY-FOUR

Mattie's flight landed safely in Bar Harbor and her rental car reception was extremely friendly. But the joy she'd felt at the beginning of the day was gone—vanished with the phone call from her grandfather. Fear gripped her heart and she focused on doing what she had to do to save him.

She had canceled her reservation at the bed-and-breakfast and changed her return flight to Asheville for later that day rather than the following morning. Time would be tight at Arnold Sinclair's home, so she'd have to make the most of it and act quickly.

The people she spoke with—the gentleman at the airport counter and the lady at the car rental place—had fixed her with sympathetic looks. She knew her face, still bruised from her encounter with the steep ditch along the road from Asheville and blotched from her tears, must have prompted questions. But fortunately, the folks she met were very pleasant, and didn't ask any. For which she was grateful. New tears threatened to crumble her façade every second and she willed herself to hold it together for a little while longer. At least until she could get more information from whatever member of the Sinclair family she met.

She walked out to pick up her car and a cold wind blasted her face—much worse than she'd anticipated. She pulled her winter coat tighter around her and fumbled through her purse for her gloves, pulling them on as she walked to the car assigned to her.

She climbed in and turned the heat on full blast, then entered the address she'd found for Arnold Sinclair into the GPS and hit "Go."

Less than an hour later she saw a sign that read *Welcome to Rogue Bluffs, Maine; Population: 292.*

Slowly she drove through the small downtown area.

Trees—almost totally bereft of leaves—lined the quaint streets that boasted diagonal parking and no meters. She passed a small department store, a hardware store, a real estate office, a bank—Machias Savings Bank, as she expected—a bar, and two restaurants. The small town, she realized, would have delighted her under normal circumstances, and she hoped she'd have time to come back one day and explore it.

The navigation device guided her all the way through town and then three miles beyond. The picture on her GPS screen, in fact, showed her driving right into the water. At the last second, before the little picture plunged her off the cliffs, she turned left into a long lane guarded by an old brick fence and then drove through a canopy of tall trees that turned the mid-morning light to dusk. She emerged back into bright sun, took the right fork of a circular drive, and came to a stop in front of a sprawling Tudor mansion surrounded by a wide wraparound porch.

Her heart hammered against her ribs. This trip had begun as important for her father's sake but had abruptly become a life-and-death situation for her grandfather's sake. Sudden fear gripped her with the realization that she didn't have a lot to go on. That maybe Jeffrey had never lived here or was here for a while, but moved ... or died ... or ...

She forced herself to stop her mind-talk and calm down.

She had to take this step first. She'd figure out the rest later. With her purse on her shoulder and her portfolio nestled in her elbow, she climbed the steps and rang the doorbell. Somewhere in the back of the house she heard the chime.

She waited.

And waited. It felt like forever.

She wavered between ringing again or knocking. Leaving wasn't an option. She had to talk with whomever lived here. She decided to knock, but with her hand in mid-air the door slowly opened.

The person on the other side of it appeared to be ancient, his face full of wrinkles and his white hair sticking straight up as if he'd had an electric shock. Or was Albert Einstein's long-lost brother.

"Hello, miss. May I help you?"

"Yes, hello," she said. She held out her hand. He just stood there. Her heart thumped into her ears, and her tears threatened to flow.

She took a deep breath and tried again. "My name is Mattie—Matilda, actually—Maguire, and I'm here from Sinclair Station, North Carolina."

The man's face showed no flicker of recognition at either name.

"I'm trying to locate a man named Jeffrey Sinclair. Would you … are you Jeffrey?"

"No, miss. We have no one here by that name." The man in front of her backed away and the door closed.

"Oh," she said to no one.

The depth of her disappointment stunned her. She had convinced herself, with practically no real facts, that she would find Jeffrey at this address. Fear overtook her, and the tears came with it.

She rang the bell again. And then knocked.

Frantically.

Several long seconds ticked by.

Then the door cracked open.

"Please, sir, please …" Mattie's eyes held his. "This is so important. How about Arnold. Arnold Sinclair? Are you Arnold?"

"No, miss."

Mattie's tears fell harder, and the door started to close again.

It can't end like this. She stuck her foot between the door and the jamb, frustration threatening to morph into anger. "Please … will you please just give me a few minutes?" A single sob escaped her throat. She turned pleading eyes to him. "I've come a long way and I'm searching for an heir to the Sinclair family estate, Clairmont Place, in North Carolina. I really thought that Jeffrey had come here to live with Arnold Sinclair. Isn't this Arnold's house?"

The door opened slightly. "Yes, miss. He used to own this house."

Clearly, the man would not be forthcoming with information.

"Did he sell it?"

"No, miss. He died."

"Does anyone else live here with you?"

The man hesitated.

"Please, sir, please," Mattie begged again, tears freezing on her cheeks. She couldn't let it go. Not yet. "If anyone else is at home, may I please speak with that person? Did Arnold Sinclair have a wife or children? Grandchildren, maybe?"

"No, miss. None of those."

"So there's no one else here?"

The man at the door didn't answer but turned at the sound of a voice from the back of the house. "Bailey, who was at the door?"

Mattie frowned. "So, someone else *is* here," she said. "Please. *Please* ... may I speak to him?"

The man moved aside, and Mattie entered. "Wait here, miss, and I'll ask if Mister Robert will see you."

"Mist—*Robert* ... of course. I should have thought of that." But the man had already shuffled away from her. Hope fluttered in her heart for the first time since finding out her grandfather had been kidnapped.

Before long, a tall, lean man in a painter's smock approached her. He also had white hair, but it was perfectly groomed. The Sinclair resemblance was unmistakable, even though his father had only been forty-five when he died.

She still had to ask him the questions.

But she knew.

Relief filled her heart and tears flooded her face.

He saw her tears and his expression changed from curiosity to concern. "Oh, my goodness, little lady, what is it? What's happened?" His eyes flickered from the bandage on her head to the bruises under her eyes and the tears pouring from them. "Did you have an accident?"

"No ... well, yes ... but yesterday in—never mind." She took a deep breath and tried to control her voice enough to speak. "So, you're the man called Robert?" she asked.

"Yes ..."

"Do you remember any other names you used to go by? Like Jeffrey? Jeffrey Sinclair?"

His blue eyes, so crisp and sharp when he expressed concern, clouded and lost their focus. It was obvious to Mattie that his mind traveled to another time, another place. She continued to cry quietly, but stood still, giving him as much time as he needed.

"Yes," he whispered. "Jeffrey. Jeffrey Sinclair." His eyes also filled with tears and Mattie's overflowed. Again. She reached in her purse and brought out tissues for both of them.

"My grandfather is Michael Maguire," she said when she could talk again.

His eyes lit. "That's a name I haven't heard for decades. I really looked up to him. He was very nice to me. I called him 'Mikey.' Did he tell you

234

that?"

She couldn't control her tears. The man in front of her could save her grandfather's life. But she didn't have much time. "Yes," she managed to whisper. "He did." She blew her nose, and he patted her shoulder awkwardly. "He needs your help, Mr. Sinclair. Please, may we talk?"

He ushered her into the east conservatory and cleared canvases from chairs. Bailey followed.

"Bailey," Jeffrey Sinclair said, "will you bring this young lady and me some tea? Make it a whole pot. And more biscuits. We may be here a long time."

Mattie and Jeffrey Sinclair shared a pot of tea. He waited for her to stop crying and filled the time by talking to her about his Uncle Arnold. He told her about his trip to Maine and his short-lived experience with the boarding school. He also told her it had been a good life for him ... that his uncle had been appreciative of his talent for drawing and kept him furnished with art supplies. And then willed the big Tudor house to him as well.

"That's kind of why I'm here," Mattie said when she could talk again. "About inheritances and heirs. And my grandfather."

He sat quietly.

"As I said earlier," she continued. "I need your help. My grandfather is in trouble and I believe you're the only one who can help him. But there's another matter, too."

She didn't trust herself to get through talking about her grandfather's kidnapping, so she quickly filled him in on the fact that Sinclair Station had been chosen for the next International G7 Summit, and that they needed a family member's signature to hold the meeting at Clairmont Place. She also told him the people of the town that bore his grandfather's name wanted to add Clairmont Place to The National Register of Historic Places. "But," she said, when she finished explaining, "we need the family's permission in order to do either of those things."

Jeffrey remained silent.

"The family member of record," Mattie continued, "was Constance Sinclair, with an address in Corfu, Greece." Mattie saw his expression harden slightly. "But when we sent the letter to her, it came back signed

'Jeffrey Sinclair,' instead of 'Constance.'" Mattie watched his face carefully as she talked. "So, my grandfather and I made a trip to Greece to verify that the person calling himself 'Jeffrey' really was. I guess you can figure out what happened."

"It was Robert."

"Yes," Mattie said. "It was Robert. Constance is dead."

Jeffrey's face relaxed.

"When my grandfather asked him questions only the real Jeffrey would have had answers to, we determined his identity pretty quickly. Now that his mother is dead, he will never again benefit from one cent of the money from the Sinclair estate. From your estate," she finished.

He looked up sharply. "My estate?"

"Yes," she said. "As far as we can determine, you are the only heir. We will need to verify that you are, indeed, the real Jeffrey." She stopped talking and fought tears once more.

And lost the battle. Sobs overtook her and her shoulders shook.

"Oh, my goodness," he said, dismay plain on his face. "What has happened?"

She had to do this. She had to finish, so she talked through her tears, working to make herself understood. "I was supposed to call my grandfather at this point, Mr. Sinclair. So he could ask you the same questions we asked Robert. But ..." She couldn't continue. Sobs swept over her again and she had no choice but to give in to them. Jeffrey watched her and the dismay on his face became misery.

"Please," she said, wiping her eyes again. "Please forgive me. But I found out this morning as I got on the plane that my grandfather has been kidnapped and is being held at gunpoint until I return ... with information from you."

The misery on his face changed to shock. "From me? I haven't seen him for close to seventy years. How on earth can I help?"

"The man who kidnapped him said something about a key and a lockbox," Mattie said in a rush, hoping to get everything out before she cried again. "Please tell me you know what that means."

He sat back in his chair. Something had changed.

"The key," he said softly. His head fell to his hand, and he sat still for a minute. Hope flared again in Mattie's heart. She waited.

He raised his eyes and looked into hers. "Yes," he said. "I believe I know what key he refers to."

Mattie sucked in her breath and reached for his hand. "Please," she said. Even to her ears, her voice sounded strangled. "Please tell me. The man who has him is really bad. He's already put my father and grandmother in the hospital and I totally believe he will hurt Gramps, too. I have to give him what he wants. Please."

Jeffrey's face held a look of pain. But he squeezed Mattie's hand. "Of course I will. I don't want anything to happen to Mikey either."

"Oh, my goodness, oh my goodness," Mattie said. "I can't thank you enough." She sniffled, blew her nose again and fumbled with her phone. "May I record you?" she asked. "This is too important, and I don't want to forget anything."

He nodded and leaned back in his chair again. "I received the key the man is referring to from my father on my eighth birthday. He had just returned from a business trip and brought me a present—art supplies—including a box with forty-eight crayons in it. I had never seen so many in one place before." His voice shook slightly, but he composed himself and continued. "After I opened my present, my father stood to leave—to take a nap in the bedroom next to mine. He did that sometimes. But before he left my room, he placed a small gold key in the drawer of my drawing table and told me to keep it our secret. And he also said that if anything ..." His voice broke slightly and he stopped speaking again. "That if anything happened to him," he continued, "I was not to tell anyone about it until I saw my Great Uncle Arnold." His eyes grew wide and bore into hers. "And I didn't. How could anyone else know about it?"

"I don't know," Mattie said. "But I can tell you this much, the man who kidnapped my grandfather was hired by a company with ties to Russia and someone from that organization told him about it."

"Yes," he said. "That does make sense."

Mattie's eyes widened.

"I had lived with my Uncle Arnold for many years before it came up. I guess I had blocked as much of that day from my memory as I could. You see, right after my father put that key in my drawing table drawer, he was killed. Within minutes. I was so traumatized I didn't speak for almost three years. When my uncle asked me about it, I had trouble remembering at first. But it came back to me, and I told him where the key was. And then he told me what it unlocked."

"What?" Mattie asked.

"A small lockbox."

"Why did the part about Russia make sense to you? How could anyone in Russia have known about a lockbox your father had?"

"My uncle explained that part, too. Apparently, he and my father traveled together that last day and visited a distant relative who gave my father the lockbox. My uncle found out later that their limousine driver was a Russian spy."

Shivers traveled the length of Mattie's spine. That was the second reference to Russia in connection with Clairmont Place in as many days.

"Between the two of us," Jeffrey Sinclair continued, "we decided to leave the contents of the lockbox untouched. So, as far as I know, the key is still where I hid it and the lockbox still where my father put it seventy years ago."

"What is it?" she asked, scarcely daring to breathe. "Can you tell me what's in it?"

"War bonds," he said, "most from World War I. Some from World War II. Easily worth tens of millions of dollars after all this time."

She sucked in her breath. No wonder David was willing to go to such lengths to get what he wanted. He told Simone "big money" was involved. Apparently, he wasn't kidding.

"I read recently," he continued, "there are billions of dollars' worth of unclaimed war bonds the government doesn't know what to do with—or how to find. The ones in that lockbox are a part of that number."

"So," Mattie began tentatively, "will you tell me where you hid the key? Believe me, Mr. Sinclair, I understand that if I tell my grandfather's kidnapper where it is, he will hand it over to his employers with Russian ties and they will take everything from that lockbox that belongs to you. But I have to save my grandfather. Will you please tell me where you hid it?"

"I will certainly tell you where the key is," he said. "I don't care about the bonds. If I did, I would have done something about them years ago. But I do remember caring a great deal about your grandfather. For Mikey." He took a long sip of his tea. "It's still at the house—the one where my father was killed. It's in my bedroom."

Again, shivers rippled down Mattie's spine.

"You don't think your stepmother might have found it and removed

238

it?" she asked. "Like before she moved to Greece?"

"No, I don't," he said. "My father was killed before he had time to talk with anyone else about it. So yes, I believe it's still there. But I must also tell you," Jeffrey continued, "that neither my uncle nor I ever knew where my father hid the lockbox. I believe it's in the house, but I don't know where."

The grip on Mattie's heart relaxed. All David asked for was the key, so she had what she needed to save her grandfather.

She continued to talk with Jeffrey, and he agreed to sign the letter for the summit. He also liked the idea of the property becoming part of the National Register of Historic Places.

"We have a really fine resource who has experience with adding properties to the register," she said. "His name is Bill Carson. You might remember him. His mother was Cook Carson at Clairmont Place. She worked there until the house was closed."

"I remember him," Jeffrey Sinclair said. "I remember thinking of him as 'Little Billy.'"

"He would love to see you again. I don't know if you noticed," Mattie said, "but an invitation to attend the opening ceremonies was with the letter I gave you. Is there any chance you might come?"

"It's funny," he said quietly. "Yesterday I would have declined. But today, your timing is perfect. North Carolina has been on my mind all day, and I realized I'd actually like to see it again." He took another long sip of tea. "You see, Bailey told me this morning he's planning to retire. Honestly, I don't relish the thought of facing another winter here, especially without my trusted Bailey by my side. Yes, it might be time."

"I know my grandfather would love that," Mattie said. "And the whole town would welcome you back with open arms."

"I believe I would like to see the place again," he said, "although I'm not sure I would want to live there. I'll sleep on it and see what I come up with."

Mattie fought her tears again, but knew they were tears of relief, of joy. The time she had left to save her grandfather was tight and she still had to convince David to keep his part of the bargain, but she was confident she could do that. And with his signature, Jeffrey Sinclair had removed the final hurdle that had worried her father as well. The fact that Jeffrey might return to the town that bore his name was simply icing on the cake.

She thanked him again and promised to call him when she returned, and her grandfather was safe. She climbed into her little car, but before she started the motor, she texted her grandfather's phone.

I have what you asked for and will be at Clairmont Place by nine o'clock. Once you prove to me that my grandfather is unharmed, I will give it to you.

Chapter Fifty-Five

Sinclair Station, North Carolina

The first step of David's plan was complete. It had worked perfectly. Michael Maguire remained hidden at the garden shed, bound and gagged, and Mattie Maguire was in Maine to find the key he needed. His job was almost finished.

He muted the sound on Michael Maguire's cell phone and stuffed it in his pocket, then left the garden shed and replaced the lock on the door. Stealthily, he surveyed the area and then drove Adelaide Maguire's car the short distance to The Cottage, where Michael lived. One of the keys on her ring unlocked the back door, so he went in and left the car keys on the kitchen table. He wanted it to look like Michael had come back home, put the keys down and simply vanished. But he kept Michael's cell phone with him.

He left the house and went deep into the woods, using the same route as earlier, sticking to thick tree growth until he came to the road, and then keeping to the shadows. He paid attention to his route since he knew he would have to come back and check on his captive periodically throughout the day. He was old, after all, and if he died before Mattie returned, David's bargaining power evaporated into thin air.

After taking Michael Maguire to the garden shed, David returned to Sally's place before she woke and surprised her with breakfast when she emerged from the shower. Her shift at the diner was a long one that day and he wanted to send her off happy. He needed to keep his options open. She had invited him to stay the night again, and he readily accepted.

As she dressed to leave, she asked him about his day—where he planned to go and what he planned to do. To his ears, it sounded like she tried to pin him down.

He hated that in women. How many times had he seen it? How many women had he been with who tried to turn a one-night stand into a one-woman commitment?

But he needed her, or at least her apartment, for a little while longer. So he evaded her questions with sweet talk and little kisses all over her neck until she stopped asking. If the rest of his day went as well as the first part had, he might be out of town on the last bus anyway. And he definitely wouldn't be staying there after tonight, no matter what happened.

He kissed her long and hard before she left for work and then busied himself with preparations for his day. He checked on Michael and gave him water. He was holding up just fine.

Then he returned to Sally's apartment and checked his gun and ammunition, rummaged around in Sally's pantry for a flashlight and found a can of black spray paint that he took as well. He had time to spare, so he searched what he believed to be the usual hiding places for cash.

No luck. Then he searched the unusual places and bingo, he hit the jackpot. Inside the largest teapot of her miniature collection were five one-hundred-dollar bills. He took them all. He hadn't spent any of the money from Matt Maguire, even though he'd been assured the bills were not marked. He'd decided to wait until he left town to test the bank president's honesty.

With everything ready, he took a nap. He figured it would be a long night.

At the edge of dusk, he awoke and made himself a sandwich, added some chips from Sally's pantry and a beer from her fridge. He didn't bother to clean up.

He found a canvas shopping bag and threw some granola bars and bottles of water in it, then added the flashlight and the can of black paint. The cash, his lock-picking tools, the remaining plastic cable ties and Michael's cell phone filled his jacket pockets.

It was time. Dusk had withered into darkness, so he left by Sally's back door.

Only a couple of miles separated David from his access to more than a million dollars. He stuck to back roads and woods as much as possible and stayed away from streetlights the rest of the time until he reached Clairmont Place.

CHAPTER FIFTY-SIX

The large, foreign-looking man had received little information from his contact in Greece about where to find his target who had, infuriatingly, escaped him twice. But the results of an intercepted phone call rewarded him with a lead to this old house at this time of night. So, at the exact moment the last ray of daylight yielded to darkness, the large man appeared at the edge of Clairmont Place.

He stuck to shadows on his way around the mansion and waited until the guard left the mouth of a shrubbery-lined walkway and headed to the other side of the house. The large man entered the path and saw that his pinpoint light illuminated a motion-activated bulb above the doorway.

He reached it quickly and the light clicked on. In the soft glow, he shoved his gloved fist through the bottom windowpane and brought it out again, cascading glass shards to both sides of the door. Without hesitation, he reached through the empty frame and unlocked the door, then hurried inside.

He was confident he could wrap his business up quickly, and finally. Fatally.

He covered the distance on the ground floor to a large, open area, and climbed a set of steps that abutted round stone walls to the floor above. At that point, he decided to simply explore. And listen.

He turned left around a huge marble staircase and roamed the length of that hallway, ducking into the last room on the right, which appeared to be a library.

He settled into the shadows and waited.

When she left the rambling Tudor house in Maine, Mattie looked quickly at the text messages she'd received. Communications from her family when they realized her grandfather was missing. She'd ignored them while she was with Jeffrey Sinclair.

Since she couldn't tell them what she knew, she didn't answer then, either.

She had to lie to them. There was no other choice. She couldn't risk her grandfather's life by letting them know what had really happened. After she met David and got her grandfather back, she could tell them everything.

High winds over the East Coast delayed her flight. Every second lost added to her fear for her grandfather's safety.

Once she landed, she decided to take a taxi back to Sinclair Station rather than wait for an Uber ride. Even then, time would be tight. She figured as long as she made it to the property on time, she could convince David to let her grandfather go.

As soon as the cab's wheels crunched gravel by the East Portico, Mattie threw bills at the driver, grabbed her overnight bag, purse, and portfolio and hopped out. She headed into the thick shrubbery that lined the path and realized, too late, that it hadn't been a great idea to come to the house alone after dark. Especially for someone scared of her own shadow.

But she'd had no choice. She had to save her gramps.

Noises assaulted her along the path. Cautiously, she turned to look over her shoulder, but saw only darkness.

"Hello?" she called out. Nothing.

She continued to walk toward the door and at the same time the motion light clicked on, her shoes crunched on the walk. She looked down. Glass shards. From the shattered windowpane.

Oh, that's how David got in.

Hair on the back of her neck rose and fear filled her chest, constricting her throat. But she reached out for the doorknob and turned it. The door swung open.

She was out of options. She had to see this through. She had to save her grandfather.

She knew the electricity in this part of the house had never been upgraded, so when the old-fashioned fuses blew, they weren't replaced. Only the upper floors and motion detector lights had working electricity.

The motion light clicked off behind her and she punched up her cell phone's flashlight.

She crept down the long hallway, shaking with fear, then climbed the receiving room stairs and trained her beam around the huge entrance hall that rose two stories above her. She tilted her phone up and a million droplets of light danced around the room, reflected from the crystal chandelier centered over the stairs.

She headed to Henry's office where she knew the lights worked.

CHAPTER FIFTY-SEVEN

"**S**o the vote on the senator's bill takes place tomorrow afternoon and we really think it will pass with flying colors. Probably first vote." Tony Adkins picked up his wine glass and drained it, then signaled the waitress.

Simone stared off into the distance, her hair wound around her index finger.

"Simone?" Tony touched her shoulder. "I guess I've been talking too much. I seem to have lost you."

"Lost me?" Simone asked.

"What can I get you, hon?" the waitress asked.

Simone gave her a small smile, but Sally's answering smile was huge. Very friendly ... almost overly friendly.

Sally left and Tony looked deeply into Simone's eyes. "I was telling you about how well the legislation is proceeding through the process. But there appeared to be something far more interesting outside. Is everything okay?"

"Oh, Tony. I'm really sorry. And ... angry."

"Angry? Because—"

"Of my brother."

"David? That's his name, right?"

"Yes. I have no idea of your impression of him, but he is ... he's ... Let's just say that he and I have always had our issues. I tried to get him to leave town, but he wouldn't. Instead, he hurt some friends of mine and I can't seem to get past the guilt. And now ... oh, Tony, you have no idea how much I have looked forward to spending more time with you. And here I am—actually doing it. But I'm still so worried about where my brother is and what he might do next that I can't even let myself relax and enjoy your company."

"So why are you angry?"

"Because every time he insinuates himself back into my life, he causes nothing but trouble. And my distraction over his next move might have ruined what could have been a good friendship between us."

"I like you, Simone," Tony said, his hand finding hers. "And I'm already enjoying your company. So please don't worry about that. Is there anything I can do to make you feel better?"

Simone smiled. "Maybe be patient until I can figure out what to do about David. He's totally unpredictable these days and I don't want to put you in danger, too."

They left the diner and Tony hugged her at the door.

She pulled out of the parking lot and drove in the direction of her apartment, cleaned and put back together after David's rampage. But the need to see Mattie's family—especially her grandmother—grew within her until it became an unshakeable urge. She had to see for herself if Miss Marilyn was okay.

She knew it was late, but she turned her car around, dashed into the grocery store for fresh flowers, and headed toward Clairmont Place.

CHAPTER FIFTY-EIGHT

David reached the edge of Clairmont Place by a different route from his previous visits and slipped around the stone fence onto the property. He stuck to the shadows, planning to make it all the way to the eastern entrance without setting off any motion lights other than that one.

He bolted from the cover of trees toward the flagstone walk when headlights swept the parking lot and shone directly on him. There was no hiding from them. He'd been seen. The car's engine stopped, and a door slammed.

"David. I can't believe you're here after what you've done to Mattie's family."

A huge smile spread across his face.

"Well, well, well … if it isn't my sweet little, double-crossing sister. I certainly didn't expect to see you here." He patted his pocket. His gun was there. Ready. Handy.

"I'm here to check on Mattie's grandmother after you beat her up."

"I didn't beat *her* up. Only Mattie's dad." He smiled again. "And look at that … you've brought flowers. How nice."

"David, please leave. Please. You've got your gun now. That should make you happy. If you will leave town, I promise I won't let anyone know where to find you."

"Oh, that won't be a problem, sis." He pulled the gun from his pocket and trained it on her. "Now that you've seen me, you're coming with me."

"David. What the hell are you thinking? Put that thing down."

"No," he said calmly. He motioned with his gun. "Come on over here beside me. We're taking a little walk. Haven't you always wanted to see

248

the inside of that big house?"

She didn't move. "Trust me, Simone, if I have to come over there to get you, you won't like it. You've messed with me enough since I've been here."

"I've messed with—are you nuts? You're the one who's been screwing up every—I can't believe you would say such a thing."

"Look," he said. "I'm not going to argue with you. And it doesn't matter now anyway. I will leave town as soon as this job is done. You can make it go faster or you can keep slowing me down like you're doing right now." He cocked his gun and held it higher, aimed at her head. "Now if you don't want to get shot," he said between clenched teeth, "get over here *now*."

She moved to his side and he grabbed her roughly by the arm. Her flowers fell to the flagstones. He propelled her toward the door, one hand firmly on her wrist, the other locked on his gun.

"You're hurting me," Simone said. She pulled away but David didn't let her go.

"Shut up!" He jerked her around in front of him and put the gun right up to her nose. "You have to keep quiet. Look, I wish it didn't have to be like this, but you brought it on yourself. So shut up and stop pulling away, and this can go quickly." He flung her back to his side and strode toward the doorway.

They got close. The motion light had already been activated and illuminated the whole path. He dropped to the ground and pulled her down beside him. "We'll wait here until that goes off."

"It was you, wasn't it, David?" Simone whispered in the dark. "The one who messed with the door here and attacked the guard?"

"Partly," he said. "I did try this door that night. And I heard somebody yell so I took off. I don't know what happened after that."

"But ..."

He brought his nose even with hers. "I told you to shut up."

"You're sick, David." Simone sniffled. "And a lot more dangerous than I ever knew you could be."

"Maybe you should try not to forget that."

The motion light over the door blinked off. David pulled the can of paint from his bag.

"Okay, we're going to run up to the door and you're going to stand perfectly still while I spray the light. We don't want an animal to come by and trigger it while we're finishing our business." He put his face right up to hers and nestled the gun under her chin. "And I am dead serious about that, Simone. You will not make noise. You will not pull away. And you will not run away. This is my last warning. I will not let you ruin this for me. Sister or not, neither will I hesitate to pull this trigger and blow you all to hell."

David pulled her to the door and spray painted the light that clicked on. He reached for the doorknob, then crunched on the shattered glass. "Your friend's more resourceful than I gave her credit for."

Simone remained silent.

David entered the mansion and dragged her along with him.

He stood for a moment to orient himself. He hadn't arranged for a specific meeting place but decided to head for the middle of the house and figure out the rest as he went along.

"This way," he said. He turned to the right and yanked Simone's arm.

"Ow. I'm not going to run. You can ease up a little."

He kept walking, shining Sally's flashlight into several rooms. He stopped for a minute and then continued down the corridor, shoving Simone ahead of him.

She stumbled and fell to her knees, knocking him off balance. His arm flailed to catch himself and his finger tightened on the trigger. The sound echoed down the hall and the bullet ricocheted, then splintered a door to his left.

Simone wrenched her arm away from him and rubbed her wrist.

"I hope you're happy," she hissed. "We could have been killed."

He grabbed her arm again and pulled her face close to his. "Shut your stupid mouth. And stop being so clumsy."

He jerked her to her feet and dragged her.

"David, please, you're hurting—"

In an instant his gun found her chin again and his nose almost touched hers. "Not. Another. Word." She nodded and meekly followed him.

He pulled her down the hallway, twisting and turning until they entered a huge open space with stairs hugging the walls on either side. She focused on not losing her footing again as he hauled her over the rough floor. He stopped in the middle of the room, then turned left. Simone followed him quickly, up the stairs, across a landing, and up more steps. His gun clinked against the stone walls.

They reached the top and he led the way past a curved marble staircase and then charged down the hallway. He turned right and faced a blank wall. He swiveled and randomly opened doors. Then closed them again. "Damn it. Stay close."

He headed in the other direction but stopped abruptly. "So, that's where she is."

CHAPTER FIFTY-NINE

David stopped so suddenly, Simone bumped into him. She peeked around him to see a set of open doors halfway down the corridor. Weak light spilled into the hallway.

David turned to her and whispered, "I'm about to finish this deal. You will keep quiet and you will not interfere. If you try anything—and I mean that … *anything*—I will kill you."

She nodded vigorously. He motioned with his gun to let her know they would be moving toward the door.

He hunched down and crept along the wall, edging closer to the lighted door.

Only inches away, he sucked in his breath.

Slowly he stood straight and released her wrist. She straightened, too, and moved beside him. David put his arm out in front of her and pushed her slightly behind him.

The dark shape of a large man loomed in their path, the barrel of the gun he pointed at them, clearly visible in the beam from Sally's flashlight.

Mattie stood perfectly still and listened as noises reached her from other parts of the huge house—a loud pop and what could have been soft voices echoing in the large receiving room, along with soft little tinkles, as if metal hit stone.

But she wasn't sure. Hair on the back of her neck rose again.

She figured David was in the house, and she was surprised she hadn't seen him yet. But she still hadn't retrieved the key.

She left the desk and went to the doors but stopped short of peering out into the hallway. She decided to wait until he called out to her.

Sudden fear overtook her, and she flattened herself against the wall with the open door covering her. Too late, she saw that her phone lay on the massive desk—the flashlight still beaming full force. She poked one foot out to dash across the room when she heard a gasp right outside the door. A beam of light in the hallway was visible from the crack between her open door and the wall. A voice followed.

"Who are you and what do you want?"

The voice was David's. *Okay ... good.* They could get this over with.

Much of her fear left her. She knew he was dangerous, but she would let him know what she'd learned, and they could find the key in Jeffrey's room together. And with her beside him, she believed she could keep his rage in check so nothing in the mansion got stolen or broken, the way it had in Simone's apartment. She actually felt relief. She could get him what he wanted and get her grandfather back. Again, she poked one foot out to go talk to him.

Until she realized he had spoken to someone else. Not her.

"Drop your gun." It was a raspy voice.

"Not until you tell me what the hell you're doing here."

"Look, buddy, I could ask you the same thing. Besides, I don't owe you no explanations. I'm here to do a job and you're in my way. You and your little lady friend there."

Little lady friend? Who is he talking about? And what is it about that voice? A slight accent, but, oh my goodness, it grates on my senses.

"No, you look, *buddy.* I've got my own thing going on here and I don't give a damn what you're up to. Just leave me alone. Let me get back to my business and you carry on with yours."

"This is your last chance. Drop your gun. And hey, I might as well make a little bonus while I'm here. Give me your wallet."

Mattie's head swam. Her vision dimmed and then blackened, sending her to the edge of oblivion. That last sentence clicked everything into place.

The raspy voice. She had no idea how it could have happened after all this time, but Paul's killer stood right outside her door. She had always known she would never forget his voice. And she had been right.

"I'm not giving you any damn thing," David said.

A shot fired. And then another. Followed by a scream.

Mattie gulped in deep breaths. She fought to keep from fainting. Her heart hammered so hard she was certain they could hear it outside the door. Her legs failed her, and she sank to the floor. Her head fell to her hands.

"Okay, little lady," the voice said. "You throw me his wallet."

"I ... I don't know where he keeps it."

"Well, look. And hurry up!"

Simone. Crying.

Mattie opened her eyes. Through the crack, she saw David lying face down on the floor, blood spurting from his temple and forming a large pool beneath him.

The sight triggered a full-scale flashback to the night Paul died.

In an instant, the room spun, and a giant hand squeezed her heart, robbed her breath. Her stomach churned and kaleidoscopic images twirled the room around her as time and time again, that raspy voice demanded Paul's wallet and keys. Countless times she heard the blast of his gun and witnessed her beloved husband lying on the concrete in a pool of his own blood. And each time the scene ended with a sheet over his face. His beautiful face ...

She hugged herself around the middle and rocked back and forth while tremors shook her body. Fear overpowered everything else and she went rigid.

Time froze. And still she sat.

For hours. Or maybe seconds. She had no way of knowing.

Roaring filled her ears until gradually more sounds penetrated.

Another shot. Another scream.

And then sobbing.

Simone. Sobbing.

"You shot me! Why? I'm trying to find it ... please, please—"

"You're taking too long. Hurry it up."

Simone sobbed again.

Her friend was in danger.

On the other side of the wall that protected Mattie.

Simone could be killed.

Just like David.

Just like Paul.

Mattie's fear left her. As quickly as it had consumed her.

She opened her eyes and saw David's gun. If she left the cover of her door, she could reach it. She could help Simone.

She moved slightly. But the fear returned and constricted her. More intensely than before.

I've never had to use a gun in a life or death situation before. I only shot at paper targets. They couldn't shoot back. What if I hesitate and he shoots me instead?

But he's already shot Simone, she argued with herself. *Are you really going to sit right here and let him kill her?*

What do you think Paul would have done? What do you think Simone would do if the situation were reversed?

Fear never left her, but Mattie forced herself to ease quietly from behind the door, careful to keep it from moving. She wasn't sure where the killer was, but she didn't want to warn him.

Simone sobbed again. Then she spoke. "Here. Here it is," she said.

The last thing Mattie saw before she fully left the cover of the door was Simone holding her hand up. To the killer.

Which showed Mattie exactly where he was.

She lunged for the gun and, remembering a move from her advanced training, flipped to her back, pointed it up, and aimed at the vague dark outline in front of her. All in one fluid motion. Without giving herself time to think, she squeezed the trigger.

A blast filled her ears and blood splattered on her pants. The dark shape fell to the floor.

Simone screamed again.

And Mattie screamed with her, then scrambled to her feet and ran out into the hallway. She stood over the body.

The bullet had pierced his jaw. His open eyes stared at her. Light brown but bordering on gold—feral—animal-like in the low light.

She nudged his head with her toe and his face contorted with pain.

"You," she spat out. All of the hate she had ever felt for him spilled out in that one word. "I'm glad you're still alive."

He tried to speak but the only sound Mattie heard was a gurgle.

"You killed my husband in a parking garage in Baltimore. Six years ago." The top part of his face registered confusion and then swiftly changed to recognition. Followed by indifference. "I swore," Mattie said, "if I ever saw you again, I would bring you to justice."

"Mattie, watch out! He's reaching for his gun!"

Mattie raised the pistol again. Thoughts swirled in her brain as time stood still. *No, I've never had to use a gun in a life and death situation before. But if he reaches his gun, he will have no qualms about killing me. The same way he did Paul.*

A sense of calm engulfed her.

She held the gun steady and pulled the trigger one more time.

Shock registered in his eyes.

For a split second.

And then faded to emptiness as blood gushed from the hole between them.

CHAPTER SIXTY

Simone threw herself into Mattie's arms, shaking so violently, Mattie worried she had gone into shock.

She placed a call to nine-one-one first and to her father second.

Within minutes, Mattie heard shouting and footsteps. She propped Simone up against the wall and went to the top of the stairs. Her father bounded up the steps and took her in his arms, holding her close for several minutes. Bryan Bennett appeared only a step behind him.

Mattie's father released her to hug Simone, stepping over the dead bodies to reach her. Bryan hugged Mattie.

"She saved my life," Simone managed to tell them between bursts of tears. "If Mattie hadn't shot that man, he would have killed me. I know he would have."

"She's right, Dad," Mattie said. "I don't know what the heck he's doing here, but I'll bet it has something to do with Robert." Her voice trembled. "He would have killed both of us."

"My goodness," Matt Maguire said. "What a day. I'm so glad you're all right, little one," he added. "But we still have to find—"

"Gramps. I know." Mattie broke down. "Dad, David kidnapped him this morning as he left Nana's hospital room."

"What? How did you know that?"

"He made Gramps call me when I was at the airport. He told me I had to find out about a key here in the house that unlocked some kind of lockbox. And once I gave it to him, he'd release Gramps. And that he'd hurt the rest of you if I told you about it or went to the police. But I assume you called Bryan, right?"

"They did," Bryan said. "We searched your grandparents' house but didn't find anything. Your mother's car was there and the keys were on the kitchen table. But nothing appeared to be out of place."

"Your grandmother is sick with worry," Mattie's father said. "They even kept her in the hospital instead of letting her come home. Honey, do you have any idea where David might have taken him?"

"No." Her tears began again, and a small sob followed. "And now he can't tell us." She shook in her father's arms before pulling back to look at him. "But we have to do something. I was able to say a few words to him this morning and he sounded awful then. I can't imagine how he must feel by now."

"We called his cell phone all day, but of course he never answered. And we talked to every business in town to see if anyone had seen him. But nobody had."

Paramedics arrived next. Simone's wound wasn't serious, but she had lost a lot of blood where the bullet penetrated her upper right arm. And Mattie had guessed correctly … she teetered on the edge of shock. A medic quickly applied a tourniquet and gave her a sedative, then helped her to a stretcher. The ambulance took her directly to the hospital.

The other paramedics lugged in large spotlights. Bryan took pictures of the crime scene and then the paramedics strapped the other shooter to a gurney first, noting he'd been hit in his left shoulder in addition to the shots Mattie fired. Bryan left with them to help navigate the stairs and Matt went outside to call his wife.

David lay on the floor, his bloody wallet inches from his fingers.

Mattie made a quick decision and bent down beside him. She figured it was tampering with evidence, but she fished a tissue out of the pack the flight attendant had given her earlier and searched his pockets. She had to. She needed to see for herself, right away, if there was something—anything—that might be a clue as to where David had hidden her grandfather.

She searched his pants first and found five crisp hundred-dollar bills. The jacket pockets yielded some small metal rods, a few plastic cable ties, a granola bar, and her grandfather's cell phone.

Bryan and the paramedics returned with the gurney for David.

Mattie stood aside. The paramedics smoothed David's jacket, bunched around his waist where she had left it after searching his pockets. They turned him over and lifted him onto the stretcher. Mattie saw a long white smudge that slashed across the seat of his pants and continued around almost to his thigh. As if he had backed into some kind of powder.

They took David away and Mattie tried to imagine what had happened to send him down the path he'd taken. Her heart filled with utter sadness that Simone had just lost her last relative. Regardless of how they got along.

Mattie and her father followed Bryan and the paramedics with David's body. They retraced the steps she had taken earlier and left through the East Portico where a canvas shopping bag leaned against the wall. They cleared the shrubbery and Mattie noticed fresh flowers strewn haphazardly on the cobblestones. She wondered idly how they got there.

She tugged on her father's sleeve. "Dad," she said softly when he turned to her, "I found Gramps's phone. In David's jacket pocket. Maybe I shouldn't have searched him, but finding Gramps is the most important thing." She stopped talking as tears threatened again. "I found these things, too." She held up the metal rods and plastic cable ties, still wrapped in a tissue. "I'm betting David used these plastic things to tie him up." Her tears spilled over and streaked down her cheeks.

"Where'd you get lock-picking tools?" Bryan asked. She jumped.

"Oh. You startled me." She turned a sheepish expression to him. "From David's pockets," she admitted. "You need to understand how important this is, Bryan. I *have* to find my gramps."

"I do understand," he said. "But we still need to follow protocol, Mattie. Regardless of how much I'd like to go tearing off to look for him, we have to be methodical. Since that stuff is already out of his pockets, how about dropping them in this bag for me?" Everything she held plopped into the paper bag—including her tissue. "Thanks. Once we get to the station, we'll enter all of this into evidence."

"So, little one, since you were the last one to talk to him," Mattie's father said, "do you have any idea where to start looking? Was there anything about your grandfather's voice on the phone to give you a clue? Or something David said?"

"No." She frowned. "Wait a minute. There were a couple of seconds when the phone changed hands that I remember hearing birds chirping. I didn't think about it at the time because I was so scared."

"So you think maybe they were outside?"

"No. Not really." She closed her eyes and tried to remember. "No," she said again, "because I also remember thinking their voices sounded kind of flat, hollow, as if they were in a small space."

"Okay," Bryan said, "let's start with David's room at the inn. We'll search it and go from there."

Mattie's eyes filled again. "We have to find him," she said. "He's been tied up all day. Probably hasn't eaten or anything."

The three of them climbed into Bryan's patrol car. "Let's take it one step at a time. Try to remember anything at all you think might help."

They talked to the owners of the inn who ushered them into David's room. A few clothes hung in the small closet, shaving supplies littered the bathroom counter, and the top of the dresser held the stub of a bus ticket and business card for "Universal Security and Surveillance."

"Not much to go on," Mattie said.

"Here's something," Bryan said. He reached under the bed and pulled out a small suitcase. "Look at this, Mr. Maguire," he said when he opened it. The case contained stacks of money, secured with bands that proclaimed Sinclair Bank & Trust. "We'll have to take this to the station first, but we'll make sure you get it all back."

They continued to search the room, picking up items and putting them down again. Bryan straightened the base of the bedside lamp and Mattie heard a small clink. Something bounced to the floor and she picked it up—a tiny round metal object with miniature components soldered onto it.

"What is this?" Mattie asked.

Bryan took it from her and studied it. "A microphone," he answered. "Better known as a bug."

"That might explain how the shooter knew where to be," Matt said.

Mattie replayed the conversation with her grandfather and David in her head. Again and again. To remember anything that might hold a clue.

"Hey," Bryan said to her after a minute. "Have I lost you?"

"I was trying to remember … anything."

"We've done all we can do here," he said. "Let's go over to the station, enter this stuff into evidence and come up with a plan. Did you have any dinner?"

She shook her head. "There wasn't time."

"You can get something from the vending machines. It's not great, but it'll be better than starving."

"Like my poor gramps probably is," she said, new tears falling. Matt patted her shoulder as they all climbed back into the police car and drove to the station.

Almost two hours passed while Bryan did his best to get police protocol back on track. As one of the shooters, Mattie also had to answer questions from the coroner and then give her statement to Bryan. Her father made phone calls, exhausting every possibility for a hiding place they could think of.

"Oh, good grief!" Mattie said after a while. "I can't stand this. How much longer will this busywork take? My grandfather's life is on the line. Are we really going to just sit here and keep—" She stopped talking abruptly and her eyes widened.

"What?" her father said. "What did you think of?"

"That we missed something … something big."

"What?"

"Bryan, didn't you say those metal rods in David's pocket were for picking locks? That's what we need to think about. Where would he go that had a lock? The door of the big house, maybe?" She stopped talking again. "I hadn't thought about that before because one of the windows in the door was broken when I got there, and the door was unlocked. I simply figured David had done it. But it could have been the other shooter. Even so," she continued, "the door would still have been locked when he hid Gramps this morning. Bryan, Gramps could be tied up in the mansion somewhere."

"I'd be surprised," Bryan said. "Although I did pull the guards off the grounds mid-morning to help search for your grandfather. What time did he call you?"

"Before six. Were your guards there then?"

"They were supposed to be. Hold on." He pulled out his phone and punched in a number. "Sam … Bennett. What time did you get to your post this morning? And did you go to The Cottage or the main house? We have reason to believe the kidnapper may have been on the property." He stopped talking. "Okay, did you see anything unusual? Anything at all?" He listened. "Really … what time was that?" Another pause while he listened. "Okay. I'm going back over there to check it out. How about grabbing Kenny and meet me there to help search?"

"What?" Mattie asked. "What did he say?" She scrambled up and grabbed her jacket.

"He said one of your family's cars came up the south drive and headed toward The Cottage. We already found that, of course, but—"

"That could have been where David stopped him. And they could have doubled back through the trees to the mansion," she said. "Oh, thank goodness we're finally doing something."

Mattie and her father followed Bryan out to his car. They reached the house and he removed a heavy-duty battery light from his trunk. They searched the first floor, room by room, calling her grandfather's name and listening for sounds that might indicate he was there.

Within minutes, two more policemen showed up and searched the other side of the house. They met in the flagstone area and climbed the stairs. At the two-story foyer, they split up again, with Mattie and Bryan taking the side of the house where the men were killed and her father searching the other side with the deputies. On Mattie's side of the house, she and Bryan moved drapes, shoved furniture, searched closets, and called Michael Maguire's name.

They found no sign of him.

They stood in the hall outside Henry Sinclair's office and Bryan shone his light across the area. Large splotches of blood stained the patterned carpet.

"What is that smell?" Mattie asked.

"Human blood," Bryan said. "Not very pleasant, is it?"

"No, it isn't. But I'm getting a whiff of something else. Something I haven't smelled in years. I wish I could remember what—wait a minute." She bent down. "Shine your light down here again," she said. She took his hand and guided the light to the right of the large patch of blood. "Here. Look."

The light picked up a small patch of white powder with several tiny aqua-colored beads in it. "That's it," she said. "That's what I smelled. Fertilizer." She stood. "And I remember seeing a white smudge on David's pants." She stood perfectly still while memories crashed through her head. "When I was little," she said softly, sorting through the sights and sounds in her brain, "I used to tag along with Gramps, and I remember how loud the birds were in the formal gardens. Even inside the garden shed—just off the lane to The Cottage." She started running, hollering over her shoulder, "That's where they keep the fertilizer. And that shed is always locked. That's where he is! I know it."

Bryan ran down the hall behind her, calling to his deputies and Mattie's father to join them. She burst through the East Portico door and ran past the shrubs along the path that bordered it, all the way to the cobblestone drive where the first rays of sun peeked through layers of pink and purple streaks. She didn't stop running until she saw the shed.

The door was closed, its lock secure.

"Gramps! Gramps," Mattie called. She banged on the door. "Gramps," she called again. "We're here. Please be in there. Please be alive ..." Her voice trailed off and she turned miserable eyes to Bryan. "I know the door is locked," she said, "but we have to check. Use the lock-picking tools. We have to get in there. Please."

"They're at the station," Bryan said. "In the evidence bin."

"Do something." The words emerged as a shriek. She shook his shoulders.

Bryan jabbed the lock with his heavy light. It didn't budge. One of the deputies aimed his gun at the lock, intent on shooting it off the door.

"No," Mattie screamed. "If Gramps is in there, you might hit him instead."

Bryan raised his battery light over his head and brought it down on the lock with all his force. It fell to the ground.

Mattie yanked the door and Bryan pushed it out of the way. They rushed in and within seconds, Mattie was on her knees, hugging her grandfather and shaking him awake. Her father was right beside her.

She pulled the gag from his mouth and Bryan cut the plastic ties that held his arms and legs. "Get an ambulance," he shouted.

"Oh, Gramps, you're all right. You're not dead." She kissed him everywhere she could reach. He leaned into her to hug her, but his arms fell back, weak and bruised. Blood oozed from cuts on the backs of both wrists and his lips were cracked and dry.

"Mr. Maguire," Bryan said, "do you think you can stand? We have an ambulance on the way, and we'll have you checked out at the hospital."

"Marilyn," he croaked. "How..."

"She's fine, Dad," Matt Maguire said. "Or at least she will be when she finds out you're all right. When you didn't come back, they kept her at the hospital one more day. You can see her yourself once you get there."

The ambulance arrived, and Mattie called her mother. "We got him, Mom," she said, "and he's okay. Let Nana know he'll be coming to the hospital right away. Bryan figures he's dehydrated, and he has cuts on the back of his wrists where the binding was. But," her voice broke with her tears, "he's alive."

CHAPTER SIXTY-ONE

"At least we don't have to worry about him getting in our way anymore," TheO said. "That El Gringo guy was a loose cannon. He could have ruined everything."

"You're sure he's dead?" The Vysakom asked.

"I'm sure."

"Level with me," The Vysokom said. "Did you hire that other shooter?"

"No," TheO said. "But he sure made it easy for us."

"Have you learned anything about him—the other shooter? Like where he came from or why he was there? Or who his target really was?"

"Bits and pieces," TheO said. "Apparently hired in Greece by the guy who pretended to be a Sinclair. And the targets were the Maguires—the groundskeeper for the property and his granddaughter. They were the only ones who knew the guy in Greece was an imposter, so he wanted to eliminate them and continue to leech money from Clairmont Place."

"Will somebody else be showing up to take his place?"

"I don't know," TheO said. "But our main worry now should be whether somebody else shows up to take the El Gringo guy's place. You think that will happen?"

"No. Now that El Gringo is dead, Hektor will be in trouble with the homeland for losing a resource. I've offered to take over whatever Hektor's mission was. It would make us look good in Moscow. Plus, we'll have time before the first international meeting, so we might as well use our connections to our advantage. You have any idea what he was looking for?"

"Again, bits and pieces," TheO said. "Something about a key. But that's all I know. I'll keep nosing around."

"Good man," The Vysokom said. "And you never know. Whatever Hektor's group was seeking could serve us well for the next couple of years during the preliminary summit meetings while we gain intelligence to send back to the homeland. By the time the actual summit is over, you and I should be able to write our tickets to any assignment in the world. Including Moscow, if that's what you want."

"I haven't thought that far ahead," TheO said.

"Maybe you should," The Vysokom responded. "You could go far, my friend, if you continue to prove yourself as well as you have to this point. I've written several good reports about you."

"Thanks," TheO said. "For now, I'm taking it day by day. We still have a lot of work to do, so I'll keep my head down and put one foot in front of the other until the time is right."

"You do that. Let's talk again when you have more information."

CHAPTER SIXTY-TWO

Michael Maguire's hospital room was full of people. Mattie had ridden with him in the ambulance. EMTs had administered fluids right away and bandaged his wrists. At the hospital, nurses brought him soft foods. All of which helped.

But when her parents entered the room, pushing Mattie's grandmother in a wheelchair, his face lit up. Tears streamed down her grandmother's face as she stood and kissed him—his forehead, his cheek, his lips, and back again. And she held tight to his hand, vowing to never let him out of her sight again.

Mattie's father left for a few minutes. When he returned, he said, "Good news, everybody. I've spoken with Dr. Harrington and both our patients will be released this afternoon." They all cheered.

"In that case," Mattie's mother said, "if it's okay with you, Marilyn, I'll go to The Cottage and prepare a big dinner to celebrate. You know I don't cook as well as you do, but I can promise you it will be festive."

"It will be wonderful, honey," Marilyn said. "Thank you. And, oh my goodness, it sure will be good to get home."

"Hey, I forgot," Mattie said. "In all the excitement of finding Gramps, I forgot to give you my news, too." She fished in her portfolio, brought out the signed permission letter, and handed it to her father. "I found him. Jeffrey Sinclair. He was living at his uncle's place in Maine. And Gramps, I didn't ask him all the questions, but trust me, I didn't need to. The first thing he said to me was, 'Did your grandfather tell you I used to call him Mikey?'"

Her grandfather smiled and nodded.

"He's the real deal, all right," Mattie continued. "He signed the letter and likes the thought of the property being put on the National Register of Historic Places, and," she said, pausing for dramatic effect, "he even thinks he'll come back to visit. His butler is retiring, and he doesn't want to face winter up there alone."

Her father enveloped her in a big bear hug. "You are really something, little one," he said. "You make me very proud. Thank you."

"Gee, Dad, thank *you*. And you're welcome. I'm so happy it worked out." She winked at her grandfather. "I'm happy *all* of it worked out."

Before she left the hospital, she went down the hall to Simone's room.

"Hey, kiddo," she said quietly. "How're you feeling?"

"Awful," Simone answered. "For the next fifteen minutes anyway, until they bring me another one of those magic pain pills." Simone's right arm hung in a sling and her left arm sported a tube with three different bags feeding into it.

"Simone, I hope you know how sorry I am about David."

"Mattie, considering what he put you and your family through, I'm really surprised you can even feel that way."

"Family is still family and he was all you had."

"We both know he brought it on himself. I'm sorry he died that way, but I wish he'd been a better person. Although he did surprise me. When he stood to face the shooter in the hallway, he put his arm out and pushed me behind him. Like he was trying to protect me." She took a deep breath and brushed away tears. "Doesn't matter now, though. At least I won't have to worry about him anymore."

A nurse entered with a little cup. "Are you ready for a pain pill?"

"Bring it on," Simone said.

"Yes, Mr. Sinclair," Mattie said. "We found him early this morning, tied up in the garden shed. He's still at the hospital now, but he'll be home this afternoon."

"Were you able to find the key for the kidnapper?" he asked.

Mattie hadn't even thought about it after David was killed. "No," she said. "A lot happened after I returned last night. In fact, the kidnapper was killed. And then I spent every second looking for Gramps. So no, the key is still where you left it." She hesitated. "Maybe you can get it when you come. Have you decided anything?"

"I have," he said. "I went into town this morning to see about a temporary replacement for Bailey and ran into some folks who are relocating here. The real estate agent wants to show them my house and they're coming over tomorrow. I told you the timing was right."

"That's wonderful news," Mattie said.

"So," Jeffrey Sinclair continued, "I decided to come to North Carolina while they're here. Tomorrow. Bailey booked rooms for us at the inn."

CHAPTER SIXTY-THREE

Knowing how close she and her grandfather had come to dying, Mattie chided herself for not fully appreciating the beauty of each day. And she resolved to change that.

She stood with Bill in the two-story foyer, millions of tiny rainbows from the chandelier reflecting around them, while she filled him in on the happenings from the previous night. She also told him about finding Jeffrey Sinclair.

A voice reached them from the floor below. "Hello?"

"Yes," Mattie said, "who is it?"

"Bryan. And Officer Scott. We wanted to talk to you for a few minutes."

"Sure," Mattie said. "Come on up."

Bryan Bennett appeared at the top of the stairs with Officer Daniel Scott right behind him. Bryan gave Mattie a quick hug. "Have you recovered from your ordeal?" he asked. She nodded. "And your grandfather?" Bryan asked. "How's he doing?"

"He'll be home from the hospital this afternoon."

She shook hands with Officer Scott. "Bryan contacted our department," Officer Scott said, "since he believed the other victim might be an international operative."

"I'm going to inspect the crime scene," Bryan said. "I'll find you later."

"Is there a place we can talk?" Officer Scott asked her.

She led the way behind the staircase, to the library, and uncovered a couple of chairs by the windows.

"How are you doing today, Miss Maguire? You really had your hands full last night," he said. "I'm surprised you're still functional."

Mattie shrugged. "It's over. And the funny thing is," she added, "I feel

270

better than I have in years. Almost … free, somehow." She caught him studying her and smiled. "I know it sounds silly, but, I've lived so much of the past few years afraid of my own shadow," she continued, "now that I know I can survive and, not only that, but take care of myself as well, I feel, I don't know … stronger … calmer." She shrugged again. "I'm not sure I understand it, but that's how I feel." She stopped talking then returned her focus to the officer. "So. You have questions?"

"Right. We did confirm that the deceased man you called your husband's killer matched the man you identified in Baltimore at the time of your husband's death. And we also confirmed that he was part of a large Greek crime syndicate that's expanded down the East Coast." He hesitated. "But you already knew that." She nodded. "We also tracked down his cell phone records and there are both calls and text messages from Greece."

"Greece, huh? From Corfu?"

Officer Scott checked his notes. "Yes. We'll need the address of the man you think arranged for the hit. Did he threaten you while you were with him?"

"He threatened my grandfather—even tried to strangle him. But once Gramps told him we knew who he really was, he sat there and cried. That's why it seems out of character for him to—wait a minute. I just remembered something."

Officer Scott leaned forward in his chair.

"After we left his villa, my grandfather and I went to dinner and I saw him walk by the restaurant. He had on big sunglasses and a large hat. And he appeared to be nervous."

"That tells me his contact was located within walking distance, so that's helpful."

"Considering how fat he is, the contact must have been *very* close. He was too out of shape to walk very far."

"That's helpful, too." Officer Scott stood and closed his notebook. "If he is the one responsible, the United States has an extradition agreement with Greece, so we can have him brought back to stand trial." He hesitated. "More than likely, the FBI will take it from here. So I guess I won't see you again. Unless you get into more trouble, that is." He grinned.

For the first time, Mattie noticed the green flecks mixed with the light brown of his eyes. And the way a single wavy clump of hair stubbornly refused to stay off his forehead, regardless of the number of times he pushed it away.

They shook hands and she wandered down the hall to see Bryan removing the yellow police tape. A couple of cleaning people stood by with buckets.

"Are you finished here, Bryan?" she asked.

"Yes. The case with David will be easy to wrap up. And Officer Scott is taking the lead on the other one. I guess he got everything he needed?"

She nodded.

"Mattie," Bryan said taking a step toward her, "I've been meaning to ask you—to tell you—to see if …" He stopped. "I'm not normally at a loss for words," he said. "Is there any chance you'd go out with me?"

Mattie hesitated. "Oh Bryan. You're so wonderful and I like you so much, but …"

"Not romantically, huh?"

"No. I'm so sorry. I wish I did. You're a great guy. But we have to work together on so many things, I don't think it would be a good idea to start something I'm pretty sure I could never finish. And I would hate for us to ever feel uncomfortable around each other."

He grinned at her. "I figured that might be your answer," he said. "But you can't blame a guy for trying."

She hugged him. "Thank you, Bryan. I will always want you for my friend. I hope that works for you."

"Of course, Mattie. Thanks for your honesty."

One of the cleaning people cleared her throat.

"Oh … sorry," Mattie said. "We'll get out of your way now. Please do what you need to and come find me when you're finished."

Mattie walked down the hallway to the beautiful foyer.

CHAPTER SIXTY-FOUR

Corfu, Greece

"I'm not paying you another dime. Your resource didn't do his job before he got himself killed." Robert held the phone tight to his ear. His hand trembled. "You need to find somebody else. Somebody who can finish the job. But don't think you can increase the fee on me. We had an agreement. The fact that you lost a resource is not my problem."

Robert disconnected the call and threw his phone onto the sofa. Carrying out the contract would be harder now, he was certain.

The stupid, bumbling idiot. He was supposed to be a professional ... the best. Now everything could be ruined.

And worse, Robert had bargained with money he didn't have. With money he would only receive if the two Americans were dead. Otherwise, he'd have to disappear. The debt was one he couldn't pay except with—

He didn't allow himself to finish the thought.

He had bought more ouzo, but only two bottles remained in the refrigerator. He opened one and drank deeply, hoping to float away to oblivion. To leave his worries and fears behind temporarily. He put the bottle to his lips again and one swallow followed another in quick succession.

His favorite chair on the balcony welcomed him and he settled into its cushions, allowing its comfortable familiarity to surround him. With two more swallows, the bottle was empty and before long, his eyes closed.

He had dreamed the same dream for the past three days.

He was back in that house. The big one. In North Carolina.

He hated that house. He always had. He had never wanted to move there in the first place, but his mother made him go.

He was six years old. The day that man died.

He was playing in the front parlor and he heard her coming.

Click-clack, click-clack. Fast. Angry. He wondered if the other boy was in trouble. He smiled.

They didn't like each other, he and the other boy. And he was often bored, so he enjoyed it when the other boy got in trouble with his mother. He thought about sneaking up the stairs behind her, but then the other man in the house followed her up the stairs and he was walking really fast.

So he decided to stay put and listen.

A lot of confusing sounds reached him after that. Lots of footsteps, heavy on the floor above—almost like jumping. And then shouting. And screaming.

He heard a couple of loud pops. And another scream.

He stood in the door of the parlor, his eyes wide, fixed on the stairs. He was terrified. He wasn't sure what had happened, but he knew it was bad. And he didn't know who would be coming back down. He started to cry. He was only six.

He woke abruptly, soaked in his own sweat. But his dream had so agitated him, he heaved himself out of the chair and lit a cigarette. He inhaled deeply.

Prior to the recurring nightmares from the past three days, he hadn't thought of that day in years. Talking to the two Americans must have triggered it.

The doorbell rang.

Followed by heavy pounding.

His heart knocked against his chest in the same rhythm as the pounding on the door. Whoever it was, they weren't friendly.

He remained still—frozen with fear, despite the fact that sweat dripped from his body and puddled on the floor under his feet.

It happened so fast.

Wood splintered and two large men burst through the door.

He had no escape.

Shots ripped into his chest and he stumbled backward with such force that his massive body hit the stone wall of the terrace and pitched over backward.

The men who shot him leaned over the wall and watched as his huge body tore into the bougainvillea climbing the walls and then bounced on the rocks below. It rolled to the edge of the Ionian Sea and lodged in the wooden bulkhead rather than plunging into the water's depths.

Four men approached the door from the villa's foyer, guns drawn. "Open up! FBI!"

They flattened against the wall and then saw the door's splintered panels, barely hanging on its hinges. They entered, their guns held high, and quickly searched every room. They found no one.

"Out here," one of the agents called. He stood on the balcony, avoiding the pool of blood and motioned toward the sea.

The path of the body was obvious. Broken vines, their flowers bloodied, drooped onto rocks—also drenched in blood. A large, swollen shape lay wedged against the bulkhead.

Expertly, the agents searched the rooms. They emptied desk and dresser drawers of any documents that appeared to be important. And then they left by the shattered front door.

Their case was closed.

CHAPTER SIXTY-FIVE

Mattie's father declared a day of celebration and arranged for lunch at the diner with the whole family. Mattie and Simone, her arm still in a sling, joined them right after the memorial service for David. Tony Adkins, the senator's aide, came in with them.

A new waitress greeted Mattie and brought her a glass of white wine while the diner's owner handed out menus. Sally, the diner's regular waitress, was nowhere in sight.

Simone touched the owner's arm. "Is Sally off today?" she asked.

Sally had shown up at David's memorial service but disappeared before Simone had a chance to thank her for coming.

"Yes," he answered. "She said she needed some personal time. But Cindy's doing a fine job. I'll tell Sally you were asking for her when she returns."

The front door opened, and Officer Daniel Scott appeared, his hat in his hand. He looked around the room hesitantly and turned to leave. Mattie jumped up. "Officer Scott," she called. She reached him and said, "We're having a small family celebration since we're all out of the hospital. For a change. Won't you join us?"

"I'm actually here on official business, Miss Maguire."

"It's time you called me Mattie."

"Right, Mattie. I'm sorry to interrupt, but I have some news."

"Do we need to go outside?" Mattie's father asked, coming up beside her. Mattie's grandfather, his wrists still bandaged, was right behind them.

Officer Scott nodded to them both. "I can tell you here. It won't take long. I just got word from my contact with the FBI that Robert Baldwin was killed in Greece. He was—"

They all turned toward the door at the sound of a sharp intake of breath where Bailey had suddenly materialized, ghost-like, as he had when Mattie saw him at the house in Maine.

"Bailey," Mattie said. She reached out and hugged him. He stood stiffly and neither rebuffed nor reciprocated.

"Sorry, miss. I didn't mean to interrupt, but Mr. Rob—that is, Mr. Jeffrey told me the story of his childhood after you left. I'm sure he never expected the real Mr. Robert would die so soon after ..."

"That's okay, Bailey. We didn't either," Mattie said. "Where is Mr. Jeffrey?"

Jeffrey Sinclair stepped through the door and looked at the group tentatively. He smiled at Mattie, but at seeing Michael Maguire, his face lit up and the two men embraced.

Mattie made the introductions and invited everyone to join them for lunch. Before returning to the dining room, Mattie hugged Jeffrey. "Welcome home, Mr. Sinclair. I really hope you decide to stay."

"Thank you, young lady. But I'll only consider it if you start calling me Jeffrey."

Mattie felt the familiar swell as the house's front façade came into view with its three-tiered deck, guarded by granite lions, and framed by tall trees. Huge stones on the highest deck formed matching staircases that curved upward in a semi-circle for two stories and then came together at the four-arch portico. Behind the portico, round, turret-like rooms rose in several levels and had always reminded her of Cinderella's castle at Walt Disney World.

She watched Jeffrey Sinclair's face as he approached the home he hadn't seen in almost seventy years. She slowed her rental car so he had time to really appreciate the view.

"I'd forgotten how beautiful it is," he whispered. "And I'm shocked it still looks so good."

"That's thanks to Gramps and his crew," Mattie said. "He always hoped some of the family would return one day." She put her hand on top of his. "We're both really glad it was you."

She parked in the circular drive and they climbed out of the car. "Will you lead the way, my dear?" he asked.

Jeffrey matched his pace to Mattie's, despite his age. Years of a lean diet, Mattie figured, and daily walks with his uncle must have kept him active and fit. He paused at the second level.

"What is it?" she asked.

"This was one of my mother's favorite spots for her flower gardens," he said softly. "Every March it was alive with the colors of spring ... yellow daffodils, purple hyacinths, red tulips, and pink crocus. She even planted lily-of-the-valley all along this walk here. I remember that especially because my father would come up behind her and put his arms around her and say, 'Planting your namesake, my sweet Lily of The Valley?'" He stood for a moment before continuing. "I loved helping her in her flower beds. So did your grandfather."

"I know. He told me. He even had a crush on her. Did he ever tell you that?"

Jeffrey laughed. "No, he didn't, but I'm not surprised. Everyone loved her."

They continued to climb and pushed through the double doors into the huge foyer. Sunlight sparkled from the ornate chandelier and reflected off the warm wood of the furniture, dust-free, thanks to the efforts of the cleaning crew.

"It really is beautiful, isn't it?" Jeffrey said softly.

"It is," she answered.

"All the years I was in Maine, I pushed it out of my mind. It's only been in the past few weeks—maybe even days—that the good memories have outweighed the bad. That I knew I would be able to stand right here without having a complete breakdown from all the trauma I suffered while I lived here."

Jeffrey smiled at her. "Do you think I could visit my old room?"

"Of course. It's been cleaned for you."

Mattie led the way up the marble staircase to the bedroom level and then down the hall to Jeffrey's room. She opened the door and stepped aside.

He hesitated at the threshold, tears gathering in his eyes.

"It's just as I remembered," he said. As if in a trance, he moved to the closet that still held small clothes and a bureau. Part of the floor was covered with a dusty throw rug.

"My pictures," he said softly. "I wonder if they're still there."

"Oh dear," Mattie said. "Bill and I came in here a few days ago, but I forgot to have the cleaning crew do your closet."

"Oh yes," he said. "'Little Billy.' I think I told you that's how I thought of him."

"And I thought of you as 'Mr. Jeffrey,'" Bill said from the door. "Nice to see you again, sir. Welcome home."

Two of the last children to live in the mansion shook hands—meeting there again as men in their seventies.

CHAPTER SIXTY-SIX

"It's been very rewarding for me," Bill said. "To be back here at the mansion. I know I was only here for a very short time as a child, but, as I told Miss Matilda, my mother kept it alive for me my whole life."

"I remember your mother," Jeffrey said. "How is she?"

"She passed away last year," Bill answered.

"I'm so sorry," Jeffrey told him. "I would have liked to spend more time with her after my father died, but Constance wouldn't allow it." He shivered.

"I know," Bill said. "My mother told me. And," he added, "there are things my mother would have told you if she had known how to find you."

"My uncle didn't want anyone to find me. In fact," he added, "that's the one nice thing Constance did for me—agreeing to let me live with Uncle Arnold. I can't imagine how horrible my life would have been had I stayed with her and her spoiled son—especially given the way you described him at the end, Mattie."

"My mother heard things," Bill continued, "from Miss Constance and her father. Things she wanted to tell your father. But cooks didn't often get audiences with Clairmont Place's owner. So she told his secretary, Charles Hudson, instead. But Mr. Sinclair dismissed their fears." Bill shook his head sadly. "If he had only known the truth about Constance and her father, everything might have been different.

"That last morning," Bill added, "the morning of your birthday, Mr. Jeffrey, my mother took coffee and pastries to your father's office and passed Constance in the foyer wearing her hat and gloves ... presumably on her way out. My mother returned to your father's office a little later to pick up his dishes. Right after that, she described it as 'all hell breaking loose.'"

280

CHAPTER SIXTY-SEVEN

1947

Cook Carson cleared the dishes and coffee service from her employer's desk, pleased to see the coffee was gone, along with most of the pastry. She was certain Mr. Sinclair had returned from his latest business trip with one of his migraines and she hoped the small breakfast had helped to ease it somewhat. She set the sugar bowl on her tray. And then she heard it.

Click-clack, click-clack.

Mrs. Sinclair moved across the marble floor, her high heels announcing her arrival to the entire household. Cook Carson picked up the tray to take back to the kitchen but before she could leave the office, Mrs. Sinclair stuck her head in and snapped at her. "Where is my husband?"

"I'm not certain, ma'am," the cook answered. "I heard him tell Mr. Hudson that he flew all night, so he may have gone upstairs to rest."

Mrs. Sinclair snorted and brushed past the cook into the office. Cook Carson bowed slightly and left for the kitchen. She unloaded her tray, but the cream pitcher was missing, and she figured Mr. Sinclair must have moved it. Rationing had ended with V-E Day, but milk and cream were still precious. She retraced her steps to the office and frowned when she saw the havoc. Drawers from Mr. Sinclair's desk stood open and his normal tidiness destroyed. A picture behind his desk skewed on the wall and his desk chair rested on its arms rather than its legs.

Alarm filled her. She knew the disarray in the office happened after Mr. Sinclair left it. And Mrs. Sinclair appeared to be distraught when she entered. Cook Carson found the cream pitcher and left hurriedly, stopping at the door to scoop up a piece of crumpled paper so she could throw it away.

She set the paper on her chopping block and went to the icebox to store the cream. When she returned, she picked up the paper to toss it when the handwriting caught her eye. It was Richard Baldwin's, recognizable from the lists he gave her for specialty items he wanted her to bring him from the market.

She was not a person to pry, but a corner of the paper revealed the words "deportation" and "disgrace." So she read the whole note.

Betsy called from Asheville attorney's office. Big trouble. Henry dictated new will and began divorce proceedings ... would substantially reduce your income. Also checked into deportation process. This could lead to disgrace. We need to talk! Right away.

She didn't understand what it all meant but remembering how upset Mrs. Sinclair had been—and what had happened to Mr. Sinclair's office, she knew she had to tell someone else about it. She hurried down the hall to Charles Hudson's office and told him everything she knew. He rose as they both heard the click-clack of Mrs. Sinclair's heels on the marble staircase.

CHAPTER SIXTY-EIGHT

2017

"Interesting," Mattie said. "I have a copy of the new will from the Asheville attorneys. But they also gave me a copy of a brochure about illegal immigration and deportation procedures. What was that about?"

"Constance's father was actually from Russia," Jeffrey told her.

"What? No ..." she said.

"That's right," Jeffrey said. "Uncle Arnold told me about it when we talked about the key and the bonds. Richard Baldwin was brought over as a tiny child and raised as an American. My father found that out the day before he was killed."

"But what could Russians have wanted from Henry Sinclair?" Mattie asked.

"What they really wanted," Jeffrey said, "were the war bonds I told you about. My father received them from Harry Sinclair, a wealthy oilman from the nineteen twenties, who made a deal with the Russian government. Apparently, he had promised to pay them millions and they were still trying to collect on it in the nineteen-forties. The Russians figured my father could lead them to the money. And as I told you earlier, he did have part of it. Still does technically, I guess. The plan my father laid out with Harry Sinclair was to go to his attorney's office to change his will, divorce Constance and send her father back to Russia. That explains the brochure for illegal immigration and deportation."

"Right," Bill said. "It also explains why the last page of the prenuptial agreement was missing. I haven't had time to tell you yet, Miss Matilda, but that piece of paper you found folded up so many times under Constance's portrait—was the missing last page."

283

"What? Why would it have been there?"

"I think she wanted it hidden because it spelled out that if Mr. Henry divorced her before they reached their two-year anniversary, she would only receive a monthly allowance—no lump sum. Of course, my guess is, in his new will, he even revoked the monthly allowance."

"But wait a minute," Mattie said. "If Constance's father was Russian, and the Russians knew that Henry Sinclair received funds from the guy in New York, why didn't her father simply get the bonds and send them to Russia as soon as Henry died?"

"All we can do is speculate at this point, of course," Jeffrey answered. "But Uncle Arnold believed that Constance was simply trying to protect her inheritance and didn't get the big picture from her father before she acted."

"What do you mean?" Mattie asked.

"As soon as she dropped the note," Bill picked up the story, "Constance ran for the stairs. And my mother figured that whatever she had in mind would be bad. So Mother found Charles Hudson and sent him after her. Of course, neither of them knew at the time that Constance had your father's gun."

"*Constance* had the gun?" Mattie asked. "But that's not … why would she have wanted to kill Henry?"

"From what Uncle Arnold told me about the plan Harry Sinclair helped my father with, the new will would have cut Constance off without a cent," Jeffrey said. "The Baldwins' only hope of continuing their lifestyle was to kill Henry before he had a chance to sign it—so the clause in the original prenup about the insurance payout could kick in. Otherwise, she'd have gotten nothing."

"But," Mattie said, "every account said Charles Hudson got there first. And that she followed him to stop him from doing anything horrible. That *he* had the gun."

"Of course," Bill said. "And where did the accounts come from?"

"Constance," Mattie and Jeffrey said in unison.

"Right," Bill answered. "Lies, all lies. And there was no one left in the house who would—who could—contradict her."

"I could have," Jeffrey said quietly.

"What?" Mattie said with a gasp.

"I saw the whole thing," Jeffrey answered.

CHAPTER SIXTY-NINE

1947

Charles Hudson took the stairs two at a time after Cook Carson told him what she had found. He didn't know why Mrs. Sinclair had gone upstairs. When he saw her earlier in her hat and gloves, he assumed she was on her way out.

But he knew his employer came home with one of his headaches, so he hoped to reach Mr. Sinclair before she did. With Mrs. Sinclair's newfound knowledge of the updated will and divorce documents, Charles worried that her explosive temper might erupt all over her husband and cause him more pain.

He ran past Jeffrey's room and burst through the doorway of the bedroom Mr. Sinclair had used recently.

But he was too late.

Constance Sinclair, still in her hat and gloves, stood at the end of the bed, a gun trained on her husband.

Mr. Sinclair's gun. The one he kept hidden in the bottom drawer of his desk.

"No," Charles screamed. He ran up behind her, but before he reached her, a gunshot blasted in his ears.

Horror surrounded his heart and his head couldn't process the scene in front of him.

Mr. Sinclair lay on the bed … a neat hole between his eyes with blood gushing from it. The bedspread under him and the wall behind him wore feathery patterns of red.

Constance held the gun steady, still aimed at her husband.

Maybe he survived somehow. I can't let her shoot him again.

Charles grabbed at her hands, reaching for the gun, their fingers entwined on the trigger. They twirled around the room in a macabre dance, pushing, grunting, each with a death-hold grip on the gun.

She screamed and fought him off, shoving him into the desk chair. It fell and crashed to the floor. Two of its legs broke. Then she turned toward him, her eyes like granite—hard, determined. Shudders traveled his spine.

In one quick motion, Mrs. Sinclair freed her fingers from the gun's trigger. His fingers remained curved around it. But immediately, her fingers closed on top of his. He, alone, touched the trigger's metal but her fingers held his captive. Charles struggled to free himself, amazed at her strength.

They continued their deadly dance around the room, locked in a mortal struggle for control of the gun. She stomped on his instep with the heel of her shoe and then wrapped her foot around his ankle. He fell and lay on the floor. His legs thrashed to find leverage. He tried to stand. He *needed* to stand.

But she flipped him to his back and shoved a knee in his chest. With both of their hands still locked on the gun, she forced his arms up until the muzzle rested against his temple.

His eyes widened and shock filled his face.

With her fingers still on top of his, Constance squeezed his finger against the trigger. An eruption of blood, and bits of brain, flew from his other temple. The kick from the heavy gun knocked her backward to the floor.

She screamed again.

Within seconds she was up and running down the stairs, her heels clicking against the marble, her throat screaming the whole time. Vaguely, she noticed her son standing in the door of the parlor as she raced by to get to the telephone. She needed to talk to her father.

"You did what?" Richard Baldwin's voice rose. He had reached the mansion within minutes of her phone call and they met in Henry Sinclair's office. "Please tell me you're lying, woman. Why would you have done such a stupid thing?"

"I did what I had to do to protect us," she snapped, pacing her husband's office.

"But you didn't. You made everything worse."

"What are you talking about?" she screamed. "I protected my five million dollars. If he had signed the new will, I'd have gotten nothing." She brought her face up to his. "And you would have been deported."

Richard Baldwin sat at Henry's desk, his head in his hands. "He came back from New York today with millions of dollars from the Sinclair oilman," Richard said. "I was supposed to convince him to tell me where he put it so I could deliver it to the homeland." He shook his head again. "All I needed was an hour with him. *Then* you could have done whatever you wanted."

Her eyes widened. "Millions? It has to be here in the house, then. Probably in his safe." She strode to the picture behind his desk and tore it from the wall. "What's the combination?"

"How the hell should I know?" he asked her. "To my knowledge, Henry and Charles were the only ones who knew it. And now, neither of them can tell us."

"We can contact the company that made it," she said, "tell them we have to get into it for Henry's insurance policy. And then we can use some of that bond money to either send to the homeland or to bribe your contact into leaving you alone. I'm sure the company will open it for me."

"Maybe," he said. "But first we need to figure out how to keep you from hanging for committing murder. Two murders. Oh, good heavens." He returned his head to his hands.

"Oh, stop worrying," she said. "That part's easy. I didn't kill them."

He raised his eyes to her. "Have you lost your mind? What do you mean?"

"Charles Hudson killed Henry while I wrestled with him to get the gun from him. I was terrified I would be next. But then he turned the gun on himself instead." She held her hands out at her sides, palms up. "Easy," she said again.

"Are you serious?"

"Of course I am. It's a cut-and-dried case. I'm the only witness."

"Are you sure?"

"I'm sure. Cook Carson was in the kitchen, the Maguires were all outside."

"What about the boys?"

"Robert was playing in the parlor. I stopped and looked in Jeffrey's room on my way past, but his table was clean, and he was nowhere in sight. I can make Robert say they were playing together." She smiled and stopped pacing. "See?" she said. "I told you. Cut-and-dried."

"Maybe," he said. "But we'll make a large donation to the sheriff's office, regardless. For insurance."

CHAPTER SEVENTY

2017

"You saw your father get shot?" Mattie's voice was soft.

"Yes," Jeffrey said. "He came to see me, and then went to the next room to nap. I snuck a look at him to make certain he was okay."

"How?" Mattie asked. "Did you go to the door of his room?"

"No. I'll show you."

Jeffrey led Mattie and Bill to his closet and pointed to the middle of the back wall. Mattie leaned down and saw a small hole. When she put her eye to it, the entire interior of the room next door was clearly visible. She shuddered.

"My mother," Jeffrey said, "made this hole here when she bought me a set of toy telephones and ran the wires from my room to her desk next door."

"So you saw … you saw …"

"Yes," Jeffrey said quietly. "After I looked at my father on the bed, I went back to my table to draw. But I heard footsteps in the hall. If I had only known …"

"I understand," Bill said. "My mother must have told me the same thing a thousand times. She said if she had only known what Constance intended to do, she wouldn't have sent Charles after her. She always felt responsible for his death."

"But," Mattie said. "But … he killed himself. Everybody said so."

"No," Jeffrey said. "*Constance* said so. And her father saw to it that no one questioned her. Or me. It was an open-and-shut case, they said. Cut-and-dried. And quickly closed."

"Oh," Mattie said. "I can't believe—"

"Believe it," Bill said. "My mother couldn't prove it, but she was absolutely certain it was Constance, and not Charles, who pulled the trigger."

"And she was right," Jeffrey said. "I heard a second set of footsteps almost right away and went back to my closet just as Constance fired the first shot." His body shuddered. "And then Charles rushed her and wrestled her for the gun. But ..."

He stopped talking and Mattie put her hand on his arm. He stood silent for another minute before continuing. "Charles had witnessed Constance murder my father, so she had to kill him, too. And, of course, she needed someone to blame. I documented the whole thing with my pictures. And hid them here."

"What? Where?" Mattie said.

Jeffrey pointed down. "In the place my mother called my 'safe room.' I hid there, along with my pictures, for hours after it happened."

"Newspaper accounts said that Constance searched your room for you to see if you saw anything."

"Right," Jeffrey said. "She made it sound like she wanted any information I may have had about Charles Hudson killing my father. But what she really wanted," he added, "was to know if I saw *her* killing my father. That's why I never said anything. I am certain in my heart she would have killed me, too. And then blamed that one on Charles as well, somehow."

He slid the small, dust-covered rug with his foot to reveal a door embedded in the floor of his closet.

"Your 'safe room,'" Mattie said. She reached down and pulled the strap to open it then fell to her knees to get a better view. Papers—some slightly yellowed, others with curled edges were scattered across its bottom. She eased herself into the space and retrieved them.

"Pictures," she said as she straightened. "They're all pictures." She lay them on the closet floor and held up a box of crayons. "These look brand new," she said.

"They are. Well, they were. My father gave them to me for my birthday. I only used them that one time. Look," he said. He reached down inside the box and brought out a tiny gold key. "This is what the man who kidnapped Mikey was after."

"It's amazing," Mattie said, "how much trouble this tiny piece of metal has caused. You should probably put it in a safe place ... well ... a *new* safe place. Maybe the people who hired David will send someone else to try and find it."

"That wouldn't do them much good," Jeffrey said. "Neither my uncle nor I had a clue where the lockbox was hidden. Still don't."

"It's in the root cellar below the kitchen," Bill said.

"What?" Mattie asked, whipping her head toward Bill. "How could you know that?"

"I don't know it for certain," Bill said. "But my mother had just left the root cellar with blackberries for a cobbler. She was behind one of the pillars getting the lard and saw Jeffrey's father go into the cellar when he first got back that morning from his trip. He was distracted and didn't see her, but she noticed he carried a small box. When he left, she stuck her head back in and saw the door to the small safe at the back hanging open. And inside was a box that looked like the one he had. So she closed the door and never said a word about it to anyone. Except me."

Mattie sat in one of the small chairs at Jeffrey's table. "Oh, my goodness," she said. "Oh, my *goodness*."

Moments of silence followed. Then Mattie said, "Jeffrey, weren't you ever tempted to tell people what really happened rather than let Constance get away with it?"

"Sure, I thought about it," Jeffrey said. "And there were times I wanted to. But since Charles Hudson didn't leave a wife or children or any other family ... and since I no longer *had* any family, I didn't see the point in putting myself in that kind of danger. So keeping quiet became a way of life with me. And Uncle Arnold agreed—he figured he couldn't help anybody by calling them out and that he'd be risking his own life—and mine—if he did. Then Constance approached my uncle with the idea of switching Robert and me, to protect me, she told him, and my uncle agreed. Then he did what they wanted, primarily calling me 'Robert' instead of my real name, as an added protection." Jeffrey's mouth curved in a small smile. "Poor Uncle Arnold didn't have a clue what he should do with an eleven-year-old boy. That's why he sent me to that school. But once he learned how badly they treated me, he kept me with him. We had a good life together."

"I'm glad you did," Mattie said. "Still, I can't believe she got away with murder for all those years."

"After a while," Jeffrey said, "neither my uncle nor I thought about it. We had enough money, so it didn't hurt us." He shook his head sadly. "I was always sorry for what it did to poor Charles's reputation, though. The whole town believed he had simply gone off the deep end by committing murder. But," he added with a shrug, "as I said, by then, the damage was done. And Charles no longer needed our help."

"But my mother and I did," Bill said quietly.

They both turned to look at him.

"What do you mean?" Mattie asked.

"Charles Hudson was my father."

Mattie's gasp was audible.

"Oh, Billy," Jeffrey said. "I had no idea." He placed his hand on the other man's arm.

"Of course you didn't," Bill said. "No one did. My mother had just found out she was pregnant with me. They planned to marry in a small civil ceremony—the afternoon he died, in fact. Afterward, since having a baby out of wedlock would have meant automatic dismissal back then, she invented a story about a quick marriage to a soldier, recently returned from World War II, who died almost right away from influenza. And household staff kept the name the family knew them by—married or not—so her name of Carson still worked. She was able to keep her job for another eight years before the house was closed for good and we moved to Asheville."

"So that's why being here and confirming the truth with Jeffrey was so important to you," Mattie said.

"Yes," he answered. "I promised my mother on her deathbed that I would clear Charles' name—if it took me the rest of my life."

Jeffrey put his hands on the other man's shoulders. "You have my word, Billy, that I will tell the world what really happened here seventy years ago. Your father's name will no longer be associated with murder."

"Thank you, Mr. Jeffrey," Bill said. "That will make both of my parents rest easier."

"And mine as well," Jeffrey answered.

CHAPTER SEVENTY-ONE

Jeffrey Sinclair's return to his family home was the talk of the town. Editors from both the Sinclair Station and Asheville newspapers interviewed him, complete with the pictures he drew and photos of the safe room where he hid them. He told the real story of how his father died, making certain that the name of William Charles Hudson was totally cleared and would never again be associated with the death of Henry Sinclair, Jr.

Local news stations picked up the story first, followed by the national stations. Segments about Jeffrey and his family appeared on all the prime-time network news shows—ABC's 20/20, CBS's 60 Minutes, and NBC's Dateline—and a New York Times best-selling author contracted with him to write a book about his life.

Jeffrey's house in Maine sold quickly and he decided to live at Clairmont Place full time—a condition, the Summit Selection Committee assured him—that would not interfere with holding the summit there. Mattie helped him hire a household staff and Bailey did, in fact, retire. Bill continued to come to the house every day and he and Jeffrey made great progress on documenting the family history and then archiving irreplaceable documents to the bank's vault.

Bill had also been correct about the location of the war bonds from Harry Sinclair. Once they were removed from the root cellar, they, too, were put in the vault at Sinclair Bank & Trust.

Jeffrey and Michael Maguire resumed their companionable friendship from seventy years earlier and spent hours walking the grounds, visiting the stables, and discussing new plant varieties.

Two weeks after Jeffrey's return, the newly repaired doorbell chimed, and Mattie headed downstairs to see who it was.

The idea flew into her head and she laughed out loud, hesitating for only a fraction of a second before swinging her leg over the banister to reach the foyer the fastest way.

Her ride was everything she dreamed it would be … wind rushing against her back and her black hair flying around her face. She was close to the end before she remembered the newel cap at the bottom of the banister had been removed for repair.

She raised her body slightly and half turned to see how close she was to the end. The smiling face of Officer Daniel Scott greeted her seconds before she flew into him. They crashed to the floor in a tangle of arms and legs.

Jeffrey leaned over the balcony. "Are you two all right?"

Mattie laughed. "Yes," she said. "Very all right." Officer Scott helped her up and Jeffrey went down to meet them.

"Okay … check," Mattie said. At their confused looks, she continued. "Sliding down that banister has been on my bucket list for more than twenty years. It was time. I had to do it."

"I'm just glad you weren't hurt. Thank you for … uh … softening her fall, officer."

"My pleasure," Officer Scott said. "I decided I needed to come see you Miss—Mattie—to try and convince you to have lunch with me. I mean, since you haven't gotten shot at lately. I didn't want to wait for that to happen again, anyway … so, lunch?"

"Sure," she said. "I would love to. How about tomorrow?"

"Done," he said. They shook on it.

The week following the sale of Jeffrey's house in Rogue Bluffs, Mattie found him in the foyer, unpacking one of the crates that arrived daily from Maine.

"I brought some tea," she said. "Vanilla Honey Chamomile … your Wednesday tea, right?"

He laughed. "Right. Bailey did a good job of training you."

He took a few sips and returned to unpacking. He eased pictures out of the large crates—mostly seascapes and landscapes of Jeffrey's northern home. But Mattie recognized the last two pictures right away.

"Oh, Jeffrey," she said. "These are beautiful." Mattie leaned them, side by side, against the largest crate. The first was of a lovely red-haired woman sitting atop a chestnut horse. A beautiful smile filled her face. "Your mother," Mattie said. "I recognize her from the portrait in your father's office."

Jeffrey stood beside her. "Yes," he said. "I was only six when she died, but that's what she looked like. I never forgot."

"And the other one—your father. That's exactly how he looked in the newspaper."

He nodded. "Life is funny," he continued. "I don't know if I told you, but the day I met you, my parents simply presented themselves to me. All at once, they were with me in my head and I knew I needed to let myself remember them—the love I had for them. And they for me." He hesitated before continuing. "They were so vivid in my mind, I *had* to paint them. There was nothing else I could do. And I've thought since then ... that maybe they came to me to—"

"To ..."

He took a deep breath. "To let me know it was okay to come home. That it was *time* to come home."

"I think you're right. I really believe in the universe giving us messages, Jeffrey. It happens to me all the time."

"But there was a whole series of them," he said. "First, I painted these pictures on the day Bailey told me he was retiring and moving to North Carolina, of all places. And then you show up later that same day and remind me of who I am and where I'm from. Quite a series of coincidences, don't you think?"

"Not necessarily," she said. "I have a theory about what we perceive as coincidences. My take is that fate has a way of fixing the injustices we suffer in life by allowing the universe to right itself. To restore 'what should have been' to 'what is.'"

"'To restore what should have been to what is,'" he repeated. "I like that."

Mattie watched his face as he processed her words. Then he inclined his head in a slight nod.

She studied his face. From his expression, she saw that he had found peace.

AUTHOR'S NOTE

A s with any fiction writing, part of it comes from the author's head and part of it is inspired by real events, people or places. Here's where you find out my inspirations for the words in this novel.

The setting of the action, Sinclair Station, is a fictional town twenty-two miles east of Asheville, North Carolina. Which would translate in real life to a spot about six miles past Black Mountain, North Carolina, and almost three miles before Old Fort, North Carolina, when traveling east from Asheville. I have a picture of the town in my head, but it was not inspired by any special town I've ever seen. Other action locations: Rogue Bluffs, Maine and Corfu, Greece are real places, but the homes I describe there—other than the wraparound porch on Arnold Sinclair's home in Maine—also exist only in my head.

I had a very interesting experience in writing this novel. The inspiration for the murders of both Henry Sinclair and Charles Hudson came from two real-life shooting deaths in February 1929 at the Greystone Mansion in Beverly Hills, California. My husband and I had visited the mansion in 2007 and heard the story of Ned Doheny, owner of the mansion, killed by his secretary, Hugh Plunkett, just four months after Ned, his wife, and their five children moved into the 46,000-square-foot home. As with my story, the testimony about the killings came from Lucy Doheny, the wife of one of the deceased. Many who heard her story considered it shaky, given the fact that the shootings took place at 11:00 pm but the first person called was the family doctor rather than the police. They weren't called until three hours later. By the time the police arrived, the story they heard was that Hugh Plunkett shot Ned Doheny and then himself. But Hugh had been shot in the back of the head—a spot almost impossible to reach by one trying to commit suicide. In addition, the bodies had been moved and everyone in the household told exactly the same story—one that appeared to be rehearsed. Regardless, within three days, the police ruled the case closed and called it a murder/suicide, just as Lucy Doheny described.

My heart went out to the Doheny family. They were very wealthy, there were so many children, and they had just moved into the magnificent mansion mere months before. But further research revealed that speculation after the 1929 murders ran rampant, with one theory that Ned Doheny did the murdering and then killed himself. And most interesting to me of all...that Lucy Doheny killed them both. Bingo. I had my inspiration. The grounds around the mansion are now owned by the City of Los Angeles and the house is closed to the public except on special occasions or when it's used as a movie set.

But here's the part that became really interesting. While working on the second iteration of the novel, I decided to add more backstory about *why* the killings might have taken place and discovered that Ned Doheny was the son of Edward Doheny, an oilman who was involved in one of the most corrupt scandals in our country's history—the Teapot Dome fiasco. I hadn't done any research on that aspect of the story earlier, so was surprised when I found out that Edward Doheny competed with another man in leasing oil-rich lands throughout the country. Between them, they made millions in the 1920s by pumping oil that had originally been reserved for the government to use in case of a national fuel crisis. Oops. In 1920, who would have figured?

But here's the part that caused my hair to stand on end. The name of the other oilman was Harry Sinclair. I had already written an entire book about my murdered character, named *Henry* Sinclair. I promise you, I had not seen the Sinclair name prior to writing the story the first time. It's as if I had picked up on someone named Sinclair...sitting patiently in the little room in my head where fictional characters wait to be chosen. But once I found Harry, the *real* Sinclair, I simply had to include the oilman in my story as a distant cousin to my Sinclair (second cousin-once removed, actually, although Henry didn't care to know that).

The story Harry tells Henry and his Uncle Arnold in Chapter Eleven is true—other than Arnold being a part of Harry's business. The part about the war bonds is also true. They were Harry's favorite form of payment and as of 2009, more than sixteen billion dollars' worth of war bonds— issued during both World War I and World War II—still have not been found or turned in. For any readers interested in more details about the

Teapot Dome scandal and the Warren Harding White House, my favorite resource was *The Teapot Dome Scandal: How Big Oil Bought the Harding White House and Tried to Steal the Country* by Laton McCartney.

The facts around the G7 Summit are also true. It became the G7 group, down from G8, in 2014 when Russia was ousted for annexing Crimea. The meeting of the most financially developed world powers is held annually in obscure places in one of the countries of the seven remaining members and cycles back to the United States in 2020. Security is always of utmost concern. But I do not know for a fact that Russia is still ticked about not being a part of the group. It just seemed reasonable to me.

The kidnapping of the Lindbergh baby did spawn the building of safe rooms for wealthy people and the description of the hole in Jeffrey's closet where his mother strung wire to hook between two toy telephones actually happened when I did that between my children's closets when they were small. The box of forty-eight crayons Jeffrey received for his eighth birthday in Chapter 21, were not actually offered for sale until 1949, which is why his father told him his gift was a prototype.

My descriptions of the outsides and some of the insides of large houses came from pictures I found on Pinterest®, but everything else… all descriptions of people, places, and things, except where already noted, came directly from my vivid imagination.

CPSIA information can be obtained
at www.ICGtesting.com
Printed in the USA
LVHW111750031220
673321LV00037B/316